NORA ROBERTS

CLOSE TO YOU

Includes *Mind Over Matter* & *Lawless*

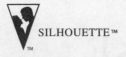

SILHOUETTE™

Recycling programs
for this product may
not exist in your area.

Close to You

ISBN-13: 978-1-335-23085-0

Copyright © 2021 by Harlequin Books S.A.

Mind Over Matter
First published in 1987. This edition published in 2021.
Copyright © 1987 by Nora Roberts

Lawless
First published in 1989. This edition published in 2021.
Copyright © 1989 by Nora Roberts

This edition published by arrangement with Harlequin Books S.A.

For questions and comments about the quality of this book, please contact us at
CustomerService@Harlequin.com.

Silhouette
22 Adelaide St. West, 40th Floor
Toronto, Ontario M5H 4E3, Canada
www.Harlequin.com

Printed in Lithuania

MIX
Paper from
responsible sources
FSC® C021394

CONTENTS

MIND OVER MATTER

Chapter 1

He'd expected a crystal ball, pentagrams and a few tea leaves. Burning candles and incense wouldn't have surprised him. Though he wouldn't admit it to anyone, he'd actually looked forward to it. As a producer of documentaries for public television, David Brady dealt in hard facts and meticulous research. Anything and everything that went into one of his productions was checked and rechecked, most often personally. The truth was, he'd thought an afternoon with a fortune teller would bring him a refreshing, even comic, relief from the daily pressure of scripts, storyboards and budgets. She didn't even wear a turban.

The woman who opened the door of the comfortable suburban home in Newport Beach looked as though she would more likely be found at a bridge table than a séance. She smelled of lilacs and dusting powder, not musk and mystery. David's impression that she was housekeeper or companion to the renowned psychic was immediately disabused.

"Hello." She offered a small, attractive hand and a smile. "I'm Clarissa DeBasse. Please come in, Mr. Brady. You're right on time."

"Miss DeBasse." David adjusted his thinking and accepted her hand. He'd done enough research so far to be prepared for the normalcy of people involved in the paranormal. "I appreciate your seeing me. Should I wonder how you know who I am?"

As their hands linked, she let impressions of him come and go, to be sorted out later. Intuitively she felt he was a man she could trust and rely on. It was enough for the moment. "I could claim precognition, but I'm afraid it's simple logic. You were expected at one-thirty." Her agent had called to remind her, or Clarissa would still be knee-deep in her vegetable garden. "I suppose it's possible you're carrying brushes and samples in that briefcase, but I have the feeling it's papers and contracts. Now I'm sure you'd like some coffee after your drive down from L.A."

"Right again." He stepped into a cozy living room with pretty blue curtains and a wide couch that sagged noticeably in the middle.

"Sit down, Mr. Brady. I just brought the tray out, so the coffee's hot."

Deciding the couch was unreliable, David chose a chair and waited while Clarissa sat across from him and poured coffee into two mismatched cups and saucers. It took him only a moment to study and analyze. He was a man who leaned heavily on first impressions. She looked, as she offered cream and sugar, like anyone's favorite aunt—rounded without being really plump, neat without being stiff. Her face was soft and pretty and had lined little in fifty-odd years. Her pale blond hair was cut stylishly and showed no gray, which David attributed to her hairdresser. She was entitled to her vanity, he thought. When she offered the cup, he noted the symphony of rings on her hands. That, at least, was in keeping with the image he had projected.

"Thank you. Miss DeBasse, I have to tell you, you're not at all what I expected."

Comfortable with herself, she settled back. "You were expecting me to greet you at the door with a crystal ball in my hands and a raven on my shoulder."

The amusement in her eyes would have had some men shifting in their chairs. David only lifted a brow. "Something like that." He sipped his coffee. The fact that it was hot was the only thing going for it. "I've read quite a bit about you in the past few weeks. I also saw a tape of your appearance on *The Barrow Show*." He probed gently for the right phrasing. "You have a different image on camera."

"That's showbiz," she said so casually he wondered if she was being sarcastic. Her eyes remained clear and friendly. "I don't generally discuss business, particularly at home, but since it seemed important that you see me, I thought we'd be more comfortable this way." She smiled again, showing the faintest of dimples in her cheeks. "I've disappointed you."

"No." And he meant it. "No, you haven't." Because his manners went only so far, he put the coffee down. "Miss DeBasse—"

"Clarissa." She beamed such a bright smile at him he had no trouble returning it.

"Clarissa, I want to be honest with you."

"Oh, that's always best." Her voice was soft and sincere as she folded her hands on her lap.

"Yeah." The childlike trust in her eyes threw him for a moment. If she was a hard-edged, money-oriented con, she was doing a good job disguising it. "I'm a very practical man. Psychic phenomena, clairvoyance, telepathy and that sort of thing, don't fit into my day-to-day life."

She only smiled at him, understanding. Whatever thoughts came into her head remained there. This time David did shift in his chair.

"I decided to do this series on parapsychology mainly for its entertainment value."

"You don't have to apologize." She lifted her hand just as a large black cat leaped into her lap. Without looking at it, Clarissa stroked it from head to tail. "You see, David, someone in my position understands perfectly the doubts and the fascination people have for...such things. I'm not a radical." As the cat curled up in her lap, she continued to pet it, looking calm and content. "I'm simply a person who's been given a gift, and a certain responsibility."

"A responsibility?" He started to reach in his pocket for his cigarettes, then noticed there were no ashtrays.

"Oh, yes." As she spoke, Clarissa opened the drawer of the coffee table and took out a small blue dish. "You can use this," she said in passing, then settled back again. "A young boy might receive a toolbox for his birthday. It's a gift. He has choices to make. He can use his new tools to learn, to build, to repair. He can also use them to saw the legs off tables. He could also put the toolbox in his closet and forget about it. A great many of us do the last, because the tools are too complicated or simply too overwhelming. Have you ever had a psychic experience, David?"

He lit a cigarette. "No."

"No?" There weren't many people who would give such a definitive no. "Never a sense of déjà vu, perhaps?"

He paused a moment, interested. "I suppose everyone's had a sense of doing something before, being somewhere before. A feeling of mixed signals."

"Perhaps. Intuition, then."

"You consider intuition a psychic gift?"

"Oh, yes." Enthusiasm lit her face and made her eyes young. "Of course it depends entirely on how it's developed, how it's channeled, how it's used. Most of us use only a fraction of what we have because our minds are so crowded with other things."

"Was it impulse that led you to Matthew Van Camp?"

A shutter seemed to come down over her eyes. "No."

Again he found her puzzling. The Van Camp case was the one that had brought her prominently into the public eye. He would have thought she would have been anxious to speak of it, elaborate, yet she seemed to close down at the mention of the name. David blew out smoke and noticed that the cat was watching him with bored but steady eyes. "Clarissa, the Van Camp case is ten years old, but it's still one of the most celebrated and controversial of your successes."

"That's true. Matthew is twenty now. A very handsome young man."

"There are some who believe he'd be dead if Mrs. Van Camp hadn't fought both her husband and the police to have you brought in on the kidnapping."

"And there are some who believe the entire thing was staged for publicity," she said so calmly as she sipped from her cup. "Alice Van Camp's next movie was quite a box-office success. Did you see the film? It was wonderful."

He wasn't a man to be eased off-track when he'd already decided on a destination. "Clarissa, if you agree to be part of this documentary, I'd like you to talk about the Van Camp case."

She frowned a bit, pouted almost, as she petted her cat. "I don't know if I can help you there, David. It was a very traumatic experience for the Van Camps, very traumatic. Bringing it all up again could be painful for them."

He hadn't reached his level of success without knowing how and when to negotiate. "If the Van Camps agreed?"

"Oh, then that's entirely different." While she considered, the cat stirred in her lap, then began to purr loudly. "Yes, entirely different. You know, David, I admire your work. I saw your documentary on child abuse. It was gripping and very upsetting."

"It was meant to be."

"Yes, exactly." She could have told him a great deal of the world was upsetting, but didn't think he was ready to understand how she knew, and how she dealt with it. "What is it you're looking for with this?"

"A good show." When she smiled he was sure he'd been right not to try to con her. "One that'll make people think and question."

"Will you?"

He tapped out his cigarette. "I produce. How much I question I suppose depends on you."

It seemed like not only the proper answer, but the truest one. "I like you, David. I think I'd like to help you."

"I'm glad to hear that. You'll want to look over the contract and—"

"No." She cut him off as he reached for his briefcase. "Details." She explained them away with a gesture of her hand. "I let my agent bother with those things."

"Fine." He'd feel more comfortable discussing terms with an agent. "I'll send them over if you give me a name."

"The Fields Agency in Los Angeles."

She'd surprised him again. The comfortable auntlike lady had one of the most influential and prestigious agencies on the Coast. "I'll have them sent over this afternoon. I'd enjoy working with you, Clarissa."

"May I see your palm?"

Every time he thought he had her cataloged, she shifted on him. Still, humoring her was easy. David offered his hand. "Am I going to take an ocean voyage?"

She was neither amused nor offended. Though she took his hand, palm up, she barely glanced at it. Instead she studied him with eyes that seemed abruptly cool. She saw a man in his early thirties, attractive in a dark, almost brooding way despite the well-styled black hair and casually elegant clothes. The bones in his face were strong, angular enough to warrant a second glance. His brows were thick, as black as his hair, and dominated surprisingly quiet eyes. Or their cool, pale green appeared quiet at first glance. She saw a mouth that was firm, full enough to gain a woman's attention. The hand in hers was wide, long fingered, artistic. It vied with a rangy, athletic build. But she saw beyond that.

"You're a very strong man, physically, emotionally, intellectually."

"Thank you."

"Oh, I don't flatter, David." It was a gentle, almost maternal reproof. "You haven't yet learned how to temper this strength with tenderness in your relationships. I suppose that's why you've never married."

She had his attention now, reluctantly. But he wasn't wearing a ring, he reminded himself. And anyone who cared to find out about his marital status had only to make a few inquiries. "The standard response is I've never met the right woman."

"In this case it's perfectly true. You need to find someone every bit as strong as you are. You will, sooner than you think. It won't be easy, of course, and it will only work between you if you both remember the tenderness I just spoke of."

"So I'm going to meet the right woman, marry and live happily ever after?"

"I don't tell the future, ever." Her expression changed again, becoming placid. "And I only read palms of people who interest me. Shall I tell you what my intuition tells me, David?"

"Please."

"That you and I are going to have an interesting and long-term relationship." She patted his hand before she released it. "I'm going to enjoy that."

"So am I." He rose. "I'll see you again, Clarissa."

"Yes. Yes, of course." She rose and nudged the cat onto the floor. "Run along now, Mordred."

"Mordred?" David repeated as the cat jumped up to settle himself on the sagging sofa cushion.

"Such a sad figure in folklore," Clarissa explained. "I always felt he got a bad deal. After all, we can't escape our destiny, can we?"

For the second time David felt her cool, oddly intimate gaze on him. "I suppose not," he murmured, and let her lead him to the door.

"I've so enjoyed our chat, David. Please come back again."

David stepped out into the warm spring air and wondered why he felt certain he would.

"Of course he's an excellent producer, Abe. I'm just not sure he's right for Clarissa."

A.J. Fields paced around her office in the long, fluid gait that always masked an overflow of nervous energy. She stopped to straighten a picture that was slightly tilted before she turned back to her associate. Abe Ebbitt was sitting with his hands folded on his round belly, as was his habit. He didn't bother to push back the glasses that had fallen down his nose. He watched A.J. patiently before he reached up to scratch one of the two clumps of hair on either side of his head.

"A.J., the offer is very generous."

"She doesn't need the money."

His agent's blood shivered at the phrase, but he continued to speak calmly. "The exposure."

"Is it the right kind of exposure?"

"You're too protective of Clarissa, A.J."

"That's what I'm here for," she countered. Abruptly she stopped, and sat on the corner of her desk. When Abe saw her brows draw together, he fell silent. He might speak to her when she was in this mood, but she wouldn't answer. He respected and admired her. Those were the reasons he, a veteran Hollywood agent, was working for the Fields Agency, instead of carving up the town on his own. He was old enough to be her father, and realized that a decade before their roles would have been reversed. The fact that he worked for her didn't bother him in the least. The best, he was fond of saying, never minded answering to the best. A minute passed, then two.

"She's made up her mind to do it," A.J. muttered, but again Abe remained silent. "I just—" Have a feeling, she thought. She hated to use that phrase. "I just hope it isn't a mistake. The wrong director, the wrong format, and she could be made to look like a fool. I won't have that, Abe."

"You're not giving Clarissa enough credit. You know better than to let your emotions color a business deal, A.J."

"Yeah, I know better." That's why she was the best. A.J. folded her arms and reminded herself of it. She'd learned at a very young age how to channel emotion. It had been more than necessary; it had been vital. When you grew up in a house where your widowed mother often forgot little details like the mortgage payment, you learned how to deal with business in a businesslike way or you went under. She was an agent because she enjoyed the wheeling and dealing. And because she was damn good at it. Her Century City office with its lofty view of Los Angeles was proof of just how good. Still, she hadn't gotten there by making deals blindly.

"I'll decide after I meet with Brady this afternoon."

Abe grinned at her, recognizing the look. "How much more are you going to ask for?"

"I think another ten percent." She picked up a pencil and tapped it against her palm. "But first I intend to find out exactly what's going into this documentary and what angles he's going for."

"Word is Brady's tough."

She sent him a deceptively sweet smile that had fire around the edges. "Word is so am I."

"He hasn't got a prayer." He rose, tugging at his belt. "I've got a meeting. Let me know how it goes."

"Sure." She was already frowning at the wall when he closed the door.

David Brady. The fact that she personally admired his work would naturally influence her decision. Still, at the right time and for the right fee, she would sign a client to play a tea bag in a thirty-second local commercial. Clarissa was a different matter. Clarissa DeBasse had been her first client. Her only client, A.J. remembered, during those first lean years. If she was protective of her, as Abe had said, A.J. felt she had a right to be. David Brady might be a successful producer of quality documentaries for public television, but he had to prove himself to A.J. Fields before Clarissa signed on the dotted line.

There'd been a time when A.J. had had to prove herself. She hadn't started out with a staff of fifteen in an exclusive suite of offices. Ten years before, she'd been scrambling for clients and hustling deals from an office that had consisted of a phone booth outside a corner deli. She'd lied about her age. Not too many people had been willing to trust their careers to an eighteen-year-old. Clarissa had.

A.J. gave a little sigh as she worked out a kink in her shoulder. Clarissa didn't really consider what she did, or what she had, a career as much as a calling. It was up to A.J. to haggle over the details.

She was used to it. Her mother had always been such a warm, generous woman. But details had never been her strong point. As a child, it had been up to A.J. to remember when the bills were due. She'd balanced the checkbook, discouraged door-to-door salesmen and juggled her schoolwork with the household budget. Not that her mother was a fool, or neglectful of her daughter. There had always been love, conversation and interest. But their roles had so often been reversed. It was the mother who would claim the stray puppy had followed her home and the daughter who had worried how to feed it.

Still, if her mother had been different, wouldn't A.J. herself be different? That was a question that surfaced often. Destiny was something that couldn't be outmaneuvered. With a laugh, A.J. rose. Clarissa would love that one, she mused.

Walking around her desk, she let herself sink into the deep, wide-armed chair her mother had given her. The chair, unlike the heavy, clean-lined desk, was extravagant and im-

Mind Over Matter

practical. Who else would have had a chair made in corn-flower-blue leather because it matched her daughter's eyes?

A.J. realigned her thoughts and picked up the DeBasse contract. It was in the center of a desk that was meticulously in order. There were no photographs, no flowers, no cute paperweights. Everything on or in her desk had a purpose, and the purpose was business.

She had time to give the contract one more thorough going-over before her appointment with David Brady. Before she met with him, she would understand every phrase, every clause and every alternative. She was just making a note on the final clause, when her buzzer rang. Still writing, A.J. cradled the phone at her ear.

"Yes, Diane."

"Mr. Brady's here, A.J."

"Okay. Any fresh coffee?"

"We have sludge at the moment. I can make some."

"Only if I buzz you. Bring him back, Diane."

She turned her notepad back to the first page, then rose as the door opened. "Mr. Brady." A.J. extended her hand, but stayed behind her desk. It was, she'd learned, important to establish certain positions of power right from the start. Besides, the time it took him to cross the office gave her an opportunity to study and judge. He looked more like someone she might have for a client than a producer. Yes, she was certain she could have sold that hard, masculine look and rangy walk. The laconic, hard-boiled detective on a weekly series; the solitary, nomadic cowboy in a feature film. Pity.

David had his own chance for study. He hadn't expected her to be so young. She was attractive in that streamlined, no-nonsense sort of way he could respect professionally and ignore personally. Her body seemed almost too slim in the sharply tailored suit that was rescued from dullness by a fire-engine-red blouse. Her pale blond hair was cut in a deceptively casual style that shagged around the ears, then angled back to sweep her collar. It suited the honey-toned skin that had been kissed by the sun—or a sunlamp. Her face was oval, her mouth just short of being too wide. Her eyes were a rich blue, accentuated by clever smudges of shadow and framed now with oversize glasses. Their hands met, held and released as hands in business do dozens of times every day.

"Please sit down, Mr. Brady. Would you like some coffee?"

"No, thank you." He took a chair and waited until she settled behind the desk. He noticed that she folded her hands over the contract. No rings, no bracelets, he mused. Just a slender, black-banded watch. "It seems we have a number of mutual acquaintances, Ms. Fields. Odd that we haven't met before."

"Yes, isn't it?" She gave him a small, noncommittal smile. "But, then, as an agent, I prefer staying in the background. You met Clarissa DeBasse."

"Yes, I did." So they'd play stroll around the bush for a while, he decided, and settled back. "She's charming. I have to admit, I'd expected someone, let's say, more eccentric."

This time A.J.'s smile was both spontaneous and generous. If David had been thinking about her on a personal level, his opinion would have changed. "Clarissa is never quite what one expects. Your project sounds interesting, Mr. Brady, but the details I have are sketchy. I'd like you to tell me just what it is you plan to produce."

"A documentary on psychic phenomena, or psi, as I'm told it's called in studies, touching on clairvoyance, parapsychology, ESP, palmistry, telepathy and spiritualism."

"Séances and haunted houses, Mr. Brady?"

He caught the faint disapproval in her tone and wondered about it. "For someone with a psychic for a client, you sound remarkably cynical."

"My client doesn't talk to departed souls or read tea leaves." A.J. sat back in the chair in a way she knew registered confidence and position. "Miss DeBasse has proved herself many times over to be an extraordinarily sensitive woman. She's never claimed to have supernatural powers."

"Supernormal."

She drew in a quiet breath. "You've done your homework. Yes, 'supernormal' is the correct term. Clarissa doesn't believe in overstatements."

"Which is one of the reasons I want Clarissa DeBasse for my program."

A.J. noted the easy use of the possessive pronoun. Not the program, but *my* program. David Brady obviously took his work personally. So much the better, she decided. Then he wouldn't care to look like a fool. "Go on."

"I've talked to mediums, palmists, entertainers, scientists, parapsychologists and carnival gypsies. You'd be amazed at the range of personalities."

A.J. stuck her tongue in her cheek. "I'm sure I would."

Though he noticed her amusement, he let it pass. "They run from the obviously fake to the absolutely sincere. I've spoken with heads of parapsychology departments in several well-known institutions. Every one of them mentioned Clarissa's name."

"Clarissa's been generous with herself." Again he thought he detected slight disapproval. "Particularly in the areas of research and testing."

And there would be no ten percent there. He decided that explained her attitude. "I intend to show possibilities, ask questions. The audience will come up with its own answers.

In the five one-hour segments I have, I'll have room to touch on everything from cold spots to tarot cards."

In a gesture she'd thought she'd conquered long ago, she drummed her fingers on the desk. "And where does Miss DeBasse fit in?"

She was his ace in the hole. But he wasn't ready to play her yet. "Clarissa is a recognizable name. A woman who's 'proved herself,' to use your phrase, to be extraordinarily sensitive. Then there's the Van Camp case."

Frowning, A.J. picked up a pencil and began to run it through her fingers. "That was ten years ago."

"The child of a Hollywood star is kidnapped, snatched from his devoted nanny as he plays in the park. The ransom call demands a half a million. The mother's frantic—the police are baffled. Thirty-six hours pass without a clue as the boy's parents desperately try to get the cash together. Over the father's objection, the mother calls a friend, a woman who did her astrological chart and occasionally reads palms. The woman comes, of course, and sits for an hour holding some of the boy's things—his baseball glove, a stuffed toy, the pajama top he'd worn to bed the night before. At the end of that hour, the woman gives the police a description of the boy's kidnappers and the exact location of the house where he's being held. She even describes the room where he's being held, down to the chipped paint on the ceiling. The boy sleeps in his own bed that night."

David pulled out a cigarette, lit it and blew out smoke, while A.J. remained silent. "Ten years doesn't take away that kind of impact, Ms. Fields. The audience will be just as fascinated today as they were then."

It shouldn't have made her angry. It was sheer foolishness to respond that way. A.J. continued to sit silently as she worked back the surge of temper. "A great many people call the Van Camp case a fraud. Dredging that up after ten years will only dredge up more criticism."

"A woman in Clarissa's position must have to deal with criticism continually." He saw the flare come into her eyes—fierce and fast.

"That may be, but I have no intention of allowing her to sign a contract that guarantees it. I have no intention of seeing my client on a televised trial."

"Hold it." He had a temper of his own and could respect hers—if he understood it. "Clarissa goes on trial every time she's in the public eye. If her abilities can't stand up to cameras and questions, she shouldn't be doing what she does. As her agent, I'd think you'd have a stronger belief in her competence."

"My beliefs aren't your concern." Intending to toss him and his contract out, A.J. started to rise, when the phone interrupted her. With an indistinguishable oath, she lifted the receiver. "No calls, Diane. No—oh." A.J. set her teeth and composed herself. "Yes, put her on."

"Oh, I'm so sorry to bother you at work, dear."

"That's all right. I'm in a meeting, so—"

"Oh, yes, I know." Clarissa's calm, apologetic voice came quietly in her ear. "With that nice David Brady."

"That's a matter of opinion."

"I had a feeling you wouldn't hit it off the first time." Clarissa sighed and stroked her cat. "I've been giving that contract business a great deal of thought." She didn't mention the dream, knowing her agent wouldn't want to hear it. "I've decided I want to sign it right away. Now, now, I know what you're going to say," she continued before A.J. could say a word. "You're the agent—you handle the business. You do whatever you think best about clauses and such, but I want to do this program."

A.J. recognized the tone. Clarissa had a feeling. There was never any arguing with Clarissa's feelings. "We need to talk about this."

"Of course, dear, all you like. You and David iron out the details. You're so good at that. I'll leave all the terms up to you, but I will sign the contract."

With David sitting across from her, A.J. couldn't take the satisfaction of accepting defeat by kicking her desk. "All right. But I think you should know I have feelings of my own."

"Of course you do. Come to dinner tonight."

She nearly smiled. Clarissa loved to feed you to smooth things over. Pity she was such a dreadful cook. "I can't. I have a dinner appointment."

"Tomorrow."

"All right. I'll see you then."

After hanging up, A.J. took a deep breath and faced David again. "I'm sorry for the interruption."

"No problem."

"As there's nothing specific in the contract regarding the Van Camp case, including that in the program would be strictly up to Miss DeBasse."

"Of course. I've already spoken to her about it."

A.J. very calmly, very deliberately bit her tongue. "I see. There's also nothing specific about Miss DeBasse's position in the documentary. That will have to be altered."

"I'm sure we can work that out." So she was going to sign, David mused, and listened to a few other minor changes A.J. requested. Before the phone rang, she'd been ready to pitch him out. He'd seen it in her eyes. He held back a smile as they negotiated another minor point. He was no clairvoyant, but he would bet his grant that Clarissa DeBasse had been on the other end of that phone. A.J. Fields had been caught right in the middle. Best place for agents, he thought, and settled back.

"We'll redraft the contract and have it to you tomorrow."

Everybody's in a hurry, she thought, and settled back herself. "Then I'm sure we can do business, Mr. Brady, if we can settle one more point."

"Which is?"

"Miss DeBasse's fee." A.J. flipped back the contract and adjusted the oversize glasses she wore for reading. "I'm afraid this is much less than Miss DeBasse is accustomed to accepting. We'll need another twenty percent."

David lifted a brow. He'd been expecting something along these lines, but he'd expected it sooner. Obviously A.J. Fields hadn't become one of the top in her profession by doing the expected. "You understand we're working in public television. Our budget can't compete with network. As producer, I can offer another five percent, but twenty is out of reach."

"And five is inadequate." A.J. slipped off her glasses and dangled them by an earpiece. Her eyes seemed larger, richer, without them. "I understand public television, Mr. Brady, and I understand your grant." She gave him a charming smile. "Fifteen percent."

Typical agent, he thought, not so much annoyed as fatalistic. She wanted ten, and ten was precisely what his budget would allow. Still, there was a game to be played. "Miss DeBasse is already being paid more than anyone else on contract."

"You're willing to do that because she'll be your biggest draw. I also understand ratings."

"Seven."

"Twelve."

"Ten."

"Done." A.J. rose. Normally the deal would have left her fully satisfied. Because her temper wasn't completely under control it was difficult to appreciate the fact that she'd gotten exactly what she'd intended to get. "I'll look for the revised contracts."

"I'll send them by messenger tomorrow afternoon. That phone call..." He paused as he rose. "You wouldn't be dealing with me without it, would you?"

She studied him a moment and cursed him for being sharp, intelligent and intuitive. All the things she needed for her client. "No, I wouldn't."

"Be sure to thank Clarissa for me." With a smile smug enough to bring her temper back to boil he offered his hand.

"Goodbye, Mr...." When their hands met this time, her voice died. Feelings ran into her with the impact of a slap, leaving her weak and breathless. Apprehension, desire, fury and delight rolled through her at the touch of flesh to flesh. She had only a moment to berate herself for allowing temper to open the door.

"Ms. Fields?" She was staring at him, through him, as though he were an apparition just risen from the floorboards. In his, her hand was limp and icy. Automatically David took her arm. If he'd ever seen a woman about to faint, he was seeing one now. "You'd better sit down."

"What?" Though shaken, A.J. willed herself back. "No, no, I'm fine. I'm sorry, I must have been thinking of something else." But as she spoke, she broke all contact with him and stepped back. "Too much coffee, too little sleep." And stay away from me, she said desperately to herself as she leaned back on the desk. Just stay away. "I'm glad we could do business, Mr. Brady. I'll pass everything along to my client."

Her color was back, her eyes were clear. Still David

hesitated. A moment before she'd looked fragile enough to crumble in his hands. "Sit down."

"I beg your—"

"Damn it, sit." He took her by the elbow and nudged her into a chair. "Your hands are shaking." Before she could do anything about it, he was kneeling in front of her. "I'd advise canceling that dinner appointment and getting a good night's sleep."

She curled her hands together on her lap to keep him from touching her again. "There's no reason for you to be concerned."

"I generally take a personal interest when a woman all but faints at my feet."

The sarcastic tone settled the flutters in her stomach. "Oh, I'm sure you do." But then he took her face in his hand and had her jerking. "Stop that."

Her skin was as soft as it looked, but he would keep that thought for later. "Purely a clinical touch, Ms. Fields. You're not my type."

Her eyes chilled. "Where do I give thanks?"

He wondered why the cool outrage in her eyes made him want to laugh. To laugh, and to taste her. "Very good," he murmured, and straightened. "Lay off the coffee," he advised, and left her alone before he did something ridiculous.

And alone, A.J. brought her knees up to her chest and pressed her face to them. What was she going to do now? she demanded as she tried to squeeze herself into a ball. What in God's name was she going to do?

Chapter 2

A.J. seriously considered stopping for a hamburger before going on to dinner at Clarissa's. She didn't have the heart for it. Besides, if she was hungry enough she would be able to make a decent showing out of actually eating whatever Clarissa prepared.

With the sunroof open, she sat back and tried to enjoy the forty-minute drive from her office to the suburbs. Beside her was a slim leather portfolio that held the contracts David Brady's office had delivered, as promised. Since the changes she'd requested had been made, she couldn't grumble. There was absolutely no substantial reason for her to object to the deal, or to her client working with Brady. All she had was a feeling. She'd been working on that since the previous afternoon.

It had been overwork, she told herself. She hadn't felt anything but a quick, momentary dizziness because she'd stood so fast. She hadn't felt anything for or about David Brady.

But she had.

A.J. cursed herself for the next ten miles before she brought herself under control.

She couldn't afford to be the least bit upset when she arrived in Newport Beach. There was no hiding such things from a woman like Clarissa DeBasse. She would have to be able to discuss not only the contract terms, but David Brady himself with complete objectivity or Clarissa would home in like radar.

For the next ten miles she considered stopping at a phone booth and begging off. She didn't have the heart for that, either.

Relax, A.J. ordered herself, and tried to imagine she was home in her apartment, doing long, soothing yoga exercises. It helped, and as the tension in her muscles eased, she turned up the radio. She kept it high until she turned the engine off in front of the tidy suburban home she'd helped pick out.

A.J. always felt a sense of self-satisfaction as she strolled up the walk. The house suited Clarissa, with its neat green lawn and pretty white shutters. It was true that with the success of her books and public appearances Clarissa could afford a house twice as big in Beverly Hills. But nothing would fit her as comfortably as this tidy brick ranch.

Shifting the brown bag that held wine under her arm, A.J. pushed open the door she knew was rarely locked. "Hello! I'm a six-foot-two, three-hundred-and-twenty-pound burglar come to steal all your jewelry. Care to give me a hand?"

"Oh, did I forget to lock it again?" Clarissa came bustling out of the kitchen, wiping her hands on an already smeared and splattered apron. Her cheeks were flushed from the heat of the stove, her lips already curved in greeting.

"Yes, you forgot to lock it again." Even with an armload of wine, A.J. managed to hug her. Then she kissed both cheeks as she tried to unobtrusively sniff out what was going on in the kitchen.

"It's meat loaf," Clarissa told her. "I got a new recipe."

"Oh." A.J. might have managed the smile if she hadn't remembered the last meat loaf so clearly. Instead she concentrated on the woman. "You look wonderful. I'd swear you were running into L.A. and sneaking into Elizabeth Arden's once a week."

"Oh, I can't be bothered with all that. It's too much worrying that causes lines and sags, anyway. You should remember that."

"So I look like a hag, do I?" A.J. dropped her portfolio on the table and stepped out of her shoes.

"You know I didn't mean that, but I can tell you're worried about something."

"Dinner," A.J. told her, evading. "I only had time for a half a sandwich at lunch."

"There, I've told you a dozen times you don't eat properly. Come into the kitchen. I'm sure everything's about ready."

Satisfied that she'd distracted Clarissa, A.J. started to follow.

"Then you can tell me what's really bothering you."

"Doesn't miss a trick," A.J. muttered as the doorbell rang.

"Get that for me, will you?" Clarissa cast an anxious glance at the kitchen. "I really should check the brussels sprouts."

"Brussels sprouts?" A.J. could only grimace as Clarissa disappeared into the kitchen. "Bad enough I have to eat the meat loaf, but brussels sprouts. I should have had the hamburger." When she opened the door her brows were already lowered.

"You look thrilled to see me."

One hand still on the knob, she stared at David. "What are you doing here?"

"Having dinner." Without waiting for an invitation, David stepped forward and stood with her in the open doorway. "You're tall. Even without your shoes."

A.J. closed the door with a quiet snap. "Clarissa didn't explain this was a business dinner."

"I think she considers it purely social." He hadn't yet figured out why he hadn't gotten the very professional Ms. Fields out of his mind. Maybe he'd get some answers before the evening was up. "Why don't we think of it that way—A.J.?"

Manners had been ingrained in her by a quietly determined mother. Trapped, A.J. nodded. "All right, David. I hope you enjoy living dangerously."

"I beg your pardon?"

She couldn't resist the smile. "We're having meat loaf." She took the bottle of champagne he held and examined the label. "This should help. Did you happen to have a big lunch?"

There was a light in her eyes he'd never noticed before. It was a laugh, a joke, and very appealing. "What are you getting at?"

She patted his shoulder. "Sometimes it's best to go into these things unprepared. Sit down and I'll fix you a drink."

"Aurora."

"Yes?" A.J. answered automatically before she bit her tongue.

"Aurora?" David repeated, experimenting with the way it sounded in his voice. "That's what the *A* stands for?"

When A.J. turned to him her eyes were narrowed. "If just

one person in the business calls me that, I'll know exactly where they got it from. You'll pay."

He ran a finger down the side of his nose, but didn't quite hide the smile. "I never heard a thing."

"Aurora, was that—" Clarissa stopped in the kitchen doorway and beamed. "Yes, it was David. How lovely." She studied both of them, standing shoulder to shoulder just inside her front door. For the instant she concentrated, the aura around them was very clear and very bright. "Yes, how lovely," she repeated. "I'm so glad you came."

"I appreciate your asking me." Finding Clarissa as charming as he had the first time, David crossed to her. He took her hand, but this time brought it to his lips. Pleasure flushed her cheeks.

"Champagne, how nice. We'll open it after I sign the contracts." She glanced over his shoulder to see A.J. frowning. "Why don't you fix yourself and David a drink, dear? I won't be much longer."

A.J. thought of the contracts in her portfolio, and of her own doubts. Then she gave in. Clarissa would do precisely what Clarissa wanted to do. In order to protect her, she had to stop fighting it and accept. "I can guarantee the vodka I bought it myself."

"Fine—on the rocks." David waited while she went to a cabinet and took out a decanter and glasses.

"She remembered the ice," A.J. said, surprised when she opened the brass bucket and found it full.

"You seem to know Clarissa very well."

"I do." A.J. poured two glasses, then turned. "She's much more than simply a client to me, David. That's why I'm concerned about this program."

He walked to her to take the glass. Strange, he thought, you only noticed her scent when you stood close, very close.

He wondered if she used such a light touch to draw men to her or to block their way. "Why the concern?"

If they were going to deal with each other, honesty might help. A.J. glanced toward the kitchen and kept her voice low. "Clarissa has a tendency to be very open with certain people. Too open. She can expose too much of herself, and leave herself vulnerable to all manner of complications."

"Are you protecting her from me?"

A.J. sipped from her drink. "I'm trying to decide if I should."

"I like her." He reached out to twine a lock of A.J.'s hair around his finger, before either of them realized his intention. He dropped his hand again so quickly she didn't have the chance to demand it. "She's a very likable woman," David continued as he turned to wander around the room. He wasn't a man to touch a business associate, especially one he barely knew, in so casual a manner. To give himself distance, he walked to the window to watch birds flutter around a feeder in the side yard. The cat was out there, he noticed, sublimely disinterested as it sunned itself in a last patch of sunlight.

A.J. waited until she was certain her voice would be properly calm and professional. "I appreciate that, but your project comes first, I imagine. You want a good show, and you'll do whatever it takes to produce one."

"That's right." The problem was, he decided, that she wasn't as tailored and streamlined as she'd been the day before. Her blouse was soft and silky, the color of poppies. If she'd had a jacket to match the snug white skirt, she'd left it in her car. She was shoeless and her hair had been tossed by the wind. He took another drink. She still wasn't his type. "But I don't believe I have a reputation for exploiting people in order to get it. I do my job, A.J., and expect the same from anyone who works with me."

"Fair enough." She finished the unwanted drink. "My job is to protect Clarissa in every way."

"I don't see that we have a problem."

"There now, everything's ready." Clarissa came out to see her guests not shoulder to shoulder, but with the entire room between them. Sensitive to mood, she felt the tension, confusion and distrust. Quite normal, she decided, for two stubborn, self-willed people on opposing ends. She wondered how long it would take them to admit attraction, let alone accept it. "I hope you're both hungry."

A.J. set down her empty glass with an easy smile. "David tells me he's starved. You'll have to give him an extra portion."

"Wonderful." Delighted, she led the way into the dining area. "I love to eat by candlelight, don't you?" She had a pair of candles burning on the table, and another half-dozen tapers on the sideboard. A.J. decided the romantic light definitely helped the looks of the meat loaf. "Aurora brought the wine, so I'm sure it's lovely. You pour, David, and I'll serve."

"It looks wonderful," he told her, and wondered why A.J. muffled a chuckle.

"Thank you. Are you from California originally, David?" Clarissa asked as she handed A.J. a platter.

"No, Washington State." He tipped Beaujolais into Clarissa's glass.

"Beautiful country." She handed Aurora a heaping bowl of mashed potatoes. "But so cold."

He could remember the long, windy winters with some nostalgia. "I didn't have any trouble acclimating to L.A."

"I grew up in the East and came out here with my husband nearly thirty years ago. In the fall I'm still the tiniest bit homesick for Vermont. You haven't taken any vegetables, Aurora. You know how I worry that you don't eat properly."

A.J. added brussels sprouts to her plate and hoped she'd be able to ignore them. "You should take a trip back this year," A.J. told Clarissa. One bite of the meat loaf was enough. She reached for the wine.

"I think about it. Do you have any family, David?"

He'd just had his first experience with Clarissa's cooking and hadn't recovered. He wondered what recipe she'd come across that called for leather. "Excuse me?"

"Any family?"

"Yes." He glanced at A.J. and saw the knowing smirk. "Two brothers and a sister scattered around Washington and Oregon."

"I came from a big family myself. I thoroughly enjoyed my childhood." Reaching out, she patted A.J.'s hand. "Aurora was an only child."

With a laugh A.J. gave Clarissa's hand a quick squeeze. "And I thoroughly enjoyed my childhood." Because she saw David politely making his way through a hill of lumpy potatoes, she felt a little tug on her conscience. A.J. waited until it passed. "What made you choose documentaries, David?"

"I'd always been fascinated by little films." Picking up the salt, he used it liberally. "With a documentary, the plot's already there, but it's up to you to come up with the angles, to find a way to present it to an audience and make them care while they're being entertained."

"Isn't it more of a learning experience?"

"I'm not a teacher." Bravely he dipped back into the meat loaf. "You can entertain with truth and speculation just as satisfyingly as you can entertain with fiction."

Somehow watching him struggle with the meal made it more palatable for her. "No urge to produce the big film?"

"I like television," he said easily, and reached for the wine. They were all going to need it. "I happen to think there's too much pap and not enough substance."

A.J.'s brow lifted, to disappear under a thin fringe of bangs. "Pap?"

"Unfortunately network television's rife with it. Shows like *Empire,* for instance, or *It Takes Two.*"

"Really." A.J. leaned forward. "*Empire* has been a top-rated show for four years." She didn't add that it was a personal favorite.

"My point exactly. If a show like that retains consistently high ratings—a show that relies on steam, glitter and contrivance—it proves that the audience is being fed a steady stream of garbage."

"Not everyone feels a show has to be educational or 'good' for it to be quality. The problem with public television is that it has its nose up in the air so often the average American ignores it. After working eight hours, fighting traffic, coping with children and dealing with car repair bills, a person's entitled to relax."

"Absolutely." Amazing, he thought, how lovely she became when you lit a little fire under her. Maybe she was a woman who needed conflict in her life. "But that same person doesn't have to shut off his or her intelligence to be entertained. That's called escapism."

"I'm afraid I don't watch enough television to see the difference," Clarissa commented, pleased to see her guests clearing their plates. "But don't you represent that lovely woman who plays on *Empire?*"

"Audrey Cummings." A.J. slipped her fingers under the cup of her wineglass and swirled it lightly. "A very accomplished actress, who's also played Shakespeare. We've just made a deal to have her take the role of Maggie in a remake of *Cat on a Hot Tin Roof*." The success of that deal was still sweet. Sipping her wine, she tilted her head at David. "For a play that deals in a lot of steam and sweat, it's amazing what longevity it's had. We can't claim it's a Verdi opera, can we?"

"There's more to public television than Verdi." He'd touched a nerve, he realized. But, then, so had she. "I don't suppose you caught the profile on Taylor Brooks? I thought it was one of the most detailed and informative on a rock star I'd ever seen." He picked up his wine in a half toast. "You don't represent him, too, do you?"

"No." She decided to play it to the hilt. "We dated casually a couple of years ago. I have a rule about keeping business and personal relationships separated."

"Wise." He lifted his wine and sipped. "Very wise."

"Unlike you, I have no prejudices when it comes to television. If I did, you'd hardly be signing one of my top clients."

"More meat loaf?" Clarissa asked.

"I couldn't eat another bite." A.J. smiled at David. "Perhaps David would like more."

"As much as I appreciate the home cooking, I can't." He tried not to register too much relief as he stood. "Let me help you clear up."

"Oh, no." Rising, Clarissa brushed his offer aside. "It relaxes me. Aurora, I think David was just a bit disappointed with me the first time we met. Why don't you show him my collection?"

"All right." Picking up her wineglass, A.J. gestured to him to follow. "You've scored points," she commented. "Clarissa doesn't show her collection to everyone."

"I'm flattered." But he took her by the elbow to stop her

as they started down a narrow hallway. "You'd prefer it if I kept things strictly business with Clarissa."

A.J. lifted the glass to her lips and watched him over the rim. She'd prefer, for reasons she couldn't name, that he stayed fifty miles from Clarissa. And double that from her. "Clarissa chooses her own friends."

"And you make damn sure they don't take advantage of her."

"Exactly. This way." Turning, she walked to a door on the left and pushed it open. "It'd be more effective by candle-light, even more with a full moon, but we'll have to make do." A.J. flicked on the light and stepped out of his view.

It was an average-size room, suitable to a modern ranch house. Here, the windows were heavily draped to block the view of the yard—or to block the view inside. It wasn't difficult to see why Clarissa would use the veil to discourage the curious. The room belonged in a tower—or a dungeon.

Here was the crystal ball he'd expected. Unable to resist, David crossed to a tall, round-topped stand to examine it. The glass was smooth and perfect, reflecting only the faintest hint of the deep blue cloth beneath it. Tarot cards, obviously old and well used, were displayed in a locked case. At a closer look he saw they'd been hand painted. A bookshelf held everything from voodoo to telekinesis. On the shelf with them was a candle in the shape of a tall, slender woman with arms lifted to the sky.

A Ouija board was set out on a table carved with pentagrams. One wall was lined with masks of pottery, ceramic, wood, even papier-mâché. There were dowsing rods and pendulums. A glass cabinet held pyramids of varying sizes. There was more—an Indian rattle, worn and fragile with age, Oriental worry beads in jet, others in amethyst.

"More what you expected?" A.J. asked after a moment.

"No." He picked up another crystal, this one small enough to rest in the palm of his hand. "I stopped expecting this after the first five minutes."

It was the right thing for him to say. A.J. sipped her wine again and tried not to be too pleased. "It's just a hobby with Clarissa, collecting the obvious trappings of the trade."

"She doesn't use them?"

"A hobby only. Actually, it started a long time ago. A friend found those tarot cards in a little shop in England and gave them to her. After that, things snowballed."

The crystal was cool and smooth in his hand as he studied her. "You don't approve?"

A.J. merely shrugged her shoulders. "I wouldn't if she took it seriously."

"Have you ever tried this?" He indicated the Ouija board. "No."

It was a lie. He wasn't sure why she told it, or why he was certain of it. "So you don't believe in any of this."

"I believe in Clarissa. The rest of this is just showmanship."

Still, he was intrigued with it, intrigued with the fascination it held for people through the ages. "You've never been tempted to ask her to look in the crystal for you?"

"Clarissa doesn't need the crystal, and she doesn't tell the future."

He glanced into the clear glass in his hand. "Odd, you'd think if she can do the other things she's reported to be able to do, she could do that."

"I didn't say she couldn't—I said she doesn't."

David looked up from the crystal again. "Explain."

"Clarissa feels very strongly about destiny, and the tampering with it. She's refused, even for outrageous fees, to predict."

"But you're saying she could."

"I'm saying she chooses not to. Clarissa considers her gift a responsibility. Rather than misuse it in any way, she'd push it out of her life."

"Push it out." He set the crystal down. "Do you mean she—a psychic—could just refuse to be one. Just block out the…let's say power, for lack of a better term. Just turn it off?"

Her fingers had dampened on the glass. A.J. casually switched it to her other hand. "To a large extent, yes. You have to be open to it. You're a receptacle, a transmitter—the extent to which you receive or transmit depends on you."

"You seem to know a great deal about it."

He was sharp, she remembered abruptly. Very sharp. A.J. smiled deliberately and moved her shoulders again. "I know a great deal about Clarissa. If you spend any amount of time with her over the next couple of months, you'll know quite a bit yourself."

David walked to her. He watched her carefully as he took the wineglass from her and sipped himself. It was warm now and seemed more potent. "Why do I get the impression that you're uncomfortable in this room. Or is it that you're uncomfortable with me?"

"Your intuition's missing the mark. If you'd like, Clarissa can give you a few exercises to sharpen it."

"Your palms are damp." He took her hand, then ran his fingers down to the wrist. "Your pulse is fast. I don't need intuition to know that."

It was important—vital—that she keep calm. She met his eyes levelly and hoped she managed to look amused. "That probably has more to do with the meat loaf."

"The first time we met you had a very strong, very strange reaction to me."

She hadn't forgotten. It had given her a very restless night. "I explained—"

"I didn't buy it," he interrupted. "I still don't. That might be because I found myself doing a lot of thinking about you."

She'd taught herself to hold her ground. She'd had to. A.J. made one last attempt to do so now, though his eyes seemed much too quiet and intrusive, his voice too firm. She took her wineglass back from him and drained it. She learned it was a mistake, because she could taste him as well as the wine. "David, try to remember I'm not your type." Her voice was cool and faintly cutting. If she'd thought about it a few seconds longer, she would have realized it was the wrong tactic.

"No, you're not." His hand cupped her nape, then slid up into her hair. "But what the hell."

When he leaned closer, A.J. saw two clear-cut choices. She could struggle away and run for cover, or she could meet him with absolute indifference. Because the second choice seemed the stronger, she went with it. It was her next mistake.

He knew how to tempt a woman. How to coax. When his lips lowered to hers they barely touched, while his hand continued to stroke her neck and hair. A.J.'s grip on the wineglass tightened, but she didn't move, not forward, not away. His lips skimmed hers again, with just the hint of his tongue. The breath she'd been holding shuddered out.

As her eyes began to close, as her bones began to soften, he moved away from her mouth to trace his lips over her jaw. Neither of them noticed when the wineglass slipped out of her hand to land on the carpet.

He'd been right about how close you had to get to be tempted by her scent. It was strong and dark and private, as though it came through her pores to hover on her skin. As he brought his lips back to hers, he realized it wasn't something he'd forget. Nor was she.

This time her lips were parted, ready, willing. Still he moved slowly, more for his own sake now. This wasn't the cool man-crusher he'd expected, but a warm, soft woman who could draw you in with vulnerability alone. He needed time to adjust, time to think. When he backed away he still hadn't touched her, and had given her only the merest hint of a kiss. They were both shaken.

"Maybe the reaction wasn't so strange after all, Aurora," he murmured. "Not for either of us."

Her body was on fire; it was icy; it was weak. She couldn't allow her mind to follow suit. Drawing all her reserves of strength, A.J. straightened. "If we're going to be doing business—"

"And we are."

She let out a long, patient breath at the interruption. "Then you'd better understand the ground rules. I don't sleep around, not with clients, not with associates."

It pleased him. He wasn't willing to ask himself why. "Narrows the field, doesn't it?"

"That's my business," she shot back. "My personal life is entirely separate from my profession."

"Hard to do in this town, but admirable. However…" He couldn't resist reaching up to play with a stray strand of hair at her ear. "I didn't ask you to sleep with me."

She caught his hand by the wrist to push it away. It both surprised and pleased her to discover his pulse wasn't any steadier than hers. "Forewarned, you won't embarrass yourself by doing so and being rejected."

"Do you think I would?" He brought his hand back up to stroke a finger down her cheek. "Embarrass myself."

"Stop it."

He shook his head and studied her face again. Attractive, yes. Not beautiful, hardly glamorous. Too cool, too stubborn. So why was he already imagining her naked and wrapped around him? "What is it between us?"

"Animosity."

He grinned, abruptly and completely charming her. She could have murdered him for it. "Maybe part, but even that's too strong for such a short association. A minute ago I was wondering what it would be like to make love with you. Believe it or not, I don't do that with every woman I meet."

Her palms were damp again. "Am I supposed to be flattered?"

"No. I just figure we'll deal better together if we understand each other."

The need to turn and run was desperate. Too desperate. A.J. held her ground. "Understand this. I represent Clarissa DeBasse. I'll look out for her interests, her welfare. If you try to do anything detrimental to her professionally or personally, I'll cut you off at the knees. Other than that, we really don't have anything to worry about."

"Time will tell."

For the first time she took a step away from him. A.J. didn't consider it a retreat as she walked over and put her hand on the light switch. "I have a breakfast meeting in the morning. Let's get the contracts signed, Brady, so we can both do our jobs."

Chapter 3

Preproduction meetings generally left his staff frazzled and out of sorts. David thrived on them. Lists of figures that insisted on being balanced appealed to the practical side of him. Translating those figures into lights, sets and props challenged his creativity. If he hadn't enjoyed finding ways to merge the two, he never would have chosen to be a producer.

He was a man who had a reputation for knowing his own mind and altering circumstances to suit it. The reputation permeated his professional life and filtered through to the personal. As a producer he was tough and, according to many directors, not always fair. As a man he was generous and, according to many women, not always warm.

David would give a director creative freedom, but only to a point. When the creative freedom tempted the director to veer from David's overall view of a project, he stopped him dead. He would discuss, listen and at times compromise. An astute director would realize that the compromise hadn't affected the producer's wishes in the least.

In a relationship he would give a woman an easy, attentive companion. If a woman preferred roses, there would be roses. If she enjoyed rides in the country, there would be rides in the country. But if she attempted to get beneath the skin, he stopped her dead. He would discuss, listen and at times compromise. An astute woman would realize the compromise hadn't affected the man in the least.

Directors would call him tough, but would grudgingly admit they would work with him again. Women would call him cool, but would smile when they heard his voice over the phone.

Neither of these things came to him through carefully thought-out strategy, but simply because he was a man who was careful with his private thoughts—and private needs.

By the time the preproduction meetings were over, the location set and the format jelled, David was anxious for results. He'd picked his team individually, down to the last technician. Because he'd developed a personal interest in Clarissa DeBasse, he decided to begin with her. His choice, he was certain, had nothing to do with her agent.

His initial desire to have her interviewed in her own home was cut off quickly by a brief memo from A.J. Fields. Miss DeBasse was entitled to her privacy. Period. Unwilling to be hampered by a technicality, David arranged for the studio to be decorated in precisely the same homey, suburban atmosphere. He'd have her interviewed there by veteran journalist Alex Marshall. David wanted to thread credibility through speculation. A man of Marshall's reputation could do it for him.

David kept in the background and let his crew take over. He'd had problems with this director before, but both projects they'd collaborated on had won awards. The end product, to David, was the bottom line.

"Put a filter on that light," the director ordered. "We may have to look like we're sitting in the furniture department in the mall, but I want atmosphere. Alex, if you'd run through your intro, I'd like to get a fix on the angle."

"Fine." Reluctantly Alex tapped out his two-dollar cigar and went to work. David checked his watch. Clarissa was late, but not late enough to cause alarm yet. In another ten minutes he'd have an assistant give her a call. He watched Alex run through the intro flawlessly, then wait while the director fussed with the lights. Deciding he wasn't needed at the moment, David opted to make the call himself. Only he'd make it to A.J.'s office. No harm in giving her a hard time, he thought as he pushed through the studio doors. She seemed to be the better for it.

"Oh, David, I do apologize."

He stopped as Clarissa hurried down the hallway. She wasn't anyone's aunt today, he thought, as she reached out to take his hands. Her hair was swept dramatically back, making her look both flamboyant and years younger. There was a necklace of silver links around her neck that held an amethyst the size of his thumb. Her makeup was artfully applied to accent clear blue eyes, just as her dress, deep and rich, accented them. This wasn't the woman who'd fed him meat loaf.

"Clarissa, you look wonderful."

"Thank you. I'm afraid I didn't have much time to prepare. I got the days mixed, you see, and was right in the middle of weeding my petunias when Aurora came to pick me up."

He caught himself looking over her shoulder and down the hall. "She's here?"

"She's parking the car." Clarissa glanced back over her shoulder with a sigh. "I know I'm a trial to her, always have been."

"She doesn't seem to feel that way."

"No, she doesn't. Aurora's so generous."

He'd reserve judgment on that one. "Are you ready, or would you like some coffee or tea first?"

"No, no, I don't like any stimulants when I'm working. They tend to cloud things." Their hands were still linked when her gaze fastened on his. "You're a bit restless, David."

She said it the moment he'd looked back, and seen A.J. coming down the hall. "I'm always edgy on a shoot," he said absently. Why was it he hadn't noticed how she walked before? Fast and fluid.

"That's not it," Clarissa commented, and patted his hand. "But I won't invade your privacy. Ah, here's Aurora. Should we start?"

"We already have," he murmured, still watching A.J.

"Good morning, David. I hope we haven't thrown you off schedule."

She was as sleek and professional as she'd been the first time he'd seen her. Why was it now that he noticed small details? The collar of her blouse rose high on what he knew was a long, slender neck. Her mouth was unpainted. He wanted to take a step closer to see if she wore the same scent. Instead he took Clarissa's arm. "Not at all. I take it you want to watch."

"Of course."

"Just inside here, Clarissa." He pushed open the door. "I'd like to introduce you to your director, Sam Cauldwell. Sam." It didn't appear to bother David that he was interrupting his director. A.J. noticed that he stood where he was and waited for Cauldwell to come to him. She could hardly censure him for it when she'd have used the same technique herself. "This is Clarissa DeBasse."

Cauldwell stemmed obvious impatience to take her hand. "A pleasure, Miss DeBasse. I read both your books to give myself a feel for your segment of the program."

"That's very kind of you. I hope you enjoyed them."

"I don't know if 'enjoyed' is the right word." He gave a quick shake of his head. "They certainly gave me something to think about."

"Miss DeBasse is ready to start whenever you're set."

"Great. Would you mind taking a seat over here. We'll take a voice test and recheck the lighting."

As Cauldwell led her away, David saw A.J. watching him like a hawk. "You make a habit of hovering over your clients, A.J.?"

Satisfied that Clarissa was all right for the moment, A.J. turned to him. "Yes. Just the way I imagine you hover over your directors."

"All in a day's work, right? You can get a better view from over here."

"Thanks." She moved with him to the left of the studio, watching as Clarissa was introduced to Alex Marshall. The veteran newscaster was tall, lean and distinguished. Twenty-five years in the game had etched a few lines on his face, but the gray threading through his hair contrasted nicely with his deep tan. "A wise choice for your narrator," she commented.

"The face America trusts."

"There's that, of course. Also, I can't imagine him putting up with any nonsense. Bring in a palm reader from Sunset Boulevard and he'll make her look like a fool regardless of the script."

"That's right."

A.J. sent him an even look. "He won't make a fool out of Clarissa."

He gave her a slow, acknowledging nod. "That's what I'm counting on. I called your office last week."

"Yes, I know." A.J. saw Clarissa laugh at something Alex said. "Didn't my assistant get back to you?"

"I didn't want to talk to your assistant."

"I've been tied up. You've very nearly recreated Clarissa's living room, haven't you?"

"That's the idea. You're trying to avoid me, A.J." He shifted just enough to block her view, so that she was forced to look at him. Because he'd annoyed her, she made the look thorough, starting at his shoes, worn canvas high-tops, up the casual pleated slacks to the open collar of his shirt before she settled on his face.

"I'd hoped you'd catch on."

"And you might succeed at it." He ran his finger down her lapel, over a pin of a half-moon. "But she's going to get in the way." He glanced over his shoulder at Clarissa.

She schooled herself for this, lectured herself and rehearsed the right responses. Somehow it wasn't as easy as she'd imagined. "David, you don't seem to be one of those men who are attracted to rejection."

"No." His thumb continued to move over the pin as he looked back at her. "You don't seem to be one of those women who pretend disinterest to attract."

"I don't pretend anything." She looked directly into his eyes, determined not a flicker of her own unease would show. "I am disinterested. And you're standing in my way."

"That's something that might get to be a habit." But he moved aside.

It took nearly another forty-five minutes of discussion, changes and technical fine-tuning before they were ready to shoot. Because she was relieved David was busy elsewhere, A.J. waited patiently. Which meant she only checked her watch half a dozen times. Clarissa sat easily on the sofa and sipped water. But whenever she glanced up and looked in her direction, A.J. was glad she'd decided to come.

The shoot began well enough. Clarissa sat with Alex on the sofa. He asked questions; she answered. They touched on clairvoyance, precognition, Clarissa's interest in astrology. Clarissa had a knack for taking long, confusing phrases and making them simple, understandable. One of the reasons she was often in demand on the lecture circuit was her ability to take the mysteries of psi and relate them to the average person. It was one area A.J. could be certain Clarissa De-Basse would handle herself. Relaxing, she took a piece of hard candy out of her briefcase in lieu of lunch.

They shot, reshot, altered angles and repeated themselves for the camera. Hours passed, but A.J. was content. Quality was the order of the day. She wanted nothing less for Clarissa.

Then they brought out the cards.

She'd nearly taken a step forward, when the slightest signal from Clarissa had her turning and staying where she was. She hated this, and always had.

"Problem?"

She hadn't realized he'd come up beside her. A.J. sent David a killing look before she riveted her attention on the set again. "We didn't discuss anything like this."

"The cards?" Surprised by her response, David, too, watched the set. "We cleared it with Clarissa."

A.J. set her teeth. "Next time, Brady, clear it with me."

David decided that whatever nasty retort he could make would wait when Alex's broadcaster's voice rose rich and clear in the studio. "Miss DeBasse, using cards to test ESP is a rather standard device, isn't it?"

"A rather limited test, yes. They're also an aid in testing telepathy."

"You've been involved in testing of this sort before, at Stanford, UCLA, Columbia, Duke, as well as institutions in England."

"Yes, I have."

"Would you mind explaining the process?"

"Of course. The cards used in laboratory tests are generally two colors, with perhaps five different shapes. Squares, circles, wavy lines, that sort of thing. Using these, it's possible to determine chance and what goes beyond chance. That is, with two colors, it's naturally a fifty-fifty proposition. If a subject hits the colors fifty percent of the time, it's accepted as chance. If a subject hits sixty percent, then it's ten percent over chance."

"It sounds relatively simple."

"With colors alone, yes. The shapes alter that. With, say, twenty-five cards in a run, the tester is able to determine by the number of hits, or correct answers, how much over chance the subject guessed. If the subject hits fifteen times out of twenty-five, it can be assumed the subject's ESP abilities are highly tuned."

"She's very good," David murmured.

"Damned right she is." A.J. folded her arms and tried not to be annoyed. This was Clarissa's business, and no one knew it better.

"Could you explain how it works—for you, that is?" Alex idly shuffled the pack of cards as he spoke to her. "Do you get a feeling when a card is held up?"

"A picture," Clarissa corrected. "One gets a picture."

"Are you saying you get an actual picture of the card?"

"An actual picture can be held in your hand." She smiled at him patiently. "I'm sure you read a great deal, Mr. Marshall."

"Yes, I do."

"When you read, the words, the phrasings make pictures in your head. This is very similar to that."

"I see." His doubt was obvious, and to David, the perfect reaction. "That's imagination."

"ESP requires a control of the imagination and a sharpening of concentration."

"Can anyone do this?"

"That's something that's still being researched. There are some who feel ESP can be learned. Others believe psychics are born. My own opinion falls in between."

"Can you explain?"

"I think every one of us has certain talents or abilities, and the degree to which they're developed and used depends on the individual. It's possible to block these abilities. It's more usual, I think, to simply ignore them so that they never come into question."

"Your abilities have been documented. We'd like to give an impromptu demonstration here, with your cooperation."

"Of course."

"This is an ordinary deck of playing cards. One of the crew purchased them this morning, and you haven't handled them. Is that right?"

"No, I haven't. I'm not very clever with games." She smiled, half apologetic, half amused, and delighted the director.

"Now if I pick a card and hold it like this." Alex pulled one from the middle of the deck and held its back to her. "Can you tell me what it is?"

"No." Her smile never faded as the director started to

signal to stop the tape. "You'll have to look at the card, Mr. Marshall, think of it, actually try to picture it in your mind." As the tape continued to roll, Alex nodded and obliged her. "I'm afraid you're not concentrating very hard, but it's a red card. That's better." She beamed at him. "Nine of diamonds."

The camera caught the surprise on his face before he turned the card over. Nine of diamonds. He pulled a second card and repeated the process. When they reached the third, Clarissa stopped, frowning.

"You're trying to confuse me by thinking of a card other than the one in your hand. It blurs things a bit, but the ten of clubs comes through stronger."

"Fascinating," Alex murmured as he turned over the ten of clubs. "Really fascinating."

"I'm afraid this sort of thing is often no more than a parlor game," Clarissa corrected. "A clever mentalist can do nearly the same thing—in a different way, of course."

"You're saying it's a trick."

"I'm saying it can be. I'm not good at tricks myself, so I don't try them, but I can appreciate a good show."

"You started your career by reading palms." Alex set down the cards, not entirely sure of himself.

"A long time ago. Technically anyone can read a palm, interpret the lines." She held hers out to him. "Lines that represent finance, emotion, length of life. A good book out of the library will tell you exactly what to look for and how to find it. A sensitive doesn't actually read a palm so much as absorb feelings."

Charmed, but far from sold, Alex held out his. "I don't quite see how you could absorb feelings by looking at the palm of my hand."

"You transmit them," she told him. "Just as you transmit

everything else, your hopes, your sorrows, your joys. I can take your palm and at a glance tell you that you communicate well and have a solid financial base, but that would hardly be earth-shattering news. But…" She held her own out to him. "If you don't mind," she began, and cupped his hand in hers. "I can look again and say that—" She stopped, blinked and stared at him. "Oh."

A.J. made a move forward, only to be blocked by David. "Let her be," he muttered. "This is a documentary, remember. We can't have it staged and tidy. If she's uncomfortable with this part of the tape we can cut it."

"If she's uncomfortable you will cut it."

Clarissa's hand was smooth and firm under Alex's, but her eyes were wide and stunned. "Should I be nervous?" he asked, only half joking.

"Oh, no." With a little laugh, she cleared her throat. "No, not at all. You have very strong vibrations, Mr. Marshall."

"Thank you. I think."

"You're a widower, fifteen, sixteen years now. You were a very good husband." She smiled at him, relaxed again. "You can be proud of that. And a good father."

"I appreciate that, Miss DeBasse, but again, it's hardly news."

She continued as if he hadn't spoken. "Both your children are settled now, which eases your mind, as it does any parent's. They never gave you a great deal of worry, though there was a period with your son, during his early twenties, when you had some rough spots. But some people take longer to find their niche, don't they?"

He wasn't smiling anymore, but staring at her as intensely as she stared at him. "I suppose."

"You're a perfectionist, in your work and in your private life. That made it a little difficult for your son. He couldn't quite live up to your expectations. You shouldn't have worried so much, but of course all parents do. Now that he's going to be a father himself, you're closer. The idea of grandchildren pleases you. At the same time it makes you think more about the future—your own mortality. But I wonder if you're wise to be thinking of retiring. You're in the prime of your life and too used to deadlines and rushing to be content with that fishing boat for very long. Now if you'd—" She stopped herself with a little shake of the head. "I'm sorry. I tend to ramble on when someone interests me. I'm always afraid of getting too personal."

"Not at all." He closed his hand into a loose fist. "Miss DeBasse, you're quite amazing."

"Cut!" Cauldwell could have gotten down on his knees and kissed Clarissa's feet. Alex Marshall considering retirement. There hadn't been so much as a murmur of it on the grapevine. "I want to see the playback in thirty minutes. Alex, thank you. It's a great start. Miss DeBasse—" He'd have taken her hand again if he hadn't been a little leery of giving off the wrong vibrations. "You were sensational. I can't wait to start the next segment with you."

Before he'd finished thanking her, A.J. was at her side. She knew what would happen, what invariably happened. One of the crew would come up and tell Clarissa about a "funny thing that happened to him." Then there would be another asking for his palm to be read. Some would be smirking, others would be curious, but inside of ten minutes Clarissa would be surrounded.

"If you're ready, I'll drive you home," A.J. began.

"Now I thought we'd settled that." Clarissa looked idly around for her purse without any idea where she'd set it. "It's too far for you to drive all the way to Newport Beach and back again."

"Just part of the service." A.J. handed her the purse she'd been holding throughout the shoot.

"Oh, thank you, dear. I couldn't imagine what I'd done with it. I'll take a cab."

"We have a driver for you." David didn't have to look at A.J. to know she was steaming. He could all but feel the heat. "We wouldn't dream of having you take a cab all the way back."

"That's very kind."

"But it won't be necessary," A.J. put in.

"No, it won't." Smoothly Alex edged in and took Clarissa's hand. "I'm hoping Miss DeBasse will allow me to drive her home—after she has dinner with me."

"That would be lovely," Clarissa told him before A.J. could say a word. "I hope I didn't embarrass you, Mr. Marshall."

"Not at all. In fact, I was fascinated."

"How nice. Thank you for staying with me, dear." She kissed A.J.'s cheek. "It always puts me at ease. Good night, David."

"Good night, Clarissa. Alex." He stood beside A.J. as they linked arms and strolled out of the studio. "A nice-looking couple."

Before the words were out of his mouth, A.J. turned on him. If it had been possible to grow fangs, she'd have grown them. "You jerk." She was halfway to the studio doors before he stopped her.

"And what's eating you?"

If he hadn't said it with a smile on his face, she might have controlled herself. "I want to see that last fifteen minutes of tape, Brady, and if I don't like what I see, it's out."

"I don't recall anything in the contract about you having editing rights, A.J."

"There's nothing in the contract saying that Clarissa would read palms, either."

"Granted. Alex ad-libbed that, and it worked very well. What's the problem?"

"You were watching, damn it." Needing to turn her temper on something, she rammed through the studio doors.

"I was," David agreed as he took her arm to slow her down. "But obviously I didn't see what you did."

"She was covering." A.J. raked a hand through her hair. "She felt something as soon as she took his hand. When you look at the tape you'll see five, ten seconds where she just stares."

"So it adds to the mystique. It's effective."

"Damn your 'effective'!" She swung around so quickly she nearly knocked him into a wall. "I don't like to see her hit that way. I happen to care about her as a person, not just a commodity."

"All right, hold it. Hold it!" He caught up to her again as she shoved through the outside door. "There didn't seem to be a thing wrong with Clarissa when she left here."

"I don't like it." A.J. stormed down the steps toward the parking lot. "First the lousy cards. I'm sick of seeing her tested that way."

"A.J., the cards are a natural. She's done that same test, in much greater intensity, for institutes all over the country."

"I know. And it makes me furious that she has to prove herself over and over. Then that palm business. Something upset her." She began to pace on the patch of lawn bordering the sidewalk. "There was something there and I didn't even have the chance to talk to her about it before that six-foot reporter with the golden voice muscled in."

"Alex?" Though he tried, for at least five seconds, to

control himself, David roared with laughter. "God, you're priceless."

Her eyes narrowed, her face paled with rage, she stopped pacing. "So you think it's funny, do you? A trusting, amazingly innocent woman goes off with a virtual stranger and you laugh. If anything happens to her—"

"Happens?" David rolled his eyes skyward. "Good God, A.J., Alex Marshall is hardly a maniac. He's a highly respected member of the news media. And Clarissa is certainly old enough to make up her own mind—and make her own dates."

"It's not a date."

"Looked that way to me."

She opened her mouth, shut it again, then whirled around toward the parking lot.

"Now wait a minute. I said wait." He took her by both arms and trapped her between himself and a parked car. "I'll be damned if I'm going to chase you all over L.A."

"Just go back inside and take a look at that take. I want to see it tomorrow."

"I don't take orders from paranoid agents or anyone else. We're going to settle this right here. I don't know what's working on you, A.J., but I can't believe you're this upset because a client's going out to dinner."

"She's not just a client," A.J. hurled back at him. "She's my mother."

Her furious announcement left them both momentarily speechless. He continued to hold her by the shoulders while she fought to even her breathing. Of course he should have seen it, David realized. The shape of the face, the eyes. Especially the eyes. "I'll be damned."

"I can only second that," she murmured, then let herself

lean back against the car. "Look, that's not for publication. Understand?"

"Why?"

"Because we both prefer it that way. Our relationship is private."

"All right." He rarely argued with privacy. "Okay, that explains why you take such a personal interest, but I think you carry it a bit too far."

"I don't care what you think." Because her head was beginning to pound, she straightened. "Excuse me."

"No." Calmly David blocked her way. "Some people might say you interfere with your mother's life because you don't have enough to fill your own."

Her eyes became very dark, her skin very pale. "My life is none of your business, Brady."

"Not at the moment, but while this project's going on, Clarissa's is. Give her some room, A.J."

Because it sounded so reasonable, her hackles rose. "You don't understand."

"No, maybe you should explain it to me."

"What if Alex Marshall presses her for an interview over dinner? What if he wants to get her alone so he can hammer at her?"

"What if he simply wanted to have dinner with an interesting, attractive woman? You might give Clarissa more credit."

She folded her arms. "I won't have her hurt."

He could argue with her. He could even try reason. Somehow he didn't think either would work quite yet. "Let's go for a drive."

"What?"

"A drive. You and me." He smiled at her. "It happens to be my car you're leaning on."

"Oh, sorry." She straightened again. "I have to get back to the office. There's some paperwork I let hang today."

"Then it can hang until tomorrow." Drawing out his keys, he unlocked the door. "I could use a ride along the beach."

So could she. She'd overreacted—there was no question of it. She needed some air, some speed, something to clear her head. Maybe it wasn't wise to take it with him, but... "Are you going to put the top down?"

"Absolutely."

It helped—the drive, the air, the smell of the sea, the blare of the radio. He didn't chat at her or try to ease her into conversation. A.J. did something she allowed herself to do rarely in the company of others. She relaxed.

How long had it been, she wondered, since she'd driven along the coast, no time frame, no destination? If she couldn't remember, then it had been too long. A.J. closed her eyes, emptied her mind and enjoyed.

Just who was she? David asked himself as he watched her relax, degree by degree, beside him. Was she the tough, no-nonsense agent with an eye out for ten percent of a smooth deal? Was she the fiercely protective, obviously devoted daughter—who was raking in that same ten percent of her mother's talent on one hand and raising the roof about exploitation the next? He couldn't figure her.

He was a good judge of people. In his business he'd be producing home movies if he weren't. Yet when he'd kissed her he hadn't found the hard-edged, self-confident woman he'd expected, but a nervous, vulnerable one. For some reason, she didn't entirely fit who she was, or what she'd chosen to be. It might be interesting to find out why.

"Hungry?"

Half dreaming, A.J. opened her eyes and looked at him. How was it he hadn't seen it before? David asked himself.

The eyes, the eyes were so like Clarissa's, the shape, the color, the…depth, he decided for lack of a better word. It ran through his head that maybe she was like Clarissa in other ways. Then he dismissed it.

"I'm sorry," she murmured, "I wasn't paying attention." But she could have described his face in minute detail, from the hard cheekbones to the slight indentation in his chin. Letting out a long breath, she drew herself in. A wise woman controlled her thoughts as meticulously as her emotions.

"I asked if you were hungry."

"Yes." She stretched her shoulders. "How far have we gone?"

Not far enough. The thought ran unbidden through his mind. Not nearly far enough. "About twenty miles. Your choice." He eased over to the shoulder of the road and indicated a restaurant on one side and a hamburger stand on the other.

"I'll take the burger. If we can sit on the beach."

"Nothing I like better than a cheap date."

A.J. let herself out. "This isn't a date."

"I forgot. You can pay for your own." He'd never heard her laugh like that before. Easy, feminine, fresh. "Just for that I'll spring." But he didn't touch her as they walked up to the stand. "What'll it be?"

"The jumbo burger, large fries and the super shake. Chocolate."

"Big talk."

As they waited, they watched a few early-evening swimmers splash in the shallows. Gulls swooped around, chattering and loitering near the stand, waiting for handouts. David left them disappointed as he gathered up the paper bags. "Where to?"

"Down there. I like to watch." A.J. walked out on the

beach and, ignoring her linen skirt, dropped down on the sand. "I don't get to the beach often enough." Kicking off her shoes, she slid stockinged feet in the sand so that her skirt hiked up to her thighs. David took a good long look before he settled beside her.

"Neither do I," he decided, wondering just how those legs—and the rest of her—might look in a bikini.

"I guess I made quite a scene."

"I guess you did." He pulled out her hamburger and handed it to her.

"I hate to," she said, and took a fierce bite. "I don't have a reputation as an abrasive or argumentative agent, just a tough one. I only lose objectivity with Clarissa."

He screwed the paper cups into the sand. "Objectivity is shot to hell when we love somebody."

"She's so good. I don't just mean at what she does, but inside." A.J. took the fries he offered and nibbled one. "Good people can get hurt so much easier than others, you know. And she's so willing to give of herself. If she gave everything she wanted, she'd have nothing left."

"So you're there to protect her."

"That's right." She turned, challenging.

"I'm not arguing with you." He held up a hand. "For some reason I'd like to understand."

With a little laugh she looked back out to sea. "You had to be there."

"Why don't you tell me what it was like? Growing up."

She never discussed it with anyone. Then again, she never sat on a beach eating hamburgers with associates. Maybe it was a day for firsts. "She was a wonderful mother. Is. Clarissa's so loving, so generous."

"Your father?"

"He died when I was eight. He was a salesman, so he

was away a lot. He was a good salesman," she added with the ghost of a smile. "We were lucky there. There were savings and a little bit of stock. Problem was the bills didn't get paid. Not that the money wasn't there. Clarissa just forgot. You'd pick up the phone and it would be dead because she'd misplaced the bill. I guess I just started taking care of her."

"You'd have been awfully young for that."

"I didn't mind." This time the smile bloomed fully. There were, as with her mother, the faintest of dimples in her cheeks. "I was so much better at managing than she. We had a little more coming in once she started reading palms and doing charts. She really just sort of blossomed then. She has a need to help people, to give them—I don't know—reassurance. Hope. Still, it was an odd time. We lived in a nice neighborhood and people would come and go through our living room. The neighbors were fascinated, and some of them came in regularly for readings, but outside the house there was a kind of distance. It was as if they weren't quite sure of Clarissa."

"It would have been uncomfortable for you."

"Now and then. She was doing what she had to do. Some people shied away from us, from the house, but she never seemed to notice. Anyway, the word spread and she became friends with the Van Camps. I guess I was around twelve or thirteen. The first time movie stars showed up at the house I was awestruck. Within a year it became a matter of course. I've known actors to call her before they'd accept a role. She'd always tell them the same thing. They had to rely on their own feelings. The one thing Clarissa will never do is make decisions for anyone else. But they still called. Then the little Van Camp boy was kidnapped. After that the press camped on the lawn, the phone never stopped. I ended up moving her out to Newport Beach. She can keep a low profile there, even when another case comes up."

"There was the Ridehour murders."

She stood up abruptly and walked closer to the sea. Rising, David walked with her. "You've no idea how she suffered through that." Emotions trembled in her voice as she wrapped her arms around herself. "You can't imagine what a toll something like that can take on a person like Clarissa. I wanted to stop her, but I knew I couldn't."

When she closed her eyes, David put a hand on her shoulder. "Why would you want to stop her if she could help?"

"She grieved. She hurt. God, she all but lived it, even before she was called in." She opened her eyes and turned to him then. "Do you understand, even before she was called in, she was involved?"

"I'm not sure I do."

"No, you can't." She gave an impatient shake of her head for expecting it. "I suppose you have to live it. In any case, they asked for help. It doesn't take any more than that with Clarissa. Five young girls dead." She closed her eyes again. "She never speaks of it, but I know she saw each one. I know." Then she pushed the thought aside, as she knew she had to. "Clarissa thinks of her abilities as a gift...but you've no idea what a curse that can be."

"You'd like her to stop. Shut down. Is that possible?"

A.J. laughed again and drew both hands through hair the wind had tossed. "Oh, yes, but not for Clarissa. I've accepted that she needs to give. I just make damn sure the wrong person doesn't take."

"And what about you?" He would have sworn something in her froze at the casual question. "Did you become an agent to protect your mother?"

She relaxed again. "Partly. But I enjoy what I do." Her eyes were clear again. "I'm good at it."

"And what about Aurora?" He brought his hands up her arms to her shoulders.

A yearning rose up in her, just from the touch. She blocked it off. "Aurora's only there for Clarissa."

"Why?"

"Because I know how to protect myself as well as my mother."

"From what?"

"It's getting late, David."

"Yeah." One hand skimmed over to her throat. Her skin was soft there, sun kissed and soft. "I'm beginning to think the same thing. I never did finish kissing you, Aurora."

His hands were strong. She'd noticed it before, but it seemed to matter more now. "It's better that way."

"I'm beginning to think that, too. Damn if I can figure out why I want to so much."

"Give it a little time. It'll pass."

"Why don't we test it out?" He lifted a brow as he looked down at her. "We're on a public beach. The sun hasn't set. If I kiss you here, it can't go any further than that, and maybe we'll figure out why we unnerve each other." When he drew her closer, she stiffened. "Afraid?" Why would the fact that she might be, just a little, arouse him?

"No." Because she'd prepared herself she almost believed it was true. He wouldn't have the upper hand this time, she told herself. She wouldn't allow it. Deliberately she lifted her arms and twined them around his neck. When he hesitated, she pressed her lips to his.

He'd have sworn the sand shifted under his feet. He was certain the crash of the waves grew in volume until it filled the air like thunder. He'd intended to control the situation like an experiment. But intentions changed as mouth met mouth. She tasted warm—cool, sweet—pungent. He had a desperate need to find out which of his senses could be trusted. Before either of them was prepared, he plunged himself into the kiss and dragged her with him.

Too fast. Her mind whirled with the thought. Too far. But her body ignored the warning and strained against him. She wanted, and the want was clearer and sharper than any want had ever been. She needed, and the need was deeper and more intense than any other need. As the feelings drummed into her, her fingers curled into his hair. Hunger for him rose so quickly she moaned with it. It wasn't right. It couldn't be right. Yet the feeling swirled through her that it was exactly right and had always been.

A gull swooped overhead and was gone, leaving only the flicker of a shadow, the echo of a sound.

When they drew apart, A.J. stepped back. With distance came a chill, but she welcomed it after the enervating heat. She would have turned then without a word, but his hands were on her again.

"Come home with me."

She had to look at him then. Passion, barely controlled, darkened his eyes. Desire, edged with temptation, roughened his voice. And she felt…too much. If she went, she would give too much.

"No." Her voice wasn't quite steady, but it was final. "I don't want this, David."

"Neither do I." He backed off then. He hadn't meant for things to go so far. He hadn't wanted to feel so much. "I'm not sure that's going to make any difference."

"We have control over our own lives." When she looked out to sea again, the wind rushed her hair back, leaving her face unframed. "I know what I want and don't want in mine."

"Wants change." Why was he arguing? She said nothing he hadn't thought himself.

"Only if we let them."

"And if I said I wanted you?"

The pulse in her throat beat quickly, so quickly she wasn't sure she could get the words around it. "I'd say you were making a mistake. You were right, David, when you said I wasn't your type. Go with your first impulse. It's usually the best."

"In this case I think I need more data."

"Suit yourself," she said as though it made no difference. "I have to get back. I want to call Clarissa and make sure she's all right."

He took her arm one last time. "You won't always be able to use her, Aurora."

She stopped and sent him the cool, intimate look so like her mother's. "I don't use her at all," she murmured. "That's the difference between us." She turned and made her way back across the sand.

Chapter 4

There was moonlight, shafts of it, glimmering. There was the scent of hyacinths—the faintest fragrance on the faintest of breezes. From somewhere came the sound of water, running, bubbling. On a wide-planked wood floor there were shadows, the shifting grace of an oak outside the window. A painting on the wall caught the eye and held it. It was no more than slashes of red and violet lines on a white, white canvas, but somehow it portrayed energy, movement, tensions with undercurrents of sex. There was a mirror, taller than most. A.J. saw herself reflected in it.

She looked indistinct, ethereal, lost. With shadows all around it seemed to her she could just step forward into the glass and be gone. The chill that went through her came not from without but from within. There was something to fear here, something as nebulous as her own reflection. Instinct told her to go, and to go quickly, before she learned what it was. But as she turned something blocked her way.

David stood between her and escape, his hands firm on her shoulders. When she looked at him she saw that his eyes were dark and impatient. Desire—his or hers—thickened the air until even breathing was an effort.

I don't want this. Did she say it? Did she simply think it? Though she couldn't be sure, she heard his response clearly enough, clipped and annoyed.

"You can't keep running, Aurora. Not from me, not from yourself."

Then she was sliding down into a dark, dark tunnel with soft edges just beginning to flame.

A.J. jerked up in bed, breathless and trembling. She didn't see moonlight, but the first early shafts of sun coming through her own bedroom windows. Her bedroom, she repeated to herself as she pushed sleep-tousled hair from her eyes. There were no hyacinths here, no shadows, no disturbing painting.

A dream, she repeated over and over. It had just been a dream. But why did it have to be so real? She could almost feel the slight pressure on her shoulders where his hands had pressed. The turbulent, churning sensation through her system hadn't faded. And why had she dreamed of David Brady?

There were several logical reasons she could comfort herself with. He'd been on her mind for the past couple of weeks. Clarissa and the documentary had been on her mind and they were all tangled together. She'd been working hard, maybe too hard, and the last true relaxation she'd had had been those few minutes with him on the beach.

Still, it was best not to think of that, of what had happened or nearly happened, of what had been said or left unsaid. It would be better, much better, to think of schedules, of work and of obligations.

There'd be no sleeping now. Though it was barely six, A.J. pushed the covers aside and rose. A couple of strong cups of black coffee and a cool shower would put her back in order. They had to. Her schedule was much too busy to allow her to waste time worrying over a dream.

Her kitchen was spacious and very organized. She allowed no clutter, even in a room she spent little time in. Counters and appliances gleamed in stark white, as much from the diligence of her housekeeper as from disuse. A.J. went down the two steps that separated the kitchen from the living area and headed for the appliance she knew best. The coffeemaker.

Turning off the automatic alarm, which would have begun the brewing at 7:05, A.J. switched it to Start. When she came out of the shower fifteen minutes later, the scent of coffee—of normalcy—was back. She drank the first cup black, for the caffeine rather than the taste. Though she was an hour ahead of schedule, A.J. stuck to routine. Nothing as foolish and insubstantial as a dream was going to throw her off. She downed a handful of vitamins, preferring them to hassling with breakfast, then took a second cup of coffee into the bedroom with her to dress. As she studied the contents of her closet, she reviewed her appointments for the day.

Brunch with a very successful, very nervous client who was being wooed for a prime-time series. It wouldn't hurt to look over the script for the pilot once more before they discussed it. A prelunch staff meeting in her own conference room was next. Then there was a late business lunch with Bob Hopewell, who'd begun casting his new feature. She had two clients she felt were tailor-made for the leads. After mentally reviewing her appointments, A.J. decided what she needed was a touch of elegance.

She went with a raw silk suit in pale peach. Sticking to routine, she was dressed and standing in front of the full-length mirrors of her closet in twenty minutes. As an afterthought, she picked up the little half-moon she sometimes wore on her lapel. As she was fastening it, the dream came back to her. She hadn't looked so confident, so—was it aloof?—in the dream. She'd been softer, hadn't she? More vulnerable.

A.J. lifted a hand to touch it to the glass. It was cool and smooth, a reflection only. Just as it had only been a dream, she reminded herself with a shake of the head. In reality she couldn't afford to be soft. Vulnerability was out of the question. An agent in this town would be eaten alive in five minutes if she allowed a soft spot to show. And a woman—a woman took terrifying chances if she let a man see that which was vulnerable. A.J. Fields wasn't taking any chances.

Tugging down the hem of her jacket, she took a last survey before grabbing her briefcase. In less than twenty minutes, she was unlocking the door to her suite of offices.

It wasn't an unusual occurrence for A.J. to open the offices herself. Ever since she'd rented her first one-room walk-up early in her career, she'd developed the habit of arriving ahead of her staff. In those days her staff had consisted of a part-time receptionist who'd dreamed of a modeling career. Now she had two receptionists, a secretary and an assistant, as well as a stable of agents. A.J. turned the switch so that light gleamed on brass pots and rose-colored walls. She'd never regretted calling in a decorator. There was class here, discreet, understated class with subtle hints of power. Left to herself, she knew she'd have settled for a couple of sturdy desks and gooseneck lamps.

A glance at her watch showed her she could get in several calls to the East Coast. She left the one light burning in the reception area and closeted herself in her own office. Within a half-hour she'd verbally agreed to have her nervous brunch appointment fly east to do a pilot for a weekly series, set out prenegotiation feelers for a contract renewal for another client who worked on a daytime drama and lit a fire under a producer by refusing his offer on a projected mini-series.

A good morning's work, A.J. decided, reflecting back on the producer's assessment that she was a nearsighted, money-grubbing python. He would counteroffer. She leaned back in her chair and let her shoes drop to the floor. When he did, her client would get over-the-title billing and a cool quarter million. He'd work for it, A.J. thought with a long stretch. She'd read the script and understood that the part would be physically demanding and emotionally draining. She understood just how much blood and sweat a good actor put into a role. As far as she was concerned, they deserved every penny they could get, and it was up to her to squeeze it from the producer's tightfisted hand.

Satisfied, she decided to delve into paperwork before her own phone started to ring. Then she heard the footsteps.

At first she simply glanced at her watch, wondering who was in early. Then it occurred to her that though her staff was certainly dedicated enough, she couldn't think of anyone who'd come to work thirty minutes before they were due. A.J. rose, fully intending to see for herself, when the footsteps stopped. She should just call out, she thought, then found herself remembering every suspense movie she'd ever seen. The trusting heroine called out, then found herself trapped in a room with a maniac. Swallowing, she picked up a heavy metal paperweight.

The footsteps started again, coming closer. Still closer.

Struggling to keep her breathing even and quiet, A.J. walked across the carpet and stood beside the door. The footsteps halted directly on the other side. With the paperweight held high, she put her hand on the knob, held her breath, then yanked it open. David managed to grab her wrist before she knocked him out cold.

"Always greet clients this way, A.J.?"

"Damn it!" She let the paperweight slip to the floor as relief flooded through her. "You scared me to death, Brady. What are you doing sneaking around here at this hour?"

"The same thing you're doing sneaking around here at this hour. I got up early."

Because her knees were shaking, she gave in to the urge to sit, heavily. "The difference is this is *my* office. I can sneak around anytime I like. What do you want?"

"I could claim I couldn't stay away from your sparkling personality."

"Cut it."

"The truth is I have to fly to New York for a location shoot. I'll be tied up for a couple of days and wanted you to pass a message on to Clarissa for me." It wasn't the truth at all, but he didn't mind lying. It was easier to swallow than the fact that he'd needed to see her again. He'd woken up that morning knowing he had to see her before he left. Admit that to a woman like A.J. Fields and she'd either run like hell or toss you out.

"Fine." She was already up and reaching for a pad. "I'll be glad to pass on a message. But next time try to remember some people shoot other people who wander into places before hours."

"The door was unlocked," he pointed out. "There was no one at reception, so I decided to see if anyone was around before I just left a note."

It sounded reasonable. Was reasonable. But it didn't suit A.J. to be scared out of her wits before 9:00 a.m. "What's the message, Brady?"

He didn't have the vaguest idea. Tucking his hands in his pockets, he glanced around her meticulously ordered, pastel-toned office. "Nice place," he commented. He noticed even the papers she'd obviously been working with on her desk were in neat piles. There wasn't so much as a paper clip out of place. "You're a tidy creature, aren't you?"

"Yes." She tapped the pencil impatiently on the pad. "The message for Clarissa?"

"How is she, by the way?"

"She's fine."

He took a moment to stroll over to study the single painting she had on the wall. A seascape, very tranquil and soothing. "I remember you were concerned about her—about her having dinner with Alex."

"She had a lovely time," A.J. mumbled. "She told me Alex Marshall was a complete gentleman with a fascinating mind."

"Does that bother you?"

"Clarissa doesn't see men. Not that way." Feeling foolish, she dropped the pad on her desk and walked to her window.

"Is something wrong with her seeing men? That way?"

"No, no, of course not. It's just…"

"Just what, Aurora?"

She shouldn't be discussing her mother, but so few people knew of their relationship, A.J. opened up before she could stop herself. "She gets sort of breathy and vague whenever she mentions him. They spent the day together on Sunday. On his boat. I don't remember Clarissa ever stepping foot on a boat."

"So she's trying something new."

"That's what I'm afraid of," she said under her breath. "Have you any idea what it's like to see your mother in the first stages of infatuation?"

"No." He thought of his own mother's comfortable relationship with his father. She cooked dinner and sewed his buttons. He took out the trash and fixed the toaster. "I can't say I have."

"Well, it's not the most comfortable feeling, I can tell you. What do I know about this man, anyway? Oh, he's smooth," she muttered. "For all I know he's been smooth with half the women in Southern California."

"Do you hear yourself?" Half-amused, David joined her at the window. "You sound like a mother fussing over her teenage daughter. If Clarissa were an ordinary middle-aged woman there'd be little enough to worry about. Don't you think the fact that she is what she is gives her an advantage? It seems she'd be an excellent judge of character."

"You don't understand. Emotions can block things, especially when it's important."

"If that's true, maybe you should look to your own emotions." He felt her freeze. He didn't have to touch her; he didn't have to move any closer. He simply felt it. "You're letting your affection and concern for your mother cause you to overreact to a very simple thing. Maybe you should give some thought to targeting some of that emotion elsewhere."

"Clarissa's all I can afford to be emotional about."

"An odd way of phrasing things. Do you ever give any thought to your own needs? Emotional," he murmured, then ran a hand down her hair. "Physical."

"That's none of your business." She would have turned away, but he kept his hand on her hair.

"You can cut a lot of people off." He felt the first edge of her anger as she stared up at him. Oddly he enjoyed it. "I think you'd be extremely good at picking up the spear and jabbing men out of your way. But it won't work with me."

"I don't know why I thought I could talk to you."

"But you did. That should give you something to consider."

"Why are you pushing me?" she demanded. Fire came into her eyes. She remembered the dream too clearly. The dream, the desire, the fears.

"Because I want you." He stood close, close enough for her scent to twine around him. Close enough so that the doubts and distrust in her eyes were very clear. "I want to make love with you for a long, long time in a very quiet place. When we're finished I might find out why I don't seem to be able to sleep for dreaming of it."

Her throat was dry enough to ache and her hands felt like ice. "I told you once I don't sleep around."

"That's good," he murmured. "That's very good, because I don't think either of us needs a lot of comparisons." He heard the sound of the front door of the offices opening. "Sounds like you're open for business, A.J. Just one more personal note. I'm willing to negotiate terms, times and places, but the bottom line is that I'm going to spend more than one night with you. Give it some thought."

A.J. conquered the urge to pick up the paperweight and heave it at him as he walked to the door. Instead she reminded herself that she was a professional and it was business hours. "Brady."

He turned, and with a hand on the knob smiled at her. "Yeah, Fields?"

"You never gave me the message for Clarissa."

"Didn't I?" The hell with the gingerbread, he decided. "Give her my best. See you around, lady."

* * *

David didn't even know what time it was when he unlocked the door of his hotel suite. The two-day shoot had stretched into three. Now all he had to do was figure out which threads to cut and remain in budget. Per instructions, the maid hadn't touched the stacks and piles of paper on the table in the parlor. They were as he'd left them, a chaotic jumble of balance sheets, schedules and production notes.

After a twelve-hour day, he'd ordered his crew to hit the sheets. David buzzed room service and ordered a pot of coffee before he sat down and began to work. After two hours, he was satisfied enough with the figures to go back over the two and a half days of taping.

The Danjason Institute of Parapsychology itself had been impressive, and oddly stuffy, in the way of institutes. It was difficult to imagine that an organization devoted to the study of bending spoons by will and telepathy could be stuffy. The team of parapsychologists they'd worked with had been as dry and precise as any staff of scientists. So dry, in fact, David wondered whether they'd convince the audience or simply put them to sleep. He'd have to supervise the editing carefully.

The testing had been interesting enough, he decided. The fact that they used not only sensitives but people more or less off the street. The testing and conclusions were done in the strictest scientific manner. How had it been put? The application of math probability theory to massive accumulation of data. It sounded formal and supercilious. To David it was card guessing.

Still, put sophisticated equipment and intelligent, highly educated scientists together, and it was understood that psychic phenomena were being researched seriously and intensely. It was, as a science, just beginning to be recognized after decades of slow, exhaustive experimentation.

Then there had been the interview on Wall Street with the thirty-two-year-old stockbroker-psychic. David let out a stream of smoke and watched it float toward the ceiling as he let that particular segment play in his mind. The man had made no secret of the fact that he used his abilities to play the market and become many times a millionaire. It was a skill, he'd explained, much like reading, writing and calculating were skills. He'd also claimed that several top executives in some of the most powerful companies in the world had used psychic powers to get there and to stay there. He'd described ESP as a tool, as important in the business world as a computer system or a slide rule.

A science, a business and a performance.

It made David think of Clarissa. She hadn't tossed around confusing technology or littered her speech with mathematical probabilities. She hadn't discussed market trends or the Dow Jones Average. She'd simply talked, person to person. Whatever powers she had…

With a shake of his head, David cut himself off. Listen to this, he thought as he ran his hands over his face. He was beginning to buy the whole business himself, though he knew from his own research that for every lab-contained experiment there were dozens of card-wielding, bell-ringing charlatans bilking a gullible audience. He drew smoke down an already raw throat before he crushed out the cigarette. If he didn't continue to look at the documentary objectively, he'd have a biased mess on his hands.

But even looking objectively, he could see Clarissa as the center of the work. She could be the hinge on which everything else hung. With his eyes half-closed, David could picture it—the interview with the somber-eyed, white-coated parapsychologists, with their no-nonsense laboratory conditions. Then a cut to Clarissa talking with Alex, covering more or less the same ground in her simpler style. Then there'd be the clip of the stockbroker in his sky-high Wall Street office, then back to Clarissa again, seated on the homey sofa. He'd have the tuxedoed mentalist they'd lined up in Vegas doing his flashy, fast-paced demonstration. Then Clarissa again, calmly identifying cards without looking at them. Contrasts, angles, information, but everything would lead back to Clarissa DeBasse. She was the hook—instinct, intuition or paranormal powers, she was the hook. He could all but see the finished product unfolding.

Still, he wanted the big pull, something with punch and drama. This brought him right back to Clarissa. He needed that interview with Alice Van Camp, and another with someone who'd been directly involved in the Ridehour case. A.J. might try to block his way. He'd just have to roll over her.

How many times had he thought of her in the past three days? Too many. How often did he catch his mind drifting back to those few moments on the beach? Too often. And how much did he want to hold her like that again, close and hard? Too much.

Aurora. He knew it was dangerous to think of her as Aurora. Aurora was soft and accessible. Aurora was passionate and giving and just a little unsure of herself. He'd be smarter to remember A.J. Fields, tough, uncompromising and prickly around the edges. But it was late and his rooms were quiet. It was Aurora he thought òf. It was Aurora he wanted.

On impulse, David picked up the phone. He punched buttons quickly, without giving himself a chance to think the action through. The phone rang four times before she answered.

"Fields."

"Good morning."

"David?" A.J. reached up to grab the towel before it slipped from her dripping hair.

"Yeah. How are you?"

"Wet." She switched the phone from hand to hand as she struggled into a robe. "I just stepped out of the shower. Is there a problem?"

The problem was, he mused, that he was three thousand miles away and was wondering what her skin would look like gleaming with water. He reached for another cigarette and found the pack empty. "No, should there be?"

"I don't usually get calls at this hour unless there is. When did you get back?"

"I didn't."

"You didn't? You mean you're still in New York?"

He stretched back in his chair and closed his eyes. Funny, he hadn't realized just how much he'd wanted to hear her voice. "Last time I looked."

"It's only ten your time. What are you doing up so early?"

"Haven't been to bed yet."

This time she wasn't quick enough to snatch the towel before it landed on her bare feet. A.J. ignored it as she dragged her fingers through the tangle of wet hair. "I see. The night life in Manhattan's very demanding, isn't it?"

He opened his eyes to glance at his piles of papers, overflowing ashtrays and empty coffee cups. "Yeah, it's all dancing till dawn."

"I'm sure." Scowling, she bent down to pick up her towel. "Well, you must have something important on your mind to break off the partying and call. What is it?"

"I wanted to talk to you."

"So I gathered." She began, more roughly than necessary, to rub the towel over her hair. "About what?"

"Nothing."

"Brady, have you been drinking?"

He gave a quick laugh as he settled back again. He couldn't even remember the last time he'd eaten. "No. Don't you believe in friendly conversations, A.J.?"

"Sure, but not between agents and producers long-distance at dawn."

"Try something new," he suggested. "How are you?"

Cautious, she sat on the bed. "I'm fine. How are you?"

"That's good. That's a very good start." With a yawn, he realized he could sleep in the chair without any trouble at all. "I'm a little tired, actually. We spent most of the day interviewing parapsychologists who use computers and mathematical equations. I talked to a woman who claims to have had a half a dozen out-of-body experiences. 'OOBs.'"

She couldn't prevent the smile. "Yes, I've heard the term."

"Claimed she traveled to Europe that way."

"Saves on airfare."

"I suppose."

She felt a little tug of sympathy, a small glimmer of amusement. "Having trouble separating the wheat from the chaff, Brady?"

"You could call it that. In any case, it looks like we're going to be running around on the East Coast awhile. A palmist in the mountains of western Maryland, a house in Virginia that's supposed to be haunted by a young girl and a cat. There's a hypnotist in Pennsylvania who specializes in regression."

"Fascinating. It sounds like you're having just barrels of fun."

"I don't suppose you have any business that would bring you out this way."

"No, why?"

"Let's just say I wouldn't mind seeing you."

She tried to ignore the fact that the idea pleased her. "David, when you put things like that I get weak in the knees."

"I'm not much on the poetic turn of phrase." He wasn't handling this exactly as planned, he thought with a scowl. Then again, he hadn't given himself time to plan. Always a mistake. "Look, if I said I'd been thinking about you, that I wanted to see you, you'd just say something nasty. I'd end up paying for an argument instead of a conversation."

"And you can't afford to go over budget."

"See?" Still, it amused him. "Let's try a little experiment here. I've been watching experiments for days and I think I've got it down."

A.J. lay back on the bed. The fact that she was already ten minutes behind schedule didn't occur to her. "What sort of experiment?"

"You say something nice to me. Now that'll be completely out of character, so we'll start with that premise.... Go ahead," he prompted after fifteen seconds of blank silence.

"I'm trying to think of something."

"Don't be cute, A.J."

"All right, here. Your documentary on women in government was very informative and completely unbiased. I felt it showed a surprising lack of male, or female, chauvinism."

"That's a start, but why don't you try something a little more personal?"

"More personal," she mused, and smiled at the ceiling. When had she last lain on her bed and flirted over the phone? Had she ever? She supposed it didn't hurt, with a distance of three thousand miles, to feel sixteen and giddy.

"How about this? If you ever decide you want to try the other end of the camera, I can make you a star."

"Too clichéd," David decided, but found himself grinning.

"You're very picky. How about if I said I think you might, just might, make an interesting companion. You're not difficult to look at, and your mind isn't really dull."

"Very lukewarm, A.J."

"Take it or leave it."

"Why don't we take the experiment to the next stage? Spend an evening with me and find out if your hypothesis is correct."

"I'm afraid I can't dump everything here and fly out to Pennsylvania or wherever to test a theory."

"I'll be back the middle of next week."

She hesitated, lectured herself, then went with impulse. "*Double Bluff* is opening here next week. Friday. Hastings Reed is a client. He's certain he's going to cop the Oscar."

"Back to business, A.J.?"

"I happen to have two tickets for the premiere. You buy the popcorn."

She'd surprised him. Switching the phone to his other hand, David was careful to speak casually. "A date?"

"Don't push your luck, Brady."

"I'll pick you up on Friday."

"Eight," she told him, already wondering if she was making a mistake. "Now go to bed. I have to get to work."

"Aurora."

"Yes?"

"Give me a thought now and then."

"Good night, Brady."

A.J. hung up the phone, then sat with it cradled in her lap. What had possessed her to do that? She'd intended to give the tickets away and catch the film when the buzz had died down. She didn't care for glittery premieres in the first place. And more important, she knew spending an evening with David Brady was foolish. And dangerous.

When was the last time she'd allowed herself to be charmed by a man? A million years ago, she remembered with a sigh. And where had that gotten her? Weepy and disgusted with herself. But she wasn't a child anymore, she remembered. She was a successful, self-confident woman who could handle ten David Bradys at a negotiating table. The problem was she just wasn't sure she could handle one of him anywhere else.

She let out a long lingering sigh before her gaze passed over her clock. With a muffled oath she was tumbling out of bed. Damn David Brady and her own foolishness. She was going to be late.

Chapter 5

She bought a new dress. A.J. told herself that as the agent representing the lead in a major motion picture premiering in Hollywood, she was obligated to buy one. But she knew she had bought it for Aurora, not A.J.

At five minutes to eight on Friday night, she stood in front of her mirror and studied the results. No chic, professional suit this time. But perhaps she shouldn't have gone so far in the other direction.

Still, it was black. Black was practical and always in vogue. She turned to the right profile, then the left. It certainly wasn't flashy. But all in all, it might have been wiser to have chosen something more conservative than the pipeline strapless, nearly backless black silk. Straight on, it was provocative. From the side it was downright suggestive. Why hadn't she noticed in the dressing room just how tightly the material clung? Maybe she had, A.J. admitted on a long breath. Maybe she'd been giddy enough, foolish enough, to buy it because it didn't make her feel like an agent or any other sort of professional. It just made her feel like a woman. That was asking for trouble.

In any case, she could solve part of the problem with the little beaded jacket. Satisfied, she reached for a heavy silver locket clipped to thick links. Even as she was fastening it, A.J. heard the door. Taking her time, she slipped into the shoes that lay neatly at the foot of her bed, checked the contents of her purse and picked up the beaded jacket. Reminding herself to think of the entire process as an experiment, she opened the door to David.

She hadn't expected him to bring her flowers. He didn't seem the type for such time-honored romantic gestures. Because he appeared to be as off-balance as she, they just stood there a moment, staring.

She was stunning. He'd never considered her beautiful before. Attractive, yes, and sexy in the coolest, most aloof sort of way. But tonight she was breathtaking. Her dress didn't glitter, it didn't gleam, but simply flowed with the long, subtle lines of her body. It was enough. More than enough.

He took a step forward. Clearing her throat, A.J. took a step back.

"Right on time," she commented, and worked on a smile.

"I'm already regretting I didn't come early."

A.J. accepted the roses and struggled to be casual, when she wanted to bury her face in them. "Thank you. They're lovely. Would you like a drink while I put them in water?"

"No." It was enough just to look at her.

"I'll just be a minute."

As she walked away, his gaze passed down her nape, over her shoulder blades and the smooth, generously exposed back to her waist, where the material of her dress again intruded. It nearly made him change his mind about the drink.

To keep his mind off tall blondes with smooth skin, he took a look around her apartment. She didn't appear to have the same taste in decorating as Clarissa.

The room was cool, as cool as its tenant, and just as streamlined. He couldn't fault the icy colors or the uncluttered lines, but he wondered just how much of herself Aurora Fields had put into the place she lived in. In the manner of her office, nothing was out of place. No frivolous mementos were set out for public viewing. The room had class and style, but none of the passion he'd found in the woman. And it told no secrets, not even in a whisper. He found himself more determined than ever to discover how many she had.

When A.J. came back she was steady. She'd arranged the roses in one of her rare extravagances, a tall, slim vase of Baccarat crystal. "Since you're prompt, we can get there a bit early and ogle the celebrities. It's different than dealing with them over a business lunch or watching a shoot."

"You look like a witch," he murmured. "White skin, black dress. You can almost smell the brimstone."

Her hands were no longer steady as she reached for her jacket. "I had an ancestor who was burned as one."

He took the jacket from her, regretting the fact that once it was on too much of her would be covered. "I guess I shouldn't be surprised."

"In Salem, during the madness." A.J. tried to ignore the way his fingers lingered as he slid the jacket over her. "Of course she was no more witch than Clarissa, but she was... special. According to the journals and documents that Clarissa gathered, she was twenty-five and very lovely. She made the mistake of warning her neighbors about a barn fire that didn't happen for two days."

"So she was tried and executed?"

"People usually have violent reactions to what they don't understand."

"We talked to a man in New York who's making a killing in the stock market by 'seeing' things before they happen."

"Times change." A.J. picked up her bag, then paused at the door. "My ancestor died alone and penniless. Her name was Aurora." She lifted a brow when he said nothing. "Shall we go?"

David slipped his hand over hers as the door shut at their backs. "I have a feeling that having an ancestor executed as a witch is very significant for you."

After shrugging, A.J. drew her hand from his to push the button for the elevator. "Not everyone has one in his family tree."

"And?"

"And let's just say I have a good working knowledge of how different opinions can be. They range from everything from blind condemnation to blind faith. Both extremes are dangerous."

As they stepped into the elevator he said consideringly, "And you work very hard to shield Clarissa from both ends."

"Exactly."

"What about you? Are you defending yourself by keeping your relationship with Clarissa quiet?"

"I don't need defending from my mother." She'd swung through the doors before she managed to bank the quick surge of temper. "It's easier for me to work for her if we keep the family relationship out of it."

"Logical. I find you consistently logical, A.J."

She wasn't entirely sure it was a compliment. "And there is the fact that I'm very accessible. I didn't want clients rushing in to ask me to have my mother tell them where they lost their diamond ring. Is your car in the lot?"

"No, we're right out front. And I wasn't criticizing, Aurora, just asking."

She felt the temper fade as quickly as it had risen. "It's all right. I tend to be a little sensitive where Clarissa's concerned. I don't see a car," she began, glancing idly past a gray limo before coming back to it with raised brows. "Well," she murmured. "I'm impressed."

"Good." The driver was already opening the door. "That was the idea."

A.J. snuggled in. She'd ridden in limos countless times, escorting clients, delivering or picking them up at airports. But she never took such cushy comfort for granted. As she let herself enjoy, she watched David take a bottle out of ice.

"Flowers, a limo and now champagne. I am impressed, Brady, but I'm also—"

"Going to spoil it," he finished as he eased the cork expertly out. "Remember, we're testing your theory that I'd make an interesting companion." He offered a glass. "How'm I doing?"

"Fine so far." She sipped and appreciated. If she'd had experience in anything, she reminded herself, it was in how to keep a relationship light and undemanding. "I'm afraid I'm more used to doing the pampering than being pampered."

"How's it feel to be on the other side?"

"A little too good." She slipped out of her shoes and let her feet sink into the carpet. "I could just sit and ride for hours."

"It's okay with me." He ran a finger down the side of her throat to the edge of her jacket. "Want to skip the movie?"

She felt the tremor start where his finger skimmed, then rush all the way to the pit of her stomach. It came home to her that she hadn't had experience with David Brady. "I think not." Draining her glass, she held it out for a refill. "I suppose you attend a lot of these."

"Premieres?" He tilted wine into her glass until it fizzed to the rim. "No. Too Hollywood."

"Oh." With a gleam in her eye, A.J. glanced slowly around the limo. "I see."

"Tonight seemed to be an exception." He toasted her, appreciating the way she sat with such careless elegance in the plush corner of the limo. She belonged there. Now. With him. "As a representative of some of the top names in the business, you must drop in on these things a few times a year."

"No." A.J.'s lips curved as she sipped from her glass. "I hate them."

"Are you serious?"

"Deadly."

"Then what the hell are we doing?"

"Experimenting," she reminded him, and set her glass down as the limo stopped at the curb. "Just experimenting."

There were throngs of people crowded into the roped off sections by the theater's entrance. Cameras were clicking, flashes popping. It didn't seem to matter to the crowd that the couple alighting from the limo weren't recognizable faces. It was Hollywood. It was opening night. The glitz was peaking. A.J. and David were cheered and applauded. She blinked twice as three paparazzi held cameras in her face.

"Incredible, isn't it?" he muttered as he steered her toward the entrance.

"It reminds me why I agent instead of perform." In an instinctive defense she wasn't even aware of, she turned away from the cameras. "Let's find a dark corner."

"I'm for that."

She had to laugh. "You never give up."

"A.J. A.J., *darling!*"

Before she could react, she found herself crushed against a soft, generous bosom. "Merinda, how nice to see you."

"Oh, I can't tell you how thrilled I am you're here." Merinda MacBride, Hollywood's current darling, drew her dramatically away. "A friendly face, you know. These things are such zoos."

She glittered from head to foot, from the diamonds that hung at her ears to the sequined dress that appeared to have been painted on by a very appreciative artist. She sent A.J. a smile that would have melted chocolate at ten paces. "You look divine."

"Thank you. You aren't alone?"

"Oh, no. I'm with Brad…." After a moment's hesitation, she smiled again. "Brad," she repeated, as if she'd decided last names weren't important. "He's fetching me a drink." Her gaze shifted and fastened on David. "You're not alone, either."

"Merinda MacBride, David Brady."

"A pleasure." He took her hand and, though she turned her knuckles up expectantly, didn't bring it to his lips. "I've seen your work and admired it."

"Why, thank you." She studied, measured and rated him in a matter of seconds. "Are we mutual clients of A.J.'s?"

"David's a producer." A.J. watched Merinda's baby-blue eyes sharpen. "Of documentaries," she added, amused. "You might have seen some of his work on public television."

"Of course." She beamed at him, though she'd never watched public television in her life and had no intention of starting. "I desperately admire producers. Especially attractive ones."

"I have a couple of scripts I think you'd be interested in," A.J. put in to draw her off.

"Oh?" Instantly Merinda dropped the sex-bomb act. A.J. Fields didn't recommend a script unless it had meat on it. "Have them sent over."

"First thing Monday."

"Well, I must find Brad before he forgets about me. David." She gave him her patented smoldering look. Documentaries or not, he was a producer. And a very attractive one. "I hope we run into each other again. Ta, A.J." She brushed cheeks. "Let's do lunch."

"Soon."

David barely waited for her to walk out of earshot. "You deal with that all the time?"

"Shh!"

"I mean *all* the time," he continued, watching as Merinda's tightly covered hips swished through the crowd. "Day after day. Why aren't you crazy?"

"Merinda may be a bit overdramatic, but if you've seen any of her films, you'll know just how talented she is."

"The woman looked loaded with talent to me," he began, but stopped to grin when A.J. scowled. "As an *actress*," he continued. "I thought she was exceptional in *Only One Day.*"

A.J. couldn't quite conquer the smile. She'd hustled for weeks to land Merinda that part. "So you have seen her films."

"I don't live in a cave. That film was the first one that didn't— let's say, focus on her anatomy."

"It was the first one I represented her on."

"She's fortunate in her choice of agents."

"Thank you, but it goes both ways. Merinda's a very hot property."

"If we're going to make it through this evening, I'd better not touch that one."

They were interrupted another half a dozen times before they could get into the theater. A.J. ran into clients, acquaintances and associates, greeted, kissed and complimented while turning down invitations to after-theater parties.

"You're very good at this." David took two seats on the aisle near the back of the theater.

"Part of the job." A.J. settled back. There was nothing she enjoyed quite so much as a night at the movies.

"A bit jaded, A.J.?"

"Jaded?"

"Untouched by the glamour of it all, unaffected by the star system. You don't get any particular thrill out of exchanging kisses and hugs with some of the biggest and most distinguished names in the business."

"Business," she repeated, as if that explained it all. "That's not being jaded—it's being sensible. And the only time I saw you awestruck was when you found yourself face-to-face with three inches of cleavage on a six-foot blonde. Shh," she muttered before he could comment. "It's started and I hate to miss the opening credits."

With the theater dark, the audience quiet, A.J. threw herself into the picture. Ever since childhood, she'd been able to transport herself with the big screen. She wouldn't have called it "escape." She didn't like the word. A.J. called it "involvement." The actor playing the lead was a client, a man she knew intimately and had comforted through two divorces. All three of his children's birthdays were noted in her book. She'd listened to him rant; she'd heard his complaints, his doubts. That was all part of the job. But the moment she saw him on film, he was, to her, the part he played and nothing else.

Within five minutes, she was no longer in a crowded theater in Los Angeles, but in a rambling house in Connecticut. And there was murder afoot. When the lights went out and thunder boomed, she grabbed David's arm and cringed in her seat. Not one to pass up an age-old opportunity, he slipped an arm around her.

When was the last time, he wondered, that he'd sat in a theater with his arm around his date? He decided it had been close to twenty years and he'd been missing a great deal. He turned his attention to the film, but was distracted by her scent. It was still light, barely discernible, but it filled his senses. He tried to concentrate on the action and drama racing across the screen. A.J. caught her breath and shifted an inch closer. The tension on the screen seemed very pedestrian compared to his own. When the lights came up he found himself regretting that there was no longer such a thing as the double feature.

"It was good, wasn't it?" Eyes brilliant with pleasure, she turned to him. "It was really very good."

"Very good," he agreed, and lifted his hand to toy with her ear. "And if the applause is any indication, your client's got himself a hit."

"Thank God." She breathed a sigh of relief before shifting away to break what was becoming a very unnerving contact. "I talked him into the part. If he'd flopped, it would have been my head."

"And now that he can expect raves?"

"It'll be because of his talent," she said easily. "And that's fair enough. Would you mind if we slipped out before it gets too crazy?"

"I'd prefer it." He rose and steered her through the pockets of people that were already forming in the aisles. They hadn't gone ten feet before A.J.'s name was called out three times.

"Where are you going? You running out?" Hastings Reed, six feet three inches of down-home sex and manhood, blocked the aisle. He was flushed with the victory of seeing himself triumph on the screen and nervous that he might have misjudged the audience reaction. "You didn't like it?"

"It was wonderful." Understanding his need for reassurance, A.J. stood on tiptoe to brush his cheek. "You were wonderful. Never better."

He returned the compliment with a bone-crushing hug. "We have to wait for the reviews."

"Prepare to accept praise humbly, and with good grace. Hastings, this is David Brady."

"Brady?" As Hastings took David's hand, his etched in bronze face creased into a frown. "Producer?"

"That's right."

"God, I love your work." Already flying, Hastings pumped David's hand six times before finally releasing it. "I'm an honorary chairman of Rights for Abused Children. Your documentary did an incredible job of bringing the issue home and making people aware. Actually, it's what got me involved in the first place."

"It's good to hear that. We wanted to make people think."

"Made me think. I've got kids of my own. Listen, keep me in mind if you ever do a follow-up. No fee." He grinned down at A.J. "She didn't hear that."

"Hear what?"

He laughed and yanked her against him again. "This lady's incredible. I don't know what I'd have done without her. I wasn't going to take this part, but she badgered me into it."

"I never badger," A.J. said mildly.

"Nags, badgers and browbeats. Thank God." Grinning,

he finally took a good look at her. "Damn if you don't look like something a man could swallow right up. I've never seen you dressed like that."

To cover a quick flush of embarrassment, she reached up to straighten his tie. "And as I recall, the last time I saw you, you were in jeans and smelled of horses."

"Guess I did. You're coming to Chasen's?"

"Actually, I—"

"You're coming. Look, I've got a couple of quick interviews, but I'll see you there in a half hour." He took two strides away and was swallowed up in the crowd.

"He's got quite an...overwhelming personality," David commented.

"To say the least." A.J. glanced at her watch. It was still early. "I suppose I should at least put in an appearance, since he'll count on it now. I can take a cab if you'd rather skip it."

"Ever hear of the expression about leaving with the guy who brought you?"

"This isn't a country dance," A.J. pointed out as they wove through the lingering crowd.

"Same rules apply. I can handle Chasen's."

"Okay, but just for a little while."

The "little while" lasted until after three.

Cases of champagne, mountains of caviar and piles of fascinating little canapés. Even someone as practical as A.J. found it difficult to resist a full-scale celebration. The music was loud, but it didn't seem to matter. There were no quiet corners to escape to. Through her clientele and David's contacts, they knew nearly everyone in the room between them. A few minutes of conversation here, another moment there, ate up hours of time. Caught up in her client's success, A.J. didn't mind.

On the crowded dance floor, she allowed herself to relax in David's arms. "Incredible, isn't it?"

"Nothing tastes so sweet as success, especially when you mix it with champagne."

She glanced around. It was hard not to be fascinated with the faces, the names, the bodies. She was part of it, a very intricate part. But through her own choice, she wasn't an intimate part. "I usually avoid this sort of thing."

He let his fingers skim lightly up her back. "Why?"

"Oh, I don't know." Weariness, wine and pleasure combined. Her cheek rested against his. "I guess I'm more of a background sort of person. You fit in."

"And you don't?"

"Ummm." She shook her head. Why was it men smelled so wonderful—so wonderfully different? And felt so good when you held and were held by one. "You're part of the talent. I just work with clauses and figures."

"And that's the way you want it?"

"Absolutely. Still, this is nice." When his hand ran down her back again, she stretched into it. "Very nice."

"I'd rather be alone with you," he murmured. Every time he held her like this he thought he would go crazy. "In some dim little room where the music was low."

"This is safer." But she didn't object when his lips brushed her temple.

"Who needs safe?"

"I do. I need safe and ordered and sensible."

"Anyone who chooses to be involved in this business tosses safe, ordered and sensible out the window."

"Not me." She drew back to smile at him. It felt so good to relax, to flow with the evening, to let her steps match his without any conscious thought. "I just make the deals and leave the chances up to others."

"Take ten percent and run?"

"That's right."

"I might have believed that a few weeks ago. The problem is I've seen you with Clarissa."

"That's entirely different."

"True enough. I also saw you with Hastings tonight. You get wrapped up with your clients, A.J. You might be able to convince yourself they're just signatures, but I know better. You're a marshmallow."

Her brows drew together. "Ridiculous. Marshmallows get swallowed."

"They're also resilient. I admire that in you." He touched his lips to hers before she could move. "I'm beginning to realize I admire quite a bit in you."

She would have pulled away then, but he kept her close easily enough and continued to sway. "I don't mix business and personal feelings."

"You lie."

"I might play with the truth," she said, abruptly dignified, "but I don't lie."

"You were ready to turn handsprings tonight when that movie hit."

A.J. tossed her hair out of her face. He saw too much too easily. A man wasn't supposed to. "Have you any idea how I can use that as a lever? I'll get Hastings a million-five for his next movie."

"You'll 'get Hastings,'" David repeated. "Even your phrasing gives you away."

"You're picking up things that aren't there."

"No, I think I'm finding things you've squirreled away. Have you got a problem with the fact that I've decided I like you?"

Off-balance, she missed a step and found herself pressed

even closer. "I think I'd handle it better if we still got on each other nerves."

"Believe me, you get on my nerves." Until his blood was on slow boil, his muscles knotting and stretching and the need racing. "There are a hundred people in this room and my mind keeps coming back to the fact that I could have you out of what there is of that dress in thirty seconds flat."

The chill arrowed down her back. "You know that's not what I meant. You'd be smarter to keep your mind on business."

"Smarter, safer. We're looking for different things, A.J."

"We can agree on that, anyway."

"We might agree on more if we gave ourselves the chance."

She didn't know exactly why she smiled. Perhaps it was because it sounded like a fantasy. She enjoyed watching them, listening to them, without really believing in them. "David." She rested her arms on his shoulders. "You're a very nice man, on some levels."

"I think I can return that compliment."

"Let me spell things out for you in the way I understand best. Number one, we're business associates at the moment. This precludes any possibility that we could be seriously involved. Number two, while this documentary is being made my first concern is, and will continue to be, Clarissa's welfare. Number three, I'm very busy and what free time I have I use to relax in my own way—which is alone. And number four, I'm not equipped for relationships. I'm selfish, critical and disinterested."

"Very well put." He kissed her forehead in a friendly fashion. "Are you ready to go?"

"Yes." A little nonplussed by his reaction, she walked off the dance floor to retrieve her jacket. They left the noise and crowd behind and stepped out into the cool early-morning air. "I forget sometimes that the glamour and glitz can be nice in small doses."

He helped her into the waiting limo. "Moderation in all things."

"Life's more stable that way." Cut off from the driver and the outside by thick smoked glass, A.J. settled back against the seat. Before she could let out the first contented sigh, David was close, his hand firm on her chin. "David—"

"Number one," he began, "I'm the producer of this project, and you're the agent for one, only one, of the talents. That means we're business associates in the broadest sense and that doesn't preclude an involvement. We're already involved."

There'd been no heat in his eyes on the dance floor, she thought quickly. Not like there was now. "David—"

"You had your say," he reminded her. "Number two, while this documentary is being made, you can fuss over Clarissa all you want. That has nothing to do with us. Number three, we're both busy, which means we don't want to waste time with excuses and evasions that don't hold water. And number four, whether you think you're equipped for relationships or not, you're in the middle of one right now. You'd better get used to it."

Temper darkened her eyes and chilled her voice. "I don't have to get used to anything."

"The hell you don't. Put a number on this."

Frustrated desire, unrelieved passion, simmering anger. She felt them all as his mouth crushed down on hers. Her first reaction was pure self-preservation. She struggled against him, knowing if she didn't free herself quickly, she'd be lost. But he seemed to know, somehow, that her struggle was against herself, not him.

He held her closer. His mouth demanded more, until, despite fears, despite doubts, despite everything, she gave.

With a muffled moan, her arms went around him. Her fingers slid up his back to lose themselves in his hair. Passion, still unrelieved, mounted until it threatened to consume. She could feel everything, the hard line of his body against hers, the soft give of the seat at her back. There was the heat of his lips as they pressed and rubbed on hers and the cool air blown in silently through the vents.

And she could taste—the lingering punch of champagne as their tongues tangled together. She could taste a darker flavor, a deeper flavor that was his flesh. Still wilder, less recognizable, was the taste of her own passion.

His mouth left hers only to search out other delights. Over the bare, vulnerable skin of her neck and shoulders he found them. His hands weren't gentle as they moved over her. His mouth wasn't tender. Her heart began to thud in a fast, chaotic rhythm at the thought of being taken with such hunger, such fury.

Driven by her own demons she let her hands move, explore and linger. When his breath was as uneven as hers their lips met again. The contact did nothing to soothe and everything to arouse. Desperate for more, she brought her teeth down to nip, to torment. With an oath, he swung her around until they were sprawled on the long, wide seat.

Her lips parted as she looked up at him. She could see the intermittent flash of streetlights as they passed overhead. Shadow and light. Shadow and light. Hypnotic. Erotic. A.J. reached up to touch his face.

She was all cream and silk as she lay beneath him. Her hair was tousled around a face flushed with arousal. The touch of her fingers on his cheek was light as a whisper and caused the need to thunder through him.

"This is crazy," she murmured.

"I know."

"It's not supposed to happen." But it was. She knew it. She had known it from the first meeting. "It can't happen," she corrected.

"Why?"

"Don't ask me." Her voice dropped to a whisper. She couldn't resist letting her fingers play along his face even as she prepared herself to deny both of them. "I can't explain. If I could you wouldn't understand."

"If there's someone else I don't give a damn."

"No, there's no one." She closed her eyes a moment, then opened them again to stare at him. "There's no one else."

Why was he hesitating? She was here, aroused, inches away from total surrender. He had only to ignore the confused plea in her eyes and take. But even with his blood hot, the need pressing, he couldn't ignore it. "It might not be now, it might not be here, but it will be, Aurora."

It would be. Had to be. The part of her that knew it fought a frantic tug-of-war with the part that had to deny it. "Let me go, David."

Trapped by his own feelings, churning with his own needs, he pulled her up. "What kind of game are you playing?"

She was cold. Freezing. She felt each separate chill run over her skin. "It's called survival."

"Damn it, Aurora." She was so beautiful. Why did she suddenly have to be so beautiful? Why did she suddenly have to look so fragile? "What does being with me, making love with me, have to do with your survival?"

"Nothing." She nearly laughed as she felt the limo cruise to a halt. "Nothing at all if it were just that simple."

"Why complicate it? We want each other. We're both

adults. People become lovers every day without doing themselves any damage."

"Some people." She let out a shuddering breath. "I'm not some people. If it were so simple, I'd make love with you right here, in the back seat of this car. I won't tell you I don't want to." She turned to look at him and the vulnerability in her eyes was haunted by regrets. "But it's not simple. Making love with you would be easy. Falling in love with you wouldn't."

Before he could move, she'd pushed open the door and was on the street.

"Aurora." He was beside her, a hand on her arm, but she shook him off. "You can't expect to just walk off after a statement like that."

"That's just what I'm doing," she corrected, and shook him off a second time.

"I'll take you up." With what willpower he had left, he held on to patience.

"No. Just go."

"We have to talk."

"No." Neither of them was prepared for the desperation in her voice. "I want you to go. It's late. I'm tired. I'm not thinking straight."

"If we don't talk this out now, we'll just have to do it later."

"Later, then." She would have promised him anything for freedom at that moment. "I want you to go now, David." When he continued to hold her, her voice quivered. "Please, I need you to go. I can't handle this now."

He could fight her anger, but he couldn't fight her fragility. "All right."

He waited until she had disappeared inside her building. Then he leaned back on the car and pulled out a cigarette. Later then, he promised himself. They'd talk. He stood where he was, waiting for his system to level. They'd talk, he assured himself again. But it was best to wait until they were both calmer and more reasonable.

Tossing away the cigarette, he climbed back into the limo. He hoped to God he could stop thinking of her long enough to sleep.

Chapter 6

She wanted to pace. She wanted to walk up and down, pull at her hair and walk some more. She forced herself to sit quietly on the sofa and wait as Clarissa poured tea.

"I'm so glad you came by, dear. It's so seldom you're able to spend an afternoon with me."

"Things are under control at the office. Abe's covering for me."

"Such a nice man. How's his little grandson?"

"Spoiled rotten. Abe wants to buy him Dodger Stadium."

"Grandparents are entitled to spoil the way parents are obliged to discipline." She kept her eyes lowered, anxious not to show her own longings and apply pressure. "How's your tea?"

"It's…different." Knowing the lukewarm compliment would satisfy Clarissa saved her from an outright lie. "What is it?"

"Rose hips. I find it very soothing in the afternoons. You seem to need a little soothing, Aurora."

A.J. set down her cup and, giving in to the need for movement, rose. She'd known when she'd deliberately cleared her calendar that she would come to Clarissa. And she'd known that she would come for help, though she'd repeatedly told herself she didn't need it.

"Momma." A.J. sat on the sofa again as Clarissa sipped tea and waited patiently. "I think I'm in trouble."

"You ask too much of yourself." Clarissa reached out to touch her hand. "You always have."

"What am I going to do?"

Clarissa sat back as she studied her daughter. She'd never heard that phrase from her before, and now that she had, she wanted to be certain to give the right answers. "You're frightened."

"Terrified." She was up again, unable to sit. "It's getting away from me. I'm losing the controls."

"Aurora, it isn't always necessary to hold on to them."

"It is for me." She looked back with a half smile. "You should understand."

"I do. Of course I do." But she'd wished so often that her daughter, her only child, would be at peace with herself. "You constantly defend yourself against being hurt because you were hurt once and decided it would never happen again. Aurora, are you in love with David?"

Clarissa would know he was at the core of it. Naturally she would know without a word being said. A.J. could accept that. "I might be if I don't pull myself back now."

"Would it be so bad to love someone?"

"David isn't just someone. He's too strong, too overwhelming. Besides…" She paused long enough to steady herself. "I thought I was in love once before."

"You were young." Clarissa came as close as she ever did to true anger. She set her cup in its saucer with a little snap. "Infatuation is a different matter. It demands more and gives less back than love."

A.J. stood in the middle of the room. There was really no place to go. "Maybe this is just infatuation. Or lust."

Clarissa lifted a brow and sipped tea calmly. "You're the only one who can answer that. Somehow I don't think you'd have cleared your calendar and come to see me in the middle of a workday if you were concerned about lust."

Laughing, A.J. walked over to drop on the sofa beside her. "Oh, Momma, there's no one like you. No one."

"Things were never normal for you, were they?"

"No." A.J. dropped her head on Clarissa's shoulder. "They were better. You were better."

"Aurora, your father loved me very much. He loved, and he accepted, without actually understanding. I can't even comprehend what my life might have been like if I hadn't given up the controls and loved him back."

"He was special," A.J. murmured. "Most men aren't."

Clarissa hesitated only a moment, then cleared her throat. "Alex accepts me, too."

"Alex?" Uneasy, A.J. sat up again. There was no mistaking the blush of color in Clarissa's cheeks. "Are you and Alex…" How did one put such a question to a mother? "Are you serious about Alex?"

"He asked me to marry him."

"What?" Too stunned for reason, A.J. jerked back and gaped. "Marriage? You barely know him. You met only weeks ago. Momma, certainly you're mature enough to realize something as important as marriage takes a great deal of thought."

Clarissa beamed at her. "What an excellent mother you'll make one day. I was never able to lecture quite like that."

"I don't mean to lecture." Mumbling, A.J. picked up her tea. "I just don't want you to jump into something like this without giving it the proper thought."

"You see, that's just what I mean. I'm sure you got that from your father's side. My family's always been just the tiniest bit flighty."

"Momma—"

"Do you remember when Alex and I were discussing palm reading for the documentary?"

"Of course." The uneasiness increased, along with a sense of inevitability. "You felt something."

"It was very strong and very clear. I admit it flustered me a bit to realize a man could be attracted to me after all these years. And I wasn't aware until that moment that I could feel like that about anyone."

"But you need time. I don't doubt anything you feel, anything you see. You know that. But—"

"Darling, I'm fifty-six." Clarissa shook her head, wondering how it had happened so quickly. "I've been content to live alone. I think perhaps I was meant to live alone for a certain amount of time. Now I want to share the rest of my life. You're twenty-eight and content and very capable of living alone. Still, you mustn't be afraid to share your life."

"It's different."

"No." She took A.J.'s hands again. "Love, affection, needs. They're really very much the same for everyone. If David is the right man for you, you'll know it. But after knowing, you have to accept."

"He may not accept me." Her fingers curled tightly around her mother's. "I have trouble accepting myself."

"And that's the only worry you've ever given me. Aurora, I can't tell you what to do. I can't look into tomorrow for you, as much as part of me wants to."

"I'm not asking that. I'd never ask you that."

"No, you wouldn't. Look into your heart, Aurora. Stop calculating risks and just look."

"I might see something I don't want to."

"Oh, you probably will." With a little laugh, Clarissa settled back on the sofa with an arm around A.J. "I can't tell you what to do, but I can tell you what I feel. David Brady is a very good man. He has his flaws, of course, but he is a good man. It's been a pleasure for me to be able to work with him. As a matter of fact, when he called this morning, I was delighted."

"Called?" Immediately alert, A.J. sat up straight. "David called you? Why?"

"Oh, a few ideas he'd had about the documentary." She fussed with the little lace napkin in her lap. "He's in Rolling Hills today. Well, not exactly in, but outside. Do you remember hearing about that old mansion no one ever seems able to live in for long? The one a few miles off the beach?"

"It's supposed to be haunted," A.J. muttered.

"Of course there are differing opinions on that. I think David made an excellent choice for his project, though, from what he told me about the background."

"What do you have to do with that?"

"That? Oh, nothing at all. We just chatted about the house. I suppose he thought I'd be interested."

"Oh." Mollified, A.J. began to relax. "That's all right then."

"We did set up a few other things. I'll be going into the studio—Wednesday," she decided. "Yes, I'm sure it's Wednesday of next week, to discuss spontaneous phenomena. And then, oh, sometime the following week, I'm to go to the Van Camps'. We'll tape in Alice's living room."

"The Van Camps'." She felt the heat rising. "He set all this up with you."

Clarissa folded her hands. "Yes, indeed. Did I do something wrong?"

"Not you." Fired up, she rose. "He knew better than to change things without clearing it with me first. You can't trust anyone. Especially a producer." Snatching up her purse, she strode to the door. "You don't go anywhere on Wednesday to discuss any kind of phenomena until I see just what he has up his sleeve." She caught herself and came back to give Clarissa a hug. "Don't worry, I'll straighten it out."

"I'm counting on it." Clarissa watched her daughter storm out of the house before she sat back, content. She'd done everything she could—set energy in motion. The rest was up to fate.

"Tell him we'll reschedule. Better yet, have Abe meet with him." A.J. shouted into her car phone as she came up behind a tractor-trailer.

"Abe has a three-thirty. I don't think he can squeeze Montgomery in at four."

"Damn." Impatient, A.J. zoomed around the tractor-trailer. "Who's free at four?"

"Just Barbara."

While keeping an eye peeled for her exit, A.J. turned that over in her mind. "No, they'd never jell. Reschedule, Diane. Tell Montgomery…tell him there was an emergency. A medical emergency."

"Check. There isn't, is there?"

Her smile was set and nothing to laugh about. "There might be."

"Sounds promising. How can I reach you?"

"You can't. Leave anything important on the machine. I'll call in and check."

"You got it. Hey, good luck."

"Thanks." Teeth gritted, A.J. replaced the receiver.

He wasn't going to get away with playing power games. A.J. knew all the rules to that one, and had made up plenty of her own. David Brady was in for it. A.J. reached for her map again. If she could ever find him.

When the first raindrop hit the windshield she started to swear. By the time she'd taken the wrong exit, made three wrong turns and found herself driving down a decrepit gravel road in a full-fledged spring storm, she was cursing fluently. Every one of them was aimed directly at David Brady's head.

One look at the house through driving rain and thunderclouds proved why he'd chosen so well. Braking viciously, A.J. decided he'd arranged the storm for effect. When she swung out of the car and stepped in a puddle of mud that slopped over her ankle, it was the last straw.

He saw her through the front window. Surprise turned to annoyance quickly at the thought of another interruption on a day that had seen everything go wrong. He hadn't had a decent night's sleep in a week, his work was going to hell and he itched just looking at her. When he pulled open the front door, he was as ready as A.J. for an altercation.

"What the hell are you doing here?"

Her hair was plastered to her face; her suit was soaked. She'd just ruined half a pair of Italian shoes. "I want to talk to you, Brady."

"Fine. Call my office and set up an appointment. I'm working."

"I want to talk to you now!" Lifting a hand to his chest,

she gave him a hefty shove back against the door. "Just where do you come off making arrangements with one of my clients without clearing it with me? If you want Clarissa in the studio next week, then you deal with me. Understand?"

He took her damp hand by the wrist and removed it from his shirt. "I have Clarissa under contract for the duration of filming. I don't have to clear anything with you."

"You'd better read it again, Brady. Dates and times are set up through her representative."

"Fine. I'll send you a schedule. Now if you'll excuse me—"

He pushed open the door, but she stepped in ahead of him. Two electricians inside the foyer fell silent and listened. "I'm not finished."

"I am. Get lost, Fields, before I have you tossed off the set."

"Watch your step, or my client might develop a chronic case of laryngitis."

"Don't threaten me, A.J." He gripped her lapels with both hands. "I've had about all I'm taking from you. You want to talk, fine. Your office or mine, tomorrow."

"Mr. Brady, we need you upstairs."

For a moment longer he held her. Her gaze was locked on his and the fury was fierce and very equal. He wanted, God, he wanted to drag her just a bit closer, wipe that maddening look off her face. He wanted to crush his mouth to hers until she couldn't speak, couldn't breathe, couldn't fight. He wanted, more than anything, to make her suffer the way he suffered. He released her so abruptly she took two stumbling steps back.

"Get lost," he ordered, and turned to mount the stairs.

It took her a minute to catch her breath. She hadn't known she could get this angry, hadn't allowed herself to become this angry in too many years to count. Emotions flared up inside her, blinding her to everything else. She dashed up the stairs behind him.

"Ms. Fields, nice to see you again." Alex stood on the top landing in front of a wall where the paint had peeled and cracked. He gave her an easy smile as he smoked his cigar and waited to be called back in front of the camera.

"And I want to talk to you, too," she snapped at him. Leaving him staring, she strode down the hall after David.

It was narrow and dark. There were cobwebs clinging to corners, but she didn't notice. In places there were squares of lighter paint where pictures had once hung. A.J. worked her way through technicians and walked into the room only steps behind David.

It hit her like a wall. No sooner had she drawn in the breath to shout at him again than she couldn't speak at all. She was freezing. The chill whipped through her and to the bone in the matter of a heartbeat.

The room was lit for the shoot, but she didn't see the cameras, the stands or the coils of cable. She saw wallpaper, pink roses on cream, and a four-poster draped in the same rose hue. There was a little mahogany stool beside the bed that was worn smooth in the center. She could smell the roses that stood fresh and a little damp in an exquisite crystal vase on a mahogany vanity that gleamed with beeswax and lemon. And she saw—much more. And she heard.

You betrayed me. You betrayed me with him, Jessica.

No! No, I swear it. Don't. For God's sake don't do this. I love you. I—

Lies! All lies. You won't tell any more.

There were screams. There was silence, a hundred times worse. A.J.'s purse hit the floor with a thud as she lifted her hands to her ears.

"A.J." David was shaking her, hands firm on her shoulders, as everyone else in the room stopped to stare. "What's wrong with you?"

She reached out to clutch his shirt. He could feel the iciness of her flesh right through the cotton. She looked at him, but her eyes didn't focus. "That poor girl," she murmured. "Oh, God, that poor girl."

"A.J." With an effort, he kept his voice calm. She was shuddering and pale, but the worst of it was her eyes, dark and glazed as they looked beyond him. She stared at the center of the room as if held in a trance. He took both of her hands in his. "A.J., what girl?"

"He killed her right here. There on the bed. He used his hands. She couldn't scream anymore because his hands were on her throat, squeezing. And then…"

"A.J." He took her chin and forced her to look at him. "There's no bed in here. There's nothing."

"It—" She struggled for air, then lifted both hands to her face. The nausea came, a too-familiar sensation. "I have to get out of here." Breaking away, she pushed through the technicians crowded in the doorway and ran. She stumbled out into the rain and down the porch steps before David caught her.

"Where are you going?" he demanded. A flash of lightning highlighted them both as the rain poured down.

"I've got to…" She trailed off and looked around blindly. "I'm going back to town. I have to get back."

"I'll take you."

"No." Panicked, she struggled, only to find herself held firmly. "I have my car."

"You're not driving anywhere like this." Half leading, half dragging, he pulled her to his car. "Now stay here," he ordered, and slammed the door on her.

Unable to gather the strength to do otherwise, A.J. huddled on the seat and shivered. She needed only a minute. She promised herself she needed only a minute to pull herself together. But however many it took David to come back, the shivering hadn't stopped. He tossed her purse in the back, then tucked a blanket around her. "One of the crew's taking your car back to town." After starting the engine, he headed down the bumpy, potholed gravel road. For several moments there was silence as the rain drummed and she sat hunched under the blanket.

"Why didn't you tell me?" he said at length.

She was better now. She took a steady breath to prove she had control. "Tell you what?"

"That you were like your mother."

A.J. curled into a ball on the seat, cradled her head in her arms and wept.

What the hell was he supposed to say? David cursed her, then himself, as he drove through the rain with her sobbing beside him. She'd given him the scare of his life when he'd turned around and seen her standing there, gasping for air and white as a sheet. He'd never felt anything as cold as her hands had been. Never seen anything like what she must have seen.

Whatever doubts he had, whatever criticisms he could make about laboratory tests, five-dollar psychics and executive clairvoyants, he knew A.J. had seen something, felt something, none of the rest of them had.

So what did he do about it? What did he say?

She wept. She let herself empty. There was no use berating herself, no use being angry with what had happened. She'd long ago resigned herself to the fact that every now and again, no matter how careful she was, no matter how tightly controlled, she would slip and leave herself open.

The rain stopped. There was milky sunlight now. A.J. kept the blanket close around her as she straightened in her seat. "I'm sorry."

"I don't want an apology. I want an explanation."

"I don't have one." She wiped her cheeks dry with her hand. "I'd appreciate it if you'd take me home."

"We're going to talk, and we're going to do it where you can't kick me out."

She was too weak to argue, too weak to care. A.J. rested her head against the window and didn't protest when they passed the turn for her apartment. They drove up into the hills, high above the city. The rain had left things fresh here, though a curling mist still hugged the ground.

He turned into a drive next to a house with cedar shakes and tall windows. The lawn was wide and trimmed with spring flowers bursting around the borders.

"I thought you'd have a place in town."

"I used to, then I decided I had to breathe." He took her purse and a briefcase from the back seat. A.J. pushed the blanket aside and stepped from the car. Saying nothing, they walked to the front door together.

Inside wasn't rustic. He had paintings on the walls and thick Turkish carpets on the floors. She ran her hand along a polished rail and stepped down a short flight of steps into the living room. Still silent, David went to the fireplace and set kindling to blaze. "You'll want to get out of those wet clothes," he said matter-of-factly. "There's a bath upstairs at the end of the hall. I keep a robe on the back of the door."

"Thank you." Her confidence was gone—that edge that helped her keep one step ahead. A.J. moistened her lips. "David, you don't have to—"

"I'll make coffee." He walked through a doorway and left her alone.

She stood there while the flames from the kindling began to lick at split oak. The scent was woodsy, comfortable. She'd never felt more miserable in her life. The kind of rejection she felt now, from David, was the kind she'd expected. It was the kind she'd dealt with before.

She stood there while she battled back the need to weep again. She was strong, self-reliant. She wasn't about to break her heart over David Brady, or any man. Lifting her chin, A.J. walked to the stairs and up. She'd shower, let her clothes dry, then dress and go home. A.J. Fields knew how to take care of herself.

The water helped. It soothed her puffy eyes and warmed her clammy skin. From the small bag of emergency cosmetics in her purse, she managed to repair the worst of the damage. She tried not to notice that the robe carried David's scent as she slipped it on. It was better to remember that it was warm and covered her adequately.

When she went back downstairs, the living area was still empty. Clinging to the courage she'd managed to build back up, A.J. went to look for him.

The hallway twisted and turned at angles when least expected. If the situation had been different, A.J. would have appreciated the house for its uniqueness. She didn't take much notice of polished paneling offset by stark white walls, or planked floors scattered with intricately patterned carpets. She followed the hallway into the kitchen. The scent of coffee eased the beginning of flutters in her stomach. She took a moment to brace herself, then walked into the light.

He was standing by the window. There was a cup of coffee in his hand, but he wasn't drinking. Something was simmering on the stove. Perhaps he'd forgotten it. A.J. crossed her arms over her chest and rubbed her hands over the sleeves of the robe. She didn't feel warm any longer.

"David?"

He turned the moment she said his name, but slowly. He wasn't certain what he should say to her, what he could say. She looked so frail. He couldn't have described his own feelings at the moment and hadn't a clue to hers. "The coffee's hot," he told her. "Why don't you sit down?"

"Thanks." She willed herself to behave as normally as he and took a seat on a stool at the breakfast bar.

"I thought you could use some food." He walked to the stove to pour coffee. "I heated up some soup."

Tension began to beat behind her eyes. "You didn't have to bother."

Saying nothing, he ladled out the soup, then brought both it and the coffee to her. "It's an old family recipe. My mother always says a bowl of soup cures anything."

"It looks wonderful," she managed, and wondered why she had to fight back the urge to cry again. "David..."

"Eat first." Taking no food for himself, he drew up a stool across from her and cradled his coffee. He lit a cigarette and sat, sipping his coffee and smoking, while she toyed with her soup. "You're supposed to eat it," he pointed out. "Not just rearrange the noodles."

"Why don't you ask?" she blurted out. "I'd rather you just asked and got it over with."

So much hurt there, he realized. So much pain. He wondered where it had its roots. "I don't intend to start an interrogation, A.J."

"Why not?" When she lifted her head, her face was defiant, her eyes strong. "You want to know what happened to me in that room."

He blew out a stream of smoke before he crushed out his cigarette. "Of course I do. But I don't think you're ready to talk about what happened in that room. At least not in detail. A.J., why don't you just talk to me?"

"Not ready?" She might have laughed if her stomach wasn't tied up in knots. "You're never ready. I can tell you what she looked like—black hair, blue eyes. She was wearing a cotton gown that buttoned all the way up to her throat, and her name was Jessica. She was barely eighteen when her husband killed her in a jealous rage, strangled her with his own hands, then killed himself in grief with the pistol in the table beside the bed. That's what you want for your documentary, isn't it?"

The details, and the cool, steady way she delivered them, left him shaken. Just who was this woman who sat across from him, this woman he'd held and desired? "What happened to you has nothing to do with the project. I think it has a great deal to do with the way you're reacting now."

"I can usually control it." She shoved the soup aside so that it lapped over the edges of the bowl. "God knows I've had years of practice. If I hadn't been so angry, so out of control when I walked in there—it probably wouldn't have happened."

"You can block it."

"Usually, yes. To a large extent, anyway."

"Why do you?"

"Do you really think this is a gift?" she demanded as she pushed away from the counter. "Oh, maybe for someone like Clarissa it is. She's so unselfish, so basically good and content with herself."

"And you?"

"I hate it." Unable to remain still, she whirled away. "You've no idea what it can be like, having people stare at you, whisper. If you're different, you're a freak, and I—" She broke off, rubbing at her temple. When she spoke again, her voice was quiet. "I just wanted to be normal. When I was little, I'd have dreams." She folded her hands together and pressed them to her lips. "They were so incredibly real, but I was just a child and thought everyone dreamed like that. I'd tell one of my friends—oh, your cat's going to have kittens. Can I have the little white one? Then weeks later, the cat would have kittens and one of them would be white. Little things. Someone would lose a doll or a toy and I'd say, well, your mother put it on the top shelf in your closet. She forgot. When they looked it would be there. Kids didn't think much of it, but it made some of the parents nervous. They thought it would be best if their children stayed away from me."

"And that hurt," he murmured.

"Yes, that hurt a lot. Clarissa understood. She was comforting and really wonderful about it, but it hurt. I still had the dreams, but I stopped talking about them. Then my father died."

She stood, the heels of her hands pressed to her eyes as she struggled to rein in her emotions. "No, please." She shook her head as she heard David shift on the stool as if to rise. "Just give me a minute." On a long breath, she dropped her hands. "I knew he was dead. He was away on a selling trip, and I woke up in the middle of the night and knew. I got up and went to Clarissa. She was sitting up in bed, wide awake. I could see on her face that she was already grieving. We didn't even say anything to each other, but I got into bed with her, and we just lay there together until the phone rang."

"And you were eight," he murmured, trying to get some grip on it.

"I was eight. After that, I started to block it off. Whenever I began to feel something, I'd just pull in. It got to the point where I could go for months—at one point, two years—

without something touching it off. If I get angry or upset to the point where I lose control, I open myself up for it."

He remembered the way she'd stormed into the house, strong and ready for a fight. And the way she'd run out again, pale and terrified. "And I make you angry."

She turned to look at him for the first time since she'd begun to speak. "It seems that way."

The guilt was there. David wasn't certain how to deal with it, or his own confusion. "Should I apologize?"

"You can't help being what you are any more than I can stop being what I am."

"Aurora, I think I understand your need to keep a handle on this thing, not to let it interfere with the day-to-day. I don't understand why you feel you have to lock it out of your life like a disease."

She'd gone this far, she thought as she walked back to the counter. She'd finish. "When I was twenty, scrambling around and trying to get my business rolling, I met this man. He had this little shop on the beach, renting surfboards, selling lotion, that sort of thing. It was so, well, exciting, to see someone that free-spirited, that easygoing, when I was working ten hours a day just to scrape by. In any case, I'd never been involved seriously with a man before. There hadn't been time. I fell flat on my face for this one. He was fun, not too demanding. Before I knew it we were on the point of being engaged. He bought me this little ring with the promise of diamonds and emeralds once we hit it big. I think he meant it." She gave a little laugh as she slid onto the stool again. "In any case, I felt that if we were going to be married we shouldn't have any secrets."

"You hadn't told him?"

"No." She said it defiantly, as if waiting for disapproval. When none came, she lowered her gaze and went on. "I introduced him to Clarissa, and then I told him that I—I told him," she said flatly. "He thought it was a joke, sort of dared me to prove it. Because I felt so strongly about having everything up front between us, well, I guess you could say I proved it. After—he looked at me as though…" She swallowed and struggled to keep the hurt buried.

"I'm sorry."

"I suppose I should have expected it." Though she shrugged it off, she picked up the spoon and began to run the handle through her fingers. "I didn't see him for days after that. I went to him with some grand gesture in mind, like giving him back his ring. It's almost funny, looking back on it now, the way he wouldn't look at me, the way he kept his distance. Too weird." She looked up again with a brittle smile. "I was just plain too weird."

And she was still hurting. But he didn't reach out to her. He wasn't quite sure how. "The wrong man at the wrong time."

A.J. gave an impatient shake of her head. "I was the wrong woman. Since then, I've learned that honesty isn't always the most advantageous route. Do you have any idea what it would do to me professionally if my clients knew? Those I didn't lose would ask me to tell them what role to audition for. People would start asking me to fly to Vegas with them so I could tell them what number to bet at the roulette table."

"So you and Clarissa downplay your relationship and you block the rest off."

"That's right." She picked up her cold coffee and downed it. "After today, I guess that goes to hell."

"I told Sam I'd discussed what had happened in that room with you, that we'd talked about the murder and coming up there had upset you." He rose to fetch the pot and freshen her coffee. "The crew may mumble about overimaginative women, but that's all."

She shut her eyes. She hadn't expected sensitivity from him, much less understanding. "Thanks."

"It's your secret if you feel it's necessary to keep it, A.J."

"It's very necessary. How did you feel when you realized?" she demanded. "Uncomfortable? Uneasy? Even now, you're tiptoeing around me."

"Maybe I am." He started to pull out a cigarette, then shoved it back into the pack. "Yeah, it makes me uneasy. It's not something I've ever had to deal with before. A man has to wonder if he'll have any secrets from a woman who can look inside him."

"Of course." She rose, back straight. "And a man's entitled to protect himself. I appreciate what you've done, David. I'm sure my clothes are dry now. I'll change if you'll call me a cab."

"No." He was up and blocking her way before she could walk out of the kitchen.

"Don't make this any more difficult for me, or for yourself."

"Damned if I want to," he muttered, and found he'd already reached for her. "I can't seem to help it. You make me uneasy," he repeated. "You've made me uneasy all along. I still want you, Aurora. That's all that seems to matter at the moment."

"You'll think differently later."

He drew her closer. "Reading my mind?"

"Don't joke."

"Maybe it's time someone did. If you want to look into my head now, you'll see that all I can think about is taking you upstairs, to my bed."

Her heart began to beat, in her chest, in her throat. "And tomorrow?"

"The hell with tomorrow." He brought his lips down to hers with a violence that left her shaken. "The hell with everything but the fact that you and I have a need for each other. You're not going home tonight, Aurora."

She let herself go, let herself risk. "No, I'm not."

Chapter 7

There was moonlight, streaks of it, glimmering. She could smell the hyacinths, light and sweet, through the open windows. The murmur of a stream winding its way through the woods beside the house was quiet, soothing. Every muscle in A.J.'s body tensed as she stepped into David's bedroom.

The painting hung on the wall as she had known it would, vivid, sensual streaks on a white canvas. The first shudder rolled through her as she turned her head and saw her own vague reflection, not in a mirror, but in a tall glass door.

"I dreamed this." The words were barely audible as she took a step back. But was she stepping back into the dream or into reality? Were they somehow both the same? Panicked, she stood where she was. Didn't she have a choice? she asked herself. Was she just following a pattern already set, a pattern that had begun the moment David Brady had walked into her office?

"This isn't what I want," she whispered, and turned—for

escape, for freedom—in denial, she couldn't have said. But he was there, blocking her way, drawing her closer, drawing her in just as she'd known he would be.

She looked up at him as she knew she had done before. His face was in shadows, as indistinct as hers had been in the glass. But his eyes were clear, highlighted by moonlight. His words were clear, highlighted by desire.

"You can't keep running, Aurora, not from yourself, not from me."

There was impatience in his voice, impatience that became all the sharper when his mouth closed over hers. He wanted, more desperately than he had allowed himself to believe. He needed, more intensely than he could afford to admit. Her uncertainty, her hesitation, aroused some deep, primitive part of him. Demand, take, possess. The thoughts twined together into one throbbing pulsebeat of desire. He didn't feel the pleasant anticipation he had with other women, but a rage, burning, almost violent. As he tasted the first hint of surrender, he nearly went mad with it.

His mouth was so hungry, his hands were so strong. The pressure of his body against hers was insistent. He held her as though she were his to take with or without consent. Yet she knew, had always known, the choice was ultimately hers. She could give or deny. Like a stone tossed into clear water, her decision now would send ripples flowing out into her life. Where they ended, how they altered the flow, couldn't be foretold. To give, she knew, was always a risk. And risk always held its own excitement, its own fear. With each second that passed, the pleasure grew more bold and ripe, until with a moan of acceptance, she brought her hands to his face and let herself go.

It was only passion, A.J. told herself while her body strained and ached. Passion followed no patterns, kept to no course. The need that grew inside her had nothing to do with dreams or hopes or wishes. It was her passion she couldn't resist, his passion she couldn't refuse. For tonight, this one night, she'd let herself be guided by it.

He knew the instant she was his. Her body didn't weaken, but strengthened. The surrender he'd expected became a hunger as urgent as his. There would be no slow seduction for either of them, no gentle persuasion. Desire was a razor's edge that promised as much pain as pleasure. They both understood it; they both acknowledged; they both accepted. Together they fell onto the bed and let the fire blaze.

His robe tangled around her. With an impatient oath, he yanked it down from her shoulder so that the tantalizing slope was exposed. His lips raced over her face, leaving hers unfulfilled while he stoked a line of heat down her throat. She felt the rasp of his cheek and moaned in approval. He sought to torment, he sought to dominate, but she met each move with equal strength. She felt the warm trace of his tongue and shivered in anticipation. Unwilling to leave the reins in his hands, she tugged at the buttons of his shirt, unfastening, tearing, until with her own patience ended, she ripped it from his back.

His flesh was taut under her palms, the muscles a tight ridge to be explored and exploited. Male, hard, strong. His scent wound its way into her senses, promising rough demands and frantic movement. She tasted furious demands, hot intentions, then her excitement bounded upward when she felt his first tremble. Painful, urgent, desperate needs poured from him into her. It was what she wanted. As ruthless as he, she sought to drag him away from his control.

The bed was like a battlefield, full of fire and smoke and passions. The spread was soft, smooth, the air touched with spring, but it meant nothing to them. Warm flesh and sharp needs, rippling muscle and rough hands. That was their world. Her breath caught, not in fear, not in protest, but in excitement, as he pulled the robe down her body. When her arms were pinned she used her mouth as a weapon to drive him beyond reason. Her hips arched, pressing against him, tormenting, tempting, thrilling. As his hands moved over her, her strength seemed to double to race with her needs.

But here in this fuming, incendiary world there would be no winner and no loser. The fire sprinted along her skin, leaving dull, tingling aches wherever his hands or lips had touched. She wanted it, reveled in it, even while she burned for more. Not content to leave the control in his hands for long, A.J. rolled on top of him and began her own siege.

He'd never known a woman could make him shudder. He'd never known a woman could make him hurt from desire alone. She was long and limber and as ravenous as he. She was naked but not vulnerable. She was passionate but not pliant. He could see her in the moonlight, her hair pale and tumbled around her face, her skin glowing from exhilaration and needs not yet met. Her hands were soft as they raked over him, but demanding enough, bold enough, to take his breath away. The lips that followed them did nothing to soothe. She yanked his slacks down with a wild impatience that had his mind spinning and his body pounding. Then before he could react, she was sprawled across him, tasting his flesh.

It was madness. He welcomed it. It was torment. He could have begged for more. Once he'd thought he had discovered a simmering, latent passion in her, but nothing had prepared him for this. She was seduction, she was lust, she was greed. With both hands in her hair, he dragged her mouth to his so that he could taste them all.

It wasn't a dream, she thought dazedly as his mouth clung to hers and his hands again took possession. No dream had ever been so tempestuous. Reality had never been so mad. Tangled with her, he rolled her to her back. Even as she gasped for air, he plunged into her so that her body arched up, taut with the first uncontrollable climax. She reached up, too stunned to realize how badly she needed to hold on to him. Wrapped tight, their strengths fed each other as surely as their hungers did.

They lay together, weak, sated, both of them vanquished.

Gradually sanity returned. A.J. saw the moonlight again. His face was buried in her hair, but his breathing had steadied, as hers had. Her arms were still around him, her body locked tight to his. She told herself to let go, to reestablish distance, but lacked the will to obey.

It had only been passion, she reminded herself. It had only been need. Both had been satisfied. Now was the time to draw away, to move apart. But she wanted to nuzzle her cheek against his, to murmur something foolish and stay just as she was until the sun came up. With her eyes closed tight she fought the urge to soften, to give that which, once given, was lost.

No, he'd never known a woman could make him shudder. He'd never known a woman could make him weak. Yes, once he'd thought he'd discovered a simmering, latent passion in her, but he hadn't expected this. He shouldn't still feel so dazed. So involved.

He hadn't been prepared for the intensity of feeling. He hadn't planned on having the need grow and multiply even after it was satisfied. That was the reason he'd lost some part of himself to her. That was, had to be, the only reason.

But when she trembled, he drew her closer.

"Cold?"

"The air's cooled." It sounded reasonable. It sounded true.

How could she explain that her body was still pumping with heat, and would be as long as he was there?

"I can shut the windows."

"No." She could hear the stream again, just smell the hyacinths. She didn't want to lose the sensations.

"Here, then." He drew away to untangle the sheets and pull them over her. It was then, in the dim light, that he noticed the pale line of smudges along her arm. Taking her elbow, he looked closer.

"Apparently I wasn't careful enough with you."

A.J. glanced down. There was regret in his voice, and a trace of a kindness she would have little defense against. If she hadn't been afraid, she would have longed to hear him speak just like that again, she would have rested her head on his shoulder. Instead, with a shrug she shifted and drew her arm away. "No permanent damage." She hoped. "I wouldn't be surprised if you found a few bruises on yourself."

He looked at her again and grinned in a way that was completely unexpected and totally charming. "It seems we both play rough."

It was too late to hold back a response to the grin. On impulse, A.J. leaned over and took a quick, none-too-gentle nip at his shoulder. "Complaining?"

She'd surprised him again. Maybe it was time for a few surprises in his life. And in hers. "I won't if you won't." Then, in a move too abrupt to evade, he rolled over her again, pinning her arms above her head with one hand.

"Look, Brady—"

"I like the idea of going one-on-one with you, A.J." He lowered his head just enough to nibble on her earlobe, until she squirmed under him.

"As long as you have the advantage." Her voice was breathy, her cheeks flushed. With his hands on her wrists he could feel the gradual acceleration of her pulse. With his body stretched full length, he could feel the dips, the curves, the fluid lines of hers. Desire began to rise again as though it had never been quenched.

"Lady, I think I might enjoy taking advantage of you on a regular basis. I know I'm going to enjoy it for the rest of the night."

She twisted one way, twisted the other, then let out a hissing breath, as he only stared down at her. Being outdone physically was nearly as bad as being outdone intellectually. "I can't stay here tonight."

"You are here," he pointed out, then took his free hand in one long stroke from her hip to her breast.

"I can't stay."

"Why?"

Because reliving pent-up passion with him and spending the night with him were two entirely different things. "Because I have to work tomorrow," she began lamely. "And—"

"I'll drop you by your apartment in the morning so you can change." The tip of her breast was already hard against his palm. He ran his thumb over it and watched passion darken her eyes.

"I have to be in the office by eight-thirty."

"We'll get up early." He lowered his head to brush kisses at either side of her mouth. "I'm not planning on getting much sleep, anyway."

Her body was a mass of nerve endings waiting to be exploited. Exploitation led to weakness, she reminded herself. And weakness to losses. "I don't spend the night with men."

"You do with this one." He brought his hand up, tracing as he went until he cupped her throat.

If she was going to lose, she'd lose with her eyes open. "Why?"

He could have given her quiet, persuasive answers. And they might have been true. Perhaps that's why he chose another way. "We haven't nearly finished with each other yet, Aurora. Not nearly."

He was right. The need was screaming through her. That she could accept. But she wouldn't accept being pressured, being cajoled or being seduced. Her terms, A.J. told herself. Then she could justify this first concession. "Let go of my hands, Brady."

Her chin was angled, her eyes direct, her voice firm. She wasn't a woman, he decided, who could be anticipated. Lifting a brow, he released her hands and waited.

With her eyes on his, she brought them to his face. Slowly her lips curved. Whether it was challenge or surrender he didn't care. "I wouldn't plan to sleep at all tonight," she warned just before she pulled his mouth to hers.

The room was still dark when A.J. roused from a light doze to draw the covers closer. There was an ache, more pleasant than annoying, in her muscles. She stretched, then shifted to glance at the luminous dial of her clock. It wasn't there. With her mind fogged with sleep, she rubbed a hand over her eyes and looked again.

Of course it wasn't there, she remembered. She wasn't there. Her clock, her apartment and her own bed were miles away. Turning again, she saw that the bed beside her was empty. Where could he have gone? she wondered as she pushed herself up. And what time was it?

She'd lost time. Hours, days, weeks, it hadn't mattered. But now she was alone, and it was time for reality again.

They'd exhausted each other, depleted each other and fed each other. She hadn't known there could be anything like the night they'd shared. Nothing real had ever been so exciting, so wild or desperate. Yet it had been very real. Her body bore the marks his hands had made while he'd been lost in passion. His taste still lingered on her tongue, his scent on her skin. It had been real, but it hadn't been reality. Reality was now, when she had to face the morning.

What she'd given, she'd given freely. She would have no regrets there. If she'd broken one of her own rules, she'd done so consciously and with deliberation. Not coolly, perhaps, but not carelessly. Neither could she be careless now. The night was over.

Because there was nothing else, A.J. picked his robe up off the floor and slipped into it. The important thing was not to be foolish, but mature. She wouldn't cuddle and cling and pretend there had been anything more between them than sex. One night of passion and mutual need.

She turned her cheek into the collar of the robe and let it linger there for a moment where his scent had permeated the cloth. Then, securing the belt, she walked out of the bedroom and down the stairs.

The living room was in shadows, but the first tongues of light filtered through the wide glass windows. David stood there, looking out, while a fire, freshly kindled, crackled beside him. A.J. felt the distance between them was like a crater, deep, wide and jagged. It took her too long to remind herself that was what she'd expected and wanted. Rather than speak, she walked the rest of the way down the stairs and waited.

"I had the place built with this window facing east so I could watch the sun rise." He lifted a cigarette and drew deep so that the tip glowed in the half-light. "No matter how many times I see it, it's different."

She wouldn't have judged him as a man drawn to sunrises. She hadn't judged him as a man who would choose a secluded house in the hills. Just how much, A.J. wondered, did she know about the man she'd spent the night with? Thrusting her hands into the pockets of the robe, her fingers brushed cardboard. A.J. curled them around the matchbook he'd stuck in there and forgotten. "I don't take much time for sunrises."

"If I happen to be right here at the right time, I usually find I can handle whatever crises the day has planned a little better."

Her fingers closed and opened, opened and closed on the matchbook. "Are you expecting any particular crisis today?"

He turned then to look at her, standing barefoot and a bit hollow-eyed in his robe. It didn't dwarf her; she was only inches shorter than he. Still, somehow it made her appear more feminine, more…accessible, he decided, than anything else he remembered. It wouldn't be possible to tell her that it had just occurred to him that he was already in the middle of a crisis. Its name was Aurora J. Fields. "You know…" He tucked his hands in the back pockets of well-broken-in jeans before he took a step closer. "We didn't spend too much time talking last night."

"No." She braced herself. "It didn't seem that conversation was what either of us wanted." Nor was it conversation she'd prepared herself to deal with. "I'm going to go up and change. I do have to be in the office early."

"Aurora." He didn't reach out to stop her this time. He only had to speak. "What did you feel that first day with me in your office?"

After letting out a long breath, she faced him again. "David, I talked about that part of my life more than I cared to last night."

He knew that was true. He'd spent some time wondering why without finding any answers. She had them. If he had to probe and prod until she gave them up, he would.

"You talked about it in connection with other people, other things. This happens to involve me."

"I'm going to be late for work," she murmured, and started up the landing.

"You make a habit of running away, Aurora."

"I'm not running." She whirled back, both hands clenched into fists in the pockets. "I simply don't see any reason to drag this all up again. It's personal. It's mine."

"And it touches me," he added calmly. "You walked into my bedroom last night and said you'd dreamed it. Had you?"

"I don't—" She wanted to deny it, but she had never been comfortable with direct lies. The fact that she couldn't use one had anger bubbling through. "Yes. Dreams aren't as easily controlled as conscious thought."

"Tell me what you dreamed."

She wouldn't give him all. A.J.'s nails dug into her palms. She'd be damned if she'd give him all. "I dreamed about your room. I could have described it for you before I'd ever gone in. Would you like to put me under a microscope now or later?"

"Self-pity isn't attractive." As her breath hissed out he stepped onto the landing with her. "You knew we were going to be lovers."

Her expression became cool, almost disinterested. "Yes."

"And you knew that day in your office when you were angry with me, frustrated with your mother, and our hands met, like this." He reached out, uncurled her fist and pressed their hands palm to palm.

Her back was against the wall, her hand caught in his. She was tired, spitting tired, of finding herself in corners. "What are you trying to prove, a theory for your documentary?"

What would she say if he told her he'd come to understand she showed her fangs only when she was most vulnerable? "You knew," he repeated, letting the venom spill off of him. "And it frightened you. Why was that?"

"I'd just had a strong, physical premonition that I was going to be the lover of a man I'd already decided was detestable. Is that reason enough?"

"For annoyance, even anger. Not for fear. You were afraid that night in the back of the limo, and again last night when you walked into the bedroom."

She tried to jerk her arm aside. "You're exaggerating."

"Am I?" He stepped closer and touched a hand to her cheek. "You're afraid now."

"That's not true." Deliberately she unclenched her other hand. "I'm annoyed because you're pressing me. We're adults who spent the night together. That doesn't give you the right to pry into my personal life or feelings."

No, it didn't. That was his own primary rule and he was breaking it. Somehow he'd forgotten that he had no rights, could expect none. "All right, that's true. But I saw the condition you were in yesterday afternoon after walking into that room."

"That's done," she said quickly, maybe too quickly. "There's no need to get into it again."

Though he was far from convinced, he let it ride. "And I listened to you last night. I don't want to be responsible for anything like that happening to you again."

"You're not responsible—I am." Her voice was calmer now. Emotions clouded things. She'd spent years discovering that. "You don't cause anything, I do, or if you like, circumstances do. David, I'm twenty-eight, and I've managed to survive this—something extra all my life."

"I understand that. You should understand that I'm thirty-six. I haven't been personally exposed to any of this up until a few weeks ago."

"I do understand." Her voice chilled, just a little. "And I understand the natural reaction is to be wary, curious or skeptical. The same way one looks at a sideshow in the circus."

"Don't put words in my mouth." His anger came as a surprise to both of them. So much of a surprise, that when he grabbed A.J. by the shoulders, she offered no protest at all. "I can't help what reaction other people have had to you. They weren't me. Damn it, I've just spent the night making love to you and I don't even know who you are. I'm afraid to touch you, thinking I might set something off. I can't keep my hands off you. I came down here this morning because if I'd lain beside you another minute I'd have taken you again while you were half-asleep."

Before she'd had a chance to weigh her own reaction, she lifted her hands up to his. "I don't know what you want."

"Neither do I." He caught himself and relaxed his grip on her. "And that's a first. Maybe I need some time to figure it out."

Time. Distance. She reminded herself that was for the best. With a nod, she dropped her hands again. "That's reasonable."

"But what isn't is that I don't want to spend that time away from you."

Chills, anxiety or excitement, rushed up her spine. "David, I—"

"I've never had a night like the one I had with you."

The weakness came quickly, to be just as quickly fought back. "You don't have to say that."

"I know I don't." With a half laugh he rubbed his hands over the shoulders he'd just clenched. "In fact, it isn't very easy to admit it. It just happens to be true, for me. Sit down a minute." He drew her down to sit on the step beside him. "I didn't have a lot of time to think last night because I was too busy being...stunned," he decided. She didn't relax when he put his arm around her, but she didn't draw away. "I've packed a lot of thinking into the past hour. There's more to you, A.J., than there is to a lot of other women. Even without the something extra. I think what I want is to have a chance to get to know the woman I intend to spend a lot of time making love with."

She turned to look at him. His face was close, his arm more gentle than she'd come to expect. He didn't look like a man who had any gentleness in him, only power and confidence. "You're taking a lot for granted."

"Yeah, I am."

"I don't think you should."

"Maybe not. I want you—you want me. We can start with that."

That was simpler. "No promises."

The protest sprang to his mind so quickly it stunned him. "No promises," he agreed, reminding himself that had always been rule number two.

She knew she shouldn't agree. The smart thing, the safe thing to do, was to cut things off now. One night, passion only. But she found herself relaxing against him. "Business and personal relationships completely separate."

"Absolutely."

"And when one of us becomes uncomfortable with the way things are going, we back off with no scenes or bad feelings."

"Agreed. Want it in writing?"

Her lips curved slightly as she studied him. "I should. Producers are notoriously untrustworthy."

"Agents are notoriously cynical."

"Cautious," she corrected, but lifted a hand to rub it along the stubble on his cheek. "We're paid to be the bad guys, after all. And speaking of which, we never finished discussing Clarissa."

"It isn't business hours," he reminded her, then turned her hand palm up and pressed his lips to it.

"Don't try to change the subject. We need to iron this out. Today."

"Between nine and five," he agreed.

"Fine, call my office and… Oh, my God."

"What?"

"My messages." Dragging both hands through her hair, she sprang up. "I never called in for my messages."

"Sounds like a national emergency," he murmured as he stood beside her.

"I was barely in the office two hours. As it was I had to reschedule appointments. Where's the phone?"

"Make it worth my while."

"David, I'm not joking."

"Neither am I." Smiling down at her, he slipped his hand into the opening of the robe and parted it. She felt her legs liquefy from the knees down.

"David." She turned her head to avoid his lips, then found herself in deeper trouble, as her throat was undefended. "It'll only take me a minute."

"You're wrong." He unfastened the belt. "It's going to take longer than that."

"For all I know I might have a breakfast meeting."

"For all you know you don't have an appointment until noon." Her hands were moving down his back, under his shirt. He wondered if she was aware. "What we both know is that we should make love. Right now."

"After," she began, but sighed against his lips.

"Before."

The robe fell to the floor at her feet. Negotiations ended.

Chapter 8

A.J. should have been satisfied. She should have been relaxed. In the ten days following her first night with David, their relationship had run smoothly. When her schedule and his allowed, they spent the evening together. There were simple evenings walking the beach, elegant evenings dining out and quiet evenings dining in. The passion that had pulled them together didn't fade. Rather, it built and intensified, driving them to quench it. He wanted her, as completely, as desperately, as a man could want a woman. Of the multitude of things she was uncertain of, she could be absolutely certain of that.

She should have been relaxed. She was tied up in knots.

Each day she had to rebuild a defense that had always been like a second skin. Each night David ripped it away again. She couldn't afford to leave her emotions unprotected in what was, by her own description, a casual, physical affair. They would continue seeing each other as long as both of them enjoyed it. No promises, no commitments. When he decided to pull away, she needed to be ready.

It was, she discovered, like waiting for the other shoe to drop. He would undoubtedly break things off sooner or later. Passions that flamed too hot were bound to burn themselves out, and they had little else. He read thick, socially significant novels and informative nonfiction. A.J. leaned toward slim, gory mysteries and glitzy bestsellers. He took her to a foreign film festival full of symbolism and subtitles. She'd have chosen the Gene Kelly–Judy Garland classic on late-night TV.

The more they got to know each other, the more distance A.J. saw. Passion was the magnet that drew them together, but she was very aware its power would fade. For her own survival, she intended to be prepared when it did.

On a business level she had to be just as prepared to deal with David Brady, producer. A.J. was grateful that in this particular relationship she knew every step and every angle. After listening to David's ideas for expanding Clarissa's role in the documentary, she'd agreed to the extra shoots. For a price. It hadn't been money she'd wanted to wheedle out of him, but the promise of promotion for Clarissa's next book, due out in midsummer.

It had taken two days of heated negotiations, tossing the ball back and forth, refusals, agreements and compromises. Clarissa would have her promotion directly on the program, and a review on *Book Talk*, the intellectual PBS weekly. David would have his extra studio shoots and his interview with Clarissa and Alice Van Camp. Both had walked away from the negotiating table smug that they had outdone the other.

Clarissa couldn't have cared less. She was busy with her plants, her recipes and, to A.J.'s mounting dismay, her wedding plans. She took the news of the promotions A.J. had sweated for with an absent "That's nice, dear," and wondered out loud if she should bake the wedding cake herself.

"Momma, a review on *Book Talk* isn't just nice." A.J. swung into the studio parking lot frustrated from the forty-minute drive during which she and Clarissa had talked at cross purposes.

"Oh, I'm sure it's going to be lovely. The publisher said they were sending advance copies. Aurora, do you think a garden wedding would be suitable? I'm afraid my azaleas might fade."

Brows lowered, she swung into a parking spot. "How many advance copies?"

"Oh, I'm really not sure. I probably wrote it down somewhere. And then it might rain. The weather's so unpredictable in June."

"Make sure they send at least three. One for the— June?" Her foot slipped off the clutch, so that the car bucked to a halt. "But that's next month."

"Yes, and I have dozens of things to do. Just dozens."

A.J.'s hands were very still on the wheel as she turned. "But didn't you say something about a fall wedding?"

"I suppose I did. You know my mums are at their best in October, but Alex is..." She flushed and cleared her throat. "A bit impatient. Aurora, I know I don't drive, but I think you've left your key on."

Muttering, she pulled it out. "Momma, you're talking about marrying a man you'll have known for less than two months."

"Do you really think time's so important?" she asked with a sweet smile. "It's more a matter of feelings."

"Feelings can change." She thought of David, of herself.

"There aren't any guarantees in life, darling." Clarissa

reached over to cover her daughter's hand with her own. "Not even for people like you and me."

"That's what worries me." She was going to talk to Alex Marshall, A.J. promised herself as she pushed her door open. Her mother was acting like a teenager going steady with the football hero. Someone had to be sensible.

"You really don't have to worry," Clarissa told her as she stepped onto the curb. "I know what I'm doing—really, I do. But talk to Alex by all means."

"Momma." With a long sigh, A.J. linked arms. "I do have to worry. And mind reading's not allowed."

"I hardly have to when it's written all over your face. Is my hair all right?"

A.J. turned to kiss her cheek. "You look beautiful."

"Oh, I hope so." Clarissa gave a nervous laugh as they approached the studio doors. "I'm afraid I've become very vain lately. But Alex is such a handsome man, isn't he?"

"Yes," A.J. agreed cautiously. He was handsome, polished smooth and personable. She wouldn't be satisfied until she found the flaws.

"Clarissa." They'd hardly stepped inside, when Alex came striding down the hall. He looked like a man approaching a lost and valued treasure. "You look beautiful."

He had both of Clarissa's hands and looked to A.J. as though he would scoop her mother up and carry her off. "Mr. Marshall." She kept her voice cool and deliberately extended her own hand.

"Ms. Fields." With obvious reluctance, he released one of Clarissa's hands to take A.J.'s. "I have to say you're more dedicated than my own agent. I was hoping to bring Clarissa down myself today."

"Oh, she likes to fuss," Clarissa put in, hoping to mollify them both. "And I'm afraid I'm so scatterbrained she has to remind me of all the little things about television interviews."

"Just relax," A.J. told her. "I'll go see if everything's set." Checking her watch as she went, she reached out to push open the thick studio doors, when David walked through.

"Good morning, Ms. Fields." The formal greeting was accompanied by the trail of his fingers over her wrist. "Sitting in again today?"

"Looking after my client, Brady. She's…" When she glanced casually over her shoulder, the words slipped back down her throat. There in the middle of the hallway was her mother caught up in a close and very passionate embrace. Stunned, she stared while dozens of feelings she couldn't identify ran through her.

"Your client appears to be well looked after," David murmured. When she didn't reply, he pulled her into a room off the hall. "Want to sit down?"

"No. No, I should—"

"Mind your own business."

Anger replaced shock very quickly. "She happens to be my mother."

"That's right." He walked to a coffee machine and poured two plastic cups. "Not your ward."

"I'm not going to stand by while she, while she—"

"Enjoys herself?" he suggested, and handed her the coffee.

"She isn't thinking." A.J. downed half the coffee in one swallow. "She's just riding on emotion, infatuation. And she's—"

"In love."

A.J. drank the rest of the coffee, then heaved the cup in the direction of the trash. "I hate it when you interrupt me."

"I know." And he grinned at her. "Why don't we have a

quiet evening tonight, at your place? We can start making love in the living room, work our way through to the bedroom and back out again."

"David, Clarissa is my mother and I'm very concerned about her. I should—"

"Be more concerned with yourself." He had his hands on her hips. "And me." They slid firm and strong up her back. "You should be very concerned with me."

"I want you to—"

"I'm becoming an expert on what you want." His mouth brushed hers, retreated, then brushed again. "Do you know your breath starts trembling whenever I do that." His voice lowered, seductive, persuading. "Then your body begins to tremble."

Weak, weaker than she should have been, she lifted both hands to his chest. "David, we have an agreement. It's business hours."

"Sue me." He kissed her again, tempting, teasing as he slipped his hands under her jacket. "What are you wearing under here, A.J.?"

"Nothing important." She caught herself swaying forward. "David, I mean it. We agreed." His tongue traced her bottom lip. "No mixing—ah—no mixing business and... oh, damn." She forgot business and agreements and responsibilities, dragging his mouth to hers.

They filled her, those wild, wanton cravings only he could bring. They tore at her, the needs, the longings, the wishes she knew could never be met. In a moment of abandon she tossed aside what should be and groped blindly for what might be.

His mouth was as hard, as ravenous, as if it were the first time. Desire hadn't faded. His hands were as strong, as possessive and demanding, as ever. Passion hadn't dimmed.

It didn't matter that the room was small and smelled of old coffee and stale cigarettes. Their senses were tangled around each other. Perfume was strong and sweet; tastes were dark and exotic.

Her arms were around his neck; her fingers were raking through his hair. Her mouth was hungry and open on his.

"Oh, excuse me." Clarissa stood in the doorway, eyes lowered as she cleared her throat. It wouldn't do to look too pleased, she knew. Just as it wouldn't be wise to mention that the vibrations bouncing around in the little room might have melted lead. "I thought you'd like to know they're ready for me."

Fumbling for dignity, A.J. tugged at her jacket. "Good. I'll be right in." She waited until the door shut, then swore pungently.

"You're even," David said lightly. "You caught her—she caught you."

Her eyes, when they met his, were hot enough to sear off a layer of skin. "It's not a joke."

"Do you know one thing I've discovered about you these past few days, A.J.? You take yourself too seriously."

"Maybe I do." She scooped her purse from the sofa, then stood there nervously working the clasp. "But has it occurred to you what would have happened if a member of the crew had opened that door?"

"They'd have seen their producer kissing a very attractive woman."

"They would have seen you kissing me during a shoot. That's totally unprofessional. Before the first coffee break, everyone in the studio would be passing around the gossip."

"So?"

"So?" Exasperated, she could only stare at him. "David, that's precisely what we agreed we didn't want. We don't want your crew or our associates speculating and gossiping about our personal relationship."

Brow lifted, eyes narrowed attentively, he listened. "I don't recall discussing that in detail."

"Of course we did." She tucked her purse under her arm, then wished she still had something in her hands. "Right at the beginning."

"As I recall, the idea was to keep our personal and professional lives separate."

"That's just what I've said."

"I didn't take that to mean you wanted to keep the fact that we're lovers a secret."

"I don't want an ad in *Variety*."

He stuck his hands in his pockets. He couldn't have said why he was angry, only that he was. "You don't leave much middle ground, do you?"

She opened her mouth to spit at him, then subsided. "I guess not." On a long breath, she took a step forward. "I want to avoid the speculation, just as I want to avoid the looks of sympathy when things change."

It didn't require telepathy to understand that she'd been waiting for the change—no, he corrected, for the end—since the beginning. Knowledge brought an unexpected, and very unwelcome, twinge of pain. "I see. All right, then, we'll try it your way." He walked to the door and held it open. "Let's go punch in."

No, he couldn't have said why he was angry. In fact, he knew he shouldn't have been. A.J.'s ground rules were logical, and if anything, they made things easier for him. Or should have made things easier for him. She made absolutely no demands and accepted none. In other relationships he'd insisted on the same thing. She refused to allow emotions to interfere with her business or his. In the past he'd felt precisely the same way.

The problem was, he didn't feel that way now.

As the shoot ground to a halt because of two defective bulbs David reminded himself it was his problem. Once he accepted that, he could work on the solution. One was to go along with the terms. The other was to change them.

David watched A.J. cross the room toward Alex. Her stride was brisk, her eyes were cool. In the conservative suit she looked like precisely what she was—a successful businesswoman who knew where she was going and how to get there. He remembered the way she looked when they made love—slim, glowing and as dangerous as a neutron bomb.

David took out a cigarette then struck a match with a kind of restrained violence. He was going to have to plan out solution number two.

"Mr. Marshall." A.J. had her speech prepared and her determination at its peak. With a friendly enough smile, she interrupted Alex's conversation with one of the grips. "Could I speak with you for a minute?"

"Of course." Because he'd been expecting it, Alex took her arm in his innate old-style manner. "Looks like we'll have time for a cup of coffee."

Together they walked back to the room where A.J. had stood with David a few hours before. This time she poured the coffee and offered the cup. But before she could start the prologue for the speech she'd been rehearsing, Alex began.

"You want to talk about Clarissa." He pulled out one of his cigars, then held it out. "Do you mind?"

"No, go ahead. Actually, Mr. Marshall, I would very much like to talk to you about Clarissa."

"She told me you were uneasy about our marriage plans." He puffed comfortably on his cigar until he was satisfied it was well started. "I admit that puzzled me a bit, until she explained that besides being her agent, you happen to be her daughter. Shall we sit down?"

A.J. frowned at the sofa, then at him. It wasn't going at all according to plan. She took her place on one end, while he settled himself on the other. "I'm glad that Clarissa explained things to you. It simplifies things. You'll understand now why I'm concerned. My mother is very important to me."

"And to me." As he leaned back, A.J. studied his profile. It wasn't difficult to see why her mother was infatuated. "You of all people can understand just how easy Clarissa is to love."

"Yes." A.J. sipped at her coffee. What was it she'd planned to say? Taking a deep breath, she moved back on track. "Clarissa is a wonderfully warm and very special person. The thing is, you've known each other for such a short time."

"It only took five minutes." He said it so simply, A.J. was left fumbling for words. "Ms. Fields," he continued, then smiled at her. "A.J.," he corrected. "It doesn't seem right for me to call you 'Ms. Fields.' After all, I'm going to be your stepfather."

Stepfather? Somehow that angle had bypassed her. She sat, coffee cup halfway to her lips, and stared at him.

"I have a son your age," he began again. "And a daughter not far behind. I think I understand some of what you're feeling."

"It's, ah, it's not a matter of my feelings."

"Of course it is. You're as precious to Clarissa as my children are to me. Clarissa and I will be married, but she'd be happier if you were pleased about it."

A.J. frowned at her coffee, then set it down. "I don't know

what to say. I thought I did. Mr. Marshall, Alex, you've been a journalist for over a quarter of a century. You've traveled all over the world, seen incredible things. Clarissa, for all her abilities, all her insights, is a very simple woman."

"An amazingly comfortable woman, especially for a man who's lived on the edge, perhaps too long. I had thought of retiring." He laughed then, but comfortably, as he remembered his own shock when Clarissa had held his hand and commented on it. "That wasn't something I'd discussed with anyone, not even my own children. I'd been looking for something more, something other than deadlines and breaking stories. In a matter of hours after being with Clarissa, I knew she was what I'd been looking for. I want to spend the rest of my life with her."

A.J. sat in silence, looking down at her hands. What more could a woman ask for, she wondered, than for a man to love her with such straightforward devotion? Couldn't a woman consider herself fortunate to have a man who accepted who she was, what she was, and loved her because of it, not in spite of?

Some of the tension dissolved and as she looked up at him she was able to smile. "Alex, has my mother fixed you dinner?"

"Why, yes." Though his tone was very sober, she caught, and appreciated, the gleam in his eyes. "Several times. In fact, she told me she's left a pot of spaghetti sauce simmering for tonight. I find Clarissa's cooking as—unique as she is."

With a laugh, A.J. held out her hand again. "I think Momma hit the jackpot." He took her hand, then surprised her by leaning over to kiss her cheek.

"Thank you."

"Don't hurt her," A.J. whispered. She clung to his hand

a moment, then composing herself rose. "We'd better get back. She'll wonder where we are."

"Being Clarissa, I'm sure she has a pretty good idea."

"That doesn't bother you?" She stopped by the door to look up at him again. "The fact that she's a sensitive?"

"Why should it? That's part of what makes Clarissa who she is."

"Yes." She tried not to think of herself, but didn't bite back the sigh in time. "Yes, it is."

When they walked back into the studio Clarissa looked over immediately. It only took a moment before she smiled. In an old habit, A.J. kissed both her cheeks. "There is one thing I have to insist on," she began without preamble.

"What is it?"

"That I give you the wedding."

Pleasure bloomed on Clarissa's cheeks even as she protested. "Oh, darling, how sweet, but it's too much trouble."

"It certainly is for a bride. You pick out your wedding dress and your trousseau and worry about looking terrific. I'll handle the rest." She kissed her again. "Please."

"If you really want to."

"I really want to. Give me a guest list and I'll handle the details. That's what I'm best at. I think they want you." She gave Clarissa a last quick squeeze before urging her back on set. A.J. took her place in the background.

"Feeling better?" David murmured as he came up beside her.

"Some." She couldn't admit to him that she felt weepy and displaced. "As soon as the shoot's finished, I start making wedding plans."

"Tomorrow's soon enough." When she sent him a puzzled look, he only smiled. "I intend to keep you busy this evening."

* * *

He was a man of his word. A.J. had barely arrived home, shed her jacket and opened the phone book to Caterers, when the bell rang. Taking the book with her, she went to answer. "David." She hooked her finger in the page so as not to lose her place. "You told me you had some things to do."

"I did them. What time is it?"

"It's quarter to seven. I didn't think you'd be by until around eight."

"Well after business hours, then." He toyed with, then loosened the top button of her blouse.

She had to smile. "Well after."

"And if you don't answer your phone, your service will pick it up after four rings?"

"Six. But I'm not expecting any calls." She stepped closer to slide her arms up his chest. "Hungry?"

"Yeah." He tested himself, seeing how long he could hold her at arm's length. It appeared to be just over thirty seconds.

"There's nothing in the kitchen except a frozen fish dinner." She closed her eyes as his lips skimmed over her jaw.

"Then we'll have to find another way to satisfy the appetite." He unhooked her skirt and, as it fell to the floor, drew his hands down her hips.

She yanked his sweater over his head and tossed it aside. "I'm sure we'll manage."

His muscles were tight as she ran her hands over him. Taut, tense all the way from his neck to his waist. With her blouse half-open, her legs clad in sheer stockings that stopped just at her thighs, A.J. pressed against him. She wanted to make him burn with just the thought of loving her. Then she was gasping for air, her fingers digging into his back as his hands took quick and complete possession.

When her legs buckled and she went limp against him,

he didn't relent. For hours and hours he'd held back, watching her sit primly in the back of the studio, looking at her make her precise notes in her book. Now he had her, alone, hot, moist and, for the first time in their lovemaking, weak.

Holding her close, he slid with her to the floor.

Unprepared, she was helpless against a riot of sensation. He took her on a desperate ride, driving her up where the air was thin, plunging her down where it was heavy and dark. She tried to cling to him but lacked the strength.

She trembled for him. That alone was enough to drive him mad. His name came helplessly through her lips. He wanted to hear it, again and again, over and over. He wanted to know she thought of nothing else. And when he pulled the remaining clothes from both of them, when he entered her with a violence neither of them could fight, he knew he thought of nothing but her.

She shuddered again and again, but he held himself back from ultimate release. Even as he drove into her, his hands continued to roam, bringing unspeakable pleasures to every inch of her body. The carpet was soft at her back, but even when her fingers curled into it she could only feel the hard thrust of her lover. She heard him say her name, once, then twice, until her eyes fluttered open. His body rose above hers, taut with muscle, gleaming from passion. His breath was heaving even as hers was. She heard it, then tasted it when his mouth crushed down to devour. Then she heard nothing but her own sobbing moan as they emptied themselves.

"I like you naked." When he'd recovered enough, David propped himself on his elbow and took a long, long look. "But I have to admit, I'm fascinated by those little stockings you wear that stop right about here." To demonstrate, he ran his fingertip along her upper thigh.

Still dazed, A.J. merely moved against his touch. "They're very practical."

With a muffled laugh, he nuzzled the side of her neck. "Yes, that's what fascinates me. Your practicality."

She opened her eyes but kept them narrowed. "That's not what I meant." Because she felt too good to make an issue of it, she curled into him.

It was one of the things that charmed him most. David wondered if he told her how soft, how warm and open to affection she was after loving, if she would pull back. Instead he held her close, stroking and pleasing them both. When he caught himself half dozing, he pulled her up.

"Come on, let's have a shower before dinner."

"A shower?" She let her head rest on his shoulder. "Why don't we just go to bed?"

"Insatiable," he decided, and scooped her up.

"David, you can't carry me."

"Why not?"

"Because." She groped. "Because it's silly."

"I always feel silly carrying naked women." In the bathroom, he stood her on her feet.

"I suppose you make a habit of it," she commented dryly, and turned on the taps with a hard twist.

"I have been trying to cut down." Smiling, he pulled her into the shower with him so that the water rained over her face.

"My hair!" She reached up once, ineffectually, to block the flow, then stopped to glare at him.

"What about it?"

"Never mind." Resigned, she picked up the soap and began to rub it lazily over her body as she watched him.

"You seem very cheerful tonight. I thought you were annoyed with me this morning."

"Did you?" He'd given some thought to strangling her. "Why would I be?" He took the soap from her and began to do the job himself.

"When we were talking…" The soap was warm and slick, his touch very thorough. "It doesn't matter. I'm glad you came by."

That was more than he'd come to expect from her. "Really?"

She smiled, then wrapped her arms around him and kissed him under the hot, steamy spray. "Yes, really. I like you, David. When you're not being a producer."

That, too, was more than he'd come to expect from her. And less than he was beginning to need. "I like you, Aurora. When you're not being an agent."

When she stepped out of the shower and reached for towels, she heard the bell ring again. "Damn." She gripped a towel at her breasts.

"I'll get it." David hooked a towel at his hips and strode out before A.J. could protest. She let out a huff of breath and snatched the robe from its hook on the door. If it was someone from the office, she'd have a lovely time explaining why David Brady, producer, was answering her door in a towel. She decided discretion was the better part of valor and stayed where she was.

Then she remembered the clothes. She closed her eyes on a moan as she imagined the carelessly strewn articles on her living room floor. Bracing herself, she walked down the hall back into the living room.

There was candlelight. On the ebony table she kept by the window, candles were already burning in silver holders on a white cloth. She saw the gleam of china, the sparkle of crystal, and stood where she was as David signed a paper handed to him by a man in a black suit.

"I hope everything is satisfactory, Mr. Brady."

"I'm sure it will be."

"We will, of course, be back for pickup at your convenience." With a bow to David, then another to A.J., he let himself out the door.

"David…" A.J. walked forward as if she weren't sure of her steps. "What is this?"

He lifted a silver cover from a plate. "It's coq au vin."

"But how did you—"

"I ordered it for eight o'clock." He checked his watch before he walked over to retrieve his pants. "They're very prompt." With the ease of a totally unselfconscious man, he dropped the towel and drew on his slacks.

She took another few steps toward the table. "It's lovely. Really lovely." There was a single rose in a vase. Moved, she reached out to touch it, then immediately brought her hand back to link it with her other. "I never expected anything like this."

He drew his sweater back over his head. "You said once you enjoyed being pampered." She looked stunned, he realized. Had he been so unromantic? A little uncertain, he walked to her. "Maybe I enjoy doing the pampering now and then."

She looked over, but her throat was closed and her eyes were filling. "I'll get dressed."

"No." Her back was to him now, but he took her by the shoulders. "No, you look fine."

She struggled with herself, pressing her lips together until she thought she could speak. "I'll just be a minute." But he was turning her around. His brows were already knit together before he saw her face.

"What's this?" He lifted a fingertip and touched a tear that clung to her lashes.

"It's nothing. I—I feel foolish. Just give me a minute."

He brushed another tear away with his thumb. "No, I don't think I should." He'd seen her weep before, but that had been a torrent. There was something soft in these tears, something incredibly sweet that drew him. "Do you always cry when a man offers you a quiet dinner?"

"No, of course not. It's just—I never expected you to do anything like this."

He brought her hand to his lips and smiled as he kissed her fingers. "Just because I'm a producer doesn't mean I can't have some class."

"That's not what I meant." She looked up at him, smiling down at her, her hands still close to his lips. She was losing. A.J. felt her heart weaken, her will weaken and her wishes grow. "That's not what I meant," she said again in a whisper, and tightened her fingers on his. "David, don't make me want too much."

It was what he thought he understood. If you wanted too much, you fell too hard. He'd avoided the same thing, maybe for the same reasons, until one late afternoon on a beach. "Do you really think either of us can stop now?"

She thought of how many times she'd been rejected, easily, coolly, nervously. Friendship, affection, love could be turned off by some as quickly as a faucet. He wanted her now, A.J. reminded herself. He cared now. It had to be enough. She touched a hand to his cheek.

"Maybe tonight we won't think at all."

Chapter 9

"**I**tem fifteen, clause B. I find the wording here too vague. As we discussed, my client feels very strongly about her rights and responsibilities as a new mother. The nanny will accompany the child to the set, at my client's expense. However, she will require regular breaks in order to feed the infant. The trailer provided by you must be equipped with a portable crib and...'" For the third time during her dictation, A.J. lost her train of thought.

"Diapers?" Diane suggested.

"What?" A.J. turned from the window to look at her secretary.

"Just trying to help. Want me to read it back to you?"

"Yes, please."

While Diane read the words back, A.J. frowned down at the contract in her hand. "'And a playpen,'" A.J. finished, and managed to smile at her secretary. "I've never seen anyone so wrapped up in motherhood."

"Doesn't fit her image, does it? She always plays the heartless sex bomb."

"This little movie of the week should change that. Okay, finish it up with 'Once the above changes are made, the contract will be passed along to my client for signing.'"

"Do you want this out today?"

"Hmm?"

"Today, A.J.?" With a puzzled smile, Diane studied her employer. "You want the letter to go right out?"

"Oh. Yes, yes, it'd better go out." She checked her watch. "I'm sorry, Diane, it's nearly five. I hadn't realized."

"No problem." Closing her notebook, Diane rose. "You seem a little distracted today. Big plans for the holiday weekend?"

"Holiday?"

"Memorial Day weekend, A.J." With a shake of her head, Diane tucked her pencil behind her ear. "You know, three days off, the first weekend of summer. Sand, surf, sun."

"No." She began rearranging the papers on her desk. "I don't have any plans." Shaking off the mood, she looked up again. Distracted? What she was was a mess. She was bogged down in work she couldn't concentrate on, tied up in knots she couldn't loosen. With a shake of her head, she glanced at Diane again and remembered there were other people in the world beside herself. "I'm sure you do. Let the letter wait. There's no mail delivery Monday, anyway. We'll send it over by messenger Tuesday."

"As a matter of fact, I do have an interesting three days planned." Diane gave her own watch a check. "And he's picking me up in an hour."

"Go home." A.J. waved her off as she shuffled through papers. "Don't get sunburned."

"A.J.—" Diane paused at the door and grinned "—I don't plan to see the sun for three full days."

When the door shut, A.J. slipped off her glasses and rubbed at the bridge of her nose. What was wrong with her? She couldn't seem to concentrate for more than five minutes at a stretch before her attention started wandering.

Overwork? she wondered as she looked down at the papers in her hand. That was an evasion; she thrived on overwork. She wasn't sleeping well. She was sleeping alone. One had virtually nothing to do with the other, A.J. assured herself as she unstacked and restacked papers. She was too much her own person to moon around because David Brady had been out of town for a few days.

But she did miss him. She picked up a pencil to work, then ended up merely running it through her fingers. There wasn't any crime in missing him, was there? It wasn't as though she were dependent on him. She'd just gotten used to his company. Wouldn't he be smug and self-satisfied to know that she'd spent half her waking hours thinking about him? Disgusted with herself, A.J. began to work in earnest. For two minutes.

It was his fault, she thought as she tossed the pencil down again. That extravagantly romantic dinner for two, then that silly little bouquet of daisies he'd sent the day he'd left for Chicago. Though she tried not to, she reached out and stroked the petals that sat cheerful and out of place on her desk. He was trying to make a giddy, romantic fool out of her—and he was succeeding.

It just had to stop. A.J. adjusted her glasses, picked up her pencil and began to work again. She wasn't going to give David Brady another thought. When the knock sounded at her door a few moments later, she was staring into space.

She blinked herself out of the daydream, swore, then called out. "Come in."

"Don't you ever quit?" Abe asked her when he stuck his head in the door.

Quit? She'd barely made a dent. "I've got a couple of loose ends. Abe, the Forrester contract comes up for renewal the first of July. I think we should start prodding. His fan mail was two to one last season, so—"

"First thing Tuesday morning I'll put the squeeze on. Right now I have to go marinate."

"I beg your pardon?"

"Big barbecue this weekend," Abe told her with a wink. "It's the only time my wife lets me cook. Want me to put a steak on for you?"

She smiled, grateful that he'd brought simpler things to her mind. Hickory smoke, freshly cut grass, burned meat. "No, thanks. The memory of the last one's a little close."

"The butcher gave me bad quality meat." He hitched up his belt and thought about spending the whole weekend in bathing trunks.

"That's what they all say. Have a good holiday, Abe. Just be prepared to squeeze hard on Tuesday."

"No problem. Want me to lock up?"

"No, I'll just be a few more minutes."

"If you change your mind about that steak, just come by."

"Thanks." Alone again, A.J. turned her concentration back to her work. She heard the sounds of her staff leaving for the day. Doors closing, scattered laughter.

David stood in the doorway and watched her. The rest of her staff was pouring out of the door as fast as they could, but she sat, calm and efficient, behind her desk. The fatigue that had had him half dozing on the plane washed away. Her hair was tidy, her suit jacket trim and smooth over her shoulders. She held the pencil in long, ringless fingers and wrote in quick, static bursts. The daisies he'd sent her days before sat in a squat vase on her desk. It was the first, the only unbusinesslike accent he'd ever seen in her office. Seeing them made him smile. Seeing her made him want.

He could see himself taking her there in her prim, organized office. He could peel that tailored, successful suit from her and find something soft and lacy beneath. With the door locked and traffic rushing by far below, he could make love with her until all the needs, all the fantasies, that had built in the days he'd been away were satisfied.

A.J. continued to write, forcing her concentration back each time it threatened to ebb. It wasn't right, she told herself, that her system would start to churn this way for no reason. The dry facts and figures she was reading shouldn't leave room for hot imagination. She rubbed the back of her neck, annoyed that tension was building there out of nothing. She would have sworn she could feel passion in the air. But that was ridiculous.

Then she knew. As surely as if he'd spoken, as surely as if he'd already touched her. Slowly, her hand damp on the pencil, she looked up.

There was no surprise in her eyes. It should have made him uneasy that she'd sensed him there when he'd made no sound, no movement. The fact that it didn't was something he would think of later. Now he could only think of how cool and proper she looked behind the desk. Of how wild and wanton she was in his arms.

She wanted to laugh, to spring up from the desk and rush across the room. She wanted to be held close and swung in dizzying circles while the pleasure of just seeing him again soared through her. Of course she couldn't. That would be foolish. Instead she lifted a brow and set her pencil on her blotter. "So you're back."

"Yeah. I had a feeling I'd find you here." He wanted to drag her up from her chair and hold her. Just hold her. He dipped his hands into his pockets and leaned against the jamb.

"A feeling?" This time she smiled. "Precognition or telepathy?"

"Logic." He smiled, too, then walked toward the desk. "You look good, Fields. Real good."

Leaning back in her chair, she gave herself the pleasure of a thorough study. "You look a little tired. Rough trip?"

"Long." He plucked a daisy from the vase and spun it by the stem. "But it should be the last one before we wrap." Watching her, he came around the desk, then, resting a hip on it, leaned over and tucked the daisy behind her ear. "Got any plans for tonight?"

If she'd had any, she would have tossed them out the window and forgotten them. With her tongue caught in her teeth, A.J. made a business out of checking her desk calender. "No."

"Tomorrow?"

She flipped the page over. "Doesn't look like it."

"Sunday?"

"Even agents need a day of rest."

"Monday?"

She flipped the next page and shrugged. "Offices are closed. I thought I'd spend the day reading over some scripts and doing my nails."

"Uh-huh. In case you hadn't noticed, office hours are over."

Her heart was drumming. Already. Her blood was warming. So soon. "I'd noticed."

In silence he held out his hand. After only a slight hesitation, A.J. put hers into it and let him draw her up. "Come home with me."

He'd asked her before, and she'd refused. Looking at him now, she knew the days of refusal were long past. Reaching down, she gathered her purse and her briefcase.

"Not tonight," David told her, and took the briefcase to set it back down.

"I want to—"

"Not tonight, Aurora." Taking her hand again, he brought it to his lips. "Please."

With a nod, she left the briefcase and the office behind.

They kept their hands linked as they walked down the hall. They kept them linked still as they rode down in the elevator. It didn't seem foolish, A.J. realized, but sweet. He hadn't kissed her, hadn't held her, and yet the tension that had built so quickly was gone again, just through a touch.

She was content to leave her car in the lot, thinking that sometime the next day, they'd drive back into town and arrange things. Pleased just to be with him again, she stopped at his car while he unlocked the doors.

"Haven't you been home yet?" she asked, noticing a suitcase in the back seat.

"No."

She started to smile, delighted that he'd wanted to see her first, but she glanced over her shoulder again as she stepped into the car. "I have a case just like that."

David settled in the seat, then turned on the ignition. "That is your case."

"Mine?" Baffled, she turned around and looked closer. "But—I don't remember you borrowing one of my suitcases."

"I didn't. Mine are in the trunk." He eased out of the lot and merged with clogged L.A. weekend traffic.

"Well, if you didn't borrow it, what's it doing in your car?"

"I stopped by your place on the way. Your housekeeper packed for you."

"Packed..." She stared at the case. When she turned to him, her eyes were narrowed. "You've got a lot of nerve, Brady. Just where do you come off packing my clothes and assuming—"

"The housekeeper packed them. Nice lady. I thought you'd be more comfortable over the weekend with some of your own things. I had thought about keeping you naked, but that's a little tricky when you take walks in the woods."

Because her jaw was beginning to ache, she relaxed it. "You thought? *You* didn't think at all. You drop by the office and calmly assume that I'll drop everything and run off with you. What if I'd had plans?"

"Then that would've been too bad." He swung easily off the ramp toward the hills.

"Too bad for whom?"

"For the plans." He punched in the car lighter and sent her a mild smile. "I have no intention of letting you out of my sight for the next three days."

"You have no intention?" The fire was rising as she shifted in her seat toward him. "What about my intention? Maybe you think it's very male and macho to just—just bundle a woman off for a weekend without asking, without any discussion, but I happen to prefer being consulted. Stop the car."

"Not a chance." David had expected this reaction. Even looked forward to it. He touched the lighter to the tip of his cigarette. He hadn't enjoyed himself this much for days. Since the last time he'd been with her.

Her breath came out in a long, slow hiss. "I don't find abductions appealing."

"Didn't think I did, either." He blew out a lazy stream of smoke. "Guess I was wrong."

She flopped back against her seat, arms folded. "You're going to be sorry."

"I'm only sorry I didn't think of it before." With his elbow resting lightly on the open window, he drove higher into the hills, with A.J. fuming beside him. The minute he stopped the car in his drive, A.J. pushed open her door, snatched her purse up and began to walk. When he grabbed her arm, she spun around, holding the pastel-dyed leather like a weapon.

"Want to fight?"

"I wouldn't give you the satisfaction." She yanked her arm out of his hold. "I'm walking back."

"Oh?" He took a quick look at the slim skirt, thin hose and fragile heels. "You wouldn't make it the first mile in those shoes."

"That's my problem."

He considered a minute, then sighed. "I guess we'll just carry through with the same theme." Before she realized his intention, he wrapped an arm around her waist and hauled her over his shoulder.

Too stunned to struggle, she blew hair out of her eyes. "Put me down."

"In a few minutes," he promised as he walked toward the house.

"Now." She whacked him smartly on the back with her purse. "This isn't funny."

"Are you kidding?" When he stuck his key in the lock,

she began to struggle. "Easy, A.J., you'll end up dropping on your head."

"I'm not going to tolerate this." She tried to kick out and found her legs pinned behind the knee. "David, this is degrading. I don't know what's gotten into you, but if you get hold of yourself now, I'll forget the whole thing."

"No deal." He started up the steps.

"I'll give you a deal," she said between her teeth as she made a futile grab for the railing. "If you put me down now, I won't kill you."

"Now?"

"Right now."

"Okay." With a quick twist of his body, he had her falling backward. Even as her eyes widened in shock, he was tumbling with her onto the bed.

"What the hell's gotten into you?" she demanded as she struggled to sit up.

"You," he said, so simply she stopped in the act of shoving him away. "You," he repeated, cupping the back of her neck. "I thought about you the whole time I was gone. I wanted you in Chicago. I wanted you in the airport, and thirty thousand feet up I still wanted you."

"You're—this is crazy."

"Maybe. Maybe it is. But when I was on that plane flying back to L.A. I realized that I wanted you here, right here, alone with me for days."

His fingers were stroking up and down her neck, soothing. Her nerves were stretching tighter and tighter. "If you'd asked," she began.

"You'd have had an excuse. You might have spent the night." His fingers inched up into her hair. "But you'd have found a reason you couldn't stay longer."

"That's not true."

"Isn't it? Why haven't you spent a weekend with me before?"

Her fingers linked and twisted. "There've been reasons."

"Yeah." He put his hand over hers. "And the main one is you're afraid to spend more than a few hours at a time with me." When she opened her mouth, he shook his head to cut her off. "Afraid if you do, I might just get too close."

"I'm not afraid of you. That's ridiculous."

"No, I don't think you are. I think you're afraid of us." He drew her closer. "So am I."

"David." The word was shaky. The world was suddenly shaky. Just passion, she reminded herself again. That's what made her head swim, her heart pound. Desire. Her arms slid up his back. It was only desire. "Let's not think at all for a while." She touched her lips to his and felt resistance as well as need.

"Sooner or later we're going to have to."

"No." She kissed him again, let her tongue trace lightly over his lips. "There's no sooner, no later." Her breath was warm, tempting, as it fluttered over him. "There's only now. Make love with me now, in the light." Her hands slipped under his shirt to tease and invite.

Her eyes were open and on his, her lips working slowly, steadily, to drive him to the edge. He swore, then pulled her to him and let the madness come.

"It's good for you."

"So's calves' liver," A.J. said breathlessly, and paused to lean against a tree. "I avoid that, too."

They'd taken the path behind his house, crossed the stream and continued up. By David's calculations they'd gone about three-quarters of a mile. He walked back to

stand beside her. "Look." He spread his arm wide. "It's terrific, isn't it?"

The trees were thick and green. Birds rustled the leaves
and sang for the simple pleasure of sound. Wildflowers
she'd never seen before and couldn't name pushed their
way through the underbrush and battled for the patches of
sunlight. It was, even to a passionately avowed city girl, a
lovely sight.

"Yes, it's terrific. You tend to forget there's anything like
this when you're down in L.A."

"That's why I moved up here." He put an arm around
her shoulders and absently rubbed his hand up and down.
"I was beginning to forget there was any place other than
the fast lane."

"Work, parties, meetings, parties, brunch, lunch and
cocktails."

"Yeah, something like that. Anyway, coming up here
after a day in the factory keeps things in perspective. If a
project bombs in the ratings, the sun's still going to set."

She thought about it, leaning into him a bit as he stroked
her arm. "If I blow a deal, I go home, lock the doors, put on
my headset and drown my brain in Rachmaninoff."

"Same thing."

"But usually I kick something first."

He laughed and kissed the top of her head. "Whatever
works. Wait till you see the view from the top."

A.J. leaned down to massage her calf. "I'll meet you back
at the house. You can draw me a picture."

"You need the air. Do you realize we've barely been out
of bed for thirty-six hours?"

"And we've probably logged about ten hours' sleep."
Straightening a bit, she stretched protesting muscles. "I
think I've had enough health and nature for the day."

He looked down at her. She wasn't A.J. Fields now, in T-shirt and jeans and scuffed boots. But he still knew how to play her. "I guess I'm in better shape than you are."

"Like hell." She pushed away from the tree.

Determined to keep up, she strode along beside him, up the winding dirt path, until sweat trickled down her back. Her leg muscles whimpered, reminding her she'd neglected her weekly tennis games for over a month. At last, aching and exhausted, she dropped down on a rock.

"That's it. I give up."

"Another hundred yards and we start circling back."

"Nope."

"A.J., it's shorter to go around this way than to turn around."

Shorter? She shut her eyes and asked herself what had possessed her to let him drag her through the woods. "I'll just stay here tonight. You can bring me back a pillow and a sandwich."

"I could always carry you."

She folded her arms. "No."

"How about a bribe?"

Her bottom lip poked out as she considered. "I'm always open to negotiations."

"I've got a bottle of cabernet sauvignon I've been saving for the right moment."

She rubbed at a streak of dirt on her knee. "What year?"

"Seventy-nine."

"A good start. That might get me the next hundred yards or so."

"Then there's that steak I took out of the freezer this morning, the one I'm going to grill over mesquite."

"I'd forgotten about that." She brought her tongue over

her top lip and thought she could almost taste it. "That should get me halfway back down."

"You drive a hard bargain."

"Thank you."

"Flowers. Dozens of them."

She lifted a brow. "By the time we get back, the florist'll be closed."

"City-oriented," he said with a sigh. "Look around you."

"You're going to pick me flowers?" Surprised, and foolishly pleased, she lifted her arms to twine them around his neck. "That should definitely get me through the front door."

Smiling, she leaned back as he stepped off the path to gather blossoms. "I like the blue ones," she called out, and laughed as he muttered at her.

She hadn't expected the weekend to be so relaxed, so easy. She hadn't known she could enjoy being with one person for so long. There were no schedules, no appointments, no pressing deals. There were simply mornings and afternoons and evenings.

It seemed absurd that something as mundane as fixing breakfast could be fun. She'd discovered that spending the time to eat it instead of rushing into the morning had a certain appeal. When you weren't alone. She didn't have a script or a business letter to deal with. And she had to admit, she hadn't missed them. She'd done nothing more mind-teasing in two days than a crossword puzzle. And even that, she remembered happily, had been interrupted.

Now he was picking her flowers. Small, colorful wildflowers. She'd put them in a vase by the window where they'd be cozy and bright. And deadly.

For an instant, her heart stopped. The birds were silent and the air was still as glass. She saw David as though she were looking through a long lens. As she watched, the light went gray. There was pain, sharp and sudden, as her knuckles scraped over the rock.

"No!" She thought she shouted, but the word came out in a whisper. She nearly slipped off the rock before she caught herself and stumbled toward him. She gasped for his name twice before it finally ripped out of her. "David! No, stop."

He straightened, but only had time to take a step toward her before she threw herself into his arms. He'd seen that blank terror in her eyes before, once before, when she'd stood in an old empty room watching something no one else could see.

"Aurora, what is it?" He held her close while she shuddered, though he had no idea how to soothe. "What's wrong?"

"Don't pick any more. David, don't." Her fingers dug hard into his back.

"All right, I won't." Hands firm, he drew her away to study her face. "Why?"

"Something's wrong with them." The fear hadn't passed. She pressed the heel of her hand against her chest as if to push it out. "Something's wrong with them," she repeated.

"They're just flowers." He showed her what he held in his hands.

"Not them. Over there. You were going to pick those over there."

He followed the direction of her gaze to a large sunny rock with flowers around the perimeter. He remembered he'd just been turning in their direction when her shouts had stopped him. "Yes, I was. Let's have a look."

"No." She grabbed him again. "Don't touch them."

"Calm down," he said quietly enough, though his own nerves were starting to jangle. Bending, he picked up a stick. Letting the flowers he'd already picked fall, he took A.J.'s hand in his and dragged the end of the stick along the edge of the rock through a thick clump of bluebells. He heard the hissing rattle, felt the jolt of the stick he held as the snake reared up and struck. A.J.'s hand went limp in his. David held on to the stick as he pulled her back to the path. He wore boots, thick and sturdy enough to protect against the snakes scattered through the hills. But he'd been picking flowers, and there had been nothing to protect the vulnerable flesh of his hands and wrists.

"I want to go back," she said flatly.

She was grateful he didn't question, didn't probe or even try to soothe. If he had, she wasn't sure what idiotic answers she'd have given him. A.J. had discovered more in that one timeless moment than David's immediate danger. She'd discovered she was in love with him. All her rules, her warnings, her precautions hadn't mattered. He could hurt her now, and she might never recover.

So she didn't speak. Because he was silent, as well, she felt the first pang of rejection. They entered through the kitchen door. David took a bottle of brandy and two water glasses out of a cupboard. He poured, handed one to A.J., then emptied half the contents of his own glass in one swallow.

She sipped, then sipped again, and felt a little steadier. "Would you like to take me home now?"

He picked up the bottle and added a dollop to his glass. "What are you talking about?"

A.J. wrapped both hands around her glass and made herself speak calmly. "Most people are uncomfortable after— after an episode. They either want to distance themselves from the source or dissect it." When he said nothing, only stared at her, she set her glass down. "It won't take me long to pack."

"You take another step," he said in a voice that was deadly calm, "and I don't know what the hell I'll do. Sit down, Aurora."

"David, I don't want an interrogation."

He hurled his glass into the sink, making her jolt at the sudden violence. "Don't we know each other any better than that by now?" He was shouting. She couldn't know it wasn't at her, but himself. "Can't we have any sort of discussion, any sort of contact, that isn't sex or negotiations?"

"We agreed—"

He said something so uncharacteristically vulgar about agreements that she stopped dead. "You very possibly saved my life." He stared down at his hand, well able to imagine what might have happened. "What am I supposed to say to you? Thanks?"

When she found herself stuttering, A.J. swallowed and pulled herself back. "I'd really rather you didn't say anything."

He walked to her but didn't touch. "I can't. Look, I'm a little shaky about this myself. That doesn't mean I've suddenly decided you're a freak." He saw the emotion come and go in her eyes before he reached out to touch her face. "I'm grateful. I just don't quite know how to handle it."

"It's all right." She was losing ground. She could feel it. "I don't expect—"

"Do." He brought his other hand to her face. "Do expect. Tell me what you want. Tell me what you need right now."

She tried not to. She'd lose one more foothold if she did. But his hands were gentle, when they never were, and his eyes offered. "Hold me." She closed her eyes as she said it. "Just hold me a minute."

He put his arms around her, drew her against him. There was no passion, no fire, just comfort. He felt her hands knead at his back until both of them relaxed. "Do you want to talk about it?"

"It was just a flash. I was sitting there, thinking about how nice it had been to do nothing. I was thinking about the flowers. I had a picture of them in the window. All at once they were black and ugly and the petals were like razors. I saw you bending over that clump of bluebells, and it all went gray."

"I hadn't bent over them yet."

"You would have."

"Yeah." He held her closer a moment. "I would have. Looks like I reneged on the last part of the deal. I don't have any flowers for you."

"It doesn't matter." She pressed her lips against his neck.

"I'll have to make it up to you." Drawing back, he took both of her hands. "Aurora…" He started to lift one, then saw the caked blood on her knuckles. "What the hell have you done to yourself?"

Blankly she looked down. "I don't know. It hurts," she said as she flexed her hand.

"Come on." He led her to the sink and began to clean off dried blood with cool water.

"Ow!" She would have jerked her hand away if he hadn't held it still.

"I've never had a very gentle touch," he muttered.

She leaned a hip against the sink. "So I've noticed."

Annoyed at seeing the rough wound on her hand, he began to dab it with a towel. "Let's go upstairs. I've got some Merthiolate."

"That stings."

"Don't be a baby."

"I'm not." But he had to tug her along. "It's only a scrape."

"And scrapes get infected."

"Look, you've already rubbed it raw. There can't be a germ left."

He nudged her into the bathroom. "We'll make sure."

Before she could stop him, he took out a bottle and dumped medicine over her knuckles. What had been a dull sting turned to fire. "Damn it!"

"Here." He grabbed her hand again and began to blow on the wound. "Just give it a minute."

"A lot of good that does," she muttered, but the pain cooled.

"We'll fix dinner. That'll take your mind off it."

"You're supposed to fix dinner," she reminded him.

"Right." He kissed her forehead. "I've got to run out for a minute. I'll start the grill when I get back."

"That doesn't mean I'm going to be chopping vegetables while you're gone. I'm going to take a bath."

"Fine. If the water's still hot when I get back, I'll join you."

She didn't ask where he was going. She wanted to, but there were rules. Instead A.J. walked into the bedroom and watched from the window as he pulled out of the drive. Weary, she sat on the bed and pulled off her boots. The afternoon had taken its toll, physically, emotionally. She didn't want to think. She didn't want to feel.

Giving in, she stretched out across the bed. She'd rest for a minute, she told herself. Only for a minute.

David came home with a handful of asters he'd begged from a neighbor's garden. He thought the idea of dropping them on A.J. while she soaked in the tub might bring the laughter back to her eyes. He'd never heard her laugh so much or so easily as she had over the weekend. It wasn't something he wanted to lose. Just as he was discovering she wasn't something he wanted to lose.

He went up the stairs quietly, then paused at the bedroom door when he saw her. She'd taken off only her boots. A pillow was crumpled under her arm as she lay diagonally across the bed. It occurred to him as he stepped into the room that he'd never watched her sleep before. They'd never given each other the chance.

Her face looked so soft, so fragile. Her hair was pale and tumbled onto her cheek, her lips unpainted and just parted. How was it he'd never noticed how delicate her features were, how slender and frail her wrists were, how elegantly feminine the curve of her neck was?

Maybe he hadn't looked, David admitted as he crossed to the bed. But he was looking now.

She was fire and thunder in bed, sharp and tough out of it. She had a gift, a curse and ability she fought against every waking moment, one that he was just beginning to understand. He was just beginning to see that it made her defensive and defenseless.

Only rarely did the vulnerabilities emerge, and then with such reluctance from her he'd tended to gloss over them. But now, just now, when she was asleep and unaware of him, she looked like something a man should protect, cherish.

The first stirrings weren't of passion and desire, but of a quiet affection he hadn't realized he felt for her. He hadn't realized it was possible to feel anything quiet for Aurora. Unable to resist, he reached down to brush the hair from her cheek and feel the warm, smooth skin beneath.

She stirred. He'd wanted her to. Heavy and sleep-glazed, her eyes opened. "David?" Even her voice was soft, feminine.

"I brought you a present." He sat on the bed beside her and dropped the flowers by her hand.

"Oh." He'd seen that before, too, he realized. That quick

surprise and momentary confusion when he'd done something foolish or romantic. "You didn't have to."

"I think I did," he murmured, half to himself. Almost as an experiment, he lowered his mouth to hers and kissed her softly, gently, with the tenderness she'd made him feel as she slept. He felt the ache move through him, sweet as a dream.

"David?" She said his name again, but this time her eyes were dark and dazed.

"Shh." His hands didn't drag through her hair now with trembles of passion, but stroked, exploring the texture. He could watch the light strike individual strands. "Lovely." He brought his gaze back to hers. "Have I ever told you how lovely you are?"

She started to reach for him, for the passion that she could understand. "It isn't necessary."

His lips met hers again, but they didn't devour and demand. This mood was foreign and made her heart pound as much with uncertainty as need. "Make love with me," she murmured as she tried to draw him down.

"I am." His mouth lingered over hers. "Maybe for the first time."

"I don't understand," she began, but he shifted so that he could cradle her in his arms.

"Neither do I."

So he began, slowly, gently, testing them both. Her mouth offered darker promises, but he waited, coaxing. His lips were patient as they moved over hers, light and soothing as they kissed her eyes closed. He didn't touch her, not yet, though he wondered what it would be like to stroke her while the light was softening, to caress as though it were all new, all fresh. Gradually he felt the tension in her body give way, he felt what he'd never felt from her before. Pliancy, surrender, warmth.

Her body seemed weightless, gloriously light and free. She felt the pleasure move through her, but sweetly, fluidly, like wine. Then he was the wine, heady and potent, drugging her with the intoxicating taste of his mouth. The hands that had clutched him in demand went lax. There was so much to absorb—the flavor of his lips as they lingered on hers; the texture of his skin as his cheek brushed hers; the scent that clung to him, part man, part woods; the dark, curious look in his eyes as he watched her.

She looked as she had when she'd slept, he thought. Fragile, so arousingly fragile. And she felt... At last he touched, fingertips only, along skin already warm. He heard her sigh his name in a way she'd never said it before. Keeping her cradled in his arms, he began to take her deeper, take himself deeper, with tenderness.

She had no strength to demand, no will to take control. For the first time her body was totally his, just as for the first time her emotions were. He touched, and she yielded. He tasted, and she gave. When he shifted her, she felt as though she could float. Perhaps she was. Clouds of pleasure, mists of soft, soft delight. When he began to undress her, she opened her eyes, needing to see him again.

The light had gone to rose with sunset. It made her skin glow as he slowly drew off her shirt. He couldn't take his eyes off her, couldn't stop his hands from touching, though he had no desire to be quick. When she reached up, he helped her pull off his own shirt, then took her injured hand to his lips. He kissed her fingers, then her palm, then her wrist, until he felt her begin to tremble. Bending, he brushed her lips with his again, wanting to hear her sigh his name. Then, watching her, waiting until she looked at him, he continued to undress her.

Slowly. Achingly slowly, he drew the jeans down her legs,

pausing now and then to taste newly exposed skin. Pulses beat at the back of her knees. He felt them, lingered there, exploited them. Her ankles were slim, fragile like her wrists. He traced them with his tongue until she moaned. Then he waited, letting her settle again as he stripped off his own jeans. He came to her, flesh against flesh.

Nothing had been like this. Nothing could be like this. The thoughts whirled in her brain as he began another deliciously slow assault. Her body was to be enjoyed and pleasured, not worshiped. But he did so now, and enticed her to do the same with his.

So strong. She'd known his strength before, but this was different. His fingers didn't grip; his hands didn't press. They skimmed, they traced, they weakened. So intense. They'd shared intensity before, but never so quietly.

She heard him say her name. Aurora. It was like a dream, one she'd never dared to have. He murmured promises in her ear and she believed them. Whatever tomorrow might bring, she believed them now. She could smell the flowers strewn over the bed and taste the excitement that built in a way it had never done before.

He slipped into her as though their bodies had never been apart. The rhythm was easy, patient, giving.

Holding himself back, he watched her climb higher. That was what he wanted, he realized, to give her everything there was to give. When she arched and shuddered, the force whipped through him. Power, he recognized it, but was driven to leash it. His mouth found hers and drew on the sweetness. How could he have known sweetness could be so arousing?

The blood was pounding in his head, roaring in his ears, yet his body continued to move slowly with hers. Balanced on the edge, David said her name a last time.

"Aurora, look at me." When her eyes opened, they were dark and aware. "I want to see where I take you."

Even when control slipped away, echoes of tenderness remained.

Chapter 10

Alice Robbins had exploded onto the screen in the sixties, a young, raw talent. She had, like so many girls before her and after her, fled to Hollywood to escape the limitations of small-town life. She'd come with dreams, with hopes and ambitions. An astrologer might have said Alice's stars were in the right quadrant. When she hit, she hit big.

She had had an early, turbulent marriage that had ended in an early, turbulent divorce. Scenes in and out of the court-room had been as splashy as anything she'd portrayed on the screen. With her marriage over and her career climbing, she'd enjoyed all the benefits of being a beautiful woman in a town that demanded, then courted, beauty. Reports of her love affairs sizzled on the pages of glossies. Glowing reviews and critical praise heaped higher with each role. But in her late twenties, when her career was reaching its peak, she found something that fulfilled her in a way success and reviews never had. Alice Robbins met Peter Van Camp.

He'd been nearly twenty years her senior, a hard-bitten, well-to-do business magnate. They'd married after a whirlwind two-week courtship that had kept the gossip columns salivating. Was it for money? Was it for power? Was it for prestige? It had been, very simply, for love.

In an unprecedented move, Alice had taken her husband's name professionally as well as privately. Hardly more than a year later, she'd given birth to a son and had, without a backward glance, put her career on hold. For nearly a decade, she'd devoted herself to her family with the same kind of single-minded drive she'd put into her acting.

When word leaked that Alice Van Camp had been lured back into films, the hype had been extravagant. Rumors of a multimillion-dollar deal flew and promises of the movie of the century were lavish.

Four weeks before the release of the film, her son, Matthew, had been kidnapped.

David knew the background. Alice Van Camp's triumphs and trials were public fodder. Her name was legend. Though she rarely consented to grace the screen, her popularity remained constant. As to the abduction and recovery of her son, details were sketchy. Perhaps because of the circumstances, the police had never been fully open and Clarissa DeBasse had been quietly evasive. Neither Alice nor Peter Van Camp had ever, until now, granted an interview on the subject. Even with their agreement and apparent cooperation, David knew he would have to tread carefully.

He was using the minimum crew, and a well-seasoned one. "Star" might be an overused term, but David was aware they would be dealing with a woman who fully deserved the title and the mystique that went with it.

Her Beverly Hills home was guarded by electric gates and a wall twice as tall as a man. Just inside the gates was a uniformed guard who verified their identification. Even after they had been passed through, they drove another half a mile to the house.

It was white, flowing out with balconies, rising up with Doric columns, softened by tall, tall trellises of roses in full bloom. Legend had it that her husband had had it built for her in honor of the last role she'd played before the birth of their son. David had seen the movie countless times and remembered her as an antebellum tease who made Scarlett O'Hara look like a nun.

There were Japanese cherry trees dripping down to sweep the lawn in long skirts. Their scent and the citrus fragrance of orange and lemon stung the air. As he pulled his car to a halt behind the equipment van, he spotted a peacock strutting across the lawn.

I wish A.J. could see this.

The thought came automatically before he had time to check it, just as thoughts of her had come automatically for days. Because he wasn't yet sure just how he felt about it, David simply let it happen.

And how did he feel about her? That was something else he wasn't quite sure of. Desire. He desired her more, even more now after he'd saturated himself with her. Friendship. In some odd, cautious way he felt they were almost as much friends as they were lovers. Understanding. It was more difficult to be as definite about that. A.J. had an uncanny ability to throw up mirrors that reflected back your own thoughts rather than hers. Still, he had come to understand that beneath the confidence and drive was a warm, vulnerable woman.

She was passionate. She was reserved. She was competent. She was fragile. And she was, David had discovered, a tantalizing mystery to be solved, one layer at a time.

Perhaps that was why he'd found himself so caught up in her. Most of the women he knew were precisely what they seemed. Sophisticated. Ambitious. Well-bred. His own taste had invariably drawn him to a certain type of woman. A.J. fit. Aurora didn't. If he understood anything about her, he understood she was both.

As an agent, he knew, she was pleased with the deal she'd made for her client, including the Van Camp segment. As a daughter, he sensed, she was uneasy about the repercussions.

But the deal had been made, David reminded himself as he walked up the wide circular steps to the Van Camp estate. As a producer, he was satisfied with the progress of his project. But as a man, he wished he knew of a way to put A.J.'s mind at rest. She excited him; she intrigued him. And as no woman had ever done before, she concerned him. He'd wondered, more often than once, if that peculiar combination equaled love. And if it did, what in hell he was going to do about it.

"Second thoughts?" Alex asked as David hesitated at the door.

Annoyed with himself, David shrugged his shoulders, then pushed the bell. "Should there be?"

"Clarissa's comfortable with this."

David found himself shifting restlessly. "That's enough for you?"

"It's enough," Alex answered. "Clarissa knows her own mind."

The phrasing had him frowning, had him searching. "Alex—"

Though he wasn't certain what he had been about to say, the door opened and the moment was lost. A formally dressed, French-accented maid took their names before leading them into a room off the main hall. The crew, not easily impressed, spoke in murmurs.

It was unapologetically Hollywood. The furnishings were big and bold, the colors flashy. On a baby grand in the center of the room was a silver candelabra dripping with crystal prisms. David recognized it as a prop from *Music at Midnight*.

"Not one for understatement," Alex commented.

"No." David took another sweep of the room. There were brocades and silks in jewel colors. Furniture gleamed like mirrors. "But Alice Van Camp might be one of the few in the business who deserves to bang her own drum."

"Thank you."

Regal, amused and as stunning as she had been in her screen debut, Alice Van Camp paused in the doorway. She was a woman who knew how to pose, and who did so without a second thought. Like others who had known her only through her movies, David's first thought was how small she was. Then she stepped forward and her presence alone whisked the image away.

"Mr. Marshall." Hand extended, Alice walked to him. Her hair was a deep sable spiked around a face as pale and smooth as a child's. If he hadn't known better, David would have said she'd yet to see thirty. "It's a pleasure to meet you. I'm a great admirer of journalists—when they don't misquote me."

"Mrs. Van Camp." He covered her small hand with both of his. "Shall I say the obvious?"

"That depends."

"You're just as beautiful face-to-face as you are on the screen."

She laughed, the smoky, sultry murmur that had made men itch for more than two decades. "I appreciate the obvious. And you're David Brady." Her gaze shifted to him and he felt the unapologetic summing up, strictly woman to man. "I've seen several of your productions. My husband prefers documentaries and biographies to films. I can't think why he married me."

"I can." David accepted her hand. "I'm an avid fan."

"As long as you don't tell me you've enjoyed my movies since you were a child." Amusement glimmered in her eyes again before she glanced around. "Now if you'll introduce me to our crew, we can get started."

David had admired her for years. After ten minutes in her company, his admiration grew. She spoke to each member of the crew, from the director down to the assistant lighting technician. When she'd finished, she turned herself over to Sam for instructions.

At her suggestion, they moved to the terrace. Patient, she waited while technicians set up reflectors and umbrellas to exploit the best effect from available light. Her maid set a table of cold drinks and snacks out of camera range. Though she didn't touch a thing, she indicated to the crew that they should enjoy. She sat easily through sound tests and blocking. When Sam was satisfied, she turned to Alex and began.

"Mrs. Van Camp, for twenty years you've been known as one of the most talented and best-loved actresses in the country."

"Thank you, Alex. My career has always been one of the most important parts of my life."

"One of the most. We're here now to discuss another part of your life. Your family, most specifically your son. A decade ago, you nearly faced tragedy."

"Yes, I did." She folded her hands. Though the sun shone down in her face, she never blinked. "A tragedy that I sincerely doubt I would have recovered from."

"This is the first interview you've given on this subject. Can I ask you why you agreed now?"

She smiled a little, leaning back in her weathered rattan chair. "Timing, in life and in business, is crucial. For several years after my son's abduction I simply couldn't speak of it. After a time, it seemed unnecessary to bring it up again. Now, if I watch the news or look in a store window and see posters of missing children, I ache for the parents."

"Do you consider that this interview might help those parents?"

"Help them find their children, no." Emotion flickered in her eyes, very real and very brief. "But perhaps it can ease some of the misery. I'd never considered sharing my feelings about my own experience. And I doubt very much if I would have agreed if it hadn't been for Clarissa DeBasse."

"Clarissa DeBasse asked you to give this interview?"

After a soft laugh, Alice shook her head. "Clarissa never asks anything. But when I spoke with her and I realized she had faith in this project, I agreed."

"You have a great deal of faith in her."

"She gave me back my son."

She said it with such simplicity, with such utter sincerity, that Alex let the sentence hang. From somewhere in the garden at her back, a bird began to trill.

"That's what we'd like to talk about here. Will you tell us how you came to know Clarissa DeBasse?"

Behind the cameras, behind the crew, David stood with his hands in his pockets and listened to the story. He remembered how A.J. had once told him of her mother's gradual association with celebrities. Alice Van Camp had come to her with a friend on a whim. After an hour, she'd gone away impressed with Clarissa's gentle style and straightforward manner. On impulse, she'd commissioned Clarissa to do her husband's chart as a gift for their anniversary. When it was done, even the pragmatic and business-oriented Peter Van Camp had been intrigued.

"She told me things about myself," Alice went on. "Not about tomorrow, you understand, but about my feelings, things about my background that had influenced me, or still worried me. I can't say I always liked what she had to say. There are things about ourselves we don't like to admit. But I kept going back because she was so intriguing, and gradually we became friends."

"You believed in clairvoyance?"

Alice's brows drew together as she considered. "I would say I first began to see her because it was fun, it was different. I'd chosen to lead a secluded life after the birth of my son, but that didn't mean I wouldn't appreciate, even need, little touches of flash. Of the unique." The frown smoothed as she smiled. "Clarissa was undoubtedly unique."

"So you went to her for entertainment."

"Oh, yes, that was definitely the motivation in the beginning. You see, at first I thought she was simply very clever. Then, as I began to know her, I discovered she was not simply clever, she was special. That certainly doesn't mean I endorse every palmist on Sunset Boulevard. I certainly can't claim to understand the testing and research that's done on the subject. I do believe, however, that there are some of us who are more sensitive, or whose senses are more finely tuned."

"Will you tell us what happened when your son was abducted?"

"June 22. Almost ten years ago." Alice closed her eyes a moment. "To me it's yesterday. You have children, Mr. Marshall?"

"Yes, I do."

"And you love them."

"Very much."

"Then you have some small glimmer of what it would be like to lose them, even for a short time. There's terror and there's guilt. The guilt is nearly as painful as the fear. You see, I hadn't been with him when he'd been taken. Jenny was Matthew's nanny. She'd been with us over five years and was very devoted to my son. She was young, but dependable and fiercely protective. When I made the decision to go back into films, we leaned on Jenny heavily. Neither my husband nor myself wanted Matthew to suffer because I was working again."

"Your son was nearly ten when you agreed to do another movie."

"Yes, he was quite independent already. Both Peter and I wanted that for him. Very often during the filming, Jenny would bring him to the studio. Even after the shooting was complete, she continued in her habit of walking to the park with him in the afternoon. If I had realized then how certain habits can be dangerous, I would have stopped it. Both my husband and myself had been careful to keep Matthew out of the limelight, not because we were afraid for him physically, but because we felt it was best that his upbringing be as normal and natural as possible. Of course he was recognized, and now and then some enterprising photographer would get a shot in."

"Did that sort of thing bother you?"

"No." When she smiled, the sultry glamour came through. "I suppose I was accustomed to such things. Peter and I didn't want to be fanatics about our privacy. And I wonder, and always have, if we'd been stricter would it have made any difference? I doubt it." There was a little sigh, as though it were a point she'd yet to resolve. "We learned later that Matthew's visits to the park were being watched."

"For a time the police suspected Jennifer Waite, your son's nanny, of working with the kidnappers."

"That was, of course, absurd. I never for a minute doubted Jenny's loyalty and devotion to Matthew. Once it was over, she was completely cleared." A trace of stubbornness came through. "She's still in my employ."

"The investigators found her story disjointed."

"The afternoon he was abducted, Jenny came home hysterical. We were the closest thing to family she had, and she blamed herself. Matthew had been playing ball with several other children while she watched. A young woman had come up to her asking for directions. She'd spun a story about missing her bus and being new in town. She'd distracted Jenny only a few moments, and that's all it took. When she looked back, Jenny saw Matthew being hustled into a car at the edge of the park. She ran after him, but he was gone. Ten minutes after she came home alone the first ransom call came in."

She lifted her hands to her lips a moment, and they trembled lightly. "I'm sorry. Could we stop here a moment?"

"Cut. Five minutes," Sam ordered the crew.

David was beside her chair before Sam had finished speaking. "Would you like something, Mrs. Van Camp? A drink?"

"No." She shook her head and looked beyond him. "It isn't as easy as I thought it would be. Ten years, and it still isn't easy."

"I could send for your husband."

"I told Peter to stay away today because he's always so uncomfortable around cameras. I wish I hadn't."

"We can wrap for today."

"Oh, no." She took a deep breath and composed herself. "I believe in finishing what I start. Matthew's a sophomore in college." She smiled up at David. "Do you like happy endings?"

He held her hand. For the moment she was only a woman. "I'm a sucker for them."

"He's bright, handsome and in love. I just needed to remember that. It could have been..." She linked her hands again and the ruby on her finger shone like blood. "It could have been much different. You know Clarissa's daughter, don't you?"

A bit off-balance at the change of subject, David shifted. "Yes."

She admired the caution. "I meant it when I said Clarissa and I are friends. Mothers worry about their children. Do you have a cigarette?"

In silence he took one out and lit it for her.

Alice blew out smoke and let some of the tension fade. "She's a hell of an agent. Do you know, I wanted to sign with her and she wouldn't have me?"

David forgot his own cigarette in simple astonishment. "I beg your pardon?"

Alice laughed again and relaxed. She'd needed a moment to remember life went on. "It was a few months after the kidnapping. A.J. figured I'd come to her out of gratitude to Clarissa. And maybe I had. In any case, she turned me down flat, even though she was scrambling around trying to rent decent office space. I admired her integrity. So much so that a few years ago I approached her again." Alice smiled at him, enjoying the fact that he listened very carefully. Apparently, she mused, Clarissa was right on target, as always. "She was established, respected. And she turned me down again."

What agent in her right mind would turn down a top name, a name that had earned through sheer talent the label of "megastar"? "A.J. never quite does what you expect," he murmured.

"Clarissa's daughter is a woman who insists on being accepted for herself, but can't always tell when she is." She crushed out the cigarette after a second quick puff. "Thanks. I'd like to continue now."

Within moments, Alice was deep into her own story. Though the camera continued to roll, she forgot about it. Sitting in the sunlight with the scent of roses strong and sweet, she talked about her hours of terror.

"We would have paid anything. Anything. Peter and I fought bitterly about calling in the police. The kidnappers had been very specific. We weren't to contact anyone. But Peter felt, and rightly so, that we needed help. The ransom calls came every few hours. We agreed to pay, but they kept changing the terms. Testing us. It was the worst kind of cruelty. While we waited, the police began searching for the car Jenny had seen and the woman she'd spoken with in the park. It was as if they'd vanished into thin air. At the end of forty-eight hours, we were no closer to finding Matthew."

"So you decided to call in Clarissa DeBasse?"

"I don't know when the idea of asking Clarissa to help came to me. I know I hadn't slept or eaten. I just kept waiting for the phone to ring. It's such a helpless feeling. I remembered, God knows why, that Clarissa had once told me where to find a diamond brooch I'd misplaced. It wasn't just a piece of jewelry to me, but something Peter had given me when Matthew was born. A child isn't a brooch, but I began to think, maybe, just maybe. I needed some hope.

"The police didn't like the idea. I don't believe Peter did, either, but he knew I needed something. I called Clarissa and I told her that Matthew had been taken." Her eyes filled. She didn't bother to blink the tears away. "I asked her if she could help me and she told me she'd try.

"I broke down when she arrived. She sat with me awhile, friend to friend, mother to mother. She spoke to Jenny, though there was no calming the poor girl down even at that point. The police were very terse with Clarissa, but she seemed to accept that. She told them they were looking in the wrong place." Unselfconsciously she brushed at the tears on her cheek. "I can tell you that didn't sit too well with the men who'd been working around the clock. She told them Matthew hadn't been taken out of the city, he hadn't gone north as they'd thought. She asked for something of Matthew's, something he would have worn. I brought her the pajamas he'd worn to bed the night before. They were blue with little cars across the top. She just sat there, running them through her hands. I remember wanting to scream at her, plead with her, to give me something. Then she started to speak very quietly.

"Matthew was only miles away, she said. He hadn't been taken to San Francisco, though the police had traced one of the ransom calls there. She said he was still in Los Angeles. She described the street, then the house. A white house with blue shutters on a corner lot. I'll never forget the way she described the room in which he was being held. It was dark, you see, and Matthew, though he always tried to be brave, was still afraid of the dark. She said there were only two people in the house, one man and the woman who had spoken to Jenny in the park. She thought there was a car in the drive, gray or green, she said. And she told me he wasn't hurt. He was afraid—" her voice shuddered, then strengthened "—but he wasn't hurt."

"And the police pursued the lead?"

"They didn't have much faith in it, naturally enough, but they sent out cars to look for the house she'd described. I don't know who was more stunned when they found it, Peter and myself or the police. They got Matthew out without a struggle because the two kidnappers with him weren't expecting any trouble. The third accomplice was in San Fransico, making all the calls. The police also found the car he'd been abducted in there.

"Clarissa stayed until Matthew was home, until he was safe. Later he told me about the room he'd been held in. It was exactly as she'd described it."

"Mrs. Van Camp, a lot of people claimed that the abduction and the dramatic rescue of your son was a publicity stunt to hype the release of your first movie since his birth."

"That didn't matter to me." With only her voice, with only her eyes, she showed her complete contempt. "They could say and believe whatever they wanted. I had my son back."

"And you believe Clarissa DeBasse is responsible for that?"

"I know she is."

"Cut," Sam mumbled to his cameraman before he walked to Alice. "Mrs. Van Camp, if we can get a few reaction shots and over-the-shoulder angles, we'll be done."

He could go now. David knew there was no real reason for him to remain during the angle changes. The shoot was essentially finished, and had been everything he could have asked for. Alice Van Camp was a consummate actress, but no one watching this segment would consider that she'd played a part. She'd been a mother, reliving an experience every mother fears. And she had, by the telling, brought the core of his project right back to Clarissa.

He thought perhaps he understood a little better why A.J. had had mixed feelings about the interview. Alice Van Camp had suffered in the telling. If his instincts were right, Clarissa would have suffered, too. It seemed to him that empathy was an intimate part of her gift.

Nevertheless he stayed behind the camera and restlessly waited until the shoot was complete. Though he detected a trace of weariness in her eyes, Alice escorted the crew to the door herself.

"A remarkable woman," Alex commented as they walked down the circular steps toward the drive.

"And then some. But you've got one yourself."

"I certainly do." Alex pulled out the cigar he'd been patiently waiting for for more than three hours. "I might be a little biased, but I believe you have one, as well."

Frowning, David paused by his car. "I haven't got A.J." It occurred to him that it was the first time he had thought of it in precisely those terms.

"Clarissa seems to think you do."

He turned back and leaned against his car. "And approves?"

"Shouldn't she?"

He pulled out a cigarette. The restlessness was growing. "I don't know."

"You were going to ask me something earlier, before we went in. Do you want to ask me now?"

It had been nagging at him. David wondered if by stating it aloud it would ease. "Clarissa isn't an ordinary woman. Does it bother you?"

Alex took a contented puff on his cigar. "It certainly intrigues me, and I'd be lying if I didn't admit I've had one or two uneasy moments. What I feel for her cancels out the fact that I have five senses and she has what we might call six. You're having uneasy moments." He smiled a little when

David said nothing. "Clarissa doesn't believe in keeping se-crets. We've talked about her daughter."

"I'm not sure A.J. would be comfortable with that."

"No, maybe not. It's more to the point what you're com-fortable with. You know the trouble with a man your age, David? You consider yourself too old to go take foolish risks and too young to trust impulse. I thank God I'm not thirty." With a smile, he walked over to hitch a ride back to town with Sam.

He was too old to take foolish risks, David thought as he pulled his door open. And a man who trusted impulse usu-ally landed flat on his face. But he wanted to see her. He wanted to see her now.

A.J.'s briefcase weighed heavily as she pulled it from the front seat. Late rush-hour traffic streamed by the front of her building. If she'd been able to accomplish more dur-ing office hours, she reminded herself as she lugged up her case, she wouldn't have to plow through papers tonight. She would have accomplished more if she hadn't been uneasy, thinking of the Van Camp interview.

It was over now, she told herself as she turned the key to lock both car doors. The filming of the documentary was all but over. She had other clients, other projects, other contracts. It was time she put her mind on them. Shifting her briefcase to her free hand, she turned and collided with David.

"I like running into you," he murmured as he slid his hands up her hips.

She'd had the wind knocked out of her. That's what she told herself as she struggled for breath and leaned into him. After a man and a woman had been intimate, after they'd been lovers, they didn't feel breathless and giddy when they saw each other. But she found herself wanting to wrap her arms around him and laugh.

"You might have cracked a rib," she told him, and contented herself with smiling up at him. "I certainly didn't expect to see you around this evening."

"Problem?"

"No." She let herself brush a hand through his hair. "I think I can work you in. How did the shoot go?"

He heard it, the barest trace of nerves. Not tonight, he told himself. There would be no nerves tonight. "It's done. You know, I like the way you smell up close." He lowered his mouth to brush it over her throat. "Up very close."

"David, we're standing in the parking lot."

"Mmm-hmm." He shifted his mouth to her ear and sent the thrill tumbling to her toes.

"David." She turned her head to ward him off and found her mouth captured by his in a long, lingering kiss.

"I can't stop thinking about you," he murmured, then kissed her again, hard, until the breath was trembling from her mouth into his. "I can't get you out of my mind. Sometimes I wonder if you've put a spell on me. Mind over matter."

"Don't talk. Come inside with me."

"We don't talk enough." He put his hand under her chin and drew her away before he gave in and buried himself in her again. "Sooner or later we're going to have to."

That's what she was afraid of. When they talked, really talked, she was sure it would be about the end. "Later, then. Please." She rested her cheek against his. "For now let's just enjoy each other."

He felt the edge of frustration compete with the first flares of desire. "That's all you want?"

No, no, she wanted more, everything, anything. If she

opened her mouth to speak of one wish, she would speak of dozens. "It's enough," she said almost desperately. "Why did you come here tonight?"

"Because I wanted you. Because I damn well can't keep away from you."

"And that's all I need." Was she trying to convince him or herself? Neither of them had the answer. "Come inside, I'll show you."

Because he needed, because he wasn't yet sure of the nature of his own needs, he took her hand in his and went with her.

Chapter 11

"Are you sure you want to do this?" A.J. felt it was only fair to give David one last chance before he committed himself.

"I'm sure."

"It's going to take the better part of your evening."

"Want to get rid of me?"

"No." She smiled but still hesitated. "Ever done anything like this before?"

He took the collar of her blouse between his thumb and forefinger and rubbed. The practical A.J. had a weakness for silk. "You're my first."

"Then you'll have to do what you're told."

He skimmed his finger down her throat. "Don't you trust me?"

She cocked her head and gave him a long look. "I haven't decided. But under the circumstances, I'll take a chance. Pull up a chair." She indicated the table behind her. There were stacks of paper, neatly arranged. A.J. picked up a pencil, freshly sharpened, and handed it to him. "The first thing you can do is mark off the names I give you. Those are the people who've sent an acceptance. I'll give you the name and the number of people under that name. I need an amount for the caterer by the end of the week."

"Sounds easy enough."

"Just shows you've never dealt with a caterer," A.J. mumbled, and took her own chair.

"What's this?" As he reached for another pile of papers, she waved his hand away.

"People who've already sent gifts, and don't mess with the system. When we finish with this, we have to deal with the guests coming in from out of town. I'm hoping to book a block of rooms tomorrow."

He studied the tidy but extensive arrangement of papers spread between them. "I thought this was supposed to be a small, simple wedding."

She sent him a mild look. "There's no such thing as a small, simple wedding. I've spent two full mornings haggling with florists and over a week off and on struggling with caterers."

"Learn anything?"

"Elopement is the wisest course. Now here—"

"Would you?"

"Would I what?"

"Elope."

With a laugh, A.J. picked up her first stack of papers. "If I ever lost a grip on myself and decided on marriage, I think I'd fly to Vegas, swing through one of those drive-in chapels and have it over with."

His eyes narrowed as he listened to her, as if he were trying to see beyond the words. "Not very romantic."

"Neither am I."

"Aren't you?" He put a hand over hers, surprising her. There was something proprietary in the gesture, and something completely natural.

"No." But her fingers linked with his. "There's not a lot of room for romance in business."

"And otherwise?"

"Otherwise romance tends to lead you to see things that aren't really there. I like illusions on the stage and screen, not in my life."

"What do you want in your life, Aurora? You've never told me."

Why was she nervous? It was foolish, but he was looking at her so closely. He was asking questions he'd never asked. And the answers weren't as simple as she'd once thought. "Success," she told him. Hadn't it always been true?

He nodded, but his thumb moved gently up and down the side of her hand. "You run a successful agency already. What else?" He was waiting, for one word, one sign. Did she need him? For the first time in his life he wanted to be needed.

"I…" She was fumbling for words. He seemed to be the only one who could make her fumble. What did he want? What answer would satisfy him? "I suppose I want to know I've earned my own way."

"Is that why you turned down Alice Van Camp as a client?"

"She told you that?" They hadn't discussed the Van Camp interview. A.J. had purposely talked around it for days.

"She mentioned it." She'd pulled her hand from his. David wondered why every time they talked, really talked, she seemed to draw further away from him.

"It was kind of her to come to me when I was just getting started and things were...rough." She shrugged her shoulders, then began to slide her pencil through her fingers. "But it was out of gratitude to my mother. I couldn't sign my first big client out of gratitude."

"Then later you turned her down again."

"It was too personal." She fought the urge to stand up, walk away from the table, and from him.

"No mixing business with personal relationships."

"Exactly. Do you want some coffee before we get started?"

"You mixed a business and personal relationship with me."

Her fingers tightened on the pencil. He watched them. "Yes, I did."

"Why?"

Though it cost her, she kept her eyes on his. He could strip her bare, she knew. If she told him she had fallen in love with him, had started the tumble almost from the first, she would have no defense left. He would have complete and total control. And she would have reneged on the most important agreement in her life. If she couldn't give him the truth, she could give him the answer he'd understand. The answer that mirrored his feelings for her.

"Because I wanted you," she said, and kept her voice cool. "I was attracted to you, and wisely or not, I gave in to the attraction."

He felt the twinge, a need unfulfilled. "That's enough for you?"

Hadn't she said he could hurt her? He was hurting her now with every word. "Why shouldn't it be?" She gave him an easy smile and waited for the ache to pass.

"Why shouldn't it be?" he murmured, and tried to accept the answer for what it was. He pulled out a cigarette, then began carefully. "I think you should know we're shooting a segment on the Ridehour case." Though his eyes stayed on hers, he saw her tense. "Clarissa agreed to discuss it."

"She told me. That should wrap the taping?"

"It should." She was holding back. Though no more than a table separated them, it might have been a canyon. "You don't like it."

"No, I don't, but I'm trying to learn that Clarissa has to make her own decisions."

"A.J., she seems very easy about it."

"You don't understand."

"Then let me."

"Before I convinced her to move, to keep her residence strictly confidential, she had closets full of letters." She took her glasses off to rub at a tiny ache in her temple. "People asking for her to help them. Some of them involved no more than asking her to locate a ring, and others were full of problems so heartbreaking they gave you nightmares."

"She couldn't help everyone."

"That's what I kept telling her. When she moved down to Newport Beach, things eased up. Until she got the call from San Francisco."

"The Ridehour murders."

"Yes." The ache grew. "There was never a question of her listening to me on that one. I don't believe she heard one argument I made. She just packed. When I saw there was no stopping her from going, I went with her." She kept her breathing even with great effort. Her hands were steady only because she locked them so tightly together. "It was one of the most painful experiences of her life. She saw." A.J. closed her eyes and spoke to him what she'd never spoken to anyone. "I saw."

When he covered her hand with his, he found it cold. He

didn't have to see her eyes to know the baffled fear would be there. Comfort, understanding. How did he show them? "Why didn't you tell me before?"

She opened her eyes. The control was there, but teetering. "It isn't something I like to remember. I've never before or since had anything come so clear, so hideously clear."

"We'll cut it."

She gave him a blank, puzzled look. "What?"

"We'll cut the segment."

"Why?"

Slowly he drew her hands apart and into his. He wanted to explain, to tell her so that she'd understand. He wished he had the words. "Because it upsets you. That's enough."

She looked down at their hands. His looked so strong, so dependable, over hers. No one except her mother had ever offered to do anything for her without an angle. Yet it seemed he was. "I don't know what to say to you."

"Don't say anything."

"No." She gave herself a moment. For reasons she couldn't understand, she was relaxed again. Tension was there, hovering, but the knots in her stomach had eased. "Clarissa agreed to this segment, so she must feel as though it should be done."

"We're not talking about Clarissa now, but you. Aurora, I said once I never wanted to be responsible for your going through something like this. I mean it."

"I think you do." It made all the difference. "The fact that you'd cut the segment because of me makes me feel very special."

"Maybe I should have told you that you are before now."

Longings rose up. She let herself feel them for only a moment. "You don't have to tell me anything. I realize that if you cut this part because of me I'd hate myself. It was a long time ago, David. Maybe it's time I learned to deal with reality a little better."

"Maybe you deal with it too well."

"Maybe." She smiled again. "In any case I think you should do the segment. Just do a good job of it."

"I intend to. Do you want to sit in on it?"

"No." She glanced down at the stacks of papers. "Alex will be there for her."

He heard it in her voice, not doubt but resignation. "He's crazy about her."

"I know." In a lightning change of mood, she picked up her pencil again. "I'm going to give them one hell of a wedding."

He grinned at her. Resiliency was only one of the things that attracted him to her. "We'd better get started."

They worked side by side for nearly two hours. It took half that time for the tension to begin to fade. They read off lists and compiled new ones. They analyzed and calculated how many cases of champagne would be adequate and argued over whether to serve salmon mousse or iced shrimp.

She hadn't expected him to become personally involved with planning her mother's wedding. Before they'd finished, she'd come to accept it to the point where she delegated him to help seat guests at the ceremony.

"Working with you's an experience, A.J."

"Hmm?" She counted the out-of-town guests one last time.

"If I needed an agent, you'd head the list."

She glanced up, but was too cautious to smile. "Is that a compliment?"

"Not exactly."

Now she smiled. When she took off her glasses, her face was abruptly vulnerable. "I didn't think so. Well, once I give these figures to the caterer, that should be it. Everyone who attends will have me to thank that they aren't eating Clarissa's Swedish meatballs. And you." She set the lists aside. "I appreciate all the help."

"I'm fond of Clarissa."

"I know. I appreciate that, too. Now I think you deserve a reward." She leaned closer and caught her tongue in her teeth. "Anything in mind?"

He had plenty in mind every time he looked at her. "We can start with that coffee."

"Coming right up." She rose, and out of habit glanced at her watch. "Oh, God."

He reached for a cigarette. "Problem?"

"*Empire*'s on."

"A definite problem."

"No, I have to watch it."

As she dashed over to the television, he shook his head. "All this time, and I had no idea you were an addict. A.J., there are places you can go that can help you deal with these things."

"Shh." She settled on the sofa, relieved she'd missed no more than the opening credits. "I have a client—"

"It figures."

"She has a lot of potential," A.J. continued. "But this is the first real break we've gotten. She's only signed for four episodes, but if she does well, they could bring her back through next season."

Resigned, he joined her on the sofa. "Aren't these repeats, anyway?"

"Not this one. It's a teaser for a spin-off that's going to run through the summer."

"A spin-off?" He propped his feet on an issue of *Variety*

on the coffee table. "Isn't there enough sex and misery in one hour a week?"

"Melodrama. It's important to the average person to see that the filthy rich have their problems. See him?" Reaching over, she dug into a bowl of candied almonds. "That's Dereck, the patriarch. He made his money in shipping— and smuggling. He's determined that his children carry on his business, by his rules. That's Angelica."

"In the hot tub."

"Yes, she's his second wife. She married him for his money and power and enjoys every minute of them. But she hates his kids."

"And they hate her right back."

"That's the idea." Pleased with him, A.J. patted his leg. "Now the setup is that Angelica's illegitimate daughter from a long-ago relationship is going to show up. That's my client."

"Like mother like daughter?"

"Oh, yes, she gets to play the perfect bitch. Her name's Lavender."

"Of course it is."

"You see, Angelica never told Dereck she had a daughter, so when Lavender shows up, she's going to cause all sorts of problems. Now Beau—that's Dereck's eldest son—"

"No more names." With a sigh, he swung his arm over the back of the sofa. "I'll just watch all the skin and diamonds."

"Just because you'd rather watch pelicans migrate— Here she is."

A.J. bit her lip. She tensed, agonizing with her client over each line, each move, each expression. And she would, David thought with a smile, fluff him off if he mentioned she had a personal involvement. Just business? Not by a long shot. She was pulling for her ingenue and ten percent didn't enter into it.

"Oh, she's good," A.J. breathed at the commercial break. "She's really very good. A season—maybe two—of this, and we'll be sifting through offers for feature films."

"Her timing's excellent." He might consider the show itself a glitzy waste of time, but he appreciated talent. "Where did she study?"

"She didn't." Smug, A.J. sat back. "She took a bus from Kansas City and ended up in my reception area with a homemade portfolio and a handful of high school plays to her credit."

He gave in and tried the candied almonds himself. "You usually sign on clients that way?"

"I usually have Abe or one of the more maternal members of my staff give them a lecture and a pat on the head."

"Sensible. But?"

"She was different. When she wouldn't budge out of the office for the second day running, I decided to see her myself. As soon as I saw her I knew. Not that way," she answered, understanding his unspoken question. "I make it a policy not to sign a client no matter what feelings might come through. She had looks and a wonderful voice. But more, she had the drive. I don't know how many auditions I sent her on in the first few weeks. But I figured if she survived that, we were going to roll." She watched the next glittery set of *Empire* appear on the screen. "And we're rolling."

"It took guts to camp out in one of the top agencies in Hollywood."

"If you don't have guts in this town, you'll be flattened in six months."

"Is that what keeps you on top, A.J.?"

"It's part of it." She found the curve of his shoulder an

easy place to rest her head. "You can't tell me you think you're where you are today because you got lucky."

"No. You start off thinking hard work's enough, then you realize you have to take risks and shed a little blood. Then just when everything comes together and a project's finished and successful, you have to start another and prove yourself all over again."

"It's a lousy business." A.J. cuddled against him.

"Yep."

"Why do you do it?" Forgetting the series, forgetting her client, A.J. turned her head to look at him.

"Masochism."

"No, really."

"Because every time I watch something I did on that little screen, it's like Christmas. And I get every present I ever wanted."

"I know." Nothing he could have said could have hit more directly home. "I attended the Oscars a couple of years ago and two of my clients won. Two of them." She let her eyes close as she leaned against him. "I sat in the audience watching, and it was the biggest thrill of my life. I know some people would say you're not asking for enough when you get your thrills vicariously, but it's enough, more than enough, to know you've had a part in something like that. Maybe your name isn't a household word, but you were the catalyst."

"Not everyone wants his name to be a household word."

"Yours could be." She shifted again to look at him. "I'm not just saying that because—" *Because I love you.* The phrase was nearly out before she checked it. When he lifted his brow at her sudden silence, she continued quickly. "Because of our relationship. With the right material, the right crew, you could be one of the top ten producers in the business."

"I appreciate that." Her eyes were so earnest, so intense. He wished he knew why. "I don't think you throw around compliments without thinking about them first."

"No, I don't. I've seen your work, and I've seen the way you work. And I've been around long enough to know."

"I don't have any desire, not at this point, anyway, to tie myself up with any of the major studios. The big screen's for fantasies." He touched her cheek. It was real; it was soft. "I prefer dealing in reality."

"So produce something real." It was a challenge—she knew it. By the look in his eyes, he knew it, as well.

"Such as?"

"I have a script."

"A.J.—"

"No, hear me out. David." She said his name in frustration when he rolled her under him on the sofa. "Just listen a minute."

"I'd rather bite your ear."

"Bite it all you want. After you listen."

"Negotiations again?" He drew himself up just to look down at her. Her eyes were lit with enthusiasm, her cheeks flushed with anticipation of excitement to come. "What script?" he asked, and watched her lips curve.

"I've done some business with George Steiger. You know him?"

"We've met. He's an excellent writer."

"He's written a screenplay. His first. It just happened to come across my desk."

"Just happened?"

She'd done him a few favors. He was asking for another. Doing favors without personal gain at the end didn't fit the image she'd worked hard on developing. "We don't need to get into that. It's wonderful, David, really wonderful. It deals with the Cherokees and what they called the Trail of Tears, when they were driven from Georgia to reservations in Oklahoma. Most of the point of view is through a small child. You sense the bewilderment, the betrayal, but there's this strong thread of hope. It's not your 'ride off into the sunset' Western, and it's not a pretty story. It's real. You could make it important."

She was selling, and doing a damn good job of it. It occurred to him she'd probably never pitched a deal while curled up on the sofa before. "A.J., what makes you think that if I were interested, Steiger would be interested in me?"

"I happened to mention that I knew you."

"Happened to again?"

"Yes." She smiled and ran her hands down to his hips. "He's seen your work and knows your reputation. David, he needs a producer, the right producer."

"And so?"

As if disinterested, she skimmed her fingertips up his back. "He asked if I'd mention it to you, all very informally."

"This is definitely informal," he murmured as he fit his body against hers. "Are you playing agent, A.J.?"

"No." Her eyes were abruptly serious as she took his face in her hands. "I'm being your friend."

She touched him, more deeply, more sweetly, than any of their loving, any of their passion. For a moment he could find nothing to say. "Every time I think I've got a track on you, you switch lanes."

"Will you read it?"

He kissed one cheek, then the other, in a gesture he'd seen her use with her mother. It meant affection, devotion.

He wondered if she understood. "I guess that means you can get me a copy."

"I just happened to have brought one home with me." With a laugh, she threw her arms around him. "David, you're going to love it."

"I'd rather love you."

She stiffened, but only for a heartbeat. Their loving was physical, she reminded herself. Deeply satisfying but only physical. When he spoke of love, it didn't mean the emotions, but the body. It was all she could expect from him, and all he wanted from her.

"Then love me now," she murmured, and found his mouth with hers. "Love me now."

She drew him to her, tempting him to take everything at once, quickly, heatedly. But he learned that pleasure taken slowly, given gently, could be so much more gratifying. Because it was still so new, she responded to tenderness with hesitation. Her stomach fluttered when he skimmed her lips with his, offering, promising. She heard her own sigh escape, a soft, giving sound that whispered across his lips. Then he murmured her name, quietly, as if it were the only sound he needed to hear.

No rush. His needs seemed to meld with her own. No hurry. Content, she let herself enjoy easy kisses that aroused the soul before they tempted the body. Relaxed, she allowed herself to thrill to the light caresses that made her strong enough to accept being weak.

She wanted to feel him against her without boundaries. With a murmur of approval, she pulled his shirt over his head, then took her hands on a long stroke down his back. There was the strength she'd understood from the beginning. A strength she respected, perhaps even more now that his hands were gentle.

When had she looked for gentleness? Her mind was already too clouded to know if she ever had. But now that she'd found it, she never wanted to lose it. Or him.

"I want you, David." She whispered the words along his cheek as she drew him closer.

Hearing her say it made his heart pound. He'd heard the words before, but rarely from her and never with such quiet acceptance. He lifted his head to look down at her. "Tell me again." As he took her chin in his hand, his voice was low and husky with emotion. "Tell me again, when I'm looking at you."

"I want you."

His mouth crushed down on hers, smothering any more words, any more thoughts. He seemed to need more; she thought she could feel it, though she didn't know what to give. She offered her mouth, that his might hungrily meet it. She offered her body, that his could greedily take it. But she held back her heart, afraid he would take that, as well, and damage it.

Clothes were peeled off as patience grew thin. He wanted to feel her against him, all the long length of her. He trembled when he touched her, but he was nearly used to trembling for her now. He ached, as he always ached. Light and subtle along her skin was the path of scent. He could follow it from her throat, to the hollow of her breasts, to the pulse at the inside of her elbows.

She shuddered against him. Her body seemed to pulse, then sigh, with each touch, each stroke. He knew where the brush of a fingertip would arouse, or the nip of his teeth would inflame. And she knew his body just as intimately. Her lips would find each point of pleasure; her palms would stroke each flame higher.

He grew to need. Each time he loved her, he came to need

not only what she would give, but what she could. Each time he was more desperate to draw more from her, knowing that if he didn't find the key, he'd beg. She could, simply because she asked for nothing, bring him to his knees.

"Tell me what you want," he demanded as she clung to him.

"You. I want you."

She was hovering above the clouds that shook with lightning and thunder. The air was thick and heavy, the heat swirling. Her body was his; she gave it willingly. But the heart she struggled so hard to defend lost itself to him.

"David." All the love, all the emotion she felt, shimmered in his name as she pressed herself against him. "Don't let me go."

They dozed, still wrapped together, still drowsily content. Though most of his weight was on her, she felt light, free. Each time they made love, the sense of her own freedom came stronger. She was bound to him, but more liberated than she had ever been in her life. So she lay quietly as his heart beat slowly and steadily against hers.

"TV's still on," David murmured.

"Uh-huh." The late-night movie whisked by, sirens blaring, guns blasting. She didn't care.

She linked her hands behind his waist. "Doesn't matter."

"A few more minutes like this and we'll end up sleeping here tonight."

"That doesn't matter, either."

With a laugh, he turned his face to kiss her neck where the skin was still heated from excitement. Reluctantly he shifted his weight. "You know, with a few minor changes, we could be a great deal more comfortable."

"In the bed," she murmured in agreement, but merely snuggled into him.

"For a start. I'm thinking more of the long term."

It was difficult to think at all when he was warm and firm against her. "Which long term?"

"Both of us tend to do a lot of running around and overnight packing in order to spend the evening together."

"Mmmm. I don't mind."

He did. The more content he became with her, the more discontent he became with their arrangement. *I love you.* The words seemed so simple. But he'd never spoken them to a woman before. If he said them to her, how quickly would she pull away and disappear from his life? Some risks he wasn't ready to take. Cautious, he approached in the practical manner he thought she'd understand.

"Still, I think we could come up with a more logical arrangement."

She opened her eyes and shifted a bit. He could see there was already a line between her brows. "What sort of arrangement?"

He wasn't approaching this exactly as he'd planned. But then he'd learned that his usual meticulous plotting didn't work when he was dealing with A.J. "Your apartment's convenient to the city, where we both happen to be working at the moment."

"Yes." Her eyes had lost that dreamy softness they always had after loving. He wasn't certain whether to curse himself or her.

"We only work five days a week. My house, on the other hand, is convenient for getting away and relaxing. It seems a logical arrangement might be for us to live here during the week and spend weekends at my place."

She was silent for five seconds, then ten, while dozens of

thoughts and twice as many warnings rushed through her mind. "A logical arrangement," he called it. Not a commitment, an "arrangement." Or more accurately, an amendment to the arrangement they'd already agreed on. "You want to live together."

He'd expected more from her, anything more. A flicker of pleasure, a gleam of emotion. But her voice was cool and cautious. "We're essentially doing that now, aren't we?"

"No." She wanted to distance herself, but his body kept hers trapped. "We're sleeping together."

And that was all she wanted. His hands itched to shake her, to shake her until she looked, really looked, at him and saw what he felt and what he needed. Instead he sat up and, in the unselfconscious way she always admired, began to dress. Feeling naked and defenseless, she reached for her blouse.

"You're angry."

"Let's just say I didn't think we'd have to go to the negotiating table with this."

"David, you haven't even given me five minutes to think it through."

He turned to her then, and the heat in his eyes had her bracing. "If you need to," he said with perfect calm, "maybe we should just drop it."

"You're not being fair."

"No, I'm not." He rose then, knowing he had to get out, get away from her, before he said too much. "Maybe I'm tired of being fair with you."

"Damn it, David." Half-dressed, she sprang up to face him. "You casually suggest that we should combine our living arrangements, then blow up because I need a few minutes to sort it through. You're being ridiculous."

"It's a habit I picked up when I starting seeing you." He

should have left. He knew he should have already walked out the door. Because he hadn't, he grabbed her arms and pulled her closer. "I want more than sex and breakfast. I want more than a quick roll in the sheets when our schedules make it convenient."

Furious, she swung away from him. "You make me sound like a—"

"No. I make us both sound like it." He didn't reach for her again. He wouldn't crawl. "I make us both sound like precisely what we are. And I don't care for it."

She'd known it would end. She'd told herself she'd be prepared when it did. But she wanted to shout and scream. Clinging to what pride she had left, she stood straight. "I don't know what you want."

He stared at her until she nearly lost the battle with the tears that threatened. "No," he said quietly. "You don't. That's the biggest problem, isn't it?"

He left her because he wanted to beg. She let him go because she was ready to.

Chapter 12

Nervous as a cat, A.J. supervised as folding chairs were set in rows in her mother's garden. She counted them— again—before she walked over to fuss with the umbrella-covered tables set in the side yard. The caterers were busy in the kitchen; the florist and two assistants were putting the finishing touches on the arrangements. Pots of lilies and tubs of roses were placed strategically around the terrace so that their scents wafted and melded with the flowers of Clarissa's garden. It smelled like a fairy tale.

Everything was going perfectly. With her hands in her pockets, she stood in the midmorning sunlight and wished for a crisis she could dig her teeth into.

Her mother was about to marry the man she loved, the weather was a blessing and all of A.J.'s preplanning was paying off. She couldn't remember ever being more miser-able. She wanted to be home, in her own apartment, with the door locked and the curtains drawn, with her head buried under the covers. Hadn't it been David who'd once told her that self-pity wasn't attractive?

Well, David was out of her life now, A.J. reminded herself. And had been for nearly two weeks. That was for the best. Without having him around, confusing her emotions, she could get on with business. The agency was so busy she was seriously considering increasing her staff. Because of the increased work load, she was on the verge of canceling her own two-week vacation in Saint Croix. She was personally negotiating two multimillion-dollar contracts and one wrong move could send them toppling.

She wondered if he'd come.

A.J. cursed herself for even thinking of him. He'd walked out of her apartment and her life. He'd walked out when she'd kept herself in a state of turmoil, struggling to keep strictly to the terms of their agreement. He'd been angry and unreasonable. He hadn't bothered to call and she certainly wasn't going to call him.

Maybe she had once, she thought with a sigh. But he hadn't been home. It wasn't likely that David Brady was mooning and moping around. A.J. Fields was too independent, and certainly too busy, to do any moping herself.

But she'd dreamed of him. In the middle of the night she'd pull herself out of dreams because he was there. She knew, better than most, that dreams could hurt.

That part of her life was over, she told herself again. It had been only an…episode, she decided. Episodes didn't always end with flowers and sunlight and pretty words. She glanced over to see one of the hired help knock over a line of chairs. Grateful for the distraction, A.J. went over to help set things to rights.

When she went back into the house, the caterers were

Mind Over Matter

busily fussing over quiche and Clarissa was sitting content-
edly in her robe, noting down the recipe.

"Momma, shouldn't you be getting ready?"

Clarissa glanced up with a vague smile and petted the
cat that curled in her lap. "Oh, there's plenty of time, isn't
there?"

"A woman never has enough time to get ready on her
wedding day."

"It's a beautiful day, isn't it? I know it's foolish to take it
as a sign, but I'd like to."

"You can take anything you want as a sign." A.J. started
to move to the stove for coffee, then changed her mind. On
impulse, she opened the refrigerator and pulled out one of
the bottles of champagne that were chilling. The caterers
muttered together and she ignored them. It wasn't every day
a daughter watched her mother marry. "Come on. I'll help
you." A.J. swung through the dining room and scooped up
two fluted glasses.

"I wonder if I should drink before. I shouldn't be fuzzy-
headed."

"You should absolutely be fuzzy-headed," A.J. corrected.
Walking into her mother's room, she plopped down on the
bed as she had as a child. "We should both be fuzzy-headed.
It's better than being nervous."

Clarissa smiled beautifully. "I'm not nervous."

A.J. sent the cork cannoning to the ceiling. "Brides have
to be nervous. I'm nervous and all I have to do is watch."

"Aurora." Clarissa took the glass she offered, then sat on
the bed beside her. "You should stop worrying about me."

"I can't." A.J. leaned over to kiss one cheek, then the
other. "I love you."

Clarissa took her hand and held it tightly. "You've always

been a pleasure to me. Not once, not once in your entire life, have you brought me anything but happiness."

"That's all I want for you."

"I know. And it's all I want for you." She loosened her grip on A.J.'s hand but continued to hold it. "Talk to me."

A.J. didn't need specifics to understand her mother meant David. She set down her untouched champagne and started to rise. "We don't have time. You need to—"

"You've had an argument. You hurt."

With a long, hopeless sigh, A.J. sank back down on the bed. "I knew I would from the beginning. I had my eyes open."

"Did you?" With a shake of her head, Clarissa set her glass beside A.J.'s so she could take both her hands. "Why is it you have such a difficult time accepting affection from anyone but me? Am I responsible for that?"

"No. No, it's just the way things are. In any case, David and I... We simply had a very intense physical affair that burned itself out."

Clarissa thought of what she had seen, what she had felt, and nearly sighed. "But you're in love with him."

With anyone else, she could have denied. With anyone else, she could have lied and perhaps have been believed. "That's my problem, isn't it? And I'm dealing with it," she added quickly, before she was tempted into self-pity again. "Today of all days we shouldn't be talking about anything but lovely things."

"Today of all days I want to see my daughter happy. How do you think he feels about you?"

It never paid to forget how quietly stubborn Clarissa could be. "He was attracted. I think he was a little intrigued because I wasn't immediately compliant, and in business we stood toe-to-toe."

Clarissa hadn't forgotten how successfully evasive her daughter could be. "I asked you how you think he feels."

"I don't know." A.J. dragged a hand through her hair and rose. "He wants me—or wanted me. We match very well in bed. And then I'm not sure. He seemed to want more—to get inside my head."

"And you don't care for that."

"I don't like being examined."

Clarissa watched her daughter pace back and forth in her quick, nervous gait. So much emotion bottled up, she thought. Why couldn't she understand she'd only truly feel it when she let it go? "Are you so sure that's what he was doing?"

"I'm not sure of anything, but I know that David is a very logical sort of man. The kind who does meticulous research into any subject that interests him."

"Did you ever consider that it was you who interested him, not your psychic abilities?"

"I think he might have been interested in one and uneasy about the other." She wished, even now, that she could be sure. "In any case, it's done now. We both understood commitment was out of the question."

"Why?"

"Because it wasn't what he—what we," she corrected herself quickly, "were looking for. We set the rules at the start."

"What did you argue about?"

"He suggested we live together."

"Oh." Clarissa paused a moment. She was old-fashioned enough to be anxious and wise enough to accept. "To some, a step like that is a form of commitment."

"No, it was more a matter of convenience." Was that what hurt? she wondered. She hadn't wanted to analyze it.

"Anyway, I wanted to think it over and he got angry. Really angry."

"He's hurt." When A.J. glanced over, surprised protest on the tip of her tongue, Clarissa shook her head. "I know. You've managed to hurt each other deeply, with nothing more than pride."

That changed things. A.J. told herself it shouldn't, but found herself weakening. "I didn't want to hurt David. I only wanted—"

"To protect yourself," Clarissa finished. "Sometimes doing one can only lead to the other. When you love someone, really love them, you have to take some risks."

"You think I should go to him."

"I think you should do what's in your heart."

Her heart. Her heart was broken open. She wondered why everyone couldn't see what was in it. "It sounds so easy."

"And it's the most frightening thing in the world. We can test, analyze and research psychic phenomena. We can set up labs in some of the greatest universities and institutions in the world, but no one but a poet understands the terror of love."

"You've always been a poet, Momma." A.J. sat down beside her again, resting her head on her mother's shoulder. "Oh, God, what if he doesn't want me?"

"Then you'll hurt and you'll cry. After you do, you'll pick up the pieces of your life and go on. I have a strong daughter."

"And I have a wise and beautiful mother." A.J. leaned over to pick up both glasses of wine. After handing one to Clarissa, she raised hers in a toast. "What shall we drink to first?"

"Hope." Clarissa clinked glasses. "That's really all there is."

* * *

A.J. changed in the bedroom her mother always kept prepared for her. It hadn't mattered that she'd spent only a handful of nights in it over nearly ten years; Clarissa had labeled it hers, and hers it remained. Perhaps she would stay there tonight, after the wedding was over, the guests gone and the newlyweds off on their honeymoon. She might think better there, and tomorrow find the courage to listen to her mother's advice and follow her heart.

What if he didn't want her? What if he'd already forgotten her? A.J. faced the mirror but closed her eyes. There were too many "what ifs" to consider and only one thing she could be certain of. She loved him. If that meant taking risks, she didn't have a choice.

Straightening her shoulders, she opened her eyes and studied herself. The dress was romantic because her mother preferred it. She hadn't worn anything so blatantly feminine and flowing in years. Lace covered her bodice and caressed her throat, while the soft blue silk peeked out of the eyelets. The skirt swept to a bell at her ankles.

Not her usual style, A.J. thought again, but there was something appealing about the old-fashioned cut and the charm of lace. She picked up the nosegay of white roses that trailed with ribbon and felt foolishly like a bride herself. What would it be like to be preparing to bond yourself with another person, someone who loved and wanted you? There would be flutters in your stomach. She felt them in her own. Your throat would be dry. She lifted a hand to it. You would feel giddy with a combination of excitement and anxiety. She put her hand on the dresser to steady herself.

A premonition? Shaking it off, she stepped back from the mirror. It was her mother who would soon promise to love, honor and cherish. She glanced at her watch, then caught her breath. How had she managed to lose so much time? If she didn't put herself in gear, the guests would be arriving with no one to greet them.

Alex's children were the first to arrive. She'd only met them once, the evening before at dinner, and they were still a bit awkward and formal with one another. But when her future sister offered to help, A.J. decided to take her at her word. Within moments, cars began pulling up out front and she needed all the help she could get.

"A.J." Alex found her in the garden, escorting guests to chairs. "You look lovely."

He looked a little pale under his tan. The sign of nerves had her softening toward him. "Wait until you see your bride."

"I wish I could." He pulled at the knot in his tie. "I have to admit I'd feel easier if she were here to hold on to. You know, I talk to millions of people every night, but this..." He glanced around the garden. "This is a whole different ball game."

"I predict very high ratings." She brushed his cheek. "Why don't you slip inside and have a little shot of bourbon?"

"I think I might." He gave her shoulder a squeeze. "I think I just might."

A.J. watched him make his way to the back door before she turned back to her duties. And there was David. He stood at the edge of the garden, where the breeze just ruffled the ends of his hair. She wondered, as her heart began to thud, that she hadn't sensed him. She wondered, as the pleasure poured through her, if she'd wished him there.

He didn't approach her. A.J.'s fingers tightened on the wrapped stems of her flowers. She knew she had to take the first step.

She was so lovely. He thought she looked like something that had stepped out of a dream. The breeze that tinted the air with the scents of the garden teased the lace at her throat. As she walked to him, he thought of every empty hour he'd spent away from her.

"I'm glad you came."

He'd told himself he wouldn't, then he'd been dressed and driving south. She'd pulled him there, through her thoughts or through his own emotions, it didn't matter. "You seem to have it all under control."

She had nothing under control. She wanted to reach out to him, to tell him, but he seemed so cool and distant. "Yes, we're nearly ready to start. As soon as I get the rest of these people seated, I can go in for Clarissa."

"I'll take care of them."

"You don't have to. I—"

"I told you I would."

His clipped response cut her off. A.J. swallowed her longings and nodded. "Thanks. If you'll excuse me, then." She walked away, into the house, into her own room, where she could compose herself before she faced her mother.

Damn it! He swung away, cursing her, cursing himself, cursing everything. Just seeing her again had made him want to crawl. He wasn't a man who could live on his knees. She'd looked so cool, so fresh and lovely, and for a moment, just a moment, he'd thought he'd seen the emotions he needed in her eyes. Then she'd smiled at him as though he were just another guest at her mother's wedding.

He wasn't going to go on this way. David forced himself to make polite comments and usher well-wishers to their seats. Today, before it was over, he and A.J. Fields were going to come to terms. His terms. He'd planned it that way, hadn't he? It was about time one of his plans concerning her worked.

The orchestra A.J. had hired after auditioning at least a half-dozen played quietly on a wooden platform on the lawn. A trellis of sweet peas stood a few feet in front of the chairs. Composed and clear-eyed, A.J. walked through the garden to take her place. She glanced at Alex and gave him one quick smile of encouragement. Then Clarissa, dressed in dusky rose silk, stepped out of the house.

She looks like a queen, A.J. thought as her heart swelled. The guests rose as she walked through, but she had eyes only for Alex. And he, A.J. noted, looked as though no one else in the world existed but Clarissa.

They joined hands, and they promised.

The ceremony was short and traditional. A.J. watched her mother pledge herself, and fought back a sense of loss that vied with happiness. The words were simple, and ultimately so complex. The vows were timeless, and somehow completely new.

With her vision misted, her throat aching, she took her mother in her arms. "Oh, be happy, Momma."

"I am. I will be." She drew away just a little. "So will you."

Before A.J. could speak, Clarissa turned away and was swept up in an embrace by her new stepchildren.

There were guests to feed and glasses to fill. A.J. found keeping busy helped put her emotions on hold. In a few hours she'd be alone. Then she'd let them come. Now she laughed, brushed cheeks, toasted and felt utterly numb.

"Clarissa." David had purposely waited until she'd had a chance to breathe before he approached her. "You're beautiful."

"Thank you, David. I'm so glad you're here. She needs you."

He stiffened and only inclined his head. "Does she?"

With a sigh, Clarissa took both of his hands. When he felt the intensity, he nearly drew away. "Plans aren't necessary," she said quietly. "Feelings are."

David forced himself to relax. "You don't play fair."

"She's my daughter. In more ways than one."

"I understand that."

It took her only a moment, then she smiled. "Yes, you do. You might let her know. Aurora's an expert at blocking feelings, but she deals well with words. Talk to her?"

"Oh, I intend to."

"Good." Satisfied, Clarissa patted his hand. "Now I think you should try the quiche. I wheedled the recipe out of the caterer. It's fascinating."

"So are you." David leaned down to kiss her cheek.

A.J. all but exhausted herself. She moved from group to group, sipping champagne and barely tasting anything from the impressive display of food. The cake with its iced swans and hearts was cut and devoured. Wine flowed and music played. Couples danced on the lawn.

"I thought you'd like to know I read Steiger's script." After stepping beside her, David kept his eyes on the dancers. "It's extraordinary."

Business, she thought. It was best to keep their conversation on business. "Are you considering producing it?"

"Considering. That's a long way from doing it. I have a meeting with Steiger Monday."

"That's wonderful." She couldn't stop the surge of pleasure for him. She couldn't help showing it. "You'll be sensational."

"And if the script ever makes it to the screen, you'll have been the catalyst."

"I like to think so."

"I haven't waltzed since I was thirteen." David slipped a hand to her elbow and felt the jolt. "My mother made me dance with my cousin, and at the time I felt girls were a lower form of life. I've changed my mind since." His arm slid around her waist. "You're tense."

She concentrated on the count, on matching her steps to his, on anything but the feel of having him hold her again. "I want everything to be perfect for her."

"I don't think you need to worry about that anymore."

Her mother danced with Alex as though they were alone in the garden. "No." She sighed before she could prevent it. "I don't."

"You're allowed to feel a little sad." Her scent was there as he remembered, quietly tempting.

"No, it's selfish."

"It's normal," he corrected. "You're too hard on yourself."

"I feel as though I've lost her." She was going to cry. A.J. steeled herself against it.

"You haven't." He brushed his lips along her temple. "And the feeling will pass."

When he was kind, she was lost. When he was gentle, she was defenseless. "David." Her fingers tightened on his shoulder. "I missed you."

It cost her to say it. The first layer of pride that covered all the rest dissolved with the words. She felt his hand tense, then gentle on her waist.

"Aurora."

"Please, don't say anything now." The control she depended on wouldn't protect her now. "I just wanted you to know."

"We need to talk."

Even as she started to agree, the announcement blared over the mike. "All unmarried ladies, line up now for the bouquet toss."

"Come on, A.J." Her new stepsister, laughing and eager, grabbed her arm and hustled her along. "We have to see who's going to be next."

She wasn't interested in bouquets or giddy young women. Her life was on the line. Distracted, A.J. glanced around for David. She looked back in time to throw up her hands defensively before her mother's bouquet landed in her face. Embarrassed, A.J. accepted the congratulations and well-meaning teasing.

"Another sign?" Clarissa commented as she pecked her daughter's cheek.

"A sign that my mother has eyes in the back of her head and excellent aim." A.J. indulged herself with burying her face in the bouquet. It was sweet, and promising. "You should keep this."

"Oh, no. That would be bad luck and I don't intend to have any."

"I'm going to miss you, Momma."

She understood—she always had—but she smiled and gave A.J. another kiss. "I'll be back in two weeks."

She barely had time for another fierce embrace before her mother and Alex dashed off in a hail of rice and cheers.

Some guests left, others lingered. When the first streaks of sunset deepened the sky she watched the orchestra pack up their instruments.

"Long day."

She turned to David and reached out a hand before she could help it. "I thought you'd gone."

"Just got out of the way for a while. You did a good job."

"I can't believe it's done." She looked over as the last of the chairs were folded and carted away.

"I could use some coffee."

She smiled, trying to convince herself to be light. "Do we have any left?"

"I put some on before I came back out." He walked with her to the house. "Where were they going on their honeymoon?"

The house was so empty. Strange, she'd never noticed just how completely Clarissa had filled it. "Sailing." She laughed a little, then found herself looking helplessly around the kitchen. "I have a hard time picturing Clarissa hoisting sails."

"Here." He pulled a handkerchief out of his pocket. "Sit down and have a good cry. You're entitled."

"I'm happy for her." But the tears began to fall. "Alex is a wonderful man and I know he loves her."

"But she doesn't need you to take care of her anymore." He handed her a mug of coffee. "Drink."

Nodding, she sipped. "She's always needed me."

"She still does." He took the handkerchief and dried her cheeks himself. "Just in a different way."

"I feel like a fool."

"The trouble with you is you can't accept that you're supposed to feel like a fool now and again."

She blew her nose, unladylike and indignant. "I don't like it."

"Not supposed to. Have you finished crying?"

She sulked a moment, sniffled, then sipped more coffee. "Yes."

"Tell me again that you missed me."

"It was a moment of weakness," she murmured into the mug, but he took it away from her.

"No more evasions, Aurora. You're going to tell me what you want, what you feel."

"I want you back." She swallowed and wished he would say something instead of just staring at her.

"Go on."

"David, you're making this difficult."

"Yeah, I know." He didn't touch her, not yet. He needed more than that. "For both of us."

"All right." She steadied herself with a deep breath. "When you suggested we live together, I wasn't expecting it. I wanted to think it through, but you got angry. Well, since you've been away, I've had a chance to think it through. I don't see why we can't live together under those terms."

Always negotiating, he thought as he rubbed a hand over his chin. She still wasn't going to take that last step. "I've had a chance to think it through, too. And I've changed my mind."

He could have slapped her and not have knocked the wind from her so successfully. Rejection, when it came, was always painful, but it had never been like this. "I see." She turned away to pick up her coffee, but her hands weren't nearly steady enough.

"You did a great job on this wedding, A.J."

Closing her eyes, she wondered why she felt like laughing. "Thanks. Thanks a lot."

"Seems to me like you could plan another standing on your head."

"Oh, sure." She pressed her fingers to her eyes. "I might go into the business."

"No, I was thinking about just one more. Ours."

The tears weren't going to fall. She wouldn't let them. It helped to concentrate on that. "Our what?"

"Wedding. Aren't you paying attention?"

She turned slowly to see him watching her with what appeared to be mild amusement. "What are you talking about?"

"I noticed you caught the bouquet. I'm superstitious."

"This isn't funny." Before she could stalk from the room he had caught her close.

"Damn right it's not. It's not funny that I've spent eleven days and twelve nights thinking of little but you. It's not funny that every time I took a step closer, you took one back. Every time I'd plan something out, the whole thing would be blown to hell after five minutes with you."

"It's not going to solve anything to shout at me."

"It's not going to solve anything until you start listening and stop anticipating. Look, I didn't want this any more than you did. I liked my life just the way it was."

"That's fine, then. I liked my life, too."

"Then we both have a problem, because nothing's going to be quite the same again."

Why couldn't she breathe? Temper never made her breathless. "Why not?"

"Guess." He kissed her then, hard, angry, as if he wanted to kick out at both of them. But it only took an instant, a heartbeat. His lips softened, his hold gentled and she was molded to him. "Why don't you read my mind? Just this once, Aurora, open yourself up."

She started to shake her head, but his mouth was on hers again. The house was quiet. Outside, the birds serenaded the lowering sun. The light was dimming and there was nothing but that one room and that one moment. Feelings poured into her, feelings that once would have brought fear. Now they offered, requested and gave her everything she'd been afraid to hope for.

"David." Her arms tightened around him. "I need you to tell me. I couldn't bear to be wrong."

Hadn't he needed words? Hadn't he tried time and again to pry them out of her? Maybe it was time to give them to her. "The first time I met your mother, she said something to me about needing to understand or discover my own tenderness. That first weekend you stayed with me, I came home and found you sleeping on the bed. I looked at you, the woman who'd been my lover, and fell in love. The problem was I didn't know how to make you fall in love with me."

"I already had. I didn't think you—"

"The problem was you did think. Too much." He drew her away, only to look at her. "So did I. Be civilized. Be careful. Wasn't that the way we arranged things?"

"It seemed like the right way." She swallowed and moved closer. "It didn't work for me. When I fell in love with you, all I could think was that I'd ruin everything by wanting too much."

"And I thought if I asked, you'd be gone before the words were out." He brushed his lips over her brow. "We wasted time thinking when we should have been feeling."

She should be cautious, but there was such ease, such quiet satisfaction, in just holding him. "I was afraid you'd never be able to accept what I am."

"So was I." He kissed one cheek, then the other. "We were both wrong."

"I need you to be sure. I need to know that it doesn't matter."

"Aurora. I love you, who you are, what you are, how you are. I don't know how else to tell you."

She closed her eyes. Clarissa and she had been right to drink to hope. That was all there was. "You just found the best way."

"There's more." He held her, waiting until she looked at him again. And he saw, as he'd needed to, her heart in her eyes. "I want to spend my life with you. Have children with you. There's never been another woman who's made me want those things."

She took his face in her hands and lifted her mouth to his. "I'm going to see to it there's never another."

"Tell me how you feel."

"I love you."

He held her close, content. "Tell me what you want."

"A lifetime. Two, if we can manage it."

* * * * *

LAWLESS

To Ruth, Marianne and Jan,
For taking me to Silverado

Chapter 1

He wanted a drink. Whiskey, cheap and warm. After six weeks on the trail, he wanted the same kind of woman. Some men usually managed to get what they wanted. He was one of them. Still, the woman could wait, Jake decided as he leaned against the bar. The whiskey couldn't.

He had another ninety long, dusty miles to go before he got home. If anybody could call a frying pan like Lone Bluff home. Some did, Jake thought as he signaled for a bottle and took his first gut-clenching gulp. Some had to.

For himself, home was usually the six feet of space where his shadow fell. But for the past few months Lone Bluff had been as good a place as any. He could get a room there, a bath and a willing woman, all at a reasonable price. It was a town where a man could avoid trouble—or find it, depending on his mood.

For now, with the dust of the trail still scratchy in his throat and his stomach empty except for a shot of whiskey,

Jake was just too tired for trouble. He'd have another drink, and whatever passed for a meal in this two-bit town blown up from the desert, then he'd be on his way.

The afternoon sunlight poured in over the swinging doors at the saloon's entrance. Someone had tacked a picture of a woman in red feathers to the wall, but that was the extent of the female company. Places like this didn't run to providing women for their clientele. Just to liquor and cards.

Even towns like this one had a saloon or two. A man could depend upon it, the way he could depend on little else. It wasn't yet noon, and half the tables were occupied. The air was thick with the smoke from the cigars the bartender sold, two for a penny. The whiskey went for a couple of bits and burned a line of fire straight from the throat to the gut. If the owner had added a real woman in red feathers, he could have charged double that and not heard a single complaint.

The place stank of whiskey, sweat and smoke. But Jake figured he didn't smell too pretty himself. He'd ridden hard from New Mexico, and he would have ridden straight through to Lone Bluff except he'd wanted to rest his horse and fill his own stomach with something other than the jerky in his saddlebags.

Saloons always looked better at night, and this one was no exception. Its bar was grimy from hundreds of hands and elbows, dulled by spilled drinks, scarred by matchtips. The floor was nothing but hard-packed dirt that had absorbed its share of whiskey and blood. He'd been in worse, Jake reflected, wondering if he should allow himself the luxury of rolling a cigarette now or wait until after a meal.

He could buy more tobacco if he had a yearning for another. There was a month's pay in his pocket. And he'd be damned if he'd ever ride cattle again. That was a life for the young and stupid—or maybe just the stupid.

When his money ran low he could always take a job riding shotgun on the stage through Indian country. The line was always looking for a man who was handy with a gun, and it was better than riding at the back end of a steer. It was the middle of 1875 and the easterners were still coming—looking for gold and land, following dreams. Some of them stopped in the Arizona Territory on their way to California because they ran out of money or energy or time.

Their hard luck, Jake thought as he downed his second whiskey. He'd been born here, and he still didn't figure it was the most hospitable place on the map. It was hot and hard and stingy. It suited him just fine.

"Redman?"

Jake lifted his eyes to the dingy glass behind the bar. He saw the man behind him. Young, wiry and edgy. His brown hat was tipped down low over his eyes, and sweat glistened on his neck. Jake nearly sighed. He knew the type too well. The kind that went out of his way looking for trouble. The kind that didn't know that if you hung around long enough it found you, anyway.

"Yeah?"

"Jake Redman?"

"So?"

"I'm Barlow, Tom Barlow." He wiped his palms on his thighs. "They call me Slim."

The way he said it, Jake was sure the kid expected the name to be recognized…shuddered over. He decided the whiskey wasn't good enough for a third drink. He dropped some money on the bar, making sure his hands were well clear of his guns.

"There a place where a man can get a steak in this town?" Jake asked the bartender.

"Down to Grody's." The man moved cautiously out of range. "We don't want any trouble in here."

Jake gave him a long, cool look. "I'm not giving you any."

"I'm talking to you, Redman." Barlow spread his legs and let his hand hover over the butt of his gun. A mean-looking scar ran across the back of his hand from his index finger to his wrist. He wore his holster high, a single rig with the leather worn smooth at the buckle. It paid to notice details.

Easy, moving no more than was necessary, Jake met his eyes. "Something you want to say?"

"You got a reputation for being fast. Heard you took out Freemont in Tombstone."

Jake turned fully. As he moved, the swinging door flew back. At least one of the saloon's customers had decided to move to safer ground. The kid was packing a .44 Colt, its black rubber grip well tended. Jake didn't doubt there were notches in it. Barlow looked like the type who would take pride in killing.

"You heard right."

Barlow's fingers curled and uncurled. Two men playing poker in the corner let their hands lie to watch and made a companionable bet on the higher-stakes game in front of them. "I'm faster. Faster than Freemont. Faster than you. I run this town."

Jake glanced around the saloon, then back into Barlow's dark, edgy eyes. "Congratulations." He would have walked away, but Barlow shifted to block him. The move had Jake narrowing his eyes. The look came into them, the hard, flat look that made a smart man give way. "Cut your teeth on somebody else. I want a steak and a bed."

"Not in my town."

Patience wasn't Jake's long suit, but he wasn't in the

mood to waste time on a gunman looking to sharpen his reputation. "You want to die over a piece of meat?"

Jake watched the grin spread over Barlow's face. He didn't think he was going to die, Jake thought wearily. His kind never did.

"Why don't you come find me in about five years?" Jake told him. "I'll be happy to put a bullet in you."

"I found you now. After I kill you, there won't be a man west of the Mississippi who won't know Slim Barlow."

For some—for many—no other reason was needed to draw and fire. "Make it easy on both of us." Jake started for the doors again. "Just tell them you killed me."

"I hear your mother was a squaw." Barlow grinned when Jake stopped and turned again. "Guess that's where you got that streak of yellow."

Jake was used to rage. It could fill a man from stomach to brain and take over. When he felt it rising up, he clamped down on it. If he was going to fight—and it seemed inevitable—he preferred to fight cold.

"My grandmother was Apache."

Barlow grinned again, then wiped his mouth with the back of his left hand. "That makes you a stinking breed, don't it? A stinking yellow breed. We don't want no Indians around here. Guess I'll have to clean up the town a little."

He went for his gun. Jake saw the move, not in Barlow's hands but in his eyes. Cold and fast and without regret, Jake drew his own. There were those who saw him who said it was like lightning and thunder. There was a flash of steel, then the roar of the bullet. He hardly moved from where he stood, shooting from the hip, trusting instinct and experience. In a smooth, almost careless movement, he replaced his gun. Tom they-call-me-Slim Barlow was sprawled on the barroom floor.

Jake passed through the swinging doors and walked to his horse. He didn't know whether he'd killed his man or not, and he didn't care. The whole damn mess had ruined his appetite.

Sarah was mortally afraid she was going to lose the miserable lunch she'd managed to bolt down at the last stop. How anyone—*anyone*—survived under these appalling conditions, she'd never know. The West, as far as she could see, was only fit for snakes and outlaws.

She closed her eyes, patted the sweat from her neck with her handkerchief, and prayed that she'd make it through the next few hours. At least she could thank God she wouldn't have to spend another night in one of those horrible stage depots. She'd been afraid she would be murdered in her bed. If one could call that miserable sheetless rope cot a bed. And privacy? Well, there simply hadn't been any.

It didn't matter now, she told herself. She was nearly there. After twelve long years, she was going to see her father again and take care of him in the beautiful house he'd built outside Lone Bluff.

When she'd been six, he'd left her in the care of the good sisters and gone off to make his fortune. There had been nights, many nights, when Sarah had cried herself to sleep from missing him. Then, as the years had passed, she'd had to take out the faded daguerreotype to remember his face. But he'd always written to her. His penmanship had been strained and childish, but there had been so much love in his letters. And so much hope.

Once a month she'd received word from her father from whatever point he'd stopped at on his journey west. After eighteen months, and eighteen letters, he'd written from the

Arizona Territory, where he'd settled, and where he would build his fortune.

He'd convinced her that he'd been right to leave her in Philadelphia, in the convent school, where she could be raised and educated as a proper young lady should. Until, Sarah remembered, she was old enough to travel across the country to live with him. Now she was nearly eighteen, and she was going to join him. Undoubtedly the house he'd built, however grand, required a woman's touch.

Since he'd never married again, Sarah imagined her father a crusty bachelor, never quite certain where his clean collars were or what the cook was serving for dinner. She'd soon fix all that.

A man in his position needed to entertain, and to entertain he needed a hostess. Sarah Conway knew exactly how to give an elegant dinner party and a formal ball.

True, what she'd read of the Arizona Territory was distressing, to say the least. Stories of ruthless gunmen and wild Indians. But, after all, this was 1875. Sarah had no doubt that even so distant a place as Arizona was under control by this time. The reports she'd read had obviously been exaggerated to sell newspapers and penny dreadfuls.

They hadn't exaggerated about the climate.

She shifted for a better position. The bulk of the woman beside her, and her own corset, gave her little room for relief. And the smell. No matter how often Sarah sprinkled lavender water on her handkerchief, there was no escaping it. There were seven passengers, crammed all but elbow-to-knee inside the rattling stagecoach. It was airless, and that accentuated the stench of sweat and foul breath and whatever liquor it was that the man across from her continued to drink. Right from the bottle. At first, his pockmarked face and grimy neckcloth had fascinated her. But when he'd offered her a drink, she had fallen back on a woman's best defense. Her dignity.

It was difficult to look dignified when her clothes were sticking to her and her hair was drooping beneath her bonnet. It was all but impossible to maintain her decorum when the plump woman beside her began to gnaw on what appeared to be a chicken leg. But when Sarah was determined, she invariably prevailed.

The good sisters had never been able to pray or punish or lecture her stubbornness out of her. Now, with her chin slightly lifted and her body braced against the bouncing sway of the coach, she kept her eyes firmly shut and ignored her fellow passengers.

She'd seen enough of the Arizona landscape, if one could call it that. As far as she could see, the entire territory was nothing but miles of sunbaked desert. True, the first cacti she'd seen had been fascinating. She'd even considered sketching a few of them. Some were as big as a man, with arms that stretched up to the sky. Others were short and squat and covered with hundreds of dangerous-looking needles. Still, after she'd seen several dozen of them, and little else, they'd lost their novelty.

The rocks were interesting, she supposed. The buttes and flat-topped mesas growing out of the sand had a certain rugged charm, particularly when they rose up into the deep, endless blue of the sky. But she preferred the tidy streets of Philadelphia, with their shops and tearooms.

Being with her father would make all the difference. She could live anywhere, as long as she was with him again. He'd be proud of her. She needed him to be proud of her. All these years she'd worked and learned and practiced so that she could become the proper, well-educated young lady he wanted his daughter to be.

She wondered if he'd recognize her. She'd sent him a small, framed self-portrait just last Christmas, but she wasn't certain it had been a truly good likeness. She'd always thought it was too bad she wasn't pretty, in the soft, round way of her dear friend Lucilla. Still, her complexion was good, and Sarah comforted herself with that. Unlike Lucilla, she never required any help from the little pots of rouge the sisters so disapproved of. In fact, there were times she thought her complexion just a bit too healthy. Her mouth was full and wide when she would have preferred a delicate Cupid's bow, and her eyes were an unremarkable brown rather than the blue that would have suited her blond hair so much better. Still, she was trim and neat—or she had been neat before she'd begun this miserable journey.

It would all be worthwhile soon. When she greeted her father and they settled into the lovely house he'd built. Four bedrooms. Imagine. And a parlor with windows facing west. Delightful. Undoubtedly, she'd have to do some redecorating. Men never thought about such niceties as curtains and throw rugs. She'd enjoy it. Once she had the glass shining and fresh flowers in the vases he would see how much he needed her. Then all the years in between would have been worthwhile.

Sarah felt a line of sweat trickle down her back. The first thing she wanted was a bath—a nice, cool bath laced with the fragrant lilac salts Lucilla had given her as a parting gift. She sighed. She could almost feel it, her body free of the tight corset and hot clothes, the water sliding over her skin. Scented. Delicious. Almost sinful.

When the coach jolted, Sarah was thrown against the fat woman to her left. Before she could right herself, a spray of rotgut whiskey soaked her skirts.

"Sir!" But before she could lecture him she heard the shot, and the screams.

"Indians!" The chicken leg went flying, and the fat woman clutched Sarah to her bosom like a shield. "We're all going to be murdered."

"Don't be absurd." Sarah struggled to free herself, not certain if she was more annoyed by the sudden dangerous speed of the coach or the spot of chicken grease on her new skirt. She leaned toward the window to call to the driver. As she did, the face of the shotgun rider slid into view, inches from hers. He hung there, upside down, for seconds only. But that was long enough for Sarah to see the blood trickling from his mouth, and the arrow in his heart. Even as the woman beside her screamed again, his body thudded to the ground.

"Indians!" she shouted again. "God have mercy."

"Apaches," the man with the whiskey said as he finished off the bottle. "Must've got the driver, too. We're on a runaway." So saying, he drew his gun, made his way to the opposite window and began firing methodically.

Dazed, Sarah continued to stare out the window. She could hear screams and whoops and the thunder of horses' hooves. Like devils, she thought dully. They sounded like devils. That was impossible. Ridiculous. The United States was nearly a century old. Ulysses S. Grant was president. Steamships crossed the Atlantic in less than two weeks. Devils simply didn't exist in this day and age.

Then she saw one, bare chested, hair flying, on a tough paint pony. Sarah looked straight into his eyes. She could see the fever in them, just as she could see the bright streaks of paint on his face and the layer of dust that covered his gleaming skin. He raised his bow. She could have counted the feathers in the arrow. Then, suddenly, he flew off the back of his horse.

It was like a play, she thought, and she had to pinch herself viciously to keep from swooning.

Another horseman came into view, riding low, with pistols in both hands. He wore a gray hat over dark hair, and his skin was nearly as dark as that of the Apache she'd seen. In his eyes, as they met hers, she saw not fever, but ice.

He didn't shoot her, as she'd been almost certain he would, but fired over his shoulder, using his right hand, then his left, even as an arrow whizzed by his head.

Amazing, she thought as a thudding excitement began to race with her terror. He was magnificent sweat and grime on his face, ice in his eyes, his lean, tense body glued to the racing horse. Then the fat lady grabbed her again and began to wail.

Jake fired behind him, clinging to the horse with his knees as easily as any Apache brave. He'd caught a glimpse of the passengers, in particular a pale, dark-eyed girl in a dark blue bonnet. His Apache cousins would've enjoyed that one, he thought dispassionately as he holstered his guns.

He could see the driver, an arrow piercing one shoulder, struggling to regain control of the horses. He was doing his best, despite the pain, but he wasn't strong enough to shove the brake down. Swearing, Jake pushed his horse on until he was close enough to the racing coach to gain a handhold.

For one endless second he hung by his fingers alone. Sarah caught a glimpse of a dusty shirt and one powerful forearm, a long, leather-clad leg and a scarred boot. Then he was up, scrambling over the top of the coach. The woman beside her screamed again, then fainted dead away when they stopped. Too terrified to sit, Sarah pushed open the door of the coach and climbed out.

The man in the gray hat was already getting down. "Ma'am," he said as he moved past her.

She pressed a hand to her drumming heart. No hero had ever been so heroic. "You saved our lives," she managed, but he didn't even glance her way.

"Redman." The passenger who'd drunk the whiskey stepped out. "Glad you stopped by."

"Lucius." Jake picked up the reins of his horse and proceeded to calm him. "There were only six of them."

"They're getting away," Sarah blurted out. "Are you just going to let them get away?"

Jake looked at the cloud of dust from the retreating horses, then back at Sarah. He had time now for a longer, more interested study. She was tiny, with *East* stamped all over her pretty face. Her hair, the color of honeycombs, was tumbling down from her bonnet. She looked as if she'd just stepped out of the schoolroom, and she smelled like a cheap saloon. He had to grin.

"Yep."

"But you can't." Her idea of a hero was rapidly crumbling. "They killed a man."

"He knew the chance he was taking. Riding the line pays good."

"They murdered him," Sarah said again, as if she were speaking to a very dull pupil. "He's lying back there with an arrow through his heart." When Jake said nothing, just walked his horse to the back of the coach, Sarah followed him. "At least you can go back and pick up that poor man's body. We can't just leave him there."

"Dead's dead."

"That's a hideous thing to say." Because she felt ill, Sarah dragged off her bonnet and used it to fan hot air around her face. "The man deserves a decent burial. I couldn't possibly— What are you doing?"

Jake spared her a glance. Mighty pretty, he decided. Even prettier without the bonnet hiding her hair. "Hitching my horse."

She dropped her arm to her side. She no longer felt ill. She was certainly no longer impressed. She was furious. "Sir, you appear to care more about that horse than you do about the man."

He stooped under the reins. For a moment they stood face-to-face, with the sun beating down and the smell of blood and dust all around them. "That's right, seeing as the man's dead and my horse isn't. I'd get back inside, ma'am. It'd be a shame if you were still standing here when the Apaches decide to come back."

That made her stop and look around uneasily. The desert was still, but for the cry of a bird she didn't recognize as a vulture. "I'll go back and get him myself," she said between her teeth.

"Suit yourself." Jake walked to the front of the coach. "Get that stupid woman inside," he told Lucius. "And don't give her any more to drink."

Sarah's mouth fell open. Before she could retaliate, Lucius had her by the arm. "Now, don't mind Jake, miss. He just says whatever he damn pleases. He's right, though. Those Apaches might turn back this way. We sure don't want to be sitting here if they do."

With what little dignity she had left, Sarah stepped back into the coach. The fat woman was still sobbing, leaning heavily against a tight-lipped man in a bowler. Sarah wedged herself into her corner as the stage jumped forward again. Securing her bonnet, she frowned at Lucius.

"Who is that horrible man?"

"Jake?" Lucius settled back. There was nothing he liked better than a good fight, particularly when he stayed alive to enjoy it. "That's Jake Redman, miss. I don't mind saying we was lucky he passed this way. Jake hits what he aims at."

"Indeed." She wanted to be aloof, but she remembered the murderous look in the Apache's eyes when he'd ridden beside the window. "I suppose we do owe him our gratitude, but he seemed cold-blooded about it."

"More'n one says he's got ice in his veins. Along with some Apache blood."

"You mean he's... Indian?"

"On his grandmother's side, I hear." Because his bottle was empty, Lucius settled for a plug of tobacco. He tucked it comfortably in his cheek. "Wouldn't want to cross him. No, ma'am, I sure wouldn't. Mighty comforting to know he's on your side when things heat up."

What kind of man killed his own kind? With a shiver, Sarah fell silent again. She didn't want to think about it.

On top of the stage, Jake kept the team to a steady pace. He preferred the freedom and mobility of having a single horse under him. The driver held a hand to his wounded shoulder and refused the dubious comfort of the coach.

"We could use you back on the line," he told Jake.

"Thinking about it." But he was really thinking about the little lady with the big brown eyes and the honey-colored hair. "Who's the girl? The young one in blue?"

"Conway. From Philadelphia." The driver breathed slow and easy against the pain. "Says she's Matt Conway's daughter."

"That so?" Miss Philadelphia Conway sure as hell didn't take after her old man. But Jake remembered that Matt bragged about his daughter back east from time to time. Especially after he started a bottle. "Come to visit her father?"

"Says she's come to stay."

Jake gave a quick, mirthless laugh. "Won't last a week. Women like that don't."

"She's planning on it." With a jerk of his thumb, the driver indicated the trunks strapped to the coach. "Most of that's hers."

With a snort, Jake adjusted his hat. "Figures."

Sarah caught her first glimpse of Lone Bluff from the stagecoach window. It spread like a jumble of rock at the base of the mountains. Hard, cold-looking mountains, she thought with a shudder, fooled—as the inexperienced always were—into thinking they were much closer than they actually were.

She'd forgotten herself enough to crane her head out. But she couldn't get another look at Jake Redman unless she pushed half her body through the opening. She really wasn't interested anyway, she assured herself. Unless it was purely for entertainment purposes. When she wrote back to Lucilla and the sisters, she wanted to be able to describe all the local oddities.

The man was certainly odd. He'd ridden like a warrior one moment, undoubtedly risking his life for a coachful of strangers. Then, the next minute, he'd dismissed his Christian duty and left a poor soul beside a lonely desert road. And he'd called her stupid.

Never in her life had anyone ever accused Sarah Conway of being stupid. In fact, both her intelligence and her breeding were widely admired. She was well-read, fluent in French and more than passably accomplished on the pianoforte.

Taking the time to retie her bonnet, Sarah reminded herself that she hardly needed approval from a man like Jake

Redman. After she was reunited with her father and took her place in the local society, it was doubtful she'd ever see him again.

She'd thank him properly, of course. Sarah drew a fresh handkerchief from her reticule and blotted her temples. Just because he had no manners was no excuse to forget her own. She supposed she might even ask her father to offer him some monetary reward.

Pleased with the idea, Sarah looked out the window again. And blinked. Surely this wasn't Lone Bluff. Her father would never have settled in this grimy excuse for a town. It was no more than a huddle of buildings and a wide patch of dust that served as a road. They passed two saloons side by side, a dry goods store and what appeared to be a rooming house. Slack-legged horses were hitched to posts, their tails switching lazily at huge black flies. A handful of young boys with dirty faces began to race alongside the coach, shouting and firing wooden pistols. Sarah saw two women in faded gingham walking arm in arm on some wooden planks that served as a sidewalk.

When the coach stopped, she heard Jake call out for a doctor. Passengers were already streaming out through the doors on both sides. Resigned, Sarah stepped out and shook out her skirts.

"Mr. Redman." The brim of her bonnet provided inadequate shade. She was forced to lift her hand over her eyes. "Why have we stopped here?"

"End of the line, ma'am." A couple of men were already lifting the driver down, so he swung himself around to unstrap the cases on top of the coach.

"End of the line? But where are we?"

He paused long enough to glance down at her. She saw

then that his eyes were darker than she'd imagined. A smoky slate gray. "Welcome to Lone Bluff."

Letting out a long, slow breath, she turned. Sunlight treated the town cruelly. It showed all the dirt, all the wear, and it heightened the pungent smell of horses.

Dear God, so this was it. The end of the line. The end of her line. It didn't matter, she told herself. She wouldn't be living in town. And surely before long the gold in her father's mine would bring more people and progress. No, it didn't matter at all. Sarah squared her shoulders. The only thing that mattered was seeing her father again.

She turned around in time to see Jake toss one of her trunks down to Lucius.

"Mr. Redman, please take care of my belongings."

Jake hefted the next case and tossed it to a grinning Lucius. "Yes, ma'am."

Biting down on her temper, she waited until he jumped down beside her. "Notwithstanding my earlier sentiments, I'm very grateful to you, Mr. Redman, for coming to our aid. You proved yourself to be quite valiant. I'm sure my father will want to repay you for seeing that I arrived safely."

Jake didn't think he'd ever heard anyone talk quite so fine since he'd spent a week in St. Louis. Tipping back his hat, he looked at her, long enough to make Sarah flush. "Forget it."

Forget it? Sarah thought as he turned his back and walked away. If that was the way the man accepted gratitude, she certainly would. With a sweep of her skirts she moved to the side of the road to wait for her father.

Jake strode into the rooming house with his saddlebag slung over his shoulder. It was never particularly clean, and it always smelled of onions and strong coffee. There were a couple of bullet holes in the wall. He'd put one of them there personally. Since the door was propped open, flies buzzed merrily in and out of the cramped entrance.

"Maggie." Jake tipped his hat to the woman who stood at the base of the stairs. "Got a room?"

Maggie O'Rourke was as tough as one of her fried steaks. She had iron-gray hair pinned back from a face that should have been too skinny for wrinkles. But wrinkles there were, a maze of them. Her tiny blue eyes seemed to peek out of the folds of a worn blanket. She ran her business with an iron fist, a Winchester repeater and an eye for a dollar.

She took one look at Jake and successfully hid her pleasure at seeing him. "Well, look what the cat dragged in," she said, the musical brogue of her native country still evident in her thin voice. "Got the law on your tail, Jake, or a woman?"

"Neither." He kicked the door shut with his boot, wondering why he always came back here. The old woman never gave him a moment's peace, and her cooking could kill a man. "You got a room, Maggie? And some hot water?"

"You got a dollar?" She held out her thin hand. When Jake dropped a coin into it, she tested it with the few good teeth she had left. It wasn't that she didn't trust Jake. She did. She just didn't trust the United States government. "Might as well take the one you had before. No one's in it."

"Fine." He started up the steps.

"Ain't had too much excitement since you left. Couple drifters shot each other over at the Bird Cage. Worthless pair, the both of them. Only one dead, though. Sheriff sent the other on his way after the doc patched him up. Young Mary Sue Brody got herself in trouble with that Mitchell boy. Always said she was a fast thing, that Mary Sue. Had a right proper wedding, though. Just last month."

Jake kept walking, but that didn't stop Maggie. One of

the privileges in running a rooming house was giving and receiving gossip.

"What a shame about old Matt Conway."

That stopped him. He turned. Maggie was still at the base of the steps, using the edge of her apron to swipe halfheartedly at the dust on the banister. "What about Matt Conway?"

"Got himself killed in that worthless mine of his. A cave-in. Buried him the day before yesterday."

Chapter 2

The heat was murderous. A plume of thin yellow dust rose each time a rider passed, then hung there to clog the still air. Sarah longed for a long, cool drink and a seat in the shade. From the looks of things, there wasn't a place in town where a lady could go to find such amenities. Even if there were, she was afraid to leave her trunks on the side of the road and risk missing her father.

She'd been so sure he would be waiting for her. But then, a man in his position could have been held up by a million things. Work at the mine, a problem with an employee, perhaps last-minute preparations for her arrival.

She'd waited twelve years, she reminded herself, resisting the urge to loosen her collar. She could wait a little longer.

A buckboard passed, spewing up more dust, so that she was forced to lift a handkerchief to her mouth. Her dark blue traveling skirt and her neat matching jacket with its fancy black braid were covered with dust. With a sigh, she glanced down at her blouse, which was drooping hopelessly and now seemed more yellow than white. It wasn't really vanity. The sisters had never given her a chance to develop any. She was concerned that her father would see her for the first time when she was travel-stained and close to exhaustion. She'd wanted to look her best for him at this first meeting. All she could do now was retie the bow at her chin, then brush hopelessly at her skirts.

She looked a fright. But she'd make it up to him. She would wear her brand-new white muslin gown for dinner tonight, the one with the charming rosebuds embroidered all over the skirt. Her kid slippers were dyed pink to match. He'd be proud of her.

If only he'd come, she thought, and take her away from here.

Jake crossed the street after losing the battle he'd waged with himself. It wasn't his business, and it wasn't his place to tell her. But for the past ten minutes he'd been watching her standing at the side of the road, waiting. He'd been able to see, too clearly, the look of hope that sprang into her eyes each time a horse or wagon approached. Somebody had to tell the woman that her father wasn't going to meet her.

Sarah saw him coming. He walked easily, despite the guns at his sides. As if they had always been there. As if they always would be. They rode low on his hips, shifting with his movements. And he kept his eyes on her in a way that she was certain a man shouldn't keep his eyes on a woman—unless she was his own. When she felt her heart flutter, she automatically stiffened her backbone.

It was Lucilla who was always talking about fluttering hearts. It was Lucilla who painted romantic pictures of lawless men and lawless places. Sarah preferred a bit more reality in her dreams.

"Ma'am." He was surprised that she hadn't already swooned under the power of the afternoon sun. Maybe she was tougher than she looked, but he doubted it.

"Mr. Redman." Determined to be gracious, she allowed her lips to curve ever so slightly at the corners.

He tucked his thumbs into the pockets of his pants. "I got some news about your father."

She smiled fully, beautifully, so that her whole face lit up with it. Her eyes turned to gold in the sunlight. Jake felt the punch, like a bullet in the chest.

"Oh, did he leave word for me? Thank you for letting me know. I might have waited here for hours."

"Ma'am—"

"Is there a note?"

"No." He wanted to get this done, and done quickly. "Matt's dead. There was an accident at his mine." He was braced for weeping, for wild wailing, but her eyes filled with fury, not tears.

"How dare you? How dare you lie to me about something like that?" She would have brushed past him, but Jake clamped a hand over her arm. Sarah's first reaction was simple indignation at being manhandled. Then she looked up at him, really looked, and said nothing.

"He was buried two days ago." He felt her recoil, then go still. The fury drained from her eyes, even as the color drained from her cheeks. "Don't go fainting on me."

It was true. She could see the truth on his face as clearly as she could see his distaste at being the one to tell her. "An accident?" she managed.

"A cave-in." He was relieved that she wasn't going to faint, but he didn't care for the glassy look in her eyes. "You'll want to talk to the sheriff."

"The sheriff?" she repeated dully.

"His office is across the street."

She just shook her head and stared at him. Her eyes *were* gold, Jake decided. The color of the brandy he sometimes drank at the Silver Star. Right now they were huge and full of hurt. He watched her bite down on her bottom lip in a gesture he knew meant she was fighting not to let go of the emotions he saw so clearly in her eyes.

If she'd fainted, he'd happily have left her on the road in the care of whatever woman happened to pass by. But she was hanging on, and it moved something in him.

Swearing, Jake shifted his grip from her arm to her elbow and guided her across the street. He was damned if he could figure out how he'd elected himself responsible.

Sheriff Barker was at his desk, bent over some paperwork and a cup of sweetened coffee. He was balding rapidly. Every morning he took the time to comb what hair he had left over the spreading bare spot on top of his head. He had the beginnings of a paunch brought on by his love of his wife's baking. He kept the law in Lone Bluff, but he didn't worry overmuch about the order. It wasn't that he was corrupt, just lazy.

He glanced up as Jake entered. Then he sighed and sent tobacco juice streaming into the spittoon in the corner. When Jake Redman was around, there was usually work to be done.

"So you're back." The wad of tobacco gave Barker a permanently swollen jaw. "Thought you might take a fancy to New Mexico." His brows lifted when Jake ushered Sarah inside. There was enough gentleman left in him to bring him to his feet. "Ma'am."

"This is Matt Conway's daughter."

"Well, I'll be damned. Begging your pardon, ma'am. I was just fixing to send you a letter."

"Sheriff." She had to pause a moment to find her balance. She would not fall apart, not here, in front of strangers.

"Barker, ma'am." He came around the desk to offer her a chair.

"Sheriff Barker." Sarah sat, praying she'd be able to stand again. "Mr. Redman has just told me that my father..." She couldn't say it. No matter how weak or cowardly it might be, she just couldn't say the words.

"Yes, ma'am. I'm mighty sorry. Couple of kids wandered on up by the mine playing games and found him. Appears he was working the mine when some of the beams gave way." When she said nothing, Barker cleared his throat and opened the top drawer of his desk. "He had this watch on him, and his tobacco." He'd had his pipe, as well, but since it had been broken—like most of Conway's bones—Barker hadn't thought anyone would want it. "We figured he'd want to be buried with his wedding ring on."

"Thank you." As if in a trance, she took the watch and the tobacco pouch from him. She remembered the watch. The tears almost won when she remembered how he'd taken it out to check the time before he'd left her in Mother Superior's lemony-smelling office. "I want to see where he's buried. My trunks will need to be taken out to his house."

"Miss Conway, if you don't mind me offering some advice, you don't want to stay way out there. It's no place for a young lady like you, all alone and all. My wife'll be happy to have you stay with us for a few days. Until the stage heads east again."

"It's kind of you to offer." She braced a hand on the chair and managed to stand again. "But I'd prefer to spend the night in my father's house." She swallowed and discovered that her throat was hurtfully dry. "Is there... Do I owe you anything for the burial?"

"No, ma'am. We take care of our own around here."

"Thank you." She needed air. With the watch clutched in her hand, she pushed through the door. Leaning against a post, she tried to catch her breath.

"You ought to take the sheriff up on his offer."

She turned her head to give Jake an even look. She could only be grateful that he made her angry enough to help her hold off her grief. He hadn't offered a word of sympathy. Not one. Well, she was glad of it.

"I'm going to stay in my father's house. Will you take me?"

He rubbed a hand over his chin. He hadn't shaved in a week. "I've got things to do."

"I'll pay you," she said quickly when he started to walk away.

He stopped and looked back at her. She was determined, all right. He wanted to see how determined. "How much?"

"Two dollars." When he only continued to look at her, she said between her teeth, "Five."

"You got five?"

Disgusted, Sarah dug in her reticule. "There."

Jake looked at the bill in her hand. "What's that?"

"It's five dollars."

"Not around here it ain't. Around here it's paper."

Sarah pushed the bill back into her reticule and pulled out a coin. "Will this do?"

Jake took the coin and turned it over in his hand, then stuck it in his pocket. "That'll do fine. I'll get a wagon."

Miserable man, she thought as he strode away. She hated him. And hated even more the fact that she needed him.

During the long, hot ride in the open wagon, she said nothing. She no longer cared about the desolation of the landscape, the heat or the cold-bloodedness of the man beside her. Her emotions seemed to have shriveled up inside her. Every mile they'd gone was just another mile behind her.

Jake Redman didn't seem to need conversation. He drove in silence, armed with a rifle across his lap, as well as the pistols he carried. There hadn't been trouble out here in quite some time, but the attack on the coach had warned him that that could change.

He'd recognized Strong Wolf in the party that had attacked the stage. If the Apache brave had decided to raid in the area, he would hit the Conway place sooner or later.

They passed no one. They saw only sand and rock and a hawk out hunting.

When he reined the horses in, Sarah saw nothing but a small adobe house and a few battered sheds on a patch of thirsty land.

"Why are we stopping here?"

Jake jumped down from the wagon. "This is Matt Conway's place."

"Don't be ridiculous." Because it didn't appear that he was going to come around and assist her, Sarah struggled down herself. "Mr. Redman, I paid you to take me to my father's home and I expect you to keep the bargain."

Before she could stop him, he dumped one of her trunks on the ground. "What do you think you're doing?"

"Delivering your luggage."

"Don't you take another piece off that wagon." Surprising them both, Sarah grabbed his shirt and pulled him around to face her. "I insist you take me to my father's house immediately."

She wasn't just stupid, Jake thought. She was irritating. "Fine." He clipped her around the waist and hauled her over his shoulder.

At first she was too shocked to move. No man had ever

touched her before. Now this, this *ruffian* had his hands all over her. And they were alone. Totally alone. Sarah began to struggle as he pushed open the door of the hut. Before she could draw the breath to scream, he was dropping her to her feet again.

"That good enough for you?"

She stared at him, visions of a hundred calamities that could befall a defenseless woman dancing in her brain. She stepped back, breathing hard, and prayed she could reason with him. "Mr. Redman, I have very little money of my own—hardly enough worth stealing."

Something came into his eyes that had her breath stopping altogether. He looked more than dangerous now. He looked fatal. "I don't steal." The light coming through the low doorway arched around him. She moistened her lips.

"Are you going to kill me?"

He nearly laughed. Instead, he leaned against the wall. Something about her was eating at him. He didn't know what or why, but he didn't like it. Not one damn bit.

"Probably not. You want to take a look around?" She just shook her head. "They told me he was buried around back, near the entrance of the mine. I'll go check on Matt's horses and water the team."

When he left, she continued to stare at the empty doorway. This was madness. Did the man expect her to believe her father had lived here, like this? She had letters, dozens of them, telling her about the house he'd been building, the house he'd finished, the house that would be waiting for her when she was old enough to join him.

The mine. If the mine was near, perhaps she could find someone there she could speak with. Taking a cautious look out the doorway, Sarah hurried out and rounded the house.

She passed what might have been the beginnings of a

small vegetable garden, withered now in the sun. There was a shed that served as a stable and an empty paddock made of a few rickety pieces of wood. She walked beyond it to where the ground began to rise with the slope of the mountain.

The entrance to the mine was easily found, though it was hardly more than a hole in the rock wall. Above it was a crudely etched plank of wood.

SARAH'S PRIDE

She felt the tears then. They came in a rush that she had to work hard to hold back. There were no workmen here, no carts shuttling along filled with rock, no picks hacking out gold. She saw it for what it was, the dream of a man who had had little else. Her father had never been a successful prospector or an important landowner. He'd been a man digging in rock and hoping for the big strike.

She saw the grave then. They had buried him only a few yards from the entrance. Someone had been kind enough to fashion a cross and carve his name on it. She knelt and ran her palm along the rubble that covered him.

He'd lied. For twelve years he'd lied to her, telling her stories about rich veins and the mother lode. He'd spun fantasies about a big house with a parlor and fine wooden floors. Had he needed to believe it? When he'd left her he'd made her a promise.

"You'll have everything your heart desires, my sweet, sweet Sarah. Everything your mother would have wanted for you."

He had kept his promise—except for one thing. One vital thing. He hadn't given her himself. All those years, all she'd really wanted had been her father.

He'd lived like this, she thought, in a mud house in the middle of nowhere, so that she could have pretty dresses and new stockings. So that she could learn how to serve tea and waltz. It must have taken nearly everything he'd managed to dig out of the rock to keep her in school back east.

Now he was dead. She could barely remember his face, and he was dead. Lost to her.

"Oh, Papa, didn't you know how little it mattered?" Lying across the grave, she let the tears come until she'd wept her heart clean.

She'd been gone a long time. Too long, Jake thought. He was just about to go after her when he saw her coming over the rise from the direction of the old mine. She paused there, looking down at the house her father had lived in for more than a decade. She'd taken off her bonnet, and she was holding it by the ribbons. For a moment she stood like a statue in the airless afternoon, her face marble-pale, her body slim and elegant. Her hair was pinned up, but a few tendrils had escaped to curl around her face. The sun slanted over it so that it glowed richly, reminding him of the hide of a young deer.

Jake blew out the last of the smoke from the cigarette he'd rolled. She was a hell of a sight, silhouetted against the bluff. She made him ache in places he didn't care to think about. Then she saw him. He could almost see her chin come up as she started down over the rough ground. Yeah, she was a hell of a sight.

"Mr. Redman." The grief was there in her red-rimmed eyes and her pale cheeks, but her voice was strong. "I apologize for the scene I caused earlier."

That tied his tongue for a moment. The way she said it, they might have been talking over tea in some cozy parlor. "Forget it. You ready to go back?"

"I beg your pardon?"

He jerked his thumb toward the wagon. Sarah noted that

all her trunks were neatly stacked on it again. "I said, are you ready to go back?"

She glanced down at her hands. Because the palms of her gloves were grimy, she tugged them off. They'd never be the same, she mused. Nothing would. She drew a long, steadying breath.

"I thought you understood me. I'm staying in my father's house."

"Don't be a fool. A woman like you's got no business out here."

"Really?" Her eyes hardened. "Be that as it may, I'm not leaving. I'd appreciate it if you'd move my trunks inside." She breezed by him.

"You won't last a day."

She stopped to look over her shoulder. Jake was forced to admit that he'd faced men over the barrel of a gun who'd had less determination in their eyes. "Is that your opinion, Mr. Redman?"

"That's a fact."

"Would you care to wager on it?"

"Look, Duchess, this is hard country even if you're born to it. Heat, snakes, mountain lions—not to mention Apaches."

"I appreciate you pointing all that out, Mr. Redman. Now my luggage."

"Damn fool woman," he muttered as he strode over to the wagon. "You want to stay out here, hell, it don't matter to me." He hefted a trunk into the house while Sarah stood a few feet back with her hands folded.

"Your language, Mr. Redman, is quite unnecessary."

He only swore with more skill as he carried in the second trunk. "Nobody's going to be around when it gets dark and you change your mind."

"I won't change my mind, but thank you so much for your concern."

"No concern of mine," he muttered, ignoring her sarcasm. He scooped up the rest of her boxes and dumped them inside the doorway. "Hope you got provisions in there, as well as fancy dresses."

"I assure you I'll be fine." She walked to the doorway herself and turned to him. "Perhaps you could tell me where I might get water."

"There's a stream half a mile due east."

Half a mile? she thought, trying not to show her dismay. "I see." Shading her eyes, she looked out. Jake mumbled another oath, took her by the shoulders and pointed in the opposite direction. "That way's east, Duchess."

"Of course." She stepped back. "Thank you again, Mr. Redman, for all your help. And good day," she added before she closed the door in his face.

She could hear him swearing at her as he unhitched the horses. If she hadn't been so weary, she might have been amused. She was certainly too exhausted to be shocked by the words he used. If she was going to stay, she was going to have to become somewhat accustomed to rough manners. She peeled off her jacket. And, she was going to stay.

If this was all she had left, she was going to make the best of it. Somehow.

She moved to the rounded opening beside the door that served as a window. From there she watched Jake ride away. He'd left her the wagon and stabled the rented horses with her father's two. For all the good it did her, Sarah thought with a sigh. She hadn't the vaguest idea of how to hitch a team, much less how to drive one.

She continued to watch Jake until he was nothing but a

cloud of dust fading in the distance. She was alone. Truly alone. She had no one, and little more than nothing.

No one but herself, she thought. And if she had only that and a mud hut, she'd find a way to make the best of it. Nobody—and certainly not Jake Redman—was going to frighten her away.

Turning, she unbuttoned her cuffs and rolled up her sleeves. The good sisters had always claimed that simple hard work eased the mind and cleansed the soul. She was about to put that claim to the test.

She found the letters an hour later. When she came across them in the makeshift loft that served as a bedroom she wiped her grimy hands as best as she could on the embroidered apron she'd dug out of one of her trunks.

He'd kept them. From the first to the last she'd written, her father had kept her letters to him. The tears threatened again, but she willed them back. Tears would do neither of them any good now. But, oh, it helped more than she could ever have explained that he'd kept her letters. To know now, when she would never see him again, that he had thought of her as she had thought of him.

He must have received the last, the letter telling him she was coming to be with him, shortly before his death. Sarah hadn't mailed it until she'd been about to board the train. She'd told herself it was because she wanted to surprise him, but she'd also wanted to be certain he wouldn't have time to forbid her to come.

Would you have, Papa? she wondered. Or would you finally have been willing to share the truth with me? Had he thought her too weak, too fragile, to share the life he'd chosen? Was she?

Sighing, she looked around. Four bedrooms, and a parlor with the windows facing west, she thought with a quiet laugh. Well, according to Jake Redman, the window did indeed face west. The house itself was hardly bigger than the room she'd shared with Lucilla at school. It was too small, certainly, for all she'd brought with her from Philadelphia, but she'd managed to drag the trunks into one corner. To please herself, she'd taken out a few of her favorite things— one of her wildflower sketches, a delicate blue glass perfume bottle, a pretty petit-point pillow and the china-faced doll her father had sent her for her twelfth birthday.

They didn't make it home, not yet. But they helped.

Setting the letters back in the tin box beside the bed, she rose. She had practical matters to think about now. The first was money. After paying the five dollars, she had only twenty dollars left. She hadn't a clue to how long that would keep her, but she doubted it would be very long. Then there was food. That was of more immediate concern. She'd found some flour, a few cans of beans, some lard and a bottle of whiskey. Pressing a hand to her stomach, Sarah decided she'd have to make do with the beans. All she had to do now was to figure out how to start a fire in the battered-looking stove.

She found a few twigs in the wood box, and a box of matches. It took her half an hour, a lot of frustration and a few words the sisters would never have approved of before she was forced to admit she was a failure.

Jake Redman. Disgusted, she scowled at the handful of charred twigs. The least the man could have done was to offer to start a cook fire for her and fetch some water. She'd already made the trip down to the stream and back once, managing to scrounge out half a bucket from its stingy trickle.

She'd eat the beans cold. She'd prove to Jake Redman that she could do very well for herself, by herself.

Sarah unsheathed her father's bowie knife, shuddered once at the sight of the vicious blade, then plunged it into the lid of the can until she'd made an opening. Too hungry to care, she sat beside the small stone hearth and devoured the beans.

She'd think of it as an adventure, she told herself. One she could write about to her friends in Philadelphia. A better one, she decided as she looked around the tiny, clean cabin, than those in the penny dreadfuls Lucilla had gotten from the library and hidden in their room.

In those, the heroine had usually been helpless, a victim waiting for the hero to rescue her in any of a dozen dashing manners. Sarah scooped out more beans. Well, she wasn't helpless, and as far as she could tell there wasn't a hero within a thousand miles.

No one would have called Jake Redman heroic—though he'd certainly looked it when he'd ridden beside the coach. He was insulting and ill-mannered. He had cold eyes and a hot temper. Hardly Sarah's idea of a hero. If she had to be rescued—and she certainly didn't—she'd prefer someone smoother, a cavalry officer, perhaps. A man who carried a saber, a gentleman's weapon.

When she'd finished the beans, she hiccuped, wiped her mouth with the back of her hand and leaned back against the hearth only to lose her balance when a stone gave way. Nursing a bruised elbow, she shifted. She would have replaced the stone, but something caught her eye. Crouching again, she reached into the small opening that was now exposed and slowly pulled out a bag.

With her lips caught tight between her teeth, she poured gold coins into her lap. Two hundred and thirty dollars. Sarah pressed both hands to her mouth, swallowed, then counted again. There was no mistake. She hadn't known until that moment how much money could mean. She could buy decent food, fuel, whatever she needed to make her way.

She poured the coins back into the bag and dug into the hole again. This time she found the deed to Sarah's Pride.

What an odd man he must have been, she thought. To hide his possessions beneath a stone.

The last and most precious item she discovered in the hiding place was her father's journal. It delighted her. The small brown book filled with her father's cramped handwriting meant more to Sarah than all the gold coins in Arizona. She hugged it to her as she'd wanted to hug her father. Before she rose with it, she replaced the gold and the deed under the stone.

She would read about one of his days each evening. It would be like a gift, something that each day would bring her a little closer to this man she'd never really known. For now she would go back to the stream, wash as best she could and gather water for the morning.

Jake watched her come out of the cabin with a pail in one hand and a lantern in the other. He'd made himself as comfortable as he needed to be among the rocks. There had been enough jerky and hardtack in his saddlebag to make a passable supper. Not what he'd planned on, exactly, but passable.

He'd be damned if he could figure out why he'd decided to keep an eye on her. The lady wasn't his problem. But even as he'd been cursing her and steering his horse toward town, he'd known he couldn't just ride off and leave her there alone.

Maybe it was because he knew what it was to lose everything. Or because he'd been alone himself for more years then he cared to remember. Or maybe, damn her, it had something to do with the way she'd looked coming down that bluff with her bonnet trailing by the ribbons and tears still drying on her face.

He hadn't thought he had a weak spot. Certainly not where women were concerned. He shoved himself to his feet. He just didn't have anything better to do.

He stayed well behind her. He knew how to move silently, over rock, through brush, in sunlight or in the dark of the moon. That was both a matter of survival and a matter of blood. In his youth he'd spent some years with his grandmother's people and he'd learned more than any white man could have learned in a lifetime about tracking without leaving a mark, about hunting without making a sound.

As for the woman, she was still wearing that fancy skirt with the bustle and shoes that were made for city sidewalks rather than rough ground. Twice Jake had to stop and wait, or even at a crawl he'd have caught up with her.

Probably break an ankle before she was through, he thought. That might be the best thing that could happen to her. Then he'd just cart her on back to town. Couldn't say he'd mind too much picking her up again. She felt good— maybe too good. He had to grin when she shrieked and landed on her fancy bustle because a rabbit darted across her path.

Nope, the pretty little duchess from Philadelphia wasn't going to last a day.

With a hand to her heart, Sarah struggled to her feet. She'd never seen a rabbit that large in her life. With a little sound of distress, she noted that she'd torn the hem of her skirt. How did the women out here manage? she wondered as she began to walk again. In this heat, a corset felt like iron and a fashionable skirt prevented anything but the most delicate walking.

When she reached the stream, she dropped down on a

rock and went to work with her buttonhook. It was heaven, absolute heaven, to remove her shoes. There was a blister starting on her heel, but she'd worry about that later. Right now all she could think about was splashing some cool water on her skin.

She glanced around cautiously. There couldn't be anyone there. The sensation of being watched was a natural one, she supposed, when a woman was alone in the wilderness and the sun was going down. She unpinned the cameo at her throat and placed it carefully in her skirt pocket. It was the one thing she had that had belonged to her mother.

Humming to keep herself company, she unbuttoned her blouse and folded it over a rock. With the greatest relief, she unfastened her corset and dropped it on top of the blouse. She could breathe, really breathe, for the first time all day. Hurrying now, she stripped down to her chemise, then unhooked her stockings.

Glorious. She closed her eyes and let out a low sound of pleasure when she stepped into the narrow, ankle-deep stream. The water, trickling down from the mountains, was cold and clear as ice.

What the hell did she think she was doing? Jake let out a low oath and averted his eyes. He didn't need this aggravation. Who would have thought the woman would strip down and play in the water with the night coming on? He glanced back to see her bend down to splash her face. There was nothing between the two of them but shadows and sunlight.

Water dampened the cotton she wore so that it clung here and there. When she bent to scoop up more water, the ruffles at the bodice sagged to tease him. Crouching behind the rock, he began to curse himself instead of her.

His own fault. Didn't he know minding your own business, and only your own, was the best way to get by? He'd just had to be riding along when the Apaches had hit the stage. He'd just had to be the one to tell her about her father. He'd just had to feel obliged to drive her out here. And then to stay.

What he should be doing was getting good and drunk at Carlotta's and spending the night in a feather bed wrestling with a woman. The kind of woman who knew what a man needed and didn't ask a bunch of fool questions. The kind of woman, Jake thought viciously, who didn't expect you to come to tea on Sunday.

He glanced back to see that one of the straps of Sarah's chemise had fallen down her arm and that her legs were gleaming and wet. Her shoulders were pale and smooth and bare.

Too long on the trail, Jake told himself. Too damn long, when a man started to hanker after skinny city women who didn't know east from west.

Sarah filled the pail as best she could, then stepped out of the stream. It was getting dark much more quickly than she'd expected. But she felt almost human again. Even the thought of the corset made her ribs ache, so she ignored it. After slipping on her blouse, she debated donning her shoes and stockings again. There was no one to see or disapprove. Instead, she hitched on her skirt and made a bundle of the rest. With the water sloshing in the pail, she made her way gingerly along the path.

She had to fight the urge to hurry. With sunset, the air was cooling rapidly. And there were sounds. Sounds she didn't recognize or appreciate. Hoots and howls and rustles. Stones dug into her bare feet, and the lantern spread more shadow than light. The half mile back seemed much, much longer than it had before.

Again she had the uncomfortable sensation that someone was watching her. Apaches? Mountain lions? Damn Jake Redman. The little adobe dwelling looked like a haven to her now. Half running, she went through the door and bolted it behind her.

The first coyote sent up a howl to the rising moon.

Sarah shut her eyes. If she lived through the night, she'd swallow her pride and go back to town.

In the rocks not far away, Jake bedded down.

Chapter 3

Soon after sunrise, Sarah awoke, stiff and sore and hungry. She rolled over, wanting to cling to sleep until Lucilla's maid brought the morning chocolate. She'd had the most awful dream about some gray-eyed man carrying her off to a hot, desolate place. He'd been handsome, the way men in dreams were supposed to be, but in a rugged, almost uncivilized way. His skin had been like bronze, taut over his face. He'd had high, almost exotic cheekbones, and the dark shadow of a beard. His hair had been untidy and as black as coal—but thick, quite thick, as it had swept down past his collar. She'd wondered, even in the dream, what it would be like to run her hands through it.

There had been something familiar about him, almost as if she'd known him. In fact, when he'd forced her to kiss him, a name had run through her mind. Then he hadn't had to force her any longer.

Drowsy, Sarah smiled. She would have to tell Lucilla

about the dream. They would both laugh about it before they dressed for the day. Lazily she opened her eyes.

This wasn't the rose-and-white room she used whenever she visited Lucilla and her family. Nor was it the familiar bedroom she had had for years at school.

Her father's house, she thought, as everything came back to her. This was her father's house, but her father was dead. She was alone. With an effort, she resisted the urge to bury her face in the pillow and weep again. She had to decide what to do, and in order to decide she had to think clearly.

For some time last night she'd been certain the best thing would be for her to return to town and use the money she had found to book passage east again. At best, Lucilla's family would welcome her. At worst, she could return to the convent. But that had been before she'd begun reading her father's journal. It had taken only the first two pages, the only two she'd allowed herself, to make her doubt.

He'd begun the journal on the day he'd left her to come west. The love and the hope he'd felt had been in every word. And the sadness. He'd still been raw with grief over the death of Sarah's mother.

For the first time she fully understood how devastated he had been by the loss of the woman they'd both shared so briefly. And how inadequate he'd felt at finding himself alone with a little girl. He'd made a promise to his wife on her deathbed that he would see that their daughter was well cared for.

She remembered the words her father had written on the yellowed paper.

She was leaving me. There was nothing I could do to stop it. Toward the end there was so much pain I prayed for God to take her quickly. My Ellen, my tiny, delicate Ellen. Her thoughts were all for me, and our sweet Sarah. I promised her. The only comfort I could give was my promise. Our daughter would have everything Ellen wanted for her. Proper schooling and church on Sunday. She would be raised the way my Ellen would have raised her. Like a lady. One day she'd have a fine house and a father she could be proud of.

He'd come here to try, Sarah thought as she tossed back the thin blanket. And she supposed he'd done as well as he could. Now she had to figure what was best. And if she was going to think, first she needed to eat.

After she'd dressed in her oldest skirt and blouse, she took stock of the cupboard again. She could not, under any circumstances, face another meal of cold beans. Perhaps he had a storage cellar somewhere, a smokehouse, anything. Sarah pushed open the door and blinked in the blinding sunlight.

At first she thought it was a mirage. But mirages didn't carry a scent, did they? This one smelled of meat roasting and coffee brewing. And what she saw was Jake Redman sitting cross-legged by a fire ringed with stones. Gathering up her skirt, she forgot her hunger long enough to stride over to him.

"What are you doing here?"

He glanced up and gave her the briefest of nods. He poured coffee from a small pot into a dented tin cup. "Having breakfast."

"You rode all the way out here to have breakfast?" She didn't know what it was he was turning on the spit, but her stomach was ready for just about anything.

"Nope." He tested the meat and judged it done. "Never left." He jerked his head in the direction of the rocks. "Bedded down over there."

"There?" Sarah eyed the rocks with some amazement. "Whatever for?"

He looked up again. The look in his eyes made her hands flutter nervously. It made her feel, though it was foolish, that he knew how she looked stripped down to her chemise. "Let's say it was a long ride back to town."

"I hardly expect you to watch over me, Mr. Redman. I explained that I could take... What is that?"

Jake was eating with his fingers and with obvious enjoyment. "Rabbit."

"Rabbit?" Sarah wrinkled her nose at the idea, but her stomach betrayed her. "I suppose you trapped it on my property."

So it was her property already. "Might've."

"If that's the case, the least you could do is offer to share."

Jake obligingly pulled off a hunk of meat. "Help yourself."

"Don't you have any... Never mind." When in Rome, Sarah decided. Taking the meat and the coffee he offered, she sat down on a rock.

"Get yourself some supper last night?"

"Yes, thank you." Never, never in her life, had she tasted anything better than this roast rabbit in the already-sweltering morning. "You're an excellent cook, Mr. Redman."

"I get by." He offered her another hunk. This time she didn't hesitate.

"No, really." She caught herself talking with her mouth full, and she didn't care. "This is delightful." Because she doubted that his saddlebags held any linens, she licked her fingers.

"Better than a can of cold beans, anyway."

She glanced up sharply, but he wasn't even looking at her.

"I suppose." She'd never had breakfast with a man before, and she decided it would be proper to engage in light conversation. "Tell me, Mr. Redman, what is your profession?"

"Never gave it much thought."

"But surely you must have some line of work."

"Nope." He leaned back against a rock and, taking out his pouch of tobacco, proceeded to roll a cigarette. She looked as fresh and neat as a daisy, he thought. You'd have thought she'd spent the night in some high-priced hotel instead of a mud hut.

Apparently making conversation over a breakfast of roasted rabbit took some skill. Patiently she smoothed her skirts and tried again. "Have you lived in Arizona long?"

"Why?"

"I—" The cool, flat look he sent her had her fumbling. "Simple curiosity."

"I don't know about back in Philadelphia." Jake took out a match, scraped it on the rock and lit the twisted end of his cigarette, studying her all the while. "But around here people don't take kindly to questions."

"I see." Her back had stiffened. She'd never encountered anyone to whom rudeness came so easily. "In a civilized society, a casual question is merely a way to begin a conversation."

"Around here it's a way to start a fight." He drew on the cigarette. "You want to fight with me, Duchess?"

"I'll thank you to stop referring to me by that name."

He grinned at her again, but lazily, the brim of his hat shadowing his eyes. "You look like one, especially when you're riled."

Her chin came up. She couldn't help it. But she answered him in calm, even tones. "I assure you, I'm not at all riled. Although you have, on several occasions already, been rude and difficult and annoying. Where I come from, Mr. Redman, a woman is entitled to a bit more charm and gallantry from a man."

"That so?" Her mouth dropped open when he slowly drew out his gun. "Don't move."

Move? She couldn't even breathe. She'd only called him rude and, sweet Mary, he was going to shoot her. "Mr. Redman, I don't—"

The bullet exploded against the rock a few inches away from her. With a shriek, she tumbled into the dirt. When she found the courage to look up, Jake was standing and lifting something dead and hideous from the rock.

"Rattler," he said easily. When she moaned and started to cover her eyes, he reached down and hauled her to her feet. "I'd take a good look," he suggested, still holding the snake in front of her. "If you stay around here, you're going to see plenty more."

It was the disdain in his voice that had her fighting off the swoon. With what little voice she had left, she asked, "Would you kindly dispose of that?"

With a muttered curse, he tossed it aside, then began to smother the fire. Sarah felt her breakfast rising uneasily and waited for it to settle. "It appears you saved my life."

"Yeah, well, don't let it get around."

"I won't, I assure you." She drew herself up straight, hiding her trembling hands in the folds of her skirts. "I appreciate the meal, Mr. Redman. Now, if you'll excuse me, I have a number of things to do."

"You can start by getting yourself into the wagon. I'll drive you back to town."

"I appreciate the offer. As a matter of fact, I would be grateful. I need some supplies."

"Look, there's got to be enough sense in that head of

yours for you to see you don't belong out here. It's a two-hour drive into town. There's nothing out here but rattlers and coyotes."

She was afraid he was right. The night she'd spent in the cabin had been the loneliest and most miserable of her life. But somewhere between the rabbit and the snake she'd made up her mind. Matt Conway's daughter wasn't going to let all his efforts and his dreams turn to dust. She was staying, Lord help her.

"My father lived here. This place was obviously important to him. I intend to stay." She doubted Jake Redman had enough heart to understand her reasons. "Now, if you'd be good enough to hitch up the wagon, I'll go change."

"Change what?"

"Why, my dress, of course. I can hardly go into town like this."

He cast a glance over her. She already looked dolled-up enough for a church social in her crisp white blouse and gingham skirt. He'd never known gingham to look quite so good on a woman before.

"Lone Bluff ain't Philadelphia. It ain't anyplace. You want the wagon hitched, I'll oblige you, but you'd better watch how it's done, because there's not going to be anyone around to do it for you next time." With that, he slung his saddlebags over his shoulder and walked away.

Very well, she thought after one last deep breath. He was quite right. It was time she learned how to do things for herself. The sooner she learned, the sooner she'd have no more need of him.

With her head held high, she followed him. She watched him guide the team out. It seemed easy enough. You simply hooked this and tied that and the deed was done. Men, she thought with a little smile. They always exaggerated the most basic chores.

"Thank you, Mr. Redman. If you'll wait just a moment, I'll be ready to go."

Didn't the woman know anything? Jake tipped his hat forward. He'd driven her out of town yesterday. If he drove her back this morning her reputation would be ruined. Even Lone Bluff had its standards. Since she'd decided to stay, at least temporarily, she'd need all the support she could get from the town women.

"I got business of my own, ma'am."

"But—" He was already moving off to saddle his own horse. Setting her teeth, Sarah stamped inside. She added another twenty dollars to what she carried in her reticule. As an afterthought she took down the rifle her father had left on the wall. She hadn't the least idea how to use it, was certain she wouldn't be able to in even the most dire circumstances, but she felt better having it.

Jake was mounted and waiting when she came out. "The road will lead you straight into town," he told her as she fastened her bonnet. "If you give Lucius a dollar he'll drive back out with you, then take the wagon and team back to the livery. Matt's got two horses of his own in the stables. Someone from town's been keeping an eye on them."

"A dollar." As if it were spun glass, she set the rifle in the wagon. "You charged me five."

He grinned at her. "I'm not Lucius." With a tip of his hat, he rode off.

It didn't take her long to climb up into the wagon. But she had to gather her courage before she touched the reins. Though she considered herself an excellent horsewoman, she'd never driven a team before. You've ridden behind them, she reminded herself as she picked up the reins. How difficult can it be?

She took the horses—or they took her—in a circle three times before she managed to head them toward the road.

Jake sat on his horse and watched her from a ridge. It was the best laugh he'd had in months.

By the time she reached Lone Bluff, Sarah was sweating profusely, her hands felt raw and cramped and her lower back was on fire. In front of the dry goods store she climbed down on legs that felt like water. After smoothing her skirts and patting her forehead dry, she spotted a young boy whittling a stick.

"Young man, do you know a man named Lucius?"

"Everybody knows old Lucius."

Satisfied, Sarah drew a coin out of her bag. "If you can find Lucius and tell him Miss Sarah Conway wishes to see him, you can have this penny."

The boy eyed it, thinking of peppermint sticks. "Yes, ma'am." He was off at a run.

At least children seemed about the same, east or west.

Sarah entered the store. There were several customers milling around, looking over the stock and gossiping. They all stopped to stare at Sarah before going back to their business. The young woman behind the counter came around to greet her.

"Good morning. May I help you?"

"Yes, I'm Sarah Conway."

"I know." When the pretty brunette smiled, dimples flashed in her cheeks. She was already envying Sarah her bonnet. "You arrived on the stage yesterday. I'm very sorry about your father. Everyone liked Matt."

"Thank you." Sarah found herself smiling back. "I'm going to need a number of supplies."

"Are you really going to stay out there, at Matt's place? Alone?"

"Yes. At least for now."

"I'd be scared to death." The brunette gave her an appraising look, then offered a hand. "I'm Liza Cody. No relation."

"I beg your pardon?"

"To Buffalo Bill. Most people ask. Welcome to Lone Bluff."

"Thank you."

With Liza's help. Sarah began to gather supplies and introductions. Within twenty minutes she'd nodded to half the women in Lone Bluff, been given a recipe for biscuits and been asked her opinion of the calico fabric just arrived from St. Joe.

Her spirits rose dramatically. Perhaps the women dressed less fashionably than their counterparts in the East, but they made her feel welcome.

"Ma'am."

Sarah turned to see Lucius, hat in hand. Beside him, the young boy was nearly dancing in anticipation of the penny. The moment it was in his hand, he raced to the jars of hard candy and began to negotiate.

"Mr...."

"Just Lucius, ma'am."

"Lucius, I was told you might be willing to drive my supplies back for me, then return the wagon and team to the livery."

He pushed his chaw into his cheek and considered. "Well, now, maybe I would."

"I'd be willing to give you a dollar for your trouble."

He grinned, showing a few yellowed—and several missing—teeth. "Glad to help, Miss Conway."

"Perhaps you'd begin by loading my supplies."

Leaving him to it, Sarah turned back to Liza. "Miss Cody."

"Liza, please."

"Liza, I wonder if you might have any tea, and I would dearly love some fresh eggs."

"Don't get much call for tea, but we've got some in the back." Liza opened the door to the rear storeroom. Three fat-bellied puppies ran out. "John Cody, you little monster. I told you to keep these pups outside."

Laughing, Sarah crouched down to greet them. "Oh, they're adorable."

"One's adorable, maybe," Liza muttered. As usual, her young brother was nowhere in sight when she needed him. "Three's unmanageable. Just last night they chewed through a sack of meal. Pop finds out, he'll take a strap to Johnny."

A brown mutt with a black circle around his left eye jumped into Sarah's lap. And captured her heart. "You're a charmer, aren't you?" She laughed as he bathed her face.

"A nuisance is more like it."

"Will you sell one?"

"Sell?" Liza stretched to reach the tea on a high shelf. "My pop'd pay you to take one."

"Really?" With the brown pup cradled in her arms, Sarah stood again. "I'd love to have one. I could use the company."

Liza added the tea and eggs to Sarah's total. "You want that one, you take it right along." She grinned when the pup licked Sarah's face again. "He certainly seems taken with you."

"I'll take very good care of him." Balancing the dog,

she took out the money to pay her bill. "Thank you for everything."

Liza counted out the coins before she placed them in the cash drawer and took out Sarah's change. Pop would be pleased, she thought. Not only because of the pup, but because Miss Conway was a cash customer. Liza was pleased because Sarah was young and pretty and would surely know everything there was to know about the latest fashions.

"It's been nice meeting you, Miss Conway."

"Sarah."

Liza smiled again and walked with Sarah to the door. "Maybe I'll ride out and see you, if you don't mind."

"I'd love it. Any time at all."

Abruptly Liza lifted a hand to pat her hair. "Good morning, Mr. Carlson."

"Liza, you're looking pretty as ever." She blushed and fluttered, though Carlson's eyes were on Sarah.

"Samuel Carlson, this is Sarah Conway."

"Delighted." Carlson's smile made his pale, handsome face even more attractive. It deepened the already-brilliant blue of his eyes. When he lifted Sarah's hand to his lips in a smooth, cavalier gesture, she was doubly glad she'd come into town.

Apparently Lone Bluff had some gentlemen after all. Samuel Carlson was slim and well dressed in a beautiful black riding coat and a spotless white shirt. His trim mustache was the same rich brown as his well-groomed hair. He had, as a gentleman should, swept off his hat at the introduction. It was a particularly fine hat, Sarah thought, black like his coat, with a silver chain for a band.

"My deepest sympathies for your loss, Miss Conway. Your father was a fine man and a good friend."

"Thank you. It's been comforting for me to learn he was well thought of."

The daughter was certainly a pretty addition to a dust hole like Lone Bluff, he thought. "Word around town is that you'll be staying with us for a while." He reached over to scratch the puppy's ears and was rewarded with a low growl.

"Hush, now." Sarah smiled an apology. "Yes, I've decided to stay. At least for the time being."

"I hope you'll let me know if there's anything I can do to help." He smiled again. "Undoubtedly life here isn't what you're used to."

The way he said it made it clear that it was a compliment. Mr. Carlson was obviously a man of the world, and of some means. "Thank you." She handed the puppy to Lucius and was gratified when Carlson assisted her into the wagon. "It was a pleasure to meet you, Mr. Carlson."

"The pleasure was mine, Miss Conway."

"Goodbye, Liza. I hope you'll come and visit soon." Sarah settled the puppy on her lap. She considered it just her bad luck that she glanced across the street at that moment. Jake was there, one hand hooked in his pocket, leaning against a post, watching. With an icy nod, she acknowledged him, then stared straight ahead as Lucius clucked to the horses.

When the wagon pulled away, the men studied each other. There was no nod of acknowledgment. They simply watched, cool and cautious, across the dusty road.

Sarah felt positively triumphant. As she stored her supplies, the puppy circled her legs, apparently every bit as pleased as she with the arrangement. Her nights wouldn't be nearly so lonely now, with the dog for company. She'd met people, was perhaps even on the way to making friends.

Her cupboard was full, and Lucius had been kind enough to show her how to fire up the old cookstove.

Tonight, after supper, she was going to write to Lucilla and Mother Superior. She would read another page or two from her father's journal before she curled up under the freshly aired blanket.

Jake Redman be damned, she thought as she bent to tickle the pup's belly. She was making it.

With a glass of whiskey at his fingertips, Jake watched Carlotta work the room. She sure was something. Her hair was the color of gold nuggets plucked from a riverbed, and her lips were as red as the velvet drapes that hung in her private room.

She was wearing red tonight, something tight that glittered as it covered her long, curvy body and clung to her smooth white breasts. Her shoulders were bare. Jake had always thought that a woman's shoulders were enough to drive a man to distraction.

He thought of Sarah, standing ankle-deep in a stream with water glistening on her skin.

He took another gulp of whiskey.

Carlotta's girls were dressed to kill, as well. The men in the Silver Star were getting their money's worth. The piano rang out, and the whiskey and the laughter poured.

The way he figured it, Carlotta ran one of the best houses in Arizona. Maybe one of the best west of the Mississippi. The whiskey wasn't watered much, and the girls weren't bad. A man could almost believe they enjoyed their work. As for Carlotta, Jake figured she enjoyed it just fine.

Money came first with her. He knew, because she'd once had enough to drink to tell him that she took a healthy cut of all her girls' pay. If the man one of her girls was with decided to slip her a little extra, that was just fine with Carlotta. She took a cut of that, as well.

She had dreams of moving her business to San Francisco and buying a place with crystal chandeliers, gilt mirrors and red carpets. Carlotta favored red. But for now, like the rest of them, Carlotta was stuck in Lone Bluff.

Tipping back more whiskey, Jake watched her. She moved like a queen, her full red lips always smiling, her cool blue eyes always watching. She was making sure her girls were persuading the men to buy them plenty of drinks. What the bartender served the working girls was hardly more than colored water, but the men paid, and paid happily, before they moved along to one of the narrow rooms upstairs.

Hell of a business, Jake thought as he helped himself to one of the cigars Carlotta provided for her paying customers. She had them shipped all the way from Cuba, and they had a fine, rich taste. Jake had no doubt she added to the price of her whiskey and her girls to pay for them. Business was business.

One of the girls sidled over to light the cigar for him. He just shook his head at the invitation. She was warm and ripe and smelled like a bouquet of roses. For the life of him he couldn't figure out why he wasn't interested.

"You're going to hurt the girls' feelings." Perfume trailing behind her, Carlotta joined Jake at the table. "Don't you see anything you like?"

He tipped his chair back against the wall. "See plenty I like."

She laughed and lifted a hand in a subtle signal. "You going to buy me a drink, Jake?" Before he could answer, one of the girls was bringing over a new bottle and a glass. No watered-down liquor for Carlotta. "Haven't seen you around in a while."

"Haven't been around."

Carlotta took a drink and let it sweep through her system. She'd take liquor over a man any day. "Going to stay around?"

"Might."

"Heard there was a little trouble on the stage yesterday. It's not like you to do good deeds, Jake." She drank again and smiled at him. In a movement as smooth as the liquor she drank, she dropped a hand to his thigh. "That's what I like about you."

"Just happened to be there."

"Also heard Matt Conway's daughter's in town." Smiling, she took the cigar from him and took a puff. "You working for her?"

"Why?"

"Word around is that you drove her on out to his place." She slowly blew out a stream of smoke from between her painted lips. "Can't see you digging in rock for gold, Jake, when it's easier just to take it."

"Far as I remember, there was never enough gold in that rock to dig for." He took the cigar back and clamped it between his teeth. "You know different?"

"I only know what I hear, and I don't hear much about Conway." She poured a second drink and downed it. She didn't want to talk about Matt Conway's mine or about what she knew. Something in the air tonight, she decided. Made her restless. Maybe she needed more than whiskey after all. "Glad you're back, Jake. Things have been too quiet around here."

Two men hankering after the same girl started to scuffle. Carlotta's tall black servant tossed them both out. She just smiled and poured a third drink. "If you're not interested in any of my girls, we could make other arrangements." She lifted the small glass in a salute before she knocked it back. "For old times' sake."

Jake looked at her. Her eyes glittered against her white skin. Her lips were parted. Above the flaming red of her dress, her breasts rose and fell invitingly. He knew what she could do to a man, with a man, when the mood was on her. It baffled and infuriated him that she didn't stir him in the least.

"Maybe some other time." He rose and, after dropping a few coins on the table, strolled out.

Carlotta's eyes hardened as she watched him. She only offered herself to a privileged few. And she didn't like to be rejected.

With the puppy snoozing at her feet, Sarah closed her father's journal. He'd written about an Indian attack on the wagon train and his own narrow escape. In simple, often stark terms, he'd written of the slaughter, the terror and the waste. Yet even after that he'd gone on, because he'd wanted to make something of himself. For her.

Shivering a bit despite her shawl, she rose to replace the book beneath the stone. If she had read those words while still in Philadelphia, she would have thought them an exaggeration. She was coming to know better.

With a half sigh, she looked down at her hands. They were smooth and well tended. They were, she was afraid, woefully inadequate to the task of carving out a life here.

It was only the night that made her feel that way, Sarah told herself as she moved to check the bolt on the door. She'd done all she could that day, and it had been enough. She'd driven to town alone, stocked the cabin and replanted the vegetable garden. Her back ached enough to tell her she'd put in a full day. Tomorrow she'd start again.

The lonely howl of a coyote made her heart thud. Gathering the puppy to her breast, she climbed up for bed.

She was in her night shift when the dog started to bark and growl. Exasperated, she managed to grab him before he could leap from the loft.

"You'll break your neck." When he strained against her hold and continued to yelp, she took him in her arms. "All right, all right. If you have to go out, I'll let you out, but you might have let me know before I went to bed." Nuzzling him, she climbed down from the loft again. She saw the fire through the window and ran to the door. "Oh, my God."

The moment she yanked it open the puppy ran out, barking furiously. With her hands to her cheeks, Sarah watched the fire rise up and eat at the old, dry wood of the shed. A scream, eerily like a woman's, pierced the night.

Her father's horses. Following instinct alone, she ran.

The horses were already wild-eyed, stamping and screaming in their stalls. Muttering a prayer, Sarah dragged the first one out and slapped its flank. The fire was moving fast, racing up the walls and onto the roof. The hay had already caught and was burning wildly.

Eyes stinging from the smoke, she groped her way to the second stall. Coughing, swearing, she fought the terrified horse as it reared and shoved against her. Then she screamed herself when a flaming plank fell behind her. Fire licked closer and closer to the hem of her shift.

Whipping off her shawl, she tossed it over the horse's eyes and dragged them both out of the shed.

Blinded by smoke, she crawled to safety. Behind her she could hear the walls collapse, could hear the roar of flames consuming wood. Gone. It was gone. She wanted to beat her fists in the dirt and weep.

It could spread. The terror of that had her pushing up

onto her hands and knees. Somehow she had to prevent the fire from spreading. She caught the sound of a horse running hard and had nearly gained her feet when something slammed into her.

Chapter 4

The night was clear, with a sharp-edged half-moon and white pinpoint stars. Jake rode easily, arguing with himself.

It was stupid, just plain stupid, for him to be heading out when he could be snuggled up against Carlotta right this minute. Except Carlotta didn't snuggle. What she did was more like devouring. With her, sex was fast and hot and un-complicated. After all, business was business.

At least he knew what Carlotta was and what to expect from her. She used men like poker chips. That was fine with Jake. Carlotta wouldn't expect posies or boxes of chocolates or Sunday calls.

Sarah Conway was a whole different matter. A woman like that wanted a man to come courting wearing a stiff collar. And probably a tie. He snorted and kicked his mount into a trot. You'd have to see that your boots were shined so you could sit around making fancy talk. With her, sex would be... He swore viciously, and the mustang pricked up his ears. You didn't have sex with a woman like that. You didn't even think about it. And even if you did...

Well, he just wasn't interested.

So what the hell was he doing riding out to her place in the middle of the night?

"Stupid," he muttered to his horse.

Overhead, a nighthawk dived and killed with hardly a sound. Life was survival, and survival meant ruthlessness. Jake understood that, accepted it. But Sarah... He shook his head. Survival to her was making sure her ribbons matched her dress.

The best thing he could do was to turn around now and head back to town. Maybe ride right on through town and go down to Tombstone for a spell. He could pick up a job there if he had a mind to. Better yet, he could travel up to the mountains, where the air was cool and smelled of pine. There wasn't anything or anyone holding him in Lone Bluff. He was a free agent, and that was the way he intended to stay.

But he didn't turn his horse around.

When he got back from the mountains, he mused—if he got back—Miss Sarah Conway, with her big brown eyes and her white shoulders, would be long gone. Just plain stubbornness was keeping her here now, anyway. Even stubbornness had to give way sometime. If she was gone, maybe he'd stop having this feeling that he was about to make a big mistake.

As far as he could see, the biggest mistakes men made were over three things—money, whiskey and women. None of the three had ever meant enough to him to worry or fight over. He didn't plan on changing that.

Even if this woman *was* different. Somehow. That was what bothered him the most. He'd always been able to figure people. It had helped keep him alive all these years. He couldn't figure Sarah Conway, or what it was about her that made him want to see that she was safe. Maybe he was getting soft, but he didn't like to think so.

He couldn't help feeling for her some, traveling all this way just to find out her father was dead. And he had to admire the way she was sticking it out, staying at the old mine. It was stupid, he mused, but you had to admire it.

With a shrug, he kept riding. He was nearly to the Conway place, anyway. He might as well take a look and make sure she hadn't shot her foot off with her daddy's rifle.

He smelled the fire before he saw it. His head came up, like a wolf's when it scents an enemy. In a similar move, the mustang reared and showed the whites of his eyes. When he caught the first flicker of flame, he kicked the horse into a run. What had the damn fool woman done now?

There had only been a few times in his life when he had experienced true fear. He didn't care for the taste of it. And he tasted it now, as his mind conjured up the image of Sarah trapped inside the burning house, the oil she'd undoubtedly spilled spreading the fire hot and fast.

Another image came back to him, an old one, an image of fire and weeping and gunplay. He'd known fear then, too. Fear and hate, and an anguish he'd sworn he'd never feel again.

There was some small relief when he saw that it was the shed burning and not the house. The heat from it roared out as the last of the roof collapsed. He slowed his horse when he spotted two riders heading up into the rocks. His gun was already drawn, his blood already cold, before he saw Sarah lying on the ground. His horse was still moving when he slid from the saddle and ran to her.

Her face was as pale as the moon, and she smelled of

smoke. As he knelt beside her, a small brown dog began to snarl at him. Jake brushed it aside when it nipped him.

"If you were going to do any guarding, you're too late."

His mouth set in a grim line, he pressed a hand to her heart. Something moved in him when he felt its slow beat. Gently he lifted her head. And felt the blood, warm on his fingers. He looked up at the rocks again, his eyes narrowed and icy. As carefully as he could, he picked her up and carried her inside.

There was no place to lay her comfortably but the cot. The puppy began to whine and jump at the ladder after Jake carried her up. Jake shushed him again and, grateful that Sarah had at least had the sense to bring in fresh water, prepared to dress her wound.

Dazed and aching, Sarah felt something cool on her head. For a moment she thought it was Sister Angelina, the soft-voiced nun who had nursed her through a fever when she had been twelve. Though she hurt, hurt all over, it was comforting to be there, safe in her own bed, knowing that someone was there to take care of her and make things right again. Sister would sometimes sing to her and would always, when she needed it, hold her hand.

Moaning a little, Sarah groped for Sister Angelina's hand. The one that closed over hers was as hard as iron. Confused, fooled for a minute into thinking her father had come back for her, Sarah opened her eyes.

At first everything was vague and wavering, as though she were looking through water. Slowly she focused on a face. She remembered the face, with its sharp lines and its taut, bronzed skin. A lawless face. She'd dreamed of it, hadn't she? Unsure, she lifted a hand to it. It was rough, unshaven and warm. Gray eyes, she thought dizzily. Gray eyes and a gray hat. Yes, she'd dreamed of him.

She managed a whisper. "Don't. Don't kiss me."

The face smiled. It was such a quick, flashing and appealing smile that she almost wanted to return it. "I guess I can control myself. Drink this."

He lifted the cup to her lips, and she took a first greedy sip. Whiskey shot through her system. "That's horrible. I don't want it."

"Put some color back in your cheeks." But he set the cup aside.

"I just want to…" But the whiskey had shocked her brain enough to clear it. Jake had to hold her down to keep her from scrambling out of bed. Her shift tangled around her knees and drooped over one shoulder.

"Hold on. You stand up now, you're going to fall on that pretty face of yours."

"Fire." She coughed, gasping from the pain in her throat. To balance herself, she grabbed him, then dropped her head weakly on his chest. "There's a fire."

"I know." Relief and pleasure surged through him as he stroked her hair. Her cheek was nestled against his heart as if it belonged there. "It's pretty well done now."

"It might spread. I've got to stop it."

"It's not going to spread." He eased her back with a gentleness that would have surprised her if she'd been aware of it. "Nothing to feed it, no wind to carry it. You lost the shed, that's all."

"I got the horses out," she murmured. Her head was whirling and throbbing. But his voice—his voice and the stroke of his hands soothed her everywhere. Comforted, she let her eyes close. "I wasn't sure I could."

"You did fine." Because he wanted to say more and didn't know how, he passed the cloth over her face. "You'd better rest now."

"Don't go." She reached for his hand again and brought it to her cheek. "Please don't go."

"I'm not going anywhere." He brushed the hair away from her face while he fought his own demons. "Go on to sleep." He needed her to. If she opened her eyes and looked at him again, if she touched him again, he was going to lose.

"The puppy was barking. I thought he needed to go out, so I—" She came to herself abruptly. He could see it in the way her eyes flew open. "Mr. Redman! What are you doing here? Here," she repeated, scandalized, as she glanced around the loft. "I'm not dressed."

He dropped the cloth back in the bowl. "It's been a trial not to notice." She was coming back, all right, he thought as he watched her eyes fire up. It was a pleasure to watch it. With some regret, he picked up the blanket and tossed it over her. "Feel better?"

"Mr. Redman." Her voice was stiff with embarrassment. "I don't entertain gentlemen in my private quarters."

He picked up the cup of whiskey and took a drink himself. Now that she seemed back to normal, it hit him how scared he'd been. Bone-scared. "Ain't much entertaining about dressing a head wound."

Sarah pushed herself up on her elbows, and the room reeled. With a moan, she lifted her fingers to the back of her neck. "I must have hit my head."

"Must have." He thought of the riders, but said nothing. "Since I picked you up off the ground and carted you all the way up here, don't you figure I'm entitled to know what happened tonight?"

"I don't really know." With a long sigh, she leaned back against the pillow she'd purchased only that morning. He was entitled to the story, she supposed. In any case, she wanted to tell someone. "I'd already retired for the night when the puppy began to bark. He seemed determined to get out, so I climbed down. I saw the fire. I don't know how it could have started. It was still light when I fed the stock, so I never even had a lamp over there."

Jake had his own ideas, but he bided his time. Sarah lifted a hand to her throbbing head and allowed herself the luxury of closing her eyes. "I ran over to get the horses out. The place was going up so fast. I've never seen anything like it. The roof was coming down, and the horses were terrified. They wouldn't come out. I'd read somewhere that horses are so frightened by fire they just panic and burn alive. I couldn't have stood that."

"So you went in after them."

"They were screaming." Her brows drew together as she remembered. "It sounded like women screaming. It was horrible."

"Yeah, I know." He remembered another barn, another fire, when the horses hadn't been so lucky.

"I remember falling when I got out the last time. I think I was choking on the smoke. I started to get up. I don't know what I was going to do. Then something hit me, I guess. One of the horses, perhaps. Or perhaps I simply fell again." She opened her eyes and studied him. He was sitting on her bed, his hair disheveled and his eyes dark and intense. Beautiful, she thought. Then she wondered if she was delirious. "Then you were here. Why are you here?"

"Riding by this way. Saw the fire." He looked into the cup of whiskey. If he was going to sit here much longer, watching what the lamplight did to her skin, he was going to need more than a cupful. "I also saw two riders heading away."

"Away?" Righteous indignation had her sitting up again, despite the headache. "You mean someone was here and didn't try to help?"

Jake gave her a long, even look. She looked so fragile, like something you put behind glass in a parlor. Fragile or not, she had to know what she was up against. "I figure they weren't here to help." He watched as the realization seeped in. There was a flicker of fear. That was what he'd expected. What he hadn't counted on and was forced to admire was the passion in her eyes.

"They came on my land? Burned down my shed? Why?"

She'd forgotten that she was wearing no more than a shift, forgotten that it was past midnight and that she was alone with a man. She sat up, and the blanket dropped to pool at her waist. Her small, round breasts rose and fell with her temper. Her hair was loose. He'd never seen it that way before. Until that moment he hadn't taken the time or the trouble to really look. A man's hands could get lost in hair like that. The thought ran through his mind and was immediately banished. It glowed warm in the lamplight, sliding over her right shoulder and streaming down her back. Anger had brought the color back to her face and the golden glow back to her eyes.

He finished off the whiskey, reminding himself that he'd do well to keep his mind on the business at hand. "Seems logical to figure they wanted to give you some trouble, maybe make you think twice about keeping this place."

"That doesn't make any sense." She leaned forward. Jake shifted uncomfortably when her thin lawn gown gapped at the throat. "Why should anyone care about an adobe house and a few sagging sheds?"

Jake set the cup down again. "You forgot the mine. Some people'll do a lot more than set a fire for gold."

With a sound of disgust, Sarah propped her elbows on her knees. "Gold? Do you think my father would have lived like this if there'd been any significant amount of gold?"

"If you believe that, why are you staying?"

The brooding look left her eyes as she glanced back at him. "I don't expect you to understand. This is all I have. All I have left of my father is this place and a gold watch." She took the watch from the tilting table beside the bed and closed her hand around it. "I intend to keep what's mine. If someone's played a nasty joke—"

Jake interrupted her. "Might've been a joke. It's more likely somebody thinks this place is worth more than you say. Trying to burn horses alive and hitting women isn't considered much of a joke. Even out here."

She lifted a hand to the wound on her head. He was saying someone had struck her. And he was right, she acknowledged with a quick shudder. He was undoubtedly right. "No one's going to scare me off my land. Tomorrow I'll report this incident to the sheriff, and I'll find a way to protect my property."

"Just what way is that?"

"I don't know." She tightened her grip on the watch. The look in her eyes said everything. "But I'll find it."

Maybe she would, he thought. And maybe, since he didn't care much for people setting fires, he'd help her. "Someone might be offering to buy this place from you," Jake murmured, thinking ahead.

"I'm not selling. And I'm not running. If and when I return to Philadelphia, it will be because I've decided that's what I want to do, not because I've been frightened away."

That was an attitude he could respect. "Fair enough. Since it appears you're going to have your hands full tomorrow, you'd best get some sleep."

"Yes." Sleep? How could she possibly close her eyes? What if they came back?

"If it's all the same to you, I'll bunk down outside."

Her eyes lifted to his and held them. The quiet understanding in them made her want to rest her head on his shoulder. He'd take care of her. She had only to ask. But she couldn't ask.

"Of course, you're welcome to. Mr. Redman…" She remembered belatedly to drag the blanket up to her shoulders. "I'm in your debt again. It seems you've come to my aid a number of times in a very short acquaintance."

"I didn't have to go out of my way much." He started to rise, then thought better of it. "I got a question for you."

Because she was feeling awkward again, she offered him a small, polite smile. "Yes?"

"Why'd you ask me not to kiss you?"

Her fingers tightened on the blanket. "I beg your pardon?"

"When you were coming to, you took a good, long look at me, and then you told me not to kiss you."

She could feel the heat rising to her cheeks. Dignity, she told herself. Even under circumstances like these, a woman must keep her dignity. "Apparently I wasn't in my right senses."

He thought that through and then unnerved her by smiling. For his own satisfaction, he reached out to touch the ends of her hair. "A man could take that two ways."

She sputtered. The lamplight shifted across his face. Light, then shadow. It made him look mysterious, exciting. Forbidden. Sarah found it almost as difficult to breathe as she did when her stays were too tight. "Mr. Redman, I assure you—"

"It made me think." He was close now, so close that she could feel his breath flutter over her lips. They parted, seemingly of their own volition. He took the time—a heartbeat, two—to flick his gaze down to them. "Maybe you've been wondering about me kissing you."

"Certainly not." But her denial lacked the ring of truth. They both knew it.

"I'll have to give it some thought myself." The trouble was, he'd been giving it too much thought already. The way she looked right now, with her hair loose around her shoulders and her eyes dark, just a little scared, made him not want to think at all. He knew that if he touched her, head wound or not, he'd climb right in the bed with her and take whatever he wanted.

He was going to kiss her. Her head swam with the idea. He had only to lean closer and his mouth would be on hers. Hard. Somehow she knew it would be hard, firm, masterful. He could take her in his arms right now and there would be nothing she could do about it. Maybe there was nothing she wanted to do about it.

Then he was standing. For the first time she noticed that he had to stoop so that his head didn't brush the roof. His body blocked the light. Her heart was thudding so hard that she was certain he must hear it. For the life of her, she couldn't be sure if it was fear or excitement. Slowly he leaned over and blew out the lamp.

In the dark, he moved down from the loft and out into the night.

Shivering, Sarah huddled under the blanket. The man was— She didn't have words to describe him. The only thing she was certain of was that she wouldn't sleep a wink.

She went out like a light.

When Sarah woke, her head felt as though it had been split open and filled with a drum-and-bugle corps. Moaning, she sat on the edge of the cot and cradled her aching head in her hands. She wished she could believe it had all been a nightmare, but the pounding at the base of her skull, and the rust-colored water in the bowl, said differently.

Gingerly she began to dress. The best she could do for herself at the moment was to see how bad the damage was and pray the horses came back. She doubted she could afford two more on her meager budget. In deference to her throbbing head, she tied her hair back loosely with a ribbon. Even the thought of hairpins made her grimace.

The power of the sun had her gasping. Small red dots danced in front of her eyes and her vision wavered and dimmed. She leaned against the door, gathering her strength, before she stepped out.

The shed was gone. In its place was rubble, a mass of black, charred wood. Determined, Sarah crossed over to it. She could still smell the smoke. If she closed her eyes she could hear the terrifying sound of fire crackling over dry wood. And the heat. She'd never forget the heat—the intensity of it, the meanness of it.

It hadn't been much of a structure, but it had been hers. In a civilized society a vandal was made to pay for the destruction of property. Arizona Territory or Philadelphia, she meant to see that justice was done here. But for now she was alone.

Alone. She stood in the yard and listened. Never before had she heard such quiet. There was a trace of wind, hot and silent. It lacked the strength to rustle the scrub that pushed its way through the rocks. The only sound she heard was the quick breathing of the puppy, who was sitting on the ground at her feet.

The horses had run off. So, Sarah thought as she turned in a circle, had Jake Redman. It was better that way, she decided—because she remembered, all too clearly, the way she had felt when he had sat on the cot in the shadowy lamp-light and touched her hair. Foolish. It was hateful to admit it, but she'd felt foolish and weak and, worst of all, willing.

There was no use being ashamed of it, but she considered herself too smart to allow it to happen again. A man like Jake Redman wasn't the type a woman could flirt harmlessly with. Perhaps she didn't have a wide and worldly experience with men, but she recognized a dangerous one when she saw him.

There were some, she had no doubt, who would be drawn to his kind. A man who killed without remorse or regret, who came and went as he pleased. But not her. When she decided to give her heart to a man, it would be to one she understood and respected.

With a sigh, she bent down to soothe the puppy, who was whimpering at her feet. There was a comfort in the way he nuzzled his face against hers. When she fell in love and married, Sarah thought, it would be to a man of dignity and breeding, a man who would cherish her, who would protect her, not with guns and fists but with honor. They would be devoted to each other, and to the family they made between them. He would be educated and strong, respected in the community.

Those were the qualities she'd been taught a woman looked for in a husband. Sarah stroked the puppy's head and wished she could conquer this strange feeling that what she'd been taught wasn't necessarily true.

What did it matter now? As things stood, she had too much to do to think about romance. She had to find a way to rebuild the shed. Then she'd have to bargain for a new wagon and team. She stirred some of the charred wood with the toe of her shoe. She was about to give in to the urge to kick it when she heard horses approaching.

Panic came first and had her spinning around, a cry for help on her lips. The sunbaked dirt and empty rocks mocked her. The Lord helped those who help themselves, she remembered, and raced into the house with the puppy scrambling behind her.

When she came out again her knees were trembling, but she was carrying her father's rifle in both hands.

Jake took one look at her, framed in the doorway, her eyes mirroring fear and fury. It came to him with a kind of dull, painful surprise that she was the kind of woman a man would die for. He slid from his horse.

"I'd be obliged, ma'am, if you'd point that someplace else."

"Oh." She nearly sagged with relief. "Mr. Redman. I thought you'd gone." He merely inclined his head and took another meaningful look at the rifle. "Oh," she said again, and lowered it. She felt foolish, not because of the gun but because when she'd looked out and seen him all her thoughts about what she wanted and didn't want had shifted ground. There he was, looking dark and reckless, with guns gleaming at his hip. And there she was, fighting back a driving instinct to run into his arms.

"You...found the horses."

He took his time tying the team to a post before he approached her. "They hadn't gone far." He took the rifle from her and leaned it against the house. The stock was damp from her nervous hands. But he'd seen more than nerves in her eyes. And he wondered.

"I'm very grateful." Because she felt awkward, she leaned down to gather the yapping puppy in her arms. Jake still hadn't shaved, and she remembered how his face had felt against the palm of her hand. Fighting a blush, she curled her fingers. "I'm afraid I don't know what to do with them until I have shelter again."

What was going on in that mind of hers? Jake wondered. "A lean-to would do well enough for the time being. Just need to rig one over a corner of the paddock."

"A lean-to, yes." It was a relief to deal with something practical. Her mind went to work quickly. "Mr. Redman, have you had breakfast?"

He tipped his hat back on his head. "Not to speak of."

"If you could fashion a temporary shelter for the horses, I'd be more than glad to fix you a meal."

He'd meant to do it anyway, but if she wanted to bargain, he'd bargain. "Can you cook?"

"Naturally. Preparing meals was a very important part of my education."

He wanted to touch her hair again. And more. Instead, he hooked his thumb in his pocket. "I ain't worried about you preparing a meal. Can you cook?"

She tried not to sigh. "Yes."

"All right, then."

When he walked away and didn't remount his horse, Sarah supposed a deal had been struck. "Mr. Redman?" He stopped to look over his shoulder. "How do you prefer your eggs?"

"Hot," he told her, then continued on his way.

She'd give him hot, Sarah decided, rattling pans. She'd give him the best damn breakfast he'd ever eaten. She took a long breath and forced herself to be calm. His way of talking was beginning to rub off on her. That would never do.

Biscuits. Delighted that she'd been given a brand-new recipe only the day before, she went to work.

Thirty minutes later, Jake came in to stand in the doorway. The scents amazed him. He'd expected to find the frying pan smoking with burnt eggs. Instead, he saw a bowl of fresh, golden-topped biscuits wrapped in a clean bandanna. Sarah was busy at the stove, humming to herself. The pup was nosing into corners, looking for trouble.

Jake had never thought much about a home for himself, but if he had it would have been like this. A woman in a pretty dress humming by the stove, the smells of good cooking rising in the air. A man could do almost anything if the right woman was waiting for him.

Then she turned. One look at her face, the elegance of it, was a reminder that a man like him didn't have a woman like her waiting for him.

"Just in time." She smiled, pleased with herself. Conquering the cookstove was her biggest accomplishment to date. "There's fresh water in the bowl, so you can wash up." She began to scoop eggs onto an ironstone plate. "I'm afraid I don't have a great deal to offer. I'm thinking of getting some chickens of my own. We had them at school, so I know a bit about them. Fresh eggs are such a comfort, don't you think?"

He lifted his head from the bowl, and water dripped down from his face. Her cheeks were flushed from cooking, and her sleeves were rolled up past her elbows, revealing slender, milk-white arms. Comfort was the last thing on his mind. Without speaking, he took his seat.

Sarah wasn't sure when he made her more nervous, when he spoke to her or when he lapsed into those long silences and just looked. Gamely she tried again. "Mrs. Cobb gave me the recipe for these biscuits yesterday. I hope they're as good as she claimed."

Jake broke one, and the steam and fragrance poured out. Watching her, he bit into it. "They're fine."

"Please, Mr. Redman, all this flattery will turn my head." She scooped up a forkful of eggs. "I was introduced to several ladies yesterday while I was buying supplies. They seem very hospitable."

"I don't know much about the ladies in town." At least not the kind Sarah was speaking of.

"I see." She took a bite of biscuit herself. It was more than fine, she thought with a pout. It was delicious. "Liza Cody—her family runs the dry goods store. I found her very amiable. She was kind enough to let me have one of their puppies."

Jake looked down at the dog, who was sniffing at his boot and thumping his tail. "That where you got this thing?"

"Yes. I wanted the company."

Jake broke off a bite of biscuit and dropped it to the dog, ignoring Sarah's muttered admonition about feeding animals from the table. "Scrawny now, but he's going to be a big one."

"Really?" Intrigued, she leaned over to look. "How can you tell?"

"His paws. He's clumsy now because they're too big for him. He'll grow into them."

"I fancy it's to my advantage to own a large dog."

"Didn't do you much good last night," he pointed out, but pleased both the pup and Sarah by scratching between the dog's floppy ears. "You give him a name yet?"

"Lafitte."

Jake paused with his fork halfway to his lips. "What the hell kind of name is that for a dog?"

"After the pirate. He had that black marking around his eye, like a patch."

"Pretty fancy name for a mutt," Jake said over a mouthful of eggs. "Bandit's better."

Sarah lifted a brow. "I'd certainly never give him a name like that."

"A pirate's a bandit, isn't he?" Jake dived into another biscuit.

"Be that as it may, the name stands."

Chewing, Jake looked down at the puppy, who was groveling a bit, obviously hoping for another handout. "Bet it makes you feel pretty stupid, doesn't it, fella?"

"Would you care for more coffee, Mr. Redman?" Frustrated, Sarah rose and, wrapping a cloth around the handle, took the pot from the stove. Without waiting for an answer, she stood beside Jake and poured.

She smelled good, he thought. Soft. Kind of subtle, like a field of wildflowers in early spring. At the ends of her stiff white sleeves, her hands were delicate. He remembered the feel of them on his cheek.

"They taught you good," he muttered.

"I beg your pardon?" She looked down at him. There was something in his eyes, a hint of what she'd seen in them the night before. It didn't make her nervous, as she'd been certain it would. It made her yearn.

"The cooking." Jake put a hand over hers to straighten the pot and keep the coffee from overflowing the cup. Then he kept it there, feeling the smooth texture of her skin and the surprisingly rapid beating of her pulse. She didn't back away, or blush, or snatch her hand from his. Instead, she simply looked back at him. The question in her eyes was one he wanted badly to answer.

She moistened her lips but kept her eyes steady. "Thank you. I'm glad you enjoyed it."

"You take too many chances, Sarah." Slowly, when he was certain she understood his meaning, he removed his hand.

With her chin up, she returned the pot to the stove. How dare he make her feel like that, then toss it back in her face?

"You don't frighten me, Mr. Redman. If you were going to hurt me, you would have done so by now."

"Maybe, maybe not. Your kind wears a man down."

"My kind?" She turned, the light of challenge in her eyes. "Just what kind would that be?"

"The soft kind. The soft, stubborn kind who's right on the edge of stepping into a man's arms."

"You couldn't be more mistaken." Her voice was icy now in defense against the blood that had heated at his words. "I haven't any interest in being in your arms, or any man's. My only interest at the moment is protecting my property."

"Could be I'm wrong." He rocked back in his chair. She was a puzzle, all right, and he'd never known how pleasurable it could be to get a woman's dander up. "We'll both find out sooner or later. Meanwhile, just how do you plan to go about protecting this place?"

Not much caring whether he was finished or not, she began to stack the plates. "I'm going to alert the sheriff, of course."

"That's not going to hurt, but it's not going to help much, either, if you get more trouble out here. The sheriff's ten miles away."

"Just what do you suggest?"

He'd already given it some thought, and he had an answer. "If I were you, I'd hire somebody to help out around here. Somebody who can give you a hand with the place, and who knows how to use a gun."

A thrill sprinted through her. She managed, just barely, to keep her voice disinterested. "Yourself, I suppose."

He grinned at her. "No, Duchess, I ain't looking for that kind of job. I was thinking of Lucius."

Frowning, she began to scrub out the frying pan. "He drinks."

"Who doesn't? Give him a couple of meals and a place to bunk down and he'll do all right for you. A woman staying out here all alone's just asking for trouble. Those men who burned your shed last night might've done more to you than give you a headache."

His meaning was clear enough, clearer still because she'd thought of that possibility herself. She'd prefer him—though only because she knew he was capable, she assured herself. But she did need someone. "Perhaps you're right."

"No perhaps about it. Someone as green as you doesn't have the sense to do more than die out here."

"I don't see why you have to insult me."

"The plain truth's the plain truth, Duchess."

Teeth clenched, she banged dishes. "I told you not to—"

"I got a question for you," he said, interrupting her easily. "What would you have done this morning if it hadn't been me bringing back the horses?"

"I would have defended myself."

"You ever shot a Henry before?"

She gave him a scandalized look. "Why in the world would I have shot anyone named Henry?"

With a long sigh, he rose. "A Henry rifle, Duchess. That's what you were pointing at my belt buckle before you fixed my eggs."

Sarah wiped the pan clean, then set it aside. "No, I haven't actually fired one, but I can't imagine it's that complicated. In any case, I never intended to shoot it."

"What did you have in mind? Dancing with it?"

She snatched up a plate. "Mr. Redman, I'm growing weary of being an amusement to you. I realize that someone like you thinks nothing of shooting a man dead and walking away. I, however, have been taught—rightfully— that killing is a sin."

"You're wrong." Something in his voice had her turning toward him again. "Surviving's never a sin. It's all there is."

"If you believe that, I'm sorry for you."

He didn't want her pity. But he did want her to stay alive. Moving over, he took the plates out of her hands. "If you see a snake, are you going to kill it or stand there and let it bite you?"

"That's entirely different."

"You might not think it's so different if you stay out here much longer. Where's the cartridges for the rifle?"

Wiping her hands on her apron, Sarah glanced at the shelf behind her. Jake took the cartridges down, checked them, then gripped her arm. "Come on. I'll give you a lesson."

"I haven't finished cleaning the dishes."

"They'll keep."

"I never said I wanted lessons," she told him as he pulled her outside.

"If you're going to pick up a gun, you ought to know how to use it." He hefted the rifle and smiled at her. "Unless you're afraid you can't learn."

Sarah untied her apron and laid it over the rail. "I'm not afraid of anything."

Chapter 5

He'd figured a challenge would be the best way to get her cooperation. Sarah marched along beside him, chin up, eyes forward. He didn't think she knew it, but when she'd held the rifle that morning she'd been prepared to pull the trigger. He wanted to make sure that when she did she hit what she aimed at.

From the rubble of the burned shed, Jake selected a few pieces of charred wood and balanced three of them against a pile of rocks.

"First thing you do is learn how to load it without shooting off your foot." Jake emptied the rifle's chamber, then slowly reloaded. "You've got to have respect for a weapon, and not go around holding it like you were going to sweep the porch with it."

To prove his point, he brought the rifle up, sighted in and fired three shots. The three pieces of scrap wood flew backward in unison. "Bullets can do powerful damage to a man," he told her as he lowered the gun again.

She had to swallow. The sound of gunfire still echoed. "I'm aware of that, Mr. Redman. I have no intention of shooting anyone."

"Most people don't wake up in the morning figuring on it." He went to the rocks again. This time he set up the largest piece of wood. "Unless you're planning on heading back to Philadelphia real soon, you'd better learn how to use this."

"I'm not going anywhere."

With a nod, Jake emptied the rifle and handed her the ammo. "Load it."

She didn't like the feel of the bullets in her hands. They were cold and smooth. Holding them, she wondered how anyone could use them against another. Metal against flesh. No, it was inconceivable.

"You going to play with them or put them in the gun?"

Because he was watching her, Sarah kept her face impassive and did as he told her.

He pushed the barrel away from his midsection. "You're a quick study."

It shouldn't have pleased her, but she felt the corners of her mouth turn up nonetheless. "So I've been told."

Unable to resist, he brushed the hair out of her eyes. "Don't get cocky." Stepping behind her, he laid the gun in her hands, then adjusted her arms. "Balance it and get a good grip on it."

"I am," she muttered, wishing he wouldn't stand quite so close. He smelled of leather and sweat, a combination that, for reasons beyond her comprehension, aroused her. One hand was firm on her arm, the other on her shoulder. Hardly a lover's touch, and yet she felt her system respond as it had never responded to the gentle, flirtatious hand-holding she'd experienced in Philadelphia. She had only to lean back the slightest bit to be pressed close against him.

Not that she wanted to be. She shifted, then grumbled under her breath when he pushed her into place again.

"Hold still. Not stiff, woman, still," he told her when her body went rigid at his touch.

"There's no need to snap at me."

"You stand like that when you fire, you're going to get a broken shoulder. Loosen up. You see the sight?"

"That little thing sticking up there?"

He closed his eyes for a moment. "Yeah, that little thing sticking up there. Use it to sight in the target. Bring the stock up some." He leaned over. Sarah pressed her lips together when his cheek brushed hers. "Steady," he murmured, re-sisting the urge to turn his face into her hair. "Wrap your finger around the trigger. Don't jerk it, just pull it back, slow and smooth."

She shut her eyes and obeyed. The rifle exploded in her hands and would have knocked her flat on her back if he hadn't been there to steady her. She screamed, afraid she'd shot herself.

"Missed."

Breathing hard, Sarah whirled around. Always a cautious man, Jake took the rifle from her. "You might have warned me." She brought her hand up to nurse her bruised shoulder. "It felt like someone hit me with a rock."

"It's always better to find things out firsthand. Try it again."

With her teeth clenched, Sarah took the rifle and man-aged to get back into position.

"This time use your arm instead of your shoulder to bal-ance it. Lean in a bit."

"My ears are ringing."

"You'll get used to it." He put a steadying hand on her waist. "It helps if you keep your eyes open. Sight low. Good. Now pull the trigger."

This time she was braced for the kick and just staggered a little. Jake kept a hand at her waist and looked over her head. "You caught a corner of it."

"I did?" She looked for herself. "I did!" Laughing, she looked over her shoulder at him. "I want to do it again." She lifted the rifle and didn't complain when Jake pushed the barrel three inches to the right. She kept her eyes wide open this time as she pressed her finger down on the trigger. She let out a whoop when the wood flew off the rocks. "I hit it."

"Looks like."

"I really hit it. Imagine." When he took the gun from her, she shook her hair back and laughed. "My arm's tingling."

"It'll pass." He was surprised he could speak. The way she looked when she laughed made his throat slam shut. He wasn't a man for pretty words, not for saying them or for thinking them. But just now it ran through his head that she looked like an angel in the sunlight, with her hair the color of wet wheat and her eyes like gold dust.

And he wanted her, as he'd wanted few things in his life. Slowly, wanting to give himself time to regain control, he walked over to the rocks to pick up the target. She had indeed hit it. The hole was nearly at the top, and far to the right of center, but she'd hit it. He walked back to drop the wood in Sarah's hands and watched her grin about it.

"Trouble is, most things you shoot at don't sit nice and still like a block of wood."

He was determined to spoil it for her, Sarah thought, studying his cool, unreadable eyes. The man was impossible to understand. One moment he was going to the trouble to teach her how to shoot the rifle, and the next he couldn't even manage the smallest of compliments because she'd learned well. The devil with him.

"Mr. Redman, it's very apparent that nothing I do pleases you." She tossed the block of wood aside. "Isn't it fortunate for both of us that it doesn't matter in the least?" With that she gathered up her skirts and began to stamp back toward the house. She managed no more than a startled gasp as he spun her around.

She knew that look, she thought dazedly as she stared at him. It was the same one she'd first seen on his face, when he'd ridden beside the stage, firing his pistol over his shoulder. She hadn't a clue as to how to deal with him now, so she took the only option that came to mind.

"Take your hands off me."

"I warned you, you took too many chances." His grip only tightened when she tried to shrug him off. "It's not smart to turn your back on a man who's holding a loaded gun."

"Did you intend to shoot me in the back, Mr. Redman?" It was an unfair remark, and she knew it. But she wanted to get away from him, quickly, until that look faded from his eyes. "I wouldn't put that, or anything else, past you. You're the rudest, most ill-mannered, most ungentlemanly man I've ever met. I'll thank you to get back on your horse and ride off my land."

He'd resisted challenges before, but he'd be damned if he'd resist this one. From the first time he'd seen her she'd started an itch in him. It was time he scratched it.

"Seems to me you need another lesson, Duchess."

"I neither need nor want anything from you. And I won't be called by that ridiculous name." Her breath came out in a whoosh when he dragged her against him. He saw her eyes go wide with shock.

"Then I won't call you anything." He was still holding the rifle. With his eyes on hers, he slid his hand up her back to gather up her hair. "I don't much like talking, anyway."

She fought him. At least she needed to believe she did. Despite her efforts, his mouth closed over hers. In that instant the sun was blocked out and she was plunged, breathless, into the deepest, darkest night.

His body was like iron. His arm bonded her against him so that she had no choice, really no choice, but to absorb the feel of him. He made her think of the rifle, slim and hard and deadly. Through the shock, the panic and the excitement she felt the fast, uneven beating of his heart against hers.

Her blood had turned into some hot, foreign liquid that made her pulse leap and her heart thud. The rough stubble of his beard scraped her face, and she moaned. From the pain, she assured herself. It couldn't be from pleasure.

And yet… Her hands were on his shoulders, holding on now rather than pushing away.

He wondered if she knew she packed a bigger kick than her father's rifle. He'd never known that anything so sweet could be so potent. That anything so delicate could be so strong. She had him by the throat and didn't even know it. And he wanted more. In a move too desperate to be gentle, he dragged her head back by the hair.

She gasped in the instant he allowed her to breathe, dragging in air, unaware that she'd been stunned into holding her breath. Then his mouth was on hers again, his tongue invading, arousing in a way she hadn't known she could be aroused, weakening in a way she hadn't believed she could be weakened.

She moaned again, but this time there was no denying the pleasure. Tentatively, then boldly, she answered the new demand. Savoring the hot, salty taste of his lips, she ran her hands along the planes of his face and into his hair. Glorious. No one had ever warned her that a kiss could make the body burn and tremble and yearn. A sound of stunned delight caught in her throat.

The sound lit fires in him that he knew could never be allowed to burn free. She was innocent. Any fool could see that. And he...he hadn't been innocent since he'd drawn his first breath. There were lines he crossed, laws he broke. But this one had to be respected. He struggled to clear his mind, but she filled it. Her arms were around his neck, pulling him closer, pulling him in. And her mouth... Sweet Lord, her mouth. His heart was hammering in his head, in his loins...all from the taste of her. Honeyed whiskey. A man could drown in it.

Afraid he would, and even more afraid he'd want to, he pushed her away. Her eyes were dark and unfocused—the way they'd been last night, when she'd started to come to. It gave him some satisfaction to see it, because he felt as though he'd been knocked cold, himself.

"Like I said, you learn fast, Sarah." His hand was shaking. Infuriated, he curled it into a fist. He had a flash, an almost painful one, of what it would be like to drag her to the ground and take everything from her. Before he could act, one way or the other, he heard the sound of an approaching wagon. "You got company coming." He handed her the rifle and walked away.

What had he done to her? Sarah put a hand to her spinning head. He'd...he'd forced himself on her. Forced her until...until he hadn't had to force her any longer. Until it had felt right to want him. Until wanting him had been all there was.

Just like the dream. But this wasn't a dream, Sarah told herself, straightening her shoulders. It was more than real, and now he was walking away from her as if it hadn't mattered to him in the least. Pride was every bit as dangerous an emotion as anger.

"Mr. Redman."

When he turned, he saw her standing there with the rifle. If the look in her eyes meant anything, she'd have dearly loved to use it.

"Apparently you take chances, too." She tilted her head. There was challenge in the gesture, as well as a touch of fury and a stab of hurt. "This rifle's still loaded."

"That's right." He touched the brim of his hat in a salute. "It's a hell of a lot harder to pull the trigger when you're aiming at flesh and blood, but go ahead. It'd be hard to miss at this range."

She wished she could. She wished she had the skill to put a bullet between his feet and watch him jump. Lifting her chin, she walked toward the house. "The difference between you and me, Mr. Redman, is that I still have morals."

"There's some truth in that." He strode easily beside her. "Seeing as you fixed me breakfast and all, why don't you call me Jake?" He swung up into the saddle as a buggy rumbled into the yard.

"Sarah?" With her hands still on the reins, Liza cast an uncertain glance at her new friend, then at the man in the saddle. She knew she wasn't supposed to approve of men like Jake Redman. But she found it difficult not to when he looked so attractive and exciting. "I hope you don't mind us coming out." A young boy jumped out of the buggy and began to chase the puppy, who was running in circles.

"Not at all. I'm delighted." Sarah shaded her eyes with her hand so that she could see Jake clearly. "Mr. Redman was just on his way."

"Those sure are some pretty guns you got there, mister." Young John Cody put a hand on the neck of Jake's gray mustang and peered up at the smooth wooden grip of one of the Colt .45s he carried. He knew who Jake Redman was—he'd heard all the stories—but he'd never managed to get this close before.

"Think so?" Ignoring the two women, Jake shifted in his saddle to get a better look at the boy. No more than ten, he figured, with awe in his eyes and a smudge of dirt on his cheek.

"Yessiree. I think that when you slap leather you're just about the fastest there is, maybe in the whole world."

"John Cody." Liza stayed in the buggy, wringing her hands. "You oughtn't to bother Mr. Redman."

Jake shot her a quick, amused look. Did she think he'd shoot the kid for talking to him? "No bother, ma'am." He glanced down at Johnny again. "You can't believe everything you hear."

But Johnny figured he knew what was what. "My ma says that since you saved that stage there's probably some good in you somewhere."

This time Liza called her brother's name in a strained, desperate whisper. Jake had to grin. He shifted his attention to Sarah long enough to see that she was standing as stiff as a rod, with one eyebrow arched.

"That's right kind of her. I'll tell the sheriff about your trouble… Miss Conway. I reckon he'll be out to see you."

"Thank you, Mr. Redman. Good day."

He tipped his hat to her, then to Liza. "See you around, Johnny." He turned his horse in a half circle and rode away.

"Yessir," Johnny shouted after him. "Yessiree."

"John Cody." Liza collected herself enough to climb out of the buggy. Johnny just grinned and raced off after the puppy again, firing an imaginary Peacemaker. "That's my brother."

"Yes, I imagined it was."

Liza gave Johnny one last look of sisterly disgust before going to Sarah. "Ma's tending the store today. She wanted you to have this. It's a loaf of her cinnamon bread."

"Oh, how kind of her." One whiff brought memories of home. "Can you stay?"

Liza gave Sarah the bread and a quick, dimpled smile. "I was hoping I could."

"Come in, please. I'll fix us some tea."

While Sarah busied herself at the stove, Liza looked around the tiny cabin. It was scrubbed clean as a whistle. "It's not as bad as I thought it would be." Instantly she lifted a hand to her mouth. "I'm sorry. Ma always says I talk too much for my own good."

"That's all right." Sarah got out two tin cups and tried not to wish they were china. "I was taken by surprise myself."

At ease again, Liza sat at the table. "I didn't expect to run into Jake Redman out here."

Sarah brought the knife down into the bread with a thwack. "Neither did I."

"He said you had trouble."

Unconsciously Sarah lifted a finger to her lips. They were still warm from his, and they tingled as her arms had from the kick of the Henry. She had trouble, all right. Since she couldn't explain the kiss to herself, she could hardly explain it to Liza. "Someone set fire to my shed last night."

"Oh, Sarah, no! Who? Why?"

"I don't know." She brought the two cups to the table. "Fortunately, Mr. Redman happened to be riding by this way."

"Do you think he might have done it?"

Sarah's brow rose as she considered the possibility. She remembered the way he'd bathed her face and tended her hurts. "No, I'm quite certain he didn't. I believe Mr. Redman takes a more direct approach."

"I guess you're right about that. I can't say he's started any trouble here in Lone Bluff, but he's finished some."

"What do you know about him?"

"I don't think anyone knows much. He rode into town about six months ago. Of course, everybody's heard of Jake Redman. Some say he's killed more than twenty men in gunfights."

"Killed?" Stunned, Sarah could only stare. "But why?"

"I don't know if there always is a why. I did hear that some rancher up north hired him on. There'd been trouble... rustling, barn-burning."

"Hired him on," Sarah murmured. "To kill."

"That's what it comes down to, I suppose. I do know that plenty of people were nervous when he rode in and took a room at Maggie O'Rourke's." Liza broke off a corner of the slice of bread Sarah had served her. "But he didn't seem to be looking for trouble. About two weeks later he found it, anyway."

A hired killer, Sarah thought, her stomach churning. And she'd kissed him, kissed him in a way no lady kissed a man who wasn't her husband. "What happened?"

"Jim Carlson was in the Bird Cage. That's one of the saloons in town."

"Carlson?"

"Yes, he's Samuel Carlson's brother. You wouldn't know it," Liza continued, pursing her lips. "Jim's nothing like Samuel. Full of spit, that one. Likes to brag and swagger and bully. Cheats at cards, but nobody had the nerve to call him on it. Until Jake." Liza drank more tea and listened with half an ear to her brother's war whoops in the yard. "The way I heard it, there were some words over the card table. Jim was drunk and a little careless with his dealing. Once Jake called him on it, some of the other men joined in. Word is, Jim drew. Everybody figured Jake would put a bullet in him there and then, but he just knocked him down."

"He didn't shoot him?" She felt a wave of relief. Perhaps he wasn't what people said he was.

"No. At least, the way I heard it, Jake just knocked him silly and gave Jim's gun to the bartender. Somebody had already hightailed it for the sheriff. By the time he got there, Jake was standing at the bar having himself a drink and Jim was picking himself up off the floor. I think Barker was going to put Jim in a cell for the night until he sobered up. But when he took hold of him, Jim pulled the gun from the sheriff's holster. Instead of getting a bullet in the back, Jake put one in Jim Carlson, then turned around and finished his drink."

Dead's dead. "Did he kill him?"

"No, though there's some in town wished he had. The Carlsons are pretty powerful around here, but there were enough witnesses, the sheriff included, to call it self-defense."

"I see." But she didn't understand the kind of justice that had to be meted out with guns and bullets. "I'm surprised Jake—Mr. Redman—hasn't moved on."

"He must like it around here. What about you? Doesn't it scare you to stay out here alone?"

Sarah thought of her first night, shivering under the blanket and praying for morning. "A little."

"After living back east." Liza gave a sigh. To her, Philadelphia sounded as glamorous and foreign as Paris or London. "All the places you've seen, the pretty clothes you must have worn."

Sarah struggled with a quick pang of homesickness. "Have you ever been east?"

"No, but I've seen pictures." Liza eyed Sarah's trunks with longing. "The women wear beautiful clothes."

"Would you like to see some of mine?"

Liza's face lit up. "I'd love to."

For the next twenty minutes Liza oohed and aahed over ruffles and lace. Her reaction caused Sarah to appreciate what she had always taken for granted. Crouched on the cabin floor, they discussed important matters such as ribbons and sashes and the proper tilt of a bonnet while Johnny was kept occupied with a hunk of bread and the puppy.

"Oh, look at this one." Delighted, Liza rose, sweeping a dress in front of her. "I wish you had a looking glass."

It was the white muslin with the rosebuds on the skirt. The dress she'd planned to wear for her first dinner with her father. He'd never see it now. She glanced at the trunks. Or any of the other lovely things he'd made certain she had in her life.

"What's wrong?" With the dress still crushed against her, Liza stepped forward. "You look so sad."

"I was thinking of my father, of how hard he worked for me."

Liza's fascination with the clothes was immediately outweighed by her sympathy. "He loved you. Often when he came in the store he'd talk about you, about what you'd written in one of your letters. I remember how he brought in this picture of you, a drawing in a little frame. He wanted everyone to see how pretty you were. He was so proud of you, Sarah."

"I miss him." With a shake of her head, Sarah blinked

back tears. "It's strange, all those years we were separated. Sometimes I could barely remember him. But since I've been here I seem to know him better, and miss him more."

Gently Liza laid a hand on her shoulder. "My pa sure riles me sometimes, but I guess I'd about die if anything happened to him."

"Well, at least I have this." She looked around the small cabin. "I feel closer to him here. I like to think about him sitting at that table and writing to me." After a long breath she managed to smile. "I'm glad I came."

Liza held out a hand. "So am I."

Rising, Sarah fluffed out the sleeves of the dress Liza was holding. "Now, let me be your looking glass. You're taller and curvier than I..." With her lips pursed, she walked in a circle around Liza. "The neckline would flatter you, but I think I'd do away with some of the ruffles in the bodice. A nice pink would be your color. It would show off your hair and eyes."

"Can you imagine me wearing a dress like that?" Closing her eyes, Liza turned in slow circles. "It would have to be at a dance. I'd have my hair curled over my shoulder and wear a velvet ribbon around my throat. Will Metcalf's eyes would fall right out."

"Who's Will Metcalf?"

Liza opened her eyes and giggled. "Just a man. He's a deputy in town. He'd like to be my beau." Mischief flashed across her face. "I might decide to let him."

"Liza loves Will," Johnny sang through the window.

"You hush up, John Cody." Rushing to the window, Liza leaned out. "If you don't, I'll tell Ma who broke Grandma's china plate."

"Liza loves Will," he repeated, unconcerned, then raced off with the puppy.

"Nothing more irritating than little brothers," she muttered. With a sigh of regret, she replaced the dress in the trunk.

Tapping a finger on her lips, Sarah came to a quick decision. She should have thought of it before, she reflected. Or perhaps it had been milling around in her mind all along. "Liza, would you like a dress like that...in pink, like that pretty muslin I saw in your store yesterday?"

"I guess I'd think I'd gone to heaven."

"What if I made it for you?"

"Made it for me?" Wide-eyed, Liza looked at the trunk, then back at Sarah. "Could you?"

"I'm very handy with a needle." Caught up in the idea, Sarah pushed through her trunks to find her measuring tape. "If you can get the material, I'll make the dress. If you like it, you can tell the other women who come in your store."

"Of course." Obediently Liza lifted her arms so that Sarah could measure her. "I'll tell everyone."

"Then some of those women might want new dresses, fashionable new dresses." Looking up, she caught the gleam of understanding in Liza's eyes.

"You bet they would."

"You get me that material and I'll make you a dress that will have Will Metcalf standing on his head."

Two hours later Sarah was pouring water over her vegetable garden. In the heat of the afternoon, with her back smarting from the chores and sun baking the dirt almost as fast as she could dampen it, she wondered if it was worth it. A garden out here would require little less than a miracle. And she would much prefer flowers.

You couldn't eat flowers, she reminded herself, and poured the last of the water out. Now she would have to walk back to the stream and fill the pail again to have water for cooking and washing.

A bath, she thought as she wiped the back of her hand over her brow. What she wouldn't give for a long bath in a real tub.

She heard the horses. It pleased her to realize that she was becoming accustomed to the sound—or lack of sound—that surrounded her new home. With her hand shading her eyes, she watched two riders come into view. It wasn't until she recognized one as Lucius that she realized she'd been holding her breath.

"Lafitte!" she called, but the dog continued to race around the yard, barking.

"Miss Conway." Sheriff Barker tipped his hat and chuckled at the snarling pup. "Got yourself a fierce-looking guard dog there."

"Makes a ruckus, anyhow," Lucius said, swinging down from his horse. Lafitte sprang at him, gripping the bottom of his pant leg with sharp puppy teeth. Bending, Lucius snatched him up by the cuff of the neck. "You mind your manners, young fella." The second he was on the ground again, Lafitte ran to hide behind Sarah's skirts.

"Heard you had some trouble out here." Barker nodded toward the remains of the shed. "This happen last night?"

"That's right. If you'd like to come inside, I was just about to get some water. I'm sure you'd like some coffee after your ride."

"I'll fetch you some water, miss," Lucius said, taking the pail from her. "Hey, boy." He grinned down at the pup. "Why don't you come along with me? I'll keep you out of trouble." After a moment's hesitation, Lafitte trotted along after him.

"Are you thinking about hiring him on?"

With her lip caught between her teeth, Sarah watched Lucius stroll off. "I was considering it."

"You'd be smart to do it." Barker took out a bandanna and wiped his neck. "Lucius has a powerful affection for the bottle, but it doesn't seem to bother him. He's honest. Did some soldiering a while back. He's amiable enough, drunk or sober."

Sarah managed a smile. "I'll take that as a recommendation, Sheriff Barker."

"Well, now." The sheriff looked back at the shed. "Why don't you tell me what happened here?"

As clearly as she could, Sarah told him everything she knew. He listened, grunting and nodding occasionally. Everything she said jibed with the story Jake had given him. But she didn't add, because she didn't know, that Jake had followed the trail of two riders into the rocks, where he'd discovered the ashes of a campfire.

"Any reason you can think of why somebody'd want to do this?"

"None at all. There's nothing here that could mean anything to anyone other than myself. Did my father have any enemies?"

Barker spit tobacco juice in the dirt. "I wouldn't think so right off. I got to tell you, Miss Conway, there ain't much I can do. I'll ask some questions and poke around some. Could be some drifters passed through and wanted to raise some hell. Begging your pardon." But he didn't think so.

"I'd wondered the same myself."

"You'll feel safer having old Lucius around."

She glanced over to see him coming back with the pail and the puppy. "I suppose you're right." But he didn't look like her idea of a protector. It was unfortunate for her that her idea of one had taken the form of Jake Redman. "I'm sure we'll do nicely," she said with more confidence than she felt.

"I'll ride out now and again and see how you're getting on." Barker pulled himself onto his horse. "You know, Miss Conway, Matt tried to grow something in that patch of dirt for as long as I can recollect." He spit again. "Never had any luck."

"Perhaps I'll have better. Good afternoon, Sheriff."

"Good day, ma'am." He lifted a hand to Lucius as he turned for home.

Chapter 6

Within a week Sarah had orders for six dresses. It took all her creativity and skill to fashion them, using her wardrobe and her imagination instead of patterns. She set aside three hours each day and three each evening for sewing. Each night when she climbed up to bed her eyes and fingers ached. Once or twice, when the exhaustion overwhelmed her, she wept herself to sleep. The grief for her father was still too raw, the country surrounding her still too rugged.

But there were other times, and they were becoming more common, when she fell asleep with a sense of satisfaction. In addition to the dresses, she'd made pretty yellow curtains for the windows and a matching cloth for the table. It was her dream, when she'd saved enough from her sewing, to buy planks for a real floor. In the meantime, she made do with what she had and was more grateful than she'd ever imagined she could be for Lucius.

He'd finished building a new shed and he was busy repairing the other outbuildings. Though he'd muttered about it, he'd agreed to build Sarah the chicken coop she wanted. At night he was content to sleep with the horses.

Sometimes he watched, tickling Lafitte's belly, as she took her daily rifle practice.

She hadn't seen Jake Redman since the day he'd given her a shooting lesson. Just as well, Sarah told herself as she pulled on her gloves. There was no one she wanted to see less. If she thought about him at all—and she hated to admit she had—it was with disdain.

A hired gun. A man with no loyalty or morals. A drifter, moving from place to place, always ready to draw his weapon and kill. To think she'd almost begun to believe there was something special about him, something good and admirable. He'd helped her, there was no denying that. But he'd probably done so out of sheer boredom. Or perhaps, she thought, remembering the kiss, because he wanted something from her. Something, she was ashamed to admit, she had nearly been willing to give.

How? Sarah picked up her hand mirror and studied her face, not out of vanity but because she hoped to see some answers there. How had he managed to make her feel that way in just a few short days, with just one embrace? Now, time after time, in the deepest part of the night, she brought herself awake because she was dreaming of him. Remembering, she thought, experiencing once again that stunning moment in the sun when his mouth had been on hers and there had been no doubt in her mind that she belonged there.

A momentary madness, she told herself, placing the mirror facedown on the table. Sunstroke, perhaps. She would never, could never, be attracted to a man who lived his life the way Jake Redman lived his.

It was time to forget him. Perhaps he had already moved

on and she would never see him again. Well, it didn't matter one way or the other. She had her own life to see to now, and with a little help from Liza it appeared she had her own business. Picking up the three bundles wrapped in brown paper, Sarah went outside.

"You real sure you don't want me to drive you to town, Miss Conway?"

Sarah put the wrapped dresses in the back of the wagon while Lucius stood at the horses' heads. "No, thank you, Lucius."

She was well aware that her driving skills were poor at best, but she'd bartered for the wagon with the owner of the livery stable. He had two daughters that she'd designed gingham frocks for, and she intended to deliver them herself. For Lucius she had a big, sunny smile.

"I was hoping you'd start on the chicken coop today. I'm going to see if Mrs. Miller will sell me a dozen young chicks."

"Yes'm." Lucius shuffled his feet and cleared his throat. "Going to be a hot, dry day."

"Yes." What day wasn't? "I have a canteen, thank you."

He waited until Sarah had gained the seat and smoothed out her skirts. "There's just one thing, Miss Conway."

Anxious to be on her way, Sarah took the reins. "Yes, Lucius, what is it?"

"I'm plumb out of whiskey."

Her brow rose, all but disappearing under the wispy bangs she wore. "And?"

"Well, seeing as you're going into town and all, I thought you could pick some up for me."

"I? You can hardly expect me to purchase whiskey."

He'd figured on her saying something of the kind. "Maybe you could get somebody to buy a bottle for you."

He gave her a gap-toothed smile and was careful not to spit. "I'd be obliged."

She opened her mouth, ready to lecture him on the evils of drink. With a sigh, she shut it again. The man worked very hard for very little. It wasn't her place to deny him his comforts, whatever they might be.

"I'll see what can be done."

His grizzled face brightened immediately. "That's right kind of you, miss. And I sure will get started on that coop." Relieved, he spit in the dirt. "You look real pretty today, miss. Just like a picture."

Her lips curved. If anyone had told her a week ago that she would grow fond of a smelly, whiskey-drinking creature like Lucius, she'd have thought them mad. "Thank you. There's chicken and fresh bread in the cabin." She held her breath and snapped the reins.

Sarah had dressed very carefully for town. If she was going to interest the ladies in ordering fashionable clothes from her, then it was wise to advertise. Her dress was a particularly flattering shade of moss green with a high neckline she'd graced with her cameo. The trim of rose-colored ribbon and the rows of flounces at the skirt made it a bit flirtatious. She'd added a matching bonnet, tilted low as much for dash as for added shade. She felt doubly pleased with her choice when her two young customers came running out of the livery and goggled at it.

Sarah left them to race home and try on their new dresses while she completed her errands.

"Sarah." Liza danced around the counter of the dry goods store to take both of her hands. "Oh, what a wonderful dress. Every woman in town's going to want one like it."

"I was hoping to tempt them." Laughing, Sarah turned in a circle. "It's one of my favorites."

"I can see why. Is everything all right with you? I haven't been able to get away for days."

"Everything's fine. There's been no more trouble." She wandered over to take a look at the bolts of fabric. "I'm certain it was just an isolated incident. As the sheriff said, it must have been drifters." Glancing over, she smiled. "Hello, Mrs. Cody," she said as Liza's mother came in from the stockroom.

"Sarah, it's nice to see you, and looking so pretty, too."

"Thank you. I've brought your dress."

"Well, that was quick work." Anne Cody took the package in her wide, capable hands and went immediately to the cash drawer.

"Oh, I don't want you to pay for it until you look and make sure it's what you wanted."

Anne smiled, showing dimples like her daughter's. "That's good business. My Ed would say you've got a head on your shoulders. Let's just take a look, then." As she unwrapped the package, two of her customers moved closer to watch.

"Why, Sarah, it's lovely." Clearly pleased, Anne held it up. The dress was dove gray, simple enough to wear for work behind the counter, yet flatteringly feminine, with touches of lace at the throat and sleeves. "My goodness, honey, you've a fine hand with a needle." Deliberately she moved from behind the counter so that the rest of her customers could get the full effect. "Look at this work, Mrs. Miller. I'll swear you won't see better."

Grinning, Liza leaned over to whisper in Sarah's ear. "She'll have a dozen orders for you in no time. Pa always says Ma could sell a legless man new boots."

"Here you are, Sarah." Anne passed her the money. "It's more than worth every penny."

"Young lady." Mrs. Miller peered through her spectacles at the stitches in Anne's new dress. "I'm going to visit my sister in Kansas City next month. I think a traveling suit of this same fabric would be flattering to me."

"Oh, yes, ma'am." Sarah beamed, ignoring the fact that very little would be flattering to Mrs. Miller's bulky figure. "You have a good eye for color. This fabric trimmed in purple would be stunning on you."

By the time she was finished, Sarah had three more orders and an armful of fabric. With one hand muffling her giggles, Liza walked out with her. "Imagine you talking that old fuddy-duddy Mrs. Miller into two dresses."

"She wants to outshine her sister. I'll have to make sure she does."

"It won't be easy, considering what you have to work with. And she's overcharging you for those chicks."

"That's all right." Sarah turned with a grin. "I'm going to overcharge her for the dresses. Do you have time to walk with me? I'd like to go down and see if this blue-and-white stripe takes Mrs. O'Rourke's fancy."

They started down the walkway. After only a few steps, Liza stopped and swept her skirts aside. Sarah watched the statuesque woman approach. In all her life she'd never seen hair that color. It gleamed like the brass knob on Mother Superior's office door. The vivid blue silk dress she wore was too snug at the bodice and entirely too low for day wear. Smooth white breasts rose out of it, the left one adorned with a small beauty mark that matched another at the corner of her red lips. She carried an unfurled parasol and strolled, her hips swaying shamelessly.

As she came shoulder-to-shoulder with Sarah, the woman stopped and looked her up and down. The tiny smile she wore became a smirk as she walked on, rolling her hips.

"My goodness." Sarah could think of little else to say as she rubbed her nose. The woman's perfume remained stubbornly behind.

"That was Carlotta. She runs the Silver Star."

"She looks...extraordinary."

"Well, she's a—you know."

"A what?"

"A woman of ill repute," Liza said in a whisper.

"Oh." Sarah's eyes grew huge. She'd heard, of course. Even in Philadelphia one heard of such women. But to actually pass one on the street... "Oh, my. I wonder why she looked at me that way."

"Probably because Jake Redman's been out your way a couple times. Jake's a real favorite with Carlotta." She shut her mouth tight. If her mother heard her talking that way she'd be skinned alive.

"I should have known." With a toss of her head Sarah started to walk again. For the life of her she didn't know why she felt so much like crying.

Mrs. O'Rourke greeted her with pleasure. Not only had it been a year since she'd had a new dress, she was determined to know all there was to know about the woman who was keeping Jake so churned up.

"I thought you might like this striped material, Mrs. O'Rourke."

"It's right nice." Maggie fingered the cotton with a large, reddened hand. "No doubt it'll make up pretty. Michael... my first husband was Michael Bailey, he was partial to a pretty dress. Died young, did Michael. Got a little drunk and took the wrong horse. Hung him for a horse thief before he sobered up."

Not certain what response was proper, Sarah murmured something inaudible. "I'm sure the colors would flatter you."

Maggie let out a bray of laughter. "Girl, I'm past the age where I care about being flattered. Buried me two husbands. Mr. O'Rourke, rest his soul, was hit by lightning back in '63. The good Lord doesn't always protect fools and drunkards, you know. Save me, I'm not in the market for another one. The only reason a woman decks herself out is to catch a man or keep one." She ran her shrewd eyes over Sarah. "Now you've got a rig on this day, you do."

Deciding to take the remark as a compliment, Sarah offered a small smile. "Thank you. If you'd prefer something else, I could—"

"I wasn't saying I didn't like the goods."

"Sarah can make you a very serviceable dress, Mrs. O'Rourke," Liza put in. "My ma's real pleased with hers. Mrs. Miller's having her make up two for her trip to Kansas City."

"That so?" Maggie knew what a pinchpenny the Miller woman was. "I reckon I could do with a new dress. Nothing fancy, mind. I don't want any of my boarders getting ideas in their heads." She let out a cackle.

"If a man got ideas about you, Maggie, he'd lose them quick enough after a bowl of your stew."

Sarah's fingers curled into her palms when she heard Jake's voice. Slowly, her body braced, she turned to face him. He was halfway down the stairs.

"Some men want something more from a woman than a bowl of stew," Maggie told him, and cackled again. "You ladies want to be wary of a man who smiles like that," she added, pointing a finger at Jake. "I ought to know, since I married two of them." As she spoke, she watched the way Jake and Sarah looked at each other. Someone had lit a fire there, she decided. She wouldn't mind fanning it a bit. "Liza, all this talk about cooking reminds me. I need another ten pounds of flour. Run on up and fetch it for me. Have your ma put it on my account."

"Yes, ma'am."

Anxious to be off, Sarah picked up the bolt of material again. "I'll get started on this right away, Mrs. O'Rourke."

"Hold on a minute. I've got a dress upstairs you can use for measuring. Needs some mending, too. I'm no hand with a needle. Liza, I can use two pounds of coffee." She motioned at the girl with the back of her hand. "Go on, off with you."

"I'll just be a minute," Liza promised as she walked out the door. Pleased with her maneuvering, Maggie started up the stairs.

"You're about as subtle as a load of buckshot," Jake murmured to her.

With the material still in her hands, Sarah watched Jake approach her. Though she was standing in the center of the room, she had the oddest sensation that her back was against the wall. He was staring at her in that way he had that made her stomach flutter and her knees shake. She promised herself that if he touched her, if he even looked as though he might touch her, she would slap him hard enough to knock his hat off.

He had images of touching her. Of tasting her. Of rolling around on the ground and filling himself with her. Seeing her now, looking like some flower that had sprung up out of the sand, he had to remind himself that they could only be images.

He figured that was no reason he couldn't needle her a bit.

"Morning, Duchess. You come by to see me?"

"Certainly not."

He couldn't help but enjoy the way her eyes fired up. Casually he brushed a finger over the fabric she held and felt her jolt. "Mighty pretty, but I like the dress you've got on better."

"It isn't for me." There was no reason in the world she should feel flattered, Sarah reminded herself. No reason at all. "Mrs. O'Rourke expressed interest in having a dress made."

"So you sew, too." His gaze traveled over her face, lingering on her mouth too long for comfort. "You're full of surprises."

"It's an honest way to make a living." Deliberately she looked down at the gun on his hip. "It's a pity not everyone can say the same."

It was difficult to say what the cool, disapproving tone made him feel. Rage, familiar and bitter-tasting. Futility, with its cold, hollow ring. Both emotions and flickers of others showed in his eyes as he stared down at her.

"So you heard about me," he said before she could follow her first impulse and lay a soothing hand on his arm. "I'm a dangerous man, Sarah." He took her chin in his hand so that her eyes stayed on his. "I draw my gun and leave women widows and children orphans. The smell of gunsmoke and death follows me wherever I go. I got Apache blood in my veins, so I don't look on killing the way a white man might. I put a bullet in a man the same way a wolf rips out throats. Because it's what I was made for. A woman like you had best keep her distance."

She heard the fury licking at his words. More, she heard frustration, a deep, raw frustration. Before he could reach the door, she was calling after him.

"Mr. Redman. Mr. Redman, please." Gathering up her skirts, she hurried after him. "Jake."

He stopped and turned as she came through the doorway.

They were outside only a step, but that was enough to have the heat and dust rising around them.

"You'd do better to stay inside until Maggie comes down for you."

"Please, wait." She laid a hand on his arm. "I don't understand what you do, or who you are, but I do know you've taken the trouble to be a help to me. Don't tell me to forget it," she said quickly. "Because I won't."

"You've got a talent for tying a man up in knots," he murmured.

"I don't mean—"

"No, I don't reckon you do. Anything else you want to say?"

"Actually, I—" She broke off when she heard a burst of wild laughter from the next building. As she looked, a man was propelled headfirst through a pair of swinging doors. He landed in a heap in the dust of the road. Even as Sarah started forward, Jake shifted to block her.

"What do you think you're doing?"

"That man might be hurt."

"He's too drunk to be hurt."

Her eyes wide, Sarah looked past Jake's shoulder and saw the drunk struggle to his feet and stagger back inside. "But it's the middle of the day."

"Just as easy to get drunk in the daylight as it is when the sun's down."

Her lips primmed. "It's just as disgraceful." Whiskey might be the work of the devil, Sarah thought, but she had promised Lucius. "I wonder if I might ask you another favor?"

"You can ask."

"I need a bottle of whiskey."

Jake took off his hat and smoothed back his hair, then replaced the hat. "I thought you didn't care for it much."

"It's not for me. It's for Lucius." She was certain she heard the sound of breaking glass from the neighboring saloon as she reached for her reticule. "I'm afraid I don't know the price."

"Lucius is good for it. Go back inside," he told her, then passed through the swinging doors.

"Quite a man, isn't he?"

Sarah lifted a hand to her heart. "Mrs. O'Rourke, you startled me."

Grinning, Maggie stepped outside. "Your mind was elsewhere." She handed Sarah a bundle. "Good-looking, Jake is. Strong back, good hands. A woman can hardly ask for more." Maggie glanced over as the din from the saloon grew louder. "You don't have a fella back east, do you?"

"A what?" Distracted, Sarah inched closer to the saloon. She hated to admit it, but she was dying to see inside. "Oh, no. At least there was no one I cared for enough to marry."

"A smart woman knows how to bring a man around to marriage and make him think it was his idea all along. You take Jake—" Maggie broke off when Sarah squealed. Two men burst through the swinging doors and rolled into the street, fists flying.

"My goodness." Her mouth hanging open, Sarah watched the two men kick and claw and pummel each other.

"I thought I told you to go inside." Jake strolled out, carrying a bottle of whiskey by the neck.

"I was just— Oh!" She saw blood fly as a fist connected with a nose. "This is dreadful. You have to stop them."

"Like hell I do. Where's your wagon?"

"But you must," Sarah insisted. "You can't simply stand here and watch two men beat each other like this."

"Duchess, if I try to break that up, both of them are going to start swinging at me." He passed her the bottle of whiskey. "I don't feel much like killing anybody today."

With a huff, Sarah thrust the bottle back into his hands and followed it with the fabric and Maggie's bundle. "Then I'll stop them myself."

"It's going to be a shame when you lose some of those pretty teeth."

Taking time only to glare at him, Sarah bent down and scooped up the spittoon Maggie kept beside her doorway. Her skirts in one hand, weapon in the other, she marched toward the middle of the melee.

"That's some woman," Maggie said with a grin. Jake merely grunted. "Got grit."

"Go water down your stew."

Maggie just laughed. "She's got you, too. Hope I'm around when she figures it out."

A little breathless, Sarah dodged the rolling bodies. The men were groaning and hissing as they struggled to land punches. The smell of stale whiskey and sweat rose from both of them. She had to scramble a bit for aim before she brought the brass down with a thunk on one head and then the other. A roar of laughter, then a few cheers, poured out the doorway of the saloon. Ignoring the sound, Sarah looked down at the two men, who were frowning at her and rubbing their heads.

"You should be ashamed of yourselves," she told them, in a tone that would have made Mother Superior proud. "Fighting in the street like a couple of schoolboys. You've done nothing but bloody your faces and make a spectacle of yourselves. Now stand up." Both men reached for their hats and struggled to their feet. "I'm sure whatever disagreement you have can be better solved by talking it out." Satisfied,

Sarah nodded politely, then glided back across the street to where Jake and Maggie stood.

"There." She handed Maggie the spittoon. Her self-satisfied smirk was for Jake alone. "It was only a matter of getting their attention, then applying reason."

He glanced over her head to where the two men were wrestling in the dirt again. "Yes, ma'am." Taking her arm, he started up the street before she could get it in her head to do something else. "Did you learn to swing like that in your fancy school?"

"I had occasion to observe the nuns' techniques for handling disagreements."

"Ever get knocked on the head with a spittoon?"

She tilted her head, her eyes laughing under the cover of her lashes. "No, but I know what a wooden ruler feels like." Sarah glanced in the dry goods as she stopped by her wagon. Inside, she could see Liza flirting with a thin, gangly man with straw-colored hair and shiny brown boots.

"Is that Will Metcalf?"

Jake stowed the rest of her things in the back of the wagon. "Yeah."

"I think Liza's quite taken with him." She bit back a sigh. Romance was as far away from her right now as the beautiful house her father had built for her in his mind. Turning, she bumped into Jake's chest. His hands came up to steady her and stayed on her arms. Not so far away, she thought again. It wasn't far away at all when it could reach out and touch you.

"You got to watch where you're going."

"I usually do. I used to." He was going to kiss her again, right there in the center of town. She could feel it. She could almost taste it.

He wanted to. He wanted five minutes alone with her, though he knew there was no use, it was no good. "Sarah—"

"Good morning, Jake." Twirling her parasol, Carlotta sauntered up to the wagon. Smiling slightly she ignored the warning look he sent her and turned her attention to Sarah. She'd already decided to hate her, for what she was, for what she had. Her smile still in place, she skimmed her gaze up and down Sarah. Pure and proper and dull, she decided. Jake would be tired of her in a week. But in the meantime it would give her pleasure to make the little priss uncomfortable.

"Aren't you going to introduce me to your friend?"

Jake ignored her and kept a hand on Sarah's arm to steer her to the front of the wagon.

Sarah didn't recognize the basic female urge, the primal urge, to face the enemy down. She only knew she wouldn't have the woman smirking at her back. "I'm Sarah Conway." She didn't offer her hand, she simply nodded. It was as much of an insult as Carlotta's sneering scrutiny.

"I know who you are." Carlotta smiled, fully, even as her eyes turned to blue ice. "I knew your pa. I knew him real well."

The blow hit home. Carlotta was delighted to see it. But when her eyes skimmed up to meet Jake's, most of the pleasure she felt died. She'd seen him look at men that way when they'd pushed him too far. With a toss of her head, she turned away. He'd come around, she told herself. Men always did.

His mouth grim, Jake reached for Sarah's arm again to help her into the wagon. The moment his fingers brushed her, she jerked away.

"Don't touch me." She had to turn, to grip the edge of the wagon, until she caught the breath Carlotta had knocked out of her. All of her illusions were shattered now. The idea of her father, her own father, with a woman like that was more than she could take.

He'd have preferred to walk away. Just turn and keep going. Infuriated, he dug his hands into his pockets. "Let me help you into the damn wagon, Sarah."

"I don't want your help." She whirled back to face him. "I don't want anything from you. Do you understand?"

"No, but then I don't figure I'm supposed to."

"Do you kiss her the same way you kissed me? Did you think of me the same way you think of her and women like her?"

His hand shot out to stop her before she could scramble into the wagon. "I wasn't thinking at all when I kissed you, and that was my mistake."

"Miss Conway." Samuel Carlson stopped his horse at the head of the wagon. His eyes stayed on Jake's as he dismounted. "Is there a problem?"

"No." Instinctively she stepped between the men. Carlson's gun had a handle of polished ivory, and it looked deadly and beautiful below his silver brocade vest. It no longer shocked her to realize that even a man as obviously cultured and educated as he wouldn't hesitate to use a weapon. "Mr. Redman's been an invaluable help to me since I arrived."

"I heard you'd had some trouble."

Sarah discovered she was digging her nails into her palms. Slowly, stiffly, she uncurled her fingers, but she could do nothing about the tension that was pounding at the base of her throat. It sprang, she knew, from the men, who stood on either side of her, watching each other, ready, almost eager.

"Yes. Fortunately, the damage wasn't extensive."

"I'm glad to hear that." At last Carlson shifted his gaze

to Sarah. She heard her own sigh of relief. "Did you ride into town alone, Miss Conway?"

"Yes, I did. As a matter of fact, I'd better be on my way."

"I'd be obliged if you'd allow me to drive you back. It's a long ride for a woman alone."

"That's kind of you, Mr. Carlson. I couldn't impose."

"No imposition at all." Taking her arm, he helped her into the seat. "I've been meaning to ride out, pay my respects. I'd consider it a favor if you'd allow me to drive you."

She was about to refuse again when she looked at Jake. There was ice in his eyes. She imagined there would be a different look in them altogether when he looked at Carlotta.

"I'd love the company," she heard herself say, and she waited while Carlson tied his horse to the rear of the wagon. "Good day, Mr. Redman." Folding her hands in her lap, she let Carlson guide her team out of town.

They talked of nothing important for most of the drive. The weather, music, the theater. It was a pleasure, Sarah told herself, to spend an hour or two in the company of a man who understood art and appreciated beauty.

"I hope you won't take offense if I offer some advice, Miss Conway."

"Advice is always welcome." She smiled at him. "Even if it's not taken."

"I hope you'll take mine. Jake Redman is a dangerous man, the kind who brings trouble to everyone around him. Stay away from him, Miss Conway, for your own good."

She said nothing for a moment, surprised by the strength of the anger that rose up in her. Carlson had said nothing but the truth, and nothing she hadn't already told herself. "I appreciate your concern."

His voice was calm and quiet and laced with regret. "But you won't take my advice."

"I don't think it will be necessary. It's unlikely I'll be seeing Mr. Redman now that I've settled in."

Carlson shook his head and smiled. "I have offended you."

"Not at all. I understand your feelings for Jake—" She corrected herself carefully. "Mr. Redman. I'm sure the trouble between him and your brother was very distressing for you."

Carlson's mouth thinned. "It pains me to say that Jim brought that incident on himself. He's young and a bit wild yet. Redman's a different matter. He lives by his gun and his reputation with it."

"That sounds like no life at all."

"Now I've stirred your sympathies. That certainly wasn't my intention." He touched a hand lightly to hers. "You're a beautiful, sensitive woman. I wouldn't want to see you hurt."

She hadn't been called beautiful in what felt like a very long time. Since a waltz, she remembered, at a ball at Lucilla's big house. "Thank you, but I assure you I'm learning very quickly to take care of myself."

As they drove into the yard, the puppy bounded up, racing around the wagon and barking. "He's grown some," Carlson commented as Lafitte snapped at his ankles.

"Hush, now." Lafitte snarled when Carlson lifted Sarah from the wagon. "He has the makings of an excellent guard dog, I think. And, thank heaven, he gets along well with Lucius. May I offer you some coffee?"

"I'd like that." Once inside, Carlson took a long look. "I've had some difficulty picturing you here. A drawing room with flowered wallpaper and blue draperies would suit you."

She laughed a little as she put the coffee on. "I think it

will be some time yet before I put up wallpaper and drap-eries. I'd like a real floor first. Please sit down."

From the tin on the shelf she took a few of the sugar cook-ies she'd baked earlier in the week. It pleased her to be able to offer him a napkin she'd sewed out of scrap material.

"It must be a lonely life for you."

"I haven't had time to be lonely, though I admit it's not what I'd hoped for."

"It's a pity your father never made the mine pay."

"It gave him hope." She thought of the journal she was reading. "He was a man who needed hope more than food."

"You're right about that." Carlson sipped at the coffee she served him. "You know, I offered to buy this place from him some time back."

"You did?" Sarah took the seat across from him. "What-ever for?"

"Sentiment." Carlson sent her an embarrassed smile. "Foolish, really. My grandfather once owned this land. He lost it in a poker game when I was a boy. It always infuriated him." He smiled again and sampled a cookie. "Of course, he had the ranch. Twelve hundred acres, with the best water that can be had in these parts. But he grumbled about los-ing that old mine until the day he died."

"There must be something about it that holds a man. It certainly held my father."

"Matt bought it from the gambler and dived right in. He always believed he'd find the mother lode, though I don't think there is one. After the old man died and I took over, I thought it might be fitting somehow for me to bring it back into the family. A tribute. But Matt, he wouldn't part with it."

"He had a dream," Sarah murmured. "It killed him, even-tually."

"I'm sorry. I've upset you. I didn't mean to."

"It's nothing. I still miss him. I suppose I always will."

"It might not be healthy for you to stay here, so close to where he died."

"It's all I have."

Carlson reached over to pat her hand. "As I said, you're a sensitive woman. I was willing to buy this place from Matt. I'd be willing to buy it from you if you feel you'd like to sell."

"Sell?" Surprised, she looked over. The sun was streaming through the yellow curtains at the window. It made a stream of gold on the floor. Before long, the strength of it would fade the material. "That's very generous of you, Mr. Carlson."

"I'd be flattered if you'd call me Samuel."

"It's very generous, and very kind, Samuel." Rising, she walked to the window. Yes, the sun would bleach it out, the same way it bleached the land. She touched a hand to the wall. The adobe stayed cool. It was a kind of miracle, she thought. Like the endurance that kept men in this place. "I don't think I'm ready to give up here."

"You don't have to decide what you want now." He rose, as well, and moved over to lay a gentle hand on her shoulder. She smiled at the gesture. It was comforting to have friends who cared.

"It's been difficult, adjusting here. Yet I feel as though I can't leave, that in leaving I'd be deserting my father."

"I know what it is to lose family. It takes time to think straight again." He turned her to face him. "I can say that I feel I knew Matt enough to be sure he'd want the best for you. If you decide you want to let it go, all you have to do is tell me. We'll leave it an open offer."

"Thank you." She turned and found herself flustered when he lifted both her hands to his lips.

"I want to help you, Sarah. I hope you'll let me."

"Miss Conway."

She jolted, then sighed when she saw Lucius in the doorway. "Yes?"

He eyed Carlson, then turned his head to spit. "You want me to put this team away?"

"Please."

Lucius stayed where he was. "How about the extra horse?"

"I'll be riding out. Thank you for the company, Sarah."

"It was a pleasure."

As they stepped outside, Carlson replaced his hat. "I hope you'll let me call again."

"Of course." Sarah was forced to snatch up the dog when he came toward her guest, snarling and snapping. "Goodbye, Samuel."

She waited until he'd started out before she put the puppy down and walked over to Lucius.

"Lucius." She leaned over to speak to him as he unhitched the horses. "You were quite rude just now."

"If you say so, miss."

"Well, I do." Frustrated, she ducked under the horses to join him. "Mr. Carlson was considerate enough to drive me back from town. You looked at him as though you wanted to shoot him in the head."

"Maybe."

"For heaven's sake. Why?"

"Some snakes don't rattle."

Casting her eyes to the sky, she gave up. Instead, she snatched the bottle of whiskey from the wagon and watched his eyes light up. "If you want this, take off your shirt."

His mouth dropped as if she'd hit him with a board. "Beg pardon, ma'am?"

"The pants, too. I want you to strip right down to the skin."

He groped at his neckcloth. "Mind if I ask why you'd be wanting me to do that, Miss Conway?"

"I'm going to wash your clothes. I've tolerated the smell of them—and you—quite long enough. While I'm washing them, you can take that extra cake of soap I bought and do the same with yourself."

"Now, miss, I—"

"If, and only if, you're clean, I'll give you this bottle. You get a pail of water and the soap and go into that shed. Toss your clothes out."

Not sure he cared for the arrangement, Lucius shifted his feet. "And if I don't?"

"Then I'll pour every drop of this into the dirt."

Lucius laid a hand on his heart as she stamped off. He was mortally afraid she'd do it.

Chapter 7

Sarah rolled up the sleeves of her oldest shirtwaist, hitched up her serviceable black skirt and went to work.

They'd be better off burned, she thought as she dunked Lucius's stiff denim pants into the stream. The water turned a mud brown instantly. With a sound of disgust, she dunked them again. It would take some doing to make them even marginally acceptable, but she was determined.

Cleanliness was next to godliness.

That had been one of the proverbs cross-stitched on Mother Superior's office wall. Well, she was going to get Lucius as close to God as was humanly possible. Whether he liked it or not.

Leaving the pants to soak, she picked up his faded blue shirt by the tips of her fingers. Deplorable, she decided as she dampened and scrubbed and soaked. Absolutely deplorable. She doubted the clothes had seen clean water in a year. Which meant Lucius's skin had been just as much in need of washing. She'd soon fix that.

She began to smile as she worked. The expression on his face when she'd threatened to empty out the whiskey had been something to see. Poor Lucius. He might look tough and crusty, but underneath he was just a sweet, misguided man who needed a woman to show him the way.

Most men did. At least that was what Lucilla had always said. As she beat Lucius's weathered shirt against the rocks, Sarah wondered what her friend would think of Jake Redman. There was certainly nothing sweet about him, no matter how deep down a woman might dig. Though he could be kind. It baffled her that time and time again he had shown her that streak of good-heartedness. Always briefly, she added, her lips thinning. Always right before he did something inexcusable.

Like kissing the breath out of her. Kissing her until her blood was hot and her mind was empty and she wanted something she didn't even understand. He'd had no right to do it, and still less to walk away afterward, leaving her trembling and confused.

She should have slapped him. With that thought in mind, Sarah slapped the shirt on the water and gave a satisfied nod at the sound. She should have knocked the arrogance right out of him, and then it should have been she who walked away.

The next time... There would be no next time, she assured herself. If Jake Redman ever touched her again, she'd...she'd...melt like butter, she admitted. Oh, she hated him for making her wish he would touch her again.

When he looked at her, something happened, something frantic, something she'd never experienced before. Her heart beat just a little too fast, and dampness sprang out on the palms of her hands. A look was all that was necessary. His eyes were so dark, so penetrating. When he looked at her it was as if he could see everything she was, or could be, or wanted to be.

It was absurd. He was a man who lived by the gun, who took what he wanted without regret or compunction. All her life she'd been taught that the line between right and wrong was clear and wide and wasn't to be crossed.

To kill was the greatest sin, the most unforgivable. Yet he had killed, and would surely kill again. Knowing it, she couldn't care for him. But care she did. And want she did. And need.

Her hands were wrist-deep in water when she brought herself back. She had no business even thinking this way. Thinking about him. If she had to think of a man, she'd do better to think of Samuel Carlson. He was well-mannered, polished. He would know the proper way to treat a lady. There would be no wild, groping kisses from a man like him. A woman would be safe, cherished, cared for.

But she wished Jake had offered to drive her home.

This was nonsense. Sarah wrung out the shirt and rubbed her nose with the back of her damp hand. She'd had enough nonsense for the time being. She would wash thoughts of Jake away just as she washed the grime and grit and the good Lord knew what from Lucius's shirt.

She wanted her life to be tidy. Perhaps it wouldn't be as grand as she'd once imagined, but it would be tidy. Even here. Sitting back on her heels, she looked around. The sun was heading toward the buttes in the west. Slowly, like a big golden ball in a sky the color of Indian paintbrush. The rocks towered, their odd, somewhat mystical shapes rising up and up, some slender as needles, others rough and thick.

There was a light smell of juniper here, and the occasional rustle that didn't alarm her as it once would have. She watched an eagle soar, its wings spread wide. King of the sky. Below, the stream gurgled, making its lazy way over the rocks.

Why, it was beautiful. She lifted a hand to her throat, surprised to discover that it was aching. She hadn't seen it before, or hadn't wanted to. There was a wild, desolate, marvelous beauty here that man hadn't been able to touch. Or hadn't dared. If the land was lawless, perhaps it deserved to be.

For the first time since she had arrived, she felt a sense of kinship, of belonging. Of peace. She'd been right to stay, because this was home. Hers. At long last, hers.

When she rose to spread the shirt over a rock, she was smiling. Then she saw the shadow, and she looked up quickly.

There were five of them. Their black hair was loose past their bare shoulders. All but one sat on a horse. It was he who stepped toward her, silent in knee-length moccasins. There was a scar, white and puckered, that ran from his temple, catching the corner of his eye, then curving like a sickle down his cheek. She saw that, and the blade of the knife he carried. Then she began to scream.

Lucius heard the rider coming and strapped his gunbelt on over his long underwear. With soap still lathered all over his face, he stepped out of the shed. Jake pulled up his mount and took a long, lazy look.

"Don't tell me it's spring already."

"Damn women." Lucius spit expertly.

"Ain't that the truth?" After easing off his horse, Jake tossed the reins over the rail. Lafitte immediately leaped up to rest his paws on his thigh. In the way dogs have, he grinned and his tongue lolled. "Going to a dance or something?"

"No, I ain't going anywhere." Lucius cast a vicious look toward the house. "She threatened me. Yes, sir, there's no two ways about it, it was a threat. Said less'n I took myself a bath and let her wash my clothes she'd pour out every last drop of whiskey in the bottle she brought."

With a grin of his own, Jake leaned against the rail and rolled a cigarette. "Maybe she's not as stupid as she looks."

"She looks okay," Lucius muttered. "Got a streak of stubborn in her, though." He wiped a soapy hand on the thigh of his long underwear. "What are you doing out here?"

"Came out to talk to you."

"Like hell. I got eyes. She ain't in there," he said when Jake continued to stare at the house.

"I said I came to talk to you." Annoyed, Jake flicked a match and lit his cigarette. "Have you done any checking in the mine?"

"I've taken a look. She don't give a body much free time." He picked up a rock and tossed it so that the puppy would have something to chase. "Always wanting something built or fixed up. Cooks right good, though." He patted his belly. "Can't complain about that."

"See anything?"

"I saw where Matt was working some, right enough. And the cave-in." He spit again. "Can't say I felt real good about digging my way past it. Now, maybe if you told me what it was I was supposed to be looking for."

"You'll know if you find it." He looked back at the house. She'd put curtains on the windows. "Does she ever go up there?"

"Goes up, not in. Sits by his grave sometimes. Breaks your heart."

"Sounds like you're going soft on her, old man." He reached down to give Lafitte a scratch on the head.

"Wouldn't talk if I was you." He only laughed when Jake looked at him. There weren't many men who would have dared. "Don't go icing up on me, boy. I've known you too long. Might interest you to know that Samuel Carlson paid a call."

Jake blew out smoke with a shrug. "I know." He waited, took another drag, then swore under his breath. "Did he stay long?"

"Long enough to make up to her. Kissing her hands, he was. Both of them."

"Is that so?" The fury burned low in his gut and spread rapidly. Eyes narrowed, he flicked the cigarette away, half finished, and watched it smolder. "Where is she?"

"Down to the stream, I imagine."

Lucius smothered a laugh and bent down to pick up Lafitte before the puppy could scramble after Jake. "I wouldn't, if'n I was you, young fella. There's going to be fireworks fit for Independence Day."

Jake wasn't sure what he was going to do, but he didn't think Sarah was going to like it. He hoped she didn't. She needed a short rein, he decided. And he was going to see to it himself. Letting Carlson paw all over her. Just the thought of it made small, jagged claws of jealousy slice through him.

When he heard her scream, both guns were out of their holsters and in his hands in a heartbeat. He took the last quarter of a mile at a run, her screams and the sound of running horses echoing in his head.

When he reached the stream he saw the dust the ponies had kicked up. Even at a distance he recognized Little Bear's profile. There was a different kind of fire in him now. It burned ice-cold as he holstered his weapons. Lafitte came tearing down the path, snarling.

"You're too late again," Jake told the dog as he sniffed the ground and whined. He turned as Lucius came running in nothing more than his gunbelt and long johns.

"What happened?" Jake said nothing. Hunkering down, Lucius studied the marks left by the struggle. "'Paches." He saw his shirt, freshly washed and drying in the sun. "Damn it all to hell." Still swearing, he raced down the path toward Jake. "Let me get on my spare shirt and my boots. They don't have much of a lead."

"I'm going alone."

"There was four of them, maybe more."

"Five." Jake strode back into the clearing. "I ride alone."

"Listen, boy, even if it was Little Bear, that don't give you no guarantees. You weren't no more than kids last time, and you chose different ways."

"It was Little Bear, and I'm not looking for guarantees." He swung into the saddle. "I'm going to get her back."

Lucius put a hand on the saddle horn. "See that you do."

"If I'm not back tomorrow sundown, go get Barker. I'll leave a trail even he can follow." He kicked his horse into a gallop and headed north.

She hadn't fainted, but she wasn't so sure that was a blessing. She'd been tossed roughly onto the back of a horse, and she was forced to grip its mane to keep from tumbling off. The Indian with the scar rode behind her, calling out to his companions occasionally and gesturing with a new government-issue Winchester. He'd dragged her by her hair to get her astride the horse, and he still seemed fascinated by it. When she felt him push his nose into it, she closed her eyes, shuddered and prayed.

They rode fast, their ponies apparently tireless and obviously surefooted, as they left the flats for the rocks and the hills. The sun was merciless here. She felt it beating down on her head as she struggled not to weep. She didn't want to die weeping. They would undoubtedly kill her. But what frightened her more than whatever death was in store for her was what they would do to her first.

She'd heard stories, horrible, barbaric stories, about what was done to captive white women. Once she'd thought them all foolishness, like the stories of bogeymen conjured up to frighten small children. Now she feared that the stories were pale reflections of reality.

They climbed higher, to where the air cooled and the mountains burst to life with pine and fast-running streams. When the horses slowed, she slumped forward, her thighs screaming from the effort of the ride. They talked among themselves in words that meant nothing to her. Time had lost all meaning, as well. It had been hours. She was only sure of that because the sun was low and just beginning to turn the western sky red. Blood red.

They stopped, and for one wild moment she thought about kicking the horse and trying to ride free. Then she was being dragged to the ground. With the breath knocked from her, she tried to get her bearings.

Three of the men were filling water skins at the stream. One seemed hardly more than a boy, but she doubted age mattered. They watered their mounts and paid no attention to her.

Pushing herself up on her elbows, she saw the scarfaced Indian arguing with one she now took to be the leader. He had a starkly beautiful face, lean and chiseled and cold. There was an eagle feather in his hair, and around his neck was a string of what looked like small bleached bones. He studied her dispassionately, then signaled to the other man.

She began to pray again, silently, desperately, as the scar-faced brave advanced on her. He dragged her to her feet and began to toy with her hair. The leader barked out an order that the brave just snarled at. He reached for her throat. Sarah held her breath as he ripped the cameo from her shirtwaist. Apparently satisfied for the moment, he pushed her toward the stream and let her drink.

She did, greedily. Perhaps death wasn't as close as she'd feared. Perhaps somehow, somehow, she could evade it. She wouldn't despair, she told herself as she soothed her burning skin with the icy water. Someone would come after her. Someone.

Jake.

She nearly cried out his name when she was dragged to her feet again. Her captor had fastened her brooch to his buckskin vest. Like a trophy, she thought. Her mother's cameo wouldn't be a trophy for a savage. Furious, she reached for it, and was slapped to the ground. She felt the shirtwaist rip away from her shoulder as she was pulled up by it. Instinctively she began to fight, using teeth and nails. She heard a cry of pain, then rolling masculine laughter. As she kicked and squirmed, her hands were bound together with a leather strap. She was sobbing now, but with rage. Tossed astride the pony again, she felt her ankles bound tight under its belly.

There was the taste of blood in her mouth, and tears in her eyes. They continued to climb.

She dozed somehow. When the pain in her arms and legs grew unbearable, it seemed the best escape. The height was dizzying. They rode along the edge of a narrow canyon that seemed to drop forever. Into hell, she thought as her eyes drooped again. Straight into hell.

Wherever they were taking her, it was a different world, one of forests and rivers and sheer cliffs. It didn't matter. She would die or she would escape. There was nothing else.

Survival. That's all there is.

She hadn't understood what Jake had meant when he'd said that to her. Now she did. There were times when there was nothing but life or death. If she could escape, and had to kill to do so, then she would kill. If she could not escape, and they were planning what she feared they were, she would find a way to kill herself.

They climbed. Endlessly, it seemed to Sarah, they rode up a winding trail and into the twilight. Around her she could hear the call of night birds, high and musical, accented by the hollow hooting of an owl. The trees glowed gold and red, and as the wind rose it sounded through them. The air chilled, working through the torn shirtwaist. Only her pride remained as she shivered in silence.

Exhaustion had her dreaming. She was riding through the forest with Lucilla, chatting about the new bonnet they had seen that morning. They were laughing and talking about the men they would fall in love with and marry. They would be tall and strong and devastatingly handsome.

She dreamed of Jake—of a dream kiss, and a real one. She dreamed of him riding to her, sweeping her up on his big gray mount and taking her away. Holding her, warming her, keeping her safe.

Then the horses stopped.

Her heart was too weary even for prayer as her ankle bonds were cut. She was pulled unresisting from the horse, then sprawled on the ground when her legs buckled under her. There was no energy left in her for weeping, so she lay still, counting each breath. She must have slept, because when she came to again she heard the crackling of a fire and the quiet murmuring of men at a meal.

Biting back a moan, she tried to push herself up. Before she could, a hand was on her shoulder, rolling her onto her back.

Her captor leaned over her, his dark eyes gleaming in the firelight. He spoke, but the words meant nothing to her. She would fight him, she promised herself. Even knowing she would lose, she would fight. He touched her hair, running his fingers through it, lifting it and letting it fall. It must have pleased him, for he grinned at her before he took out his knife.

She thought, almost hoped, that he would slit her throat and be done with it. Instead, he began to cut her skirt away. She kicked, as viciously as she could, but he only parried the blows, then locked her legs with his own. Hearing her skirt rip, she struck out blindly with her bound hands. As he raised his own to strike her, there was a call from the campfire. Her kidnappers rose, bows and rifles at the ready.

She saw the rider come out of the gloom and into the flickering light. Another dream, she thought with a little sob. Then he looked at her. Strength poured back into her body, and she scrambled to her feet.

"Jake!"

She would have run to him, but she was yanked ruthlessly back. He gave no sign, barely glanced her way as he walked his horse toward the group of Apaches. He spoke, but the words were strange, incomprehensible to her.

"Much time has passed, Little Bear."

"I felt breath on my back today." Little Bear lowered his rifle and waited. "I thought never to see you again, Gray Eyes."

Slowly, ignoring the rage bubbling inside him, Jake dismounted. "Our paths have run apart. Now they come together again." He looked steadily into eyes he knew as well as he knew his own. There was between them a love few men would have understood. "I remember a promise made between boys. We swore in blood that one would never lift a hand against the other."

"The promise sworn in blood has not been forgotten." Little Bear held out his hand. They gripped firm, hand to elbow. "Will you eat?"

With a nod, Jake sat by the fire to share the venison. Out of the corner of his eye, he saw Sarah huddled on the ground, watching. Her face was pale with fear and exhaustion. He could see bruises of fatigue under eyes that were glazed with it. Her clothes were torn, and he knew, as he ate and drank, that she must be cold. But if he wanted her alive, there were traditions to be observed.

"Where is the rest of our tribe?"

"Dead. Lost. Running." Little Bear stared broodingly into the fire. "The long swords have cut us down like deer. Those who are left are few and hide in the mountains. Still they come."

"Crooked Arm? Straw Basket?"

"They live. North, where the winters are long and the game is scarce." He turned his head again, and Jake saw a cold, depthless anger—one he understood. "The children do not laugh, Gray Eyes, nor do the women sing."

They talked, as the fire blazed, of shared memories, of people both had loved. Their bond was as strong as it had been when Jake had lived and learned and felt like an Apache. But they both knew that time had passed.

When the meal was over, Jake rose from the fire. "You

have taken my woman, Little Bear. I have come to take her back."

Little Bear held up a hand before the scarred man beside him could speak. "She is not my prisoner, but Black Hawk's. It is not for me to return her to you."

"Then the promise can be kept between us." He turned to Black Hawk. "You have taken my woman."

"I have not finished with her." He put a hand on the hilt of his knife. "I will keep her."

He could have bargained with him. A rifle was worth more than a woman. But bargaining would have cost him face. He had claimed Sarah as his, and there was only one way to take her back.

"The one who lives will keep her." He unstrapped his guns, handing them to Little Bear. There were few men he would have trusted with his weapons. "I will speak with her." He moved to Sarah as Black Hawk began to chant in preparation for the fight.

"I hope you enjoyed your meal," she said, sniffing. "I actually thought you might have come to rescue me."

"I'm working on it."

"Yes, I could see that. Sitting by the fire, eating, telling stories. My hero."

His grin flashed as he hauled her against him for a long, hard kiss. "You're a hell of a woman, Sarah. Just sit tight and let me see what I can do."

"Take me home." Pride abandoned, she gripped the front of his shirt. "Please, just take me home."

"I will." He squeezed her hands as he removed them from his shirt. Then he rose, and he, too, began to chant. If there was magic, he wanted his share.

They stood side by side in the glow of the fire as the youngest warrior bound their left wrists together. The glitter of knives had Sarah pushing herself to her feet. Little Bear closed a hand over her arm.

"You cannot stop it," he said in calm, precise English.

"No!" She struggled as she watched the blades rise. "Oh, God, no!" They came down, whistling.

"I will spill your white blood, Gray Eyes," Black Hawk murmured as their blades scraped, edge to edge.

Locked wrist to wrist, they hacked, dodged, advanced. Jake fought in grim silence. If he lost, even as his blood poured out, Black Hawk would celebrate his victory by raping Sarah. The thought of it, the fury of it, broke his concentration, and Black Hawk pushed past his guard and sliced down his shoulder. Blood ran warm down his arm. Concentrating on the scent of it, he blocked Sarah from his mind and fought to survive.

In the frigid night air, their faces gleamed with sweat. The birds had flown away at the sound of blades and the smell of blood. The only sound now was the harsh breathing of the two men locked in combat, intent on the kill. The other men formed a loose circle around them, watching, the inevitability of death accepted.

Sarah stood with her bound hands at her mouth, holding back the need to scream and scream until she had no air left. At the first sight of Jake's blood she had closed her eyes tight. But fear had had them wide again in an instant.

Little Bear still held her arm, his grip light but inescapable. She already understood that she was to be a kind of prize for the survivor. As Jake narrowly deflected Black Hawk's blade, she turned to the man beside her.

"Please, if you stop it, let him live, I'll go with you willingly. I won't fight or try to escape."

For a moment, Little Bear took his eyes away from the

combat. Gray Eyes had chosen his woman well. "Only death stops it now."

As she watched, both men tumbled to the ground. She saw Black Hawk's knife plunge into the dirt an inch from Jake's face. Even as he drew it out, Jake's knife was ripping into his flesh. They rolled toward the fire.

Jake didn't feel the heat, only an ice-cold rage. The fire seared the skin on his arm before he yanked free. The hilt of his knife was slick with his own sweat but the blade dripped red with his opponent's blood.

The horses whinnied and shied when the men rolled too close. Then they were in the shadows. Sarah could see only a dark blur and the sporadic gleam of a knife. But she could hear desperate grunts and the scrape of metal. Then she heard nothing but the sound of a man breathing hard. One man. With her heart in her throat, she waited to see who would come back into the light.

Bruised, bloodied, Jake walked to her. Saying nothing, he cut through her bonds with the blade of the stained knife. Still silent, he pushed it into his boot and took his guns back from Little Bear.

"He was a brave warrior," Little Bear said.

With pain and triumph singing through him, Jake strapped on his gunbelt. "He died a warrior's death." He offered his hand again. "May the spirits ride with you, brother."

"And with you, Gray Eyes."

Jake held out a hand for Sarah. When he saw that she was swaying on her feet, he picked her up and carried her to his horse. "Hold on," he told her, swinging up into the saddle behind her. He rode out of camp without looking back, knowing he would never see Little Bear again.

She didn't want to cry, but she couldn't stop. Her only

comfort was that her tears were silent and he couldn't hear them. Or so she thought. They'd ridden no more than ten minutes at a slow walk when he turned her around in the saddle to cradle her against him.

"You've had a bad time, Duchess. Go on and cry for a while."

So she wept shamelessly, her cheeks pressed against his chest, the movement of the horse lulling her. "I was so afraid." Her voice hitching, she clung to him. "He was going to—"

"I know. You don't want to think about it." He didn't. If he did, he'd lose the already-slippery grip he had on his control. "It's all over now."

"Will they come after us?"

"No."

"How can you be sure?" As the tears passed, the fear doubled back.

"It wouldn't be honorable."

"Honorable?" She lifted her head to look at him. In the moonlight his face looked hard as rock. "But they're Indians."

"That's right. They'll stand by their honor a lot longer than any white man."

"But—" She had forgotten for a moment the Apache in him. "You seemed to know them."

"I lived with them five years. Little Bear, the one with the eagle feather, is my cousin." He stopped and dismounted. "You're cold. I'll build a fire and you can rest awhile." He pulled a blanket out of his saddlebag and tossed it over her shoulders. Too tired to argue, Sarah wrapped it tight around herself and sat on the ground.

He had a fire burning quickly and started making coffee. Without hesitation, Sarah bit into the jerky he gave her and warmed her hands over the flames.

"The one you...fought with. Did you know him?"

"Yeah."

He'd killed for her, she thought, and had to struggle not to weep again. Perhaps it had been a member of his own family, an old friend. "I'm sorry," she managed.

"For what?" He poured coffee into a cup, then pushed it into her trembling hands.

"For all of it. They were just there, all at once. There was nothing I could do." She drank, needing the warmth badly. "When I was in school, we would read the papers, hear stories. I never really believed it. I was certain that the army had everything under control."

"You read about massacres," he said with a dull fury in his voice that had her looking up again. "About settlers slaughtered and wagon trains attacked. You read about savages scalping children. It's true enough. But did you read any about soldiers riding into camps and butchering, raping women, putting bullets in babies long after treaties were signed and promises made? Did you hear stories about poisoned food and contaminated blankets sent to the reservations?"

"But that can't be."

"The white man wants the land, and the land isn't his— or wasn't." He took out his knife and cleaned it in the dirt. "He'll take it, one way or the other."

She didn't want to believe it, but she could see the truth in his eyes. "I never knew."

"It won't go on much longer. Little Bear and men like him are nearly done."

"How did you choose? Between one life and the other?"

He moved his shoulders. "There wasn't much choice.

There's not enough Apache in me to have been accepted as a warrior. And I was raised white, mostly. Red man. That's what they called my father when he was coming up outside an army post down around Tucson. He kept it. Maybe it was pride, maybe it wasn't."

He stopped, annoyed with himself. He'd never told anyone so much.

"You up to riding?"

She wanted him to go on, to tell her everything there was to tell about himself. Instinct held her back. If she pushed, she might never learn. "I can try." Smiling, she reached out to touch his arm. "I want to— Oh, you're bleeding."

He glanced down. "Here and there."

"Let me see. I should have tended these already." She was up on her knees, pulling away the rent material of his sleeve.

"Nothing a man likes better than to have his clothes ripped off by a pretty woman."

"I'll thank you to behave yourself," she told him, but she couldn't muffle a chuckle.

It was good to hear her laugh, even if only a little. Most of the horror had faded from her eyes. But he wanted it gone, all of it. "Heard you made Lucius strip down to the skin. He claimed you threatened him."

This time her laughter was warmer. "The man needed to be threatened. I wish you'd seen his face when I told him to take off his pants."

"I don't suppose you'd like me to do the same."

"Just the shirt should do. This arm certainly needs to be bandaged." She rose and, modesty prevailing, turned her back before she lifted the hem of her skirt to rip her petticoat.

"I'm obliged." He eased painfully out of his shirt. "I've

been wondering, Duchess, just how many of those petticoats do you wear?"

"That's certainly not a subject for discussion. But it's
fortunate that I..." She turned back to him, and the words
slipped quietly down her throat. She'd never seen a man's
chest before, had certainly never thought a man could be so
beautiful. But he was firm and lean, with the dark skin taut
over his rib cage and gleaming in the firelight. She felt the
heat flash inside her, pressing and throbbing in her center
and then spreading through her like a drug.

An owl hooted behind her and made her jolt. "I'll need
some water." She was forced to clear her throat. "Those
wounds should be cleaned."

With his eyes still on hers, he lifted the canteen. Saying
nothing, she knelt beside him again to tend the cut that ran
from his shoulder to his elbow.

"This is deep. You'll want a doctor to look at it."

"Yes, ma'am."

Her eyes flicked up to his, then quickly away. "It's likely
to scar."

"I've got others."

Yes, she could see that. His was the body of a hero,
scarred, disciplined and magnificent. "I've caused you a
great deal of trouble."

"More than I figured on," he murmured as her fingers
glided gently over his skin.

She tied the first bandage, then gave her attention to the
slice in his side. "This one doesn't look as serious, but it
must be painful."

Her voice had thickened. He could feel the flutter of her
breath on his skin. He winced as she cleaned the wound,
but it was the firelight on her hair that was making him

ache. He held his breath when she reached around him to secure the bandage.

"There are some nicks," she murmured. Fascinated, she touched her palm to his chest. "You'll need some salve."

He knew what he needed. His hand closed over her wrist. Her pulse jumped, but she only stared, as if she were mesmerized by the contrast of his skin against hers. Dazed, she watched her own fingers spread and smooth over the hard line of his chest.

The fire had warmed it, warmed her. Slowly she lifted her head and looked at him. His eyes were dark, darker than she'd ever seen them. Storm clouds, she thought. Or gunsmoke. She thought she could hear her heart pounding in her head. Then there was no sound. No sound at all.

He reached for her face, just to rub his palm over her cheek. Nothing in his life had ever seemed so soft or looked so beautiful. The fire was in her eyes, glowing, heating. There was passion there. He knew enough of women to recognize it. Her cheeks, drained of color by fatigue, were as delicate as glass.

He leaned toward her, his eyes open, ready for her to shy away.

She leaned toward him, her pulse pounding, waiting for him to take.

An inch apart, they hesitated, his breath merging with hers. Softly, more softly than either of them would have thought he could, he brushed his lips over hers. And heard her sigh. Gently, with hands more used to molding the grips of guns, he drew her to him. And felt her give. Her lips parted, as they would only for him.

Boldly, as she had never known she could, she ran her hands up his chest. Was he trembling? She murmured to him, lost in the wonder of it. His body was rigid with tension, even as he took the kiss deeper, gloriously deeper. She tasted the hot flavor of desire on his lips as they moved, restless and hungry, over hers.

Eager for more, she pressed against him, letting her arms link tight behind him, and her mouth tell him everything.

He felt the need burst through him like wildfire, searing his mind and loins and heart. Her name tore out of him as he twisted her in his arms and plundered her mouth. The flames beside them leaped, caught by the wind, and sent sparks shooting into the air. He felt her body strain against his, seeking more. Desperate, he tugged at the torn neck of her blouse.

She could only gasp when he covered her breast with his hand. His palm was rough with calluses, and the sensation made her arch and ache. Then his mouth was on her, hot and wet and greedy as it trailed down. Helpless, she dragged her hands through his hair.

She had faced death. This was life. This was love.

His lips raced over her until she was a mass of nerves and need. Recklessly she dragged his mouth back to hers and drove them both toward delirium. His hands were everywhere, pressing, bruising, exciting. With her breath hammering in and out of her lungs, she began to tremble.

His mouth was buried at her throat. The taste of her had seeped into him, and now it was all he knew, all he wanted to know. She was shuddering. Over and over, beneath his own, her body shook. Jake dug his fingers into the dirt as he fought to drag himself back. He'd forgotten what he was. What she was. Hadn't he proven that by nearly taking her on the ground? He heard her soft, breathless moan as he rolled away from her.

She was dizzy, dazed, desperate. With her eyes half

closed, she reached out. The moment she touched him, he was moving away, standing.

"Jake."

He felt as though he'd been shot, low in the gut, and would bleed for the rest of his life. In silence, he smothered the fire and began to break camp.

Sarah suddenly felt the cold, and she wrapped her arms around herself. "What's wrong?"

"We've got to ride."

"But…" Her skin still tingled where his hands had scraped over it. "I thought…that is, it seemed as though…"

"Damn it, woman, I said we've got to ride." He yanked a duster out of his saddlebag and tossed it to her. "Put that on."

She held it against her as she watched him secure his saddlebags again. She wouldn't cry. Biting her lip hard to make sure, she vowed she would never cry over him. He didn't want her. It had just been a whim. He preferred another kind of woman. After dragging the duster around her shoulders, she walked to the horse.

"I can mount," she said coldly when he took her arm.

With a nod, he stepped back, then vaulted into the saddle behind her.

Chapter 8

The crack of the rifle echoed over the rock and sent a lone hawk wheeling. Sarah gritted her teeth, cocked the lever and squeezed again. The empty whiskey bottle exploded. She was improving, she decided as she mopped her brow and reloaded. And she was determined to get better still.

Lucius wandered over, Lafitte dancing at his heels. "You got a good eye there, Miss Sarah."

"Thank you." She lowered the rifle to give the pup a scratch. Jake was right. He was going to be a big one. "I believe I do."

No one was going to have to rescue her again, not from a rattlesnake, not from Apache marauders, not from the wrath of God himself. In the two weeks since Jake had dropped her, without a word and apparently without a thought, on her doorstep, she'd increased her daily rifle practice. Her aim had sharpened a great deal since she'd taken to imagining that the empty bottles and cans were Jake's grinning face.

"I told you, Lucius, there's no need for you to watch my every move. What happened before wasn't your fault."

"I can't help feeling it was. You hired me on to keep a lookout around here. Then the first time my pants're down— so to speak, Miss Sarah—you're in trouble."

"I'm back now, and unharmed."

"And I'm mighty grateful for it. If Jake hadn't just ridden up… I'd have tried to get you back, Miss Sarah, but he was the man for it."

She bit back the unkind remark that sprang to mind. He had saved her, had risked his life to do so. Whatever had happened afterward couldn't diminish that.

"I'm very grateful to Mr. Redman, Lucius."

"Jake just done what he had to."

She remembered the knife fight with a shudder. "I sincerely hope he won't be required to do anything like it again."

"That's why I'm going to keep a better eye on you. I tell you the God's truth now, Miss Sarah, worrying after a woman's a troublesome thing. I ain't had to bother since my wife died."

"Why, Lucius, I never knew you'd been married."

"Some years back. Quiet Water was her name. She was mighty dear to me."

"You had an Indian wife?" Wanting to hear more, Sarah sat down on a rock, spreading her skirts.

He didn't talk about it often, at least not when he was sober. But he found he was making himself comfortable and telling his tale. "Yes, ma'am. She was Apache, one of Little Bear's tribe. Fact is, she'd've been some kind of aunt to him. I met her when I'd come out here to do some soldiering. Fought Cheyenne, mostly. That would have been back in '62. Didn't mind the fighting, but I sure got tired of the marching. I headed south some to do a little prospecting. Anyways, I met up with John Redman. That was Jake's pa."

"You knew Jake's father?"

"Knew him right well. Partnered up for a while. He and his missus had hit some hard times. Lot of people didn't care much for the idea of him being half-Apache." With a little laugh, he shrugged. "He told me once that some of his tribe didn't care much for the idea of him being half-white. So there you go."

"What kind of man was he?"

"Hardheaded, but real quiet. Didn't say much less'n you said something first. Could be funny. Sometimes it wouldn't occur to you for a minute or two that he'd made a joke. He was good for a laugh. Guess he was the best friend I ever had." He took out his bottle and was relieved when Sarah said nothing. "John had in mind to do some ranching, so I lent a hand here and there. That's how I came to meet Quiet Water."

Casually Sarah pleated her skirt. "I suppose you knew Jake as a boy."

"I'll say I did." Lucius let go a whistling laugh. "Tough little cuss. Could look a hole right through you. Ain't changed much. He was spending some time with his grandma's people. Would've thought he was one of them then, 'cept for the eyes. Course, he wasn't. They knew it and he knew it. Like John said, it's hard not being one or the other. I used to wonder what would've happened if Quiet Water and me had had kids."

"What happened to her, Lucius?"

"I had gone off looking for gold." His eyes narrowed as he stared off into the sun. "Seems a regiment rode through early one morning. Some settler claimed his stock was stolen, and that the Apaches had done it. So the soldiers came in, looking for trouble, hating Indians. Killed most everybody but those who made it up into the rocks."

"Oh, Lucius. Lucius, I'm so sorry." Unable to find words, she took both his hands in hers.

"When I come back, it was done. I was half-crazy, I guess. Rode around for days, not going anywhere. I guess I was hoping somebody'd come along and shoot me. Then I headed to the Redman place. They'd been burned out."

"Oh, dear God."

"Nothing left but charred wood and ashes."

"How horrible." She tightened her grip on his hands. "Oh, Lucius, it wasn't the soldiers?"

"No. Leastwise they weren't wearing uniforms. Seemed like some men from town got liquored up and decided they didn't want no breed that close by. John and his missus had had trouble before, like I said, but this went past hard words and threats. They started out to burn the barn, raise hell. One of them started shooting. Maybe they'd meant to all along, there's no saying. When it was over, they'd burned them out and left the family for dead."

Horror made her eyes dark and huge. "Jake. He would have been just a boy."

"Thirteen, fourteen, I reckon. But he was past being a boy. I found him where he'd buried his folks. He was just sitting there, between the two fresh graves. Had his pa's hunting knife in his hands. Still carries it."

She knew the knife. She'd seen it stained with blood, for her. But now all she could think of was the boy. "Oh, the poor child. He must have been so frightened."

"No, ma'am. I don't believe frightened's the word. He was chanting, like in a trance the Indians sometimes use. War chant, it was. He figured on going into town and finding the men who killed his folks."

"But you said he was only thirteen."

"I said he was past being a boy. Best I could do was talk him out of it for a time, till he learned to handle a gun better. He learned mighty fast. I ain't never seen a man do with a gun what Jake can do."

Though it was hot out, she rubbed the chill from her arms. "Did he...go back for them?"

"I don't rightly know. I never asked. I thought it best we move on until he had some years on him, so we headed south. Didn't know what to do for him. Bought him a horse, and we rode together awhile. I always figured he'd hook up with the wrong kind, but Jake was never much for hooking up with anybody. He'd've been about sixteen when we parted ways. Heard about him off and on. Then he rode into Lone Bluff a few months back."

"To lose everything that way." A tear ran down her cheek. "It's a wonder he's not filled with hate."

"He's got it in him, but it's cold. Me, I use the bottle, wash it away now and then. Jake uses something in here." He tapped his temple. "That boy holds more inside than anybody should have to. He ever lets it out, people better stand back."

She understood what he meant. Hadn't she seen it, that flat, dangerous look that came into his eyes? That expressionless stare that was more passionate than fury, more deadly than rage.

"You care for him."

"He's all I got that you might call family. Yeah, I got an affection for the boy." Lucius squinted over at her. "I figure you do, too."

"I don't know what I feel for him." That was a lie. She knew very well what she felt, how she felt. She was even coming to understand why she felt. He wasn't the man she had once imagined she would love, but he was the only man she ever would. "It doesn't matter what I feel," she said, "if he doesn't feel it back."

"Maybe he does. It might be hard for him to say it right out, but I always figure a woman's got a sense about those things."

"Not always." With a little sigh, she rose. "There's work to be done, Lucius."

"Yes'm."

"There is one question. What have you been doing in the mine?"

"The mine, Miss Sarah?"

"You said yourself I have a good eye. I know you've been going in there. I'd like to know why."

"Well, now." Fabricating wasn't Lucius's strong suit. He coughed and shifted his feet and peered off at nothing. "Just having a look around."

"For gold?"

"Could be."

"Do you think you'll find any?"

"Matt always figured there was a rich vein in that rock, and when Jake—" He broke off.

"When Jake what? Asked you to look?"

"Maybe he might have suggested it sometime."

"I see." Sarah looked up to the top of the ridge. She had always wondered what Jake wanted, she thought, her heart shattering. Perhaps she knew now. Gold seemed to pull at the men she loved. "I have no objection to you working the mine, Lucius. In fact, I think it's an excellent idea. You must let me know if you require any tools." When she looked back at him, her eyes were as cool and hard as any man's. "The next time you ride into town, you might mention to Jake that Sarah's Pride is mine."

"Yes, ma'am, if you'd like."

"I insist." She looked toward the road. "There's a buggy coming."

Lucius spit and hoped it wasn't Carlson. As far as he was concerned, the man had been too free with his visits to Sarah in the past few weeks.

It wasn't Carlson. As the buggy drew closer, Sarah saw it was a woman holding the reins. Not Liza, she realized with a pang of disappointment. The woman was dark and delicate and a stranger to her.

"Good morning." Sarah set the rifle against the wall of the house.

"Good morning, ma'am." The young woman sat in the buggy and sent Sarah a nervous smile. "You sure live a ways out."

"Yes." Since her visitor didn't seem in a hurry to alight, Sarah walked to the buggy. "I'm Sarah Conway."

"Yes, ma'am, I know. I'm Alice. Alice Johnson." She gave the puppy a bright, cheerful smile, then looked at Sarah again. "Pleased to meet you."

"It's nice to meet you, too, Miss Johnson. Would you like to come in for some tea?"

"Oh, no, ma'am, I couldn't."

Baffled by Alice's horrified expression, Sarah tried again. "Perhaps you're lost?"

"No, I've come to talk with you, but I couldn't come in. It wouldn't be fitting."

"Oh? Why?"

"Well, you see, Miss Conway, I'm one of Carlotta's girls."

Carlotta? Wide-eyed, Sarah looked her visitor over again. She was hardly more than a girl, a year or more younger than Sarah herself. Her face was scrubbed clean, and her dress was certainly modest. As Sarah stared, thick lashes lowered over her dark eyes and a blush rushed into her cheeks.

"Do you mean you work at the Silver Star?"

"Yes, ma'am, for nearly three months now."

"But—" Sarah swallowed the words when she saw Alice bite her lip. "Miss Johnson, if you've come to see me, I suggest we talk inside. It's much too hot to stand in the sun."

"I couldn't. Really, it wouldn't be fitting, Miss Conway."

"Fitting or not, I don't wish sunstroke on either of us. Please, come in." Leaving the decision in the hands of her visitor, Sarah walked inside.

Alice hesitated. It didn't feel right, not when Miss Conway was a real lady. But if she went back and couldn't tell Carlotta that she'd done what she'd been sent for, she'd get slapped around for sure. Carlotta always knew when you lied. And you always paid for it.

Sarah heard the timid footsteps as she put water on to boil. Before she could turn and offer Alice a seat, the girl was bubbling.

"Oh, my, isn't this pretty? You've got a real nice place here, Miss Conway. Curtains and all."

"Thank you." Her smile was full and genuine. It was the first time she'd had company who had thought so. "I'm more and more at home here. Please, sit down, Miss Johnson. I'm making tea."

"It's real kind of you, but I don't feel right, you giving me tea. It ain't proper."

"This is my house, and you're my guest. Of course it's proper. I hope you'll enjoy these cookies. I made them only yesterday."

With her fingers plucking nervously at her skirt, Alice sat. "Thank you, ma'am. And don't worry. I won't tell a soul I came in and sat at your table."

Intrigued, Sarah poured the tea. "Why don't you tell me what brought you out to see me?"

"Carlotta. She's been looking at all the dresses you've been making for the ladies in town. They're real pretty, Miss Conway."

"Thank you."

"Just the other day, after Jake left—"

"Jake?"

"Yes'm." Hoping she was holding the cup properly, Alice drank. "He comes into the Silver Star pretty regular. Carlotta's real fond of him. She don't work much herself, you know. Unless it's somebody like Jake."

"Yes, I see." She waited for what was left of her heart to break. Instead, it swelled with fury. "I suppose she might find a man like him appealing."

"She surely does. All the girls got a fondness for Jake."

"I'm sure," she murmured.

"Well, like I was saying, Carlotta got it into her head one day after he left that we should have us some new clothes. Something classy, like ladies would wear. She told me Jake said you could sew some up for us."

"Did he?"

"Yes, ma'am. She said she thought Jake had a real fine idea there, and she sent me on out to see about it. I got me all the measurements."

"I'm sorry, Miss Johnson, I really couldn't. Be sure to tell Carlotta that I appreciate the offer."

"There's eight of us girls, miss, and Carlotta said she'd pay you in advance. I got the money."

"That's generous, but I can't do it. Would you like more tea?"

"I don't—" Confused, Alice looked at her cup. She didn't know anyone who'd ever said no to Carlotta. "If it's not too much trouble." She wanted to stretch out her visit, though she knew that, and the message she'd be taking back, would make Carlotta box her ears.

"Miss Johnson—"

"You can call me Alice, Miss Conway. Everybody does."

"Alice, then. Would you mind telling me how it was you came to work for Carlotta? You're very young to be…on your own."

"My daddy sold me off."

"*Sold* you?"

"There was ten of us at home, and another on the way. Every time he got drunk he whipped one of us or made another. He got drunk a lot. Few months back, a man passed through and Daddy sold me for twenty dollars. I ran off as soon as I could. When I got to Lone Bluff I went to work for Carlotta. I know it ain't right and proper, but it's better than what I had. I get my meals and a bed to myself when I'm finished work." She gave a quick, uncomfortable shrug. "Most of the men are all right."

"Your father had no right to sell you, Alice."

"Sometimes there's right and there's what's done."

"If you wanted to leave Carlotta, I'm sure there would be other work for you in town. Proper work."

"Begging your pardon, Miss Conway, but that ain't true. None of the town ladies would hire me for anything. And they shouldn't. Why, how would they know if I'd been with one of their husbands?"

It was sound thinking, but Sarah shook her head. "If you decide to leave, I'll find work for you."

Alice stared at her, wide-eyed. "That's kind of you. I knew you were a real lady, Miss Conway, and I'm obliged. I'd better be heading back."

"If you'd like to visit again, I'd be happy to see you," Sarah told her as she walked her out.

"No, ma'am, that wouldn't be proper. Thank you for the tea, Miss Conway."

Sarah thought a great deal about Alice's visit. That night, as she read her father's journal by lamplight, she tried to imagine what it had been like. To be sold, she thought with an inward shudder. By her own father, like a horse or a steer. It was true that she, too, had spent years of her life without a real family, but she had always known her father loved her. What he had done, he had done with her best interests at heart.

Once she would have condemned Alice's choice out of hand. But now she thought she understood. It was all the girl knew. The cycle had begun with her father's callousness, and the girl was caught in it, helplessly moving in the same circle, selling herself time after time because she knew nothing else.

Had it been the same for Jake? Had the cruelty he'd lived through as a child forced him into a life of restlessness and violence? The scars he carried must run deep. And the hate. Sarah looked into the soft glow of the lamp. As Lucius had said, the hate ran cold.

She should have hated him. She wanted to, she wished the strong, destructive emotion would come, filling all the cracks in her feelings, blocking out everything else. With hate, a coolheaded, sharply honed hate, she would have felt in control again. She needed badly to feel in control again. But she didn't hate him. She couldn't.

Even though she knew he had spent the night with another woman, kissing another woman's lips, touching another woman's skin, she couldn't hate him. But she could grieve for her loss, for the death of a beauty that had never had a chance to bloom fully.

She had come to understand what they might have had together. She had almost come to accept that they belonged together, whatever their differences, whatever the risks. He would always live by his gun and by his own set of rules, but with her, briefly, perhaps reluctantly, he had shown such kindness, such tenderness.

There was a place for her in his heart. Sarah knew it. Beneath the rough-hewn exterior was a man who believed in justice, who was capable of small, endearing kindnesses. He'd allowed her to see that part of him, a part she knew he'd shared with few others.

Then why, the moment she had begun to soften toward him, to accept him for what and who he was, had he turned to another woman? A woman whose love could be bought with a handful of coins?

What did it matter? With a sigh, she closed her father's journal and prepared for bed. She had only fooled herself into believing he could care for her. Whatever kindness Jake had shown her would always war with his lawless nature and his restless heart. She wanted a home, a man by her side and children at her feet. As long as she loved Jake, she would go on wanting and never having.

Somehow, no matter how hard it was, no matter how painful, she would stop loving him.

Jake hated himself for doing it, but he rode toward Sarah's place, a dozen excuses forming in his head. He wanted to talk to Lucius and check on the progress in the mine. He wanted to make sure she hadn't been bitten by a snake. He'd wanted a ride, and her place was as good as any.

They were all lies.

He just wanted to see her. He just wanted to look at her, hear her talk, smell her hair. He'd stayed away from her for two weeks, hadn't he? He had a right... He had no rights, he told himself as he rode into the yard. He had no rights, and no business thinking about her the way he was thinking about her, wanting her the way he wanted her.

She deserved a man who could make her promises and keep them, who could give her the kind of life she'd been born to live.

He wasn't going to touch her again. That was a promise he'd made himself when he'd ridden away from her the last time. If he touched her, he wouldn't pull back. That would only cause them both more misery.

He'd hurt her. He had seen that plain enough when he'd left her. But that was nothing compared to what he would have done if he'd stayed.

It was quiet. Jake pulled up his mount and took a long, cautious look around, his hand hovering over the butt of his gun. The dog wasn't yapping, nor was there any smoke rising from the chimney. The saddle creaked as he dismounted.

He didn't knock, but pushed open the door and listened. There wasn't a sound from inside. He could see, as his eyes scanned from one corner to the next, that the cabin was empty and as tidy as a church. The curtains she'd sewed had already begun to fade, but they moved prettily in the hot wind. His shoulders relaxed.

She'd done something here. That was something else he had to admire about her. She'd taken less than nothing and made it a home. There were pictures on the walls. One was a watercolor of wildflowers in soft, dreamy hues. It looked like her, he thought as he took a closer study. All dewy and fresh and delicate. Flowers like that would wither fast if they weren't tended.

He moved to the next, his brows drawing together as he scanned it. It was a pencil drawing—a sketch, he figured she'd call it. He recognized the scene, the high, arrogant buttes, the sun-bleached rock. If you looked west from the stream you'd see it. It wasn't an empty place. The Apache knew the spirits that lived there. But oddly, as he studied the lines and shadows, he thought Sarah might know them, too. He would never have imagined her taking the time to draw something so stark and strong, much less hang it on the wall so that she would see it every time she turned around.

Somehow—he couldn't quite figure out the why of it—it suited her every bit as much as the wildflowers.

Annoyed with himself, he turned away. She knew something about magic, he figured. Didn't the cabin smell of her, so that his stomach kept tying itself in knots? He'd be better off out in the air—fifty miles away.

A book caught his eye as he started out. Without giving a thought to her privacy, he opened it. Apparently she'd started a diary. Unable to resist, he scanned the first page.

She'd described her arrival in Lone Bluff. He had to grin as he read over her recounting of the Apache raid and his timely arrival. She'd made him sound pretty impressive, even if she'd noted what she called his "infuriating and unchristian behavior."

There was a long passage about her father, and her feelings about him. He passed it by. Grief was to be respected, unless it needed to be shared. He chuckled out loud as she described her first night, the cold can of beans and the sounds that had kept her awake and trembling until morning. There were bits and pieces he found entertaining enough about the townspeople and her impressions of life in the West. Then he caught his name again.

"Jake Redman is an enigma." He puzzled over the word,

sure he'd never heard it before. It sounded a little too fancy to be applied to him.

I don't know if one might call him a diamond in the rough, though rough he certainly is. Honesty forces me to admit that he has been of some help to me and shown glimmers of kindness. I can't resolve my true feelings about him, and I wonder why I find it necessary to try. He is a law unto himself and a man wholly lacking in manners and courtesy. His reputation is distressing, to say the least. He is what is referred to as a gunslinger, and he wears his weapons as smoothly as a gentleman wears a watch fob. Yet I believe if one dug deeply enough one might discover a great deal of goodness there. Fortunately, I have neither the time nor the inclination to do the digging.

Despite his manner and his style of living there is a certain, even a strong, attractiveness about him. He has fine eyes of clear gray, a mouth that some women might call poetic, particularly when he smiles, and truly beautiful hands.

He stopped there to frown down at his hands. They'd been called a lot of things, but beautiful wasn't one of them. He wasn't sure he cared for it. Still, she sure did have a way with words.

He turned the page and would have read on, but the slightest of sounds at his back had him whirling, his guns gripped firmly in his hands.

Lucius swore long and skillfully as he lowered his own pistol. "I ain't lived this long to have you blow holes in me."

Jake slipped his guns home. "You'd better be careful how you come up on a man. Didn't you see my horse?"

"Yeah, I saw it. Just making sure. Didn't expect to find you poking around in here." He glanced down at the book. Without a word, Jake shut it.

"I didn't expect to find the place deserted."

"I've been up to the mine." Lucius pulled a small bottle of whiskey from his pocket.

"And?"

"It's interesting." He took a long pull, then wiped his mouth with the back of his hand. "I can't figure how Matt got himself caught in that cave-in. He was pretty sharp, and I recollect them beams being secure enough. Looks to me like someone worked pretty hard to bring them down."

With a nod, Jake glanced at the watercolor on the wall. "Have you said anything to her yet?"

"Nope." He didn't think it was the best time to tell Jake that Sarah had found him out. "There's something else I haven't mentioned." His face split into a grin as Jake looked at him. "There's gold in there, boy. Just like Matt always claimed. He'd found the mother lode." Lucius took a swig from the bottle, then corked it. "You figured on that?"

"Just a hunch."

"Want me to keep it under my hat?"

"For the time being."

"I don't care much for playing tricks on Miss Sarah, but I reckon you've got your reasons."

"I've got them."

"I won't ask you what they are. I won't ask you neither what reasons you got for not coming around lately. Miss Sarah, she's been looking a mite peaked since you brought her back from the hills."

"She's sick?" he asked, too quickly.

Lucius rubbed a hand over his mouth to hide a grin. "I figure she's got a fever, all right. Heart fever."

"She'll get over it," Jake muttered as he walked outside.

"You're looking peaked yourself." When Jake didn't answer, he tried again. "Sure is some woman. Looks soft, but that streak of stubborn keeps her going. See there?" He pointed to the vegetable patch. "She's got something growing there. Never thought I'd see a speck of green, but there you go. She waters that thing every day. Stubborn. A stubborn woman's just bound to make things happen."

"Where is she?"

Lucius had been hoping he'd ask. "Gone off driving with Carlson. He's been coming around here near every day. Drinks tea." He spit. "Kisses her fingers and calls her right out by her first name." It warmed his heart to see Jake's eyes harden. "Said something about taking her to see his ranch. Been gone better than an hour now."

"I don't know when I've spent a more pleasant day." Sarah rose from the glossy mahogany table in Carlson's dining room. "Or had a more delightful meal."

"The pleasure has been mine." Carlson took her hand. "All mine."

Sarah smiled and gently took her hand away. "You have such a beautiful home. I never expected to see anything like it out here."

"My grandfather loved beautiful things." He took her elbow. "I inherited that love from him. Most of the furniture was shipped in from Europe. We had to make some concessions to the land." He patted a thick adobe wall. "But there's no reason to sacrifice all our comforts. This painting—" He guided her to a portrait of a pale, elegant woman in blue silk. "My mother. She was my grandfather's pride and joy. His wife died before this house was completed. Everything he did from that day was for his daughter."

"She's lovely."

"She was. Even my grandfather's love and devotion couldn't keep her alive. The women in my family have always been delicate. This land is hard, too hard for the fragile. It baked the life out of her. I suppose that's why I worry about you."

"I'm not as delicate as you might think." She thought of the ride into the mountains with her hands and feet bound.

"You're strong-willed. I find that very attractive."

He took her hand again. Before she could decide how to respond, a man strode into the house. He was shorter and leaner than Carlson, but there was enough of a resemblance around the mouth and eyes for her to recognize him. His hat was pushed back so that it hung around his neck by its strap. Yellow dust coated his clothes. He hooked his thumbs in the pockets of his pants and looked at her in a way that made her blood chill.

"Well, now, what have we got here?"

"Miss Conway." There was a warning, mild but definite, in Carlson's voice. "My brother Jim. You'll have to excuse him. He's been working the cattle."

"Sam handles the money, I handle the rest. You didn't tell me we were having company." He swaggered closer. He carried the scents of leather and tobacco, but she found nothing appealing about it. "Such nice-looking company."

"I invited Miss Conway to lunch."

"And it was lovely, but I really should be getting back." And away, she thought, from Jim Carlson.

"You don't want to rush off the minute I get in." Grinning, Jim laid a dirty hand on the polished surface of a small table. "We don't get enough company here, at least not your kind. You're just as pretty as a picture." He glanced at his brother with a laugh Sarah didn't understand. "Just as pretty as a picture."

"You'd better wash up." Though his voice was mild, Carlson sent him a hard look. "We have some business to discuss when I get back."

"It's all business with Sam." Jim winked at Sarah. "Now, me, I got time for other things."

Sarah swallowed a sigh of relief when Carlson took her elbow again. "Good day, Mr. Carlson."

Jim watched her retreating back. "Yeah, good day to you. A real good day."

"You'll have to excuse him." Carlson helped Sarah into the waiting buggy. "Jim's a bit rough around the edges. I hope he didn't upset you."

"No, not at all," she said, struggling to keep a polite smile. With her hands folded in her lap, she began to chat about whatever came to mind.

"You seem to be adjusting well to your new life," Carlson commented.

"Actually, I'm enjoying it."

"For selfish reasons, I'm glad to hear it. I was afraid you'd lose heart and leave." He let the horses prance as he turned to smile at her. "I'm very glad you're staying." He pulled up so that they could have a last look at the ranch from the rise. The house spread out, rising two stories, glowing pink in the sunlight, its small glass windows glimmering. Neat paddocks and outbuildings dotted the land, which was cut through by a blue stream and ringed by hills.

"It's lovely, Samuel. You must be very proud of it."

"Pride isn't always enough. A place like this needs to be shared. I've regretted not having a family of my own to fill it. Until now I'd nearly given up hoping I'd find a woman to share it with me." He took her hand and brought it to his lips. "Sarah, nothing would make me happier than if that woman were you."

She wasn't sure she could speak, though she could hardly claim to be surprised. He'd made no secret about the fact that he was courting her. She studied his face in silence. He was everything she had dreamed of. Handsome, dashing, dependable, successful. Now he was offering her everything she had dreamed of. A home, a family, a full and happy life.

She wanted to say yes, to lift a hand to his cheek and smile. But she couldn't. She looked away, struggling to find the right words.

She saw him then. He was hardly more than a silhouette on the horizon. An anonymous man on horseback. But she knew without seeing his face, without hearing his voice, that it was Jake. That knowledge alone made her pulse beat fast and her body yearn.

Deliberately she turned away. "Samuel, I can't begin to tell you how flattered I am by your offer."

He sensed refusal, and though anger tightened within him, he only smiled. "Please, don't give me an answer now. I'd like you to think about it. Believe me, Sarah, I realize we've known each other only a short time and your feelings might not be as strong as mine. Give me a chance to change that."

"Thank you." She didn't object when he kissed her hand again. "I will think about it." That she promised herself. "I'm very grateful you're patient. There's so much on my mind right now. I've nearly got my life under control again, and now that I'm going to open the mine—"

"The mine?" His hand tightened on hers. "You're going to open the mine?"

"Yes." She gave him a puzzled look. "Is something wrong?"

"No, no, it's only that it's dangerous." It was a measure of his ambition that he was able to bring himself under control so quickly. "And I'm afraid doing so might distress you more than you realize. After all, the mine killed your father."

"I know. But it also gave him life. I feel strongly that he would have wanted me to continue there."

"Will you do something for me?"

"I'll try."

"Think about it carefully. You're too important to me. I would hate to have you waste yourself on an empty dream." With another smile, he clucked to the horses. "And if you marry me, I'll see that the mine is worked without causing you any heartache."

"I will think about it." But her mind was crowded with other thoughts as she looked over her shoulder at the lone rider on the hill.

Chapter 9

Sarah had never been more excited about a dance in her life. Nor had she ever worked harder. The moment the plans had been announced for a town dance to celebrate Independence Day, the orders for dresses began to pour in. She left all the chores to Lucius and sewed night and day.

Her fingers were cramped and her eyes burned, but she had earned enough to put through an order for the wood floor she wanted so badly.

After the floor, Sarah thought, she would order glass for the windows and a proper set of dishes. Then, when time and money allowed, she was going to have Lucius build her a real bedroom. With a little laugh, she closed her eyes and imagined it. If the mine came through, she would have that house with four bedrooms and a parlor, but for now she'd settle for a real floor beneath her feet.

Soon, she thought. But before floors and windows came the dance.

She might have made every frock as pretty and as fashionable as her skill allowed, but she wasn't about to be outdone. On the afternoon of the dance she took out her best silk dress. It was a pale lavender blue, the color of moonbeams in a forest. White lace flirted at the square-cut bodice that accented the line of her throat and a hint of shoulder. There were pert bows of a deeper lavender at the edge of each poufed sleeve.

She laced her stays so tightly that her ribs hurt, telling herself it would be worth it. With her hand mirror, she struggled to see different parts of herself and put them together in her mind for a complete image. The flounced skirt with the bows was flattering, she decided, and the matching velvet ribbon at her throat was a nice touch. She would have pinned her cameo to it, but that, like so much else, had been lost.

She wouldn't think about that tonight, she told herself as she patted her hair. She'd swept it up, and its weight had caused her to use every hairpin she could find. But, she thought with a nod, it looked effortless, curling ever so slightly at her ears and temples.

It was important that she look her best. Very important, she added, pulling on her long white gloves. If Jake was there, she wanted him to see just what he'd tossed aside. She swept on her white lace shawl, checked the contents of her reticule, then stepped outside.

"Glory be." Lucius stood by the wagon with his hat in his hand. He'd cleaned up without her having to remind him, and had even taken a razor to his chin. When she smiled at him, he decided that if he'd been ten years younger he'd have given Jake a run for his money.

"Lucius, how handsome you look."

"Hell, Miss Sarah. I mean—" He cleared his throat. "You sure look a sight."

Recognizing that as a compliment, Sarah smiled and held out a hand. With as much style as he could muster, Lucius helped her into the wagon.

"You're going to set them on their ears."

"I hope so." At least she hoped she set one person on his ear. "You're going to save a dance for me, aren't you, Lucius?"

"I'd be pleased to. If I do say so, I dance right well, drunk or sober."

"Perhaps you'll try it sober tonight."

Jake saw them ride into town. He was sitting at his window, smoking and watching some of the cowboys racing in the streets, waving their hats, shooting off guns and howling.

Independence Day, he thought, blowing smoke at the sky. Most of them figured they had a right to freedom and the land they'd claimed. He'd come to accept that they, and others like them, would take the Arizona Territory and the rest of the West. Black Hawk, and others like him, would never stop the rush.

And he was neither invader nor invaded.

Maybe that was why he had never tried to put his mark on the land. Not since he'd lost what his father had tried to build. It was better to keep whatever you owned light, light enough that it fit on your horse.

The town was full of noise and people. Most of the cowhands were going to get three-quarters drunk, and they were liable to end up shooting themselves instead of the targets Cody had set up for the marksmanship contest. He didn't much care. He just sat at the window and watched.

Then he saw her. It hurt. Unconsciously he rubbed a hand over his heart, where the ache centered. She laughed. He could hear the sound float right up to him and shimmer like water over his skin. The wanting, the pure strength of it, made him drag his eyes away. For survival.

But he looked back, unable to stop himself. She stepped out of the wagon and laughed again as Liza Cody ran out of her father's store. She twirled in a circle for Liza, and he saw all of her, the white skin of her throat, the hint of high, round breasts, the tiny waist, the glow in her eyes. The cigarette burned down to his fingers, and he cursed. But he didn't stop looking.

"You going to sit in the window all day or take me down like you promised?" Maggie came farther into the room, her hands on her hips. The boy hadn't heard a word. She tugged on his shoulder, ignored the name he called her and repeated herself.

"I never promised to do anything."

"You promised, all right, the night I poured you into that bed when you came in so drunk you couldn't stand."

He remembered the night clearly enough. It had been a week after he'd brought Sarah back from the mountains. A week since he'd been going to the Silver Star, trying to work up enough interest to take Carlotta or any other woman to bed. Drinking had been simpler, but getting blind drunk was something he'd never done before and didn't intend to do again.

"I could have gotten myself into bed well enough."

"You couldn't even crawl up the stairs. If there's one thing I know, it's a man who's too drunk to think. Now, are you going to take me down or are you going to back down?"

He grumbled but pushed himself away from the window. "Nothing worse than a nagging woman."

She only grinned and handed him his hat.

They had no more than stepped outside when John Cody

came racing up. "Mr. Redman. Mr. Redman. I've been waiting for you."

"Yeah?" He pulled the boy's hat over his face. "Why's that?"

Delighted with the attention, Johnny grinned. "The contest. My pa's having a contest. Best shooting gets a brand-new saddle blanket. A red one. You're going to win, ain't you?"

"I wasn't figuring on it."

"How come? Nobody shoots better'n you. It's a real nice blanket, too."

"Go on, Jake." Maggie gave him a slap on the arm. "The boy's counting on you."

"I don't shoot for sport." He meant to walk on, but he saw Johnny's face fall. "A red blanket?"

The boy's eyes lit instantly. "Yessiree, about the prettiest one I ever seen."

"I guess we could look." Before the sentence was complete, Johnny had him by the hand and was pulling him across the street.

At the back of the store Cody had set up empty bottles and cans of varying sizes. Each contestant stood behind a line drawn in the dirt and took his best six shots. Broken glass littered the ground already.

"It costs two bits to enter," Johnny told him. "I got a short bit if you need it."

Jake looked at the dime the boy offered. The gesture touched him in a way that only those who had been offered very little through life would have understood. "Thanks, but I think I got two bits."

"You can shoot better than Jim Carlson. He's winning now." Johnny glanced over to where Jim was showing off a fancy railman's spin with his shiny new Smith & Wesson .44. "Can you do that?"

"Why? It doesn't help you shoot any better." He flipped a quarter to Johnny. "Why don't you go put my name down?"

"Yessir. Yessiree." He took time out to have a friendly shoving match with another boy, then raced away.

"Going to shoot for the blanket?" Lucius asked from behind him.

"Thinking about it." But he was watching Jim Carlson. He remembered that Jim rode a big white gelding. Jake had seen the gleam of a white horse riding away the night Sarah's shed had burned.

Lucius tipped his hat to Maggie. "Ma'am."

"That you, Lucius? I don't believe I've ever seen you with that beard shaved."

He colored up and stepped away. "I guess a man can shave now and then without a body gawking at him."

"I forgot you had a face under there," Jake commented as he watched Will Metcalf hit four out of six bottles. "You looking for a new red blanket, too?"

"Nope. Just thought I'd come around and tell you Burt Donley rode into town."

Only his eyes changed. "Is that so? I thought he was in Laramie."

"Not anymore. He came this way while you were in New Mexico. Started working for Carlson."

In an easy move, Jake turned and scanned the area behind him. "Donley doesn't punch cattle."

"Hasn't been known to. Could be Carlson hired him to do something else."

"Could be," Jake murmured, watching Donley walk toward the crowd.

He was a big man, burly at the shoulders, thick at the

waist. He wore his graying hair long, so long it merged with his beard. And he was fast. Jake had good reason to know just how fast. If the law hadn't stepped in two years before, one of them would be dead now.

"Heard you had some trouble a while back."

"Some." Through the crowd, Jake's eyes met Donley's. They didn't need words. There was unfinished business between them.

As she stood beside Liza, Sarah watched Jake. And shivered. Something had come into his eyes. Something cold and deadly and inevitable. Then the crowd roared when the next contestant shattered all six bottles.

"Oh, look." Liza gave Sarah a quick shake. "Jake's going to shoot. I know it's wrong, but I've always wanted to see how he does it. You hear such stories. There was one—" Her mouth fell open when he drew his right hand and fired.

"I didn't even see him take it out," she whispered. "It was just in his hand, quick as a blink."

"He hit them all." Sarah wrapped her shawl tighter around her. He had hardly moved. His gun was still smoking when he slid it back in place.

Donley strode over, flipped a quarter and waited until more targets were set. Sarah watched his big hand curl over the butt of his gun. Then he drew and fired.

"Goodness. He hit all of them, too. That leaves Dave Jeffrey, Jim Carlson, Jake and Burt Donley."

"Who is he?" she asked, wondering why Jake looked like he wanted to kill him. "The big man in the leather vest."

"Donley? He works for Samuel Carlson. I've heard talk about him, too. The same kind of talk as you hear about Jake. Only…"

"Only?"

"Well, you know how I told you Johnny's been tagging

after Jake, pestering him and talking his ear off? I can't say it worries me any. But if he got within ten feet of Burt Donley I'd skin him alive."

The crowd shifted as Cody brought the line back five feet. When the first man aimed and fired, missing two bottles, Sarah saw Johnny tug on Jake's arm and whisper something. To her surprise, Jake grinned and ruffled the boy's hair. There it was again, she thought. That goodness. That basic kindness. Yet she remembered the look that had come into his eyes only moments before.

Who are you? she wanted to ask.

As if he'd heard her, Jake turned his head. Their eyes met and held. She felt a flood of emotions rise up uncontrollably and again wished she could hate him for that alone.

"You keep looking at her like that," Maggie murmured at his side, "you're going to have to marry her or ride fast in the other direction."

"Shut up, Maggie."

She smiled as sweetly as if he'd kissed her cheek. "Just thought you'd like to know that Sam Carlson ain't too pleased by the way you two are carrying on."

Jake's gaze shifted and met Carlson's. He had come up to stand behind Sarah and lay a proprietary hand on her shoulder. Jake considered allowing himself the pleasure of shooting him for that alone. "He's got no claim."

"Not for lack of trying. Better move fast, boyo."

The onlookers cheered again as Jim Carlson nipped five out of six targets.

Taking his time, Jake reloaded his pistol, then moved to the line. The six shots sounded almost like one. When he lowered his Colt, six bottles had been shattered.

Donley took his place. Six shots, six hits.

The line was moved farther back.

"They can't do it from here," Liza whispered to Sarah. "No one could."

Sarah just shook her head. It wasn't a game anymore. There was something between the two men, something much deeper, much darker, than a simple contest of skill. Others sensed it, too. She could hear the murmur of the crowd and see the uneasy looks.

Jake moved behind the line. He scanned the targets, judging the distance, taking mental aim. Then he did what he did best. He drew and fired on instinct. Bottles exploded, one by one. There was nothing left but a single jagged base. Without pausing, he drew his other gun and shattered even that.

There was silence as Donley stepped forward. He drew, and the gun kicked in his hand with each shot. When he was done, a single bottle remained unbroken.

"Congratulations, Redman." Cody brought the blanket over, hoping to dispel some of the tension. Relief made him let out his breath audibly when Sheriff Barker strolled over.

"That was some shooting, boys." He gave each man a casual nod. Will Metcalf stood at his shoulder as directed. "Good to get it out of your system with a few bottles. Either one of you catches a bullet tonight, there's sure no way I can doubt who put it there."

The warning was given with a smile that was friendly enough. Behind Sarah, Carlson gave a quick shake of his head. Without speaking, Donley made his way through the crowd, which parted for him.

"I ain't never seen nobody shoot like that." Johnny looked up at Jake with awe and wonder in his eyes.

Jake tossed the blanket to him. "There you go."

His eyes widened even farther. "I can have it?"

"You got a horse, don't you?"

"Yes, sir, I got me a bay pony."

"Red ought to look real nice on a bay. Why don't you go see?"

With a whoop, Johnny raced off, only to be caught by his mother. After a minor scuffle, he turned back, grinning. "Thanks, Mr. Redman. Thanks a lot."

"You sure did please that boy pink," Barker commented.

"I don't need a blanket."

Barker only shook his head. "You're a puzzle, Jake. I can't help but have a liking for you."

"That's a puzzle to me, Sheriff. Most lawmen got other feelings."

"Maybe so. Either way, I'd be obliged if you'd keep those guns holstered tonight. You wouldn't want to tell me what there is between you and Donley?"

Jake sent him an even look. "No."

"Didn't figure you would." He spit out tobacco juice. "Well, I'm going to have me some chicken and dance with my wife."

There were a dozen tables lined up along one side of the big canvas tent. Even before the music started, more than half of the food was gone. Women, young and old, were flirting, pleased to be shown off in their best dresses. When the fiddle started, couples swarmed onto the floor. Liza, in her pink muslin, grabbed Will's hand and pulled him with her. Carlson, dashing in his light brown suit and string tie, bowed to Sarah.

"I'd be honored if you'd step out with me, Sarah."

With a little laugh, she gave him a formal curtsy. "I'd be delighted."

The music was fast and cheerful. Despite the heat, the dancing followed suit. At the front of the tent the musicians fiddled and plucked and strummed tirelessly, and the caller wet his whistle with free beer. Couples swung and sashayed and kicked up their heels in a reel. It was different from the dances Sarah had attended in Philadelphia. Wonderfully different, she thought as she twirled in Lucius's arms. Hoots and hollers accompanied the music, as well as hand-clapping, foot-stamping and whistles.

"You were right, Lucius." Laughing, she laid a hand on her speeding heart when the music stopped.

"I was?"

"Yes, indeed. You're a fine dancer. And this is the best party I've ever been to." She leaned over impulsively and kissed his cheek.

"Well, now." His face turned beet red with embarrassed pleasure. "Why don't I fetch you a cup of that punch?"

"That would be lovely."

"Sarah!" Liza's face was nearly as pink as Lucius's when she rushed over and grabbed Sarah's arm.

"My goodness, what's wrong?"

"Nothing. Nothing in the world is wrong." Impatient, Liza dragged Sarah to a corner of the tent. "I just got to tell somebody or bust."

"Then tell me. I'd hate to see you rip the seams of that dress."

"I was just outside, taking a little air." She looked quickly right, then left. "Will came out after me. He kissed me."

"He did?"

"Twice. I guess my heart just about stopped."

One brow lifted, Sarah struggled with a smile. "I suppose that means you've decided to let him be your beau."

"We're getting married," Liza blurted out.

"Oh, Liza, really? That's wonderful." Delighted, Sarah threw her arms around her friend. "I'm so happy for you. When?"

"Well, he's got to talk to Pa first." Liza chewed her lip as she glanced toward her father. "But I know it's going to be all right. Pa likes Will."

"Of course he does. Liza, I can't tell you how happy I am for you."

"I know." When her eyes filled, Liza blinked and sniffled. "Oh, Lordy, I don't want to cry now."

"No, don't, or I'll start."

Laughing, Liza hugged her again. "I can't wait. I just can't wait. It'll be your turn before long. The way Samuel Carlson can't take his eyes off you. I have to admit, I used to have a crush on him." She gave a quick, wicked smile. "Mostly, I thought about using him to make Will jealous."

"I'm not going to marry Samuel. I don't think I'm ever going to get married."

"Oh, nonsense. If not Samuel, there's bound to be a man around here who'll catch your eye."

The musicians began to play again. A waltz. Half smiling, Sarah listened. "The trouble is," she heard herself saying, "one has, but he isn't the kind who thinks about marriage."

"But who—" Liza broke off when she saw Sarah's eyes go dark. "Oh, my," she said under her breath as she watched Jake come into the tent and cross the room.

There might have been no one else there. No one at all. The moment he'd walked in everything had faded but the music, and him. She didn't see Carlson start toward her to claim the waltz. Nor did she see his jaw clench when he noted where her attention was focused. She only saw Jake coming toward her.

He didn't speak. He just stopped in front of her and held out a hand. Sarah flowed like water into his arms.

She thought it must be a dream. He was holding her, spinning her around and around the room while the music swelled in her head. His eyes never left hers. Without thinking, she lifted her hand from his shoulder to touch his face. And watched his eyes darken like storm clouds.

Flustered by her own behavior, she dropped her hand again. "I didn't imagine you would dance."

"My mother liked to."

"You haven't—" She broke off. It was shameless. The devil with it. "You haven't been by to see me."

"No."

He was never any help, Sarah thought. "Why?"

"You know why." He was crazy to be doing even this. Holding her, torturing himself. She had lowered her eyes at his words, but she raised them again now. The look was clear and challenging.

"Are you afraid to see me?"

"No." That was a lie, and he didn't lie often. "But you should be."

"You don't frighten me, Jake."

"You haven't got the sense to be scared, Sarah." When the music stopped, he held her a moment longer. "If you did, you'd run like hell any time I got close."

"You're the one doing the running." She drew out of his arms and walked away.

It was difficult to hold on to her composure, difficult not to fume and stamp and scream as she would have liked. With her teeth gritted, she stood up for the next dance with the first man who asked her. When she looked again, Jake was gone.

"Sarah." Carlson appeared at her side with a cup of lemonade.

"Thank you." Her small silk fan was hardly adequate for the July heat. "It's a lovely party, isn't it?"

"Yes. More so for me because you're here."

She sipped, using the drink as an excuse not to respond.

"I don't want to spoil your evening, Sarah, but I feel I must speak my mind."

"Of course. What is it?"

"You're stepping on very dangerous ground with Jake Redman."

"Oh." Her dander rose, and she fought it down again. "How is that, Samuel?"

"You must know him for what he is, my dear. A killer, a hired gun. A man like that will treat you with no more respect than he would a woman who was…less of a lady."

"Whatever you think of him, Samuel, Mr. Redman has come to my aid a number of times. If nothing else, I consider him a friend."

"He's no one's friend. Stay away from him, Sarah, for your own sake."

Her spine shot ramrod-straight. "That doesn't sound like advice any longer, but like a demand."

Recognizing the anger in her eyes, he shifted ground. "Consider it a request." He took her hand. "I like to think we have an understanding, Sarah."

"I'm sorry." Gently she took her hand from his. "We don't. I haven't agreed to marry you, Samuel. Until I do I feel no obligation to honor a request. Now, if you'll excuse me, I'd like some air. Alone."

Knowing she had been unnecessarily short with him, she hurried out of the tent.

The moon was up now, and nearly full. Taking the deep, long breaths Sister Madeleine had always claimed would calm an unhealthy temper, she studied it. Surely the moon had been just as big and white in the East. But it had never seemed so. Just as the sky had never seemed so vast or so crowded with stars. Or the men as impossible.

The breathing wasn't going to work, she discovered. She'd walk off her anger instead. She'd taken no more than five steps when the shadow of a man brought her up short. She watched Jake flick away a cigarette.

"It's a hot night for walking."

"Thank you for pointing that out," she said stiffly, and continued on her way.

"There's a lot of drinking going on tonight. A lot of men in town who don't get much chance to see pretty women, much less hold on to one. Walking alone's not smart."

"Your advice is noted." She stormed away, only to have her arm gripped.

"Do you have to be so ornery?"

"Yes." She yanked her arm free. "Now, if that's all you have to say, I'd like to be alone."

"I got more to say." He bit off the words, then dug into his pocket. "This belongs to you."

"Oh." She took the cameo, closing her fingers around it. "I thought it was gone. The Apache with the scar. He'd taken it. He was wearing it when—" When you killed him, she thought.

"I took it back. I've been meaning to give it to you, but it slipped my mind." That was another lie. He'd kept it because he'd wanted to have something of her, even for a little while.

"Thank you." She opened her bag and slipped the cameo inside. "It means a great deal to me." The sound of high, wild feminine laughter tightened her lips. Apparently there was a party at the Silver Star tonight, as well. She wouldn't soften toward him, not now, not ever again. "I'm surprised you're still here. I'd think a dance would be a bit tame for your tastes. Don't let me keep you."

"Damn it, I said I don't want you walking around alone." Sarah looked down at the hand that had returned to her arm. "I don't believe I'm obliged to take orders from you. Now let go of me."

"Go back inside."

"I'll go where I want, when I want." She jerked free a second time. "And with whom I want."

"If you're talking about Carlson, I'm going to tell you now to stay away from him."

"Are you?" The temper that had bubbled inside her when one man had warned her boiled over at the nerve of this one. "You can tell me whatever you choose, but *I* don't choose to listen. I'll see Samuel when it pleases me to see him."

"So he can kiss your hand?" The anger he was keeping on a short rein strained for freedom. "So you can have the town talking about you spending the day at his place?"

"You have quite a nerve," she whispered. "You, who spends your time with—that woman. Paying her for attention. How dare you insinuate that there's anything improper in my behavior?" She stepped closer to stab a finger at his chest. "If I allow Samuel to kiss my hand, that's my affair. He's asked me to marry him."

The last thing she expected was to be hauled off her feet so that her slippers dangled several inches from the ground. "What did you say?"

"I said he asked me to marry him. Put me down."

He gave her a shake that sent hairpins flying. "I warn you, Duchess, you think long and hard about marrying him, because the same day you're his wife, you're his widow. That's a promise."

She had to swallow her heart, which was lodged in her throat. "Is a gun your answer for everything?"

Slowly, his eyes on hers, he set her down. "Stay here."

"I don't—"

He shook her again. "By God, you'll stay here. Right here, or I'll tie you to a rail like a bad-tempered horse."

Scowling after him, she rubbed the circulation back into her arms. Of all the rude, high-handed— Then her eyes grew wide. Oh, dear Lord, she thought. He's going to kill someone. Flinging a hand to her throat, she started to run. He caught her on his way back, when she was still two feet from the tent.

"Don't you ever listen?"

"I thought—I was afraid—"

"That I was going to put a bullet in Carlson's heart?" His mouth thinned. So she cared that much, to come running to save him. "There's time for that yet." Taking a firmer grip on her arm, he pulled her with him.

"What are you doing?"

"Taking you home."

"You are not." She tried and failed to dig in her heels. "I'm not going with you, and I'm not ready to go home."

"Too bad." Impatient with her struggles, he swooped her up.

"Stop this at once and put me down. I'll scream."

"Go right ahead." He dumped her on the wagon seat. She scrambled for the reins, but he was faster.

"Lucius will take me home when I choose to go home."

"Lucius is staying in town." Jake cracked the reins. "Now why don't you sit back and enjoy the ride? And keep quiet," he added when she opened her mouth. "Or I swear I'll gag you."

Chapter 10

Dignity. Despite the circumstances… No, Sarah thought, correcting herself, *because* of the circumstances, she would maintain her dignity. It might be difficult at the speed Jake was driving, and given the state of her own temper, but she would never, never forget she was a lady.

She wished she were a man so she could knock him flat.

Control. Jake kept his eyes focused over the horses' heads as they galloped steadily and wished it was as easy to control himself. It wasn't easy, but he'd used his control as effectively as he had his Colts for most of his life. He wasn't about to lose it now and do something he'd regret.

He thought it was a shame that a man couldn't slug a woman.

In stony silence, they drove under the fat, full moon. Some might consider it a night for romance, Sarah thought with a sniff. Not her. She was certain she'd never see another full moon without becoming furious. Dragging her off in the middle of a party, she fumed, trying to give her orders on her personal affairs. Threatening to tie her up like—like a horse, she remembered. Of all the high-handed, arrogant, ill-mannered— Taking a long, cautious breath, she blocked her thoughts.

She'd lose more than her dignity if she allowed herself to dwell on Jake Redman.

The dog sent up a fast, frantic barking as they drove into the yard. He scented Sarah and the tall man who always scratched him between the ears. Tongue lolling, he jumped at the side of the wagon, clearly pleased to have his mistress home. One look had him subsiding and slinking off again. She'd worn that same look when he'd tried to sharpen his teeth on one of her kid slippers.

The moment Jake had pulled the horses up in front of the house, Sarah gathered her skirts to step down. Haste and temper made her careless, and she caught the hem. Before she could remind herself about her dignity, she was tugging it free. She heard the silk rip.

"Now see what you've done."

Just as angry, but without the encumbrances, Jake climbed down from the opposite side. "If you'd have held on a minute, I'd have given you a hand."

"Oh, really?" With her chin lifted, she marched around the front of the wagon. "You've never done a gentlemanly thing in your life. You eat with your hat on, swear and ride in and out of here without so much as a good day or a good-bye."

He decided she looked much more likely to bite than her scrawny dog. "Those are powerful faults."

"Faults?" She lifted a brow and stepped closer. "I haven't begun to touch on your faults. If I began, I'd be a year older before I could finish. How dare you toss me in the wagon like a sack of meal and bring me back here against my wishes?"

She was stunning in the moonlight, her cheeks flushed with anger, her eyes glowing with it. "I got my reasons."

"Do you? I'd be fascinated to hear them."

So would he. He wasn't sure what had come over him, unless it was blind jealousy. That wasn't a thought he wanted to entertain. "Go to bed, Duchess."

"I have no intention of going anywhere." She grabbed his arm before he could lead the horses away. "And neither will you until you explain yourself. You accosted me, man-handled me and threatened to kill Samuel Carlson."

"It wasn't a threat." He took her hand by the wrist and dragged it away from his arm. "The next time he touches you, I'll kill him."

He meant it, Sarah realized. She stood rooted to the spot. The ways of the West might still be new to her, but she recognized murder when she saw it in a man's eyes. With her shawl flying behind her, she raced after him.

"Are you mad?"

"Maybe."

"What concern is my relationship with Samuel Carlson to you? I assure you that if I didn't wish Samuel, or any man, to touch me, I would not be touched."

"So you like it?" The horses shied nervously when he spun around to her. "You like having him hold you, put his hands over you, kiss you."

She would have suffered the tortures of hell rather than admit that Carlson had done no more than kiss her fingers. And that the only man who had done more was standing before her now. She stepped forward until she was toe-to-toe with him.

"I'll risk repeating myself and say that it's none of your business."

The way she lifted that chin, he thought, she was just asking to have it punched. "I figure it is." He dragged the horses inside the shed to unharness them.

"You figure incorrectly." Sarah followed him inside. Dignified or not, she was going to have her say. "What I do is my business, and mine alone. I've done nothing I'm ashamed of, and certainly nothing I feel requires justification to you. If I allow Samuel to court me, you have no say in the matter whatsoever."

"Is that what you call it?" He dragged the first horse into its stall. "Courting?"

She went icily still. "Have you another name for it?"

"Maybe I've been wrong about you." He took the second horse by the bridle as he studied Sarah. "I thought you were a bit choosier. Then again, you didn't pull back when I put my hands on you." He grabbed her wrist before she could have the satisfaction of slapping his face.

"How dare you?" Her breath heaved through her lips. "How dare you speak to me that way?" When she jerked free, her shawl fell to the ground unnoticed. "No, I didn't object when you touched me. By God, I wish I had. You make me feel—" The words backed up in her throat. Sarah dug her fingers into her palms until she could choke them free. "You made me feel things I still don't understand. You made me trust you, and those feelings, when it was all a lie. You made me want you when you didn't want me back. After you'd done that, you turned away as though it had meant nothing."

Pain clawed through his gut. What she was saying was true. The hurt shining from her eyes was real. "You're better off," he said quietly as he led the horse into a stall.

"I couldn't agree more." She wanted to weep. "But if you think that gives you any right to interfere in my life, you're wrong. Very wrong."

"You jumped mighty fast from my arms to his." Bitterness hardened the words even as he cursed himself for saying them.

"I?" It was too much—much more than she could bear. Driven by fury, she grabbed his shirt with both hands. "It wasn't I who jumped, it was you. You left me here without a word, then rode straight to the Silver Star. You kissed me, then rubbed my taste from your mouth so that you could kiss her."

"Who?" He caught her by the shoulder before she could rush back outside. "Who?"

"I have nothing more to say to you."

"You started it. Now finish it. Whose bed do you have me jumping in, Sarah?"

"Carlotta's." She threw the name at him with all the hurt and fury that was bottled up inside of her. "You left me to go to her. If that wasn't enough hurt and humiliation, you told her to hire me."

"Hire you?" Shock had his fingers tightening, bruising her flesh. "What the hell are you talking about?"

"You know very well you told her she should hire me to sew dresses for her and her—the others."

"Sew?" He didn't know if he should laugh or curse. Slowly he released his grip and let his hands fall to his sides. "Whatever else you think about me, you should know I'm not stupid."

"I don't know what I think about you." She was fighting back tears now, and it infuriated her.

It was the gleam of those tears that had him explaining when he would have preferred to keep silent. "I never told Carlotta to hire you, for anything. And I haven't been with—" He broke off, swearing. Before he could stride out, she snatched his arm again. She'd conquered her tears, but she couldn't stop her heart from pounding.

"Are you telling me that you haven't been to the Silver Star?"

"No. I'm not telling you that."

"I see." With a bitter little laugh, she rubbed her temple. "So you've simply found, and bought, another woman who suits you. Poor Carlotta. She must be devastated."

"It would take a hell of a lot more than that. And I haven't bought anything in the Silver Star but whiskey since you— since I got back to town."

"Why?" She had to force even a whisper through her lips.

"That's my business." Cursing himself, he started out again, only to have her rush to stop him.

"I asked you a question."

"I gave you my answer." He scooped up her shawl and pushed it into her hands. "Now go to bed."

She tossed the filmy lace on the ground again. "I'm not going anywhere, and neither are you until you tell me why you haven't been with her, or anyone."

"Because I can't stop thinking about you." Enraged, he shoved her back against the wall with a force that had pins scattering and her hair tumbling wild and free to her waist. He wanted to frighten her, frighten her half as much as she frightened him. "You're not safe with me, Duchess." He leaned close to her, dragging a hand roughly through her hair. "Remember that."

She pressed her damp hands against the wall. It wasn't fear she felt. The emotion was strong and driving, but it wasn't fear. "You don't want me."

"Wanting you's eating holes in me." His free hand slid

up to circle her neck. "I'd rather be shot than feel the way you make me feel."

"How do I make you feel?" she murmured.

"Reckless." It was true, but it wasn't everything. "And that's not smart, not for either of us. I'll hurt you." He squeezed lightly, trying to prove it to them both. "And I won't give a damn. So you better run while I still have a mind to let you."

"I'm not running." Even if she had wanted to, it would have been impossible. Her legs were weak and trembling. She was already out of breath. "But you are." Knowing exactly what she was doing, what she was risking, she raised her chin. "Threats come easily to you. If you were the kind of man you say you are, and you wanted me, you'd take me. Right here, right now."

His eyes darkened. They were almost black as they bored into hers. She didn't wince as his fingers tightened painfully in her hair. Instead, she kept her chin up and dared him.

"Damn you." He brought his mouth down hard on hers. To scare her, he told himself as he pressed her back against the wall and took his fill. To make her see once and for all what he was. Ruthless, knowing she would bruise, he dragged his hands over her. He touched her the way he would have touched a girl at the Silver Star. Boldly, carelessly. He wanted to bring her to tears, to make her sob and tremble and beg him to leave her alone.

Maybe then he would be able to.

He heard her muffled cry against his mouth and tried to pull back. Her arms circled him, drawing him in.

She gave herself totally, unrestrainedly, to the embrace. He was trying to hurt her, she knew. But he couldn't. She would make him see that being in his arms would never cause her pain. She gasped, forced to grip him tighter to keep her balance, when his mouth roamed down her throat, spreading luxuriant heat. The scraping of his teeth against her skin had her moaning. Too aroused to be shocked by her own actions, she tugged at his shirt. She wanted to touch his skin again, wanted to feel the warmth of it.

He was losing himself in her. No, he was already lost. Her scent, the fragility of it, had his senses spinning. Her mouth, the hunger of it, clawed at his control. Then she said his name—it was a sigh, a prayer—and broke the last bonds.

He pulled her down into the hay, desperate for her. The silk of her dress rustled against his hands as he dragged it from her shoulders. A wildness was on him, peeling away right and wrong as he tore the silk away to find her.

Terror rose up to grab her by the throat. But it wasn't terror of him. It was terror of the need that had taken possession of her. It ruled her, drove her beyond what could and could not be. As ruthless as he, she ripped at his shirt.

He was yanking at her laces, cursing them, cursing himself. Impatient with encumbrances, he shrugged out of his shirt, then sucked in his breath when her fingers dug into his flesh to pull him closer.

Hot, quick kisses raced over her face. She couldn't catch her breath, not even when he tore her laces loose. They rolled over on the hay as they fought to free themselves, and each other, of the civilized barrier of clothing. She arched when he filled his hands with her breasts, too steeped in pleasure to be ashamed of her nakedness. Her pulse hammered at dozens of points, making her thoughts spin and whirl and center only on him.

She was willow-slim, soft as the silk he'd torn, delicate as glass. For all her fragility, he couldn't fight her power over him. He could smell the hay, the horses, the night. He could see her eyes, her hair, her skin, as the moonlight pushed

Lawless

through the chinks in the shed to shimmer over them. Once more, just once more, he tried to bring himself to sanity. For her sake. For his own.

Then she lifted her arms to him and took him back.

He was lean and firm and strong. Sarah tossed her common sense aside and gave herself to the need, to the love. His eyes were dark, dangerously dark. His skin gleamed like copper in the shadowed light. She saw the scar that ran down his arm. As his mouth came bruisingly back to hers, she ran a gentle finger over it.

There was no turning back for either of them. The horses scraped the ground restlessly in their stalls. In the hills, a coyote sent up a wailing, lonesome song. They didn't hear. She heard her name as he whispered it. But that was all.

The hay scratched her bare skin as he covered her body with his own. She only sighed. He felt the yielding, gloried in it. He tasted the heat and the honey as he drew her breast into his mouth. A breathless moan escaped her at this new intimacy. Then his tongue began to stroke, to tease.

The pleasure built, painful, beautiful, tugging at her center as his teeth tugged at her nipples. It was unbearable. It was glorious. She wanted to tell him, wanted to explain somehow, but she could only say his name over and over.

He felt her thigh tremble when he stroked a hand along it. Then he heard her gasp of surprise, her moan of desire, when he touched what no man had ever dared to touch.

His. He took her as gently as his grinding need would allow toward her first peak. She was his. She cried out, her body curving like a bow as she crested. The breath burned in his lungs as he crushed his mouth to hers and took her flying again.

She held on, rocked, dazed and desperate. So this was love. This was what a man and woman brought to each other in the privacy of the night. It was more, so much more, than she had ever dreamed. Tears streamed from her eyes to mix with the sweat that slicked her body and his.

"Please," she murmured against his mouth, unsure of what she was asking. "Please."

He didn't want to hurt her. With that part of his mind that still functioned he prayed he could take her painlessly. His breathing harsh and ragged, he entered her slowly, trying to soothe her with his mouth and his hands.

Lights exploded behind her eyes, brilliant white lights that flashed into every color she'd ever seen or imagined. The heat built and built until she was gasping from it, unaware that her nails had scraped down his back and dug in.

Then she was running, racing, speeding, toward something unknown, something urgently desired. Like life. Like breath. Like love. Instinct had her hips moving. Joy had her arms embracing.

She lost her innocence in a wild burst of pleasure that echoed endlessly.

The moonlight slanted across her face as she slept. He watched her. Though his body craved sleep, his mind couldn't rest. She looked almost too beautiful to be real, curled into the hay, her hair spread out, her skin glowing, covered by nothing more than the thin velvet ribbon around her neck.

He'd recognized the passion in her from the beginning. He had suppressed his own for too long not to recognize it when it was suppressed in another. She'd come to him openly, honestly, innocently. And of all the sins he'd ever committed, the greatest had been taking that innocence from her.

He'd had no right. He pressed his fingers against his eyes.

He'd had no choice. The kind of need he'd felt for her—still felt, he realized—left no choice.

He was in love with her. He nearly laughed out loud. That kind of thinking was dangerous. Dangerous to Sarah. The things he loved always seemed to end up dead, destroyed. His gaze shifted. Her dress was bundled in a heap near her feet. On the pale silk lay his gunbelt.

That said it all, Jake decided. He and Sarah didn't belong together any more than his Colts and her silk dress did. He didn't belong with anyone.

He shifted, started to rise, but Sarah stirred and reached for his hand. "Jake."

"Yeah." Just the way she said his name made desire quicken in him.

Slowly, a smile curving her lips, she opened her eyes. She hadn't been dreaming, she thought. He was here, with her. She could smell the hay, feel it. She could see the glint of his eyes in the shadowed light. Her smile faded.

"What's wrong?"

"Nothing's wrong." Turning away, he reached for his pants.

"Why are you angry?"

"I'm not angry." He yanked his pants over his hips as he rose. "Why the hell should I be angry?"

"I don't know." She was determined to be calm. Nothing as beautiful as what had happened between them was going to be spoiled by harsh words. She found her chemise, noted that one shoulder strap was torn and slipped it on. "Are you going somewhere?"

He picked up his gunbelt because it troubled him to see it with her things. "I don't think I'd care to walk back to town, and Lucius has my horse."

"I see. Is that the only reason you're staying?"

He turned, ready to swear at her. She was standing very straight, her hair drifting like clouds around her face and shoulders. Her chemise skimmed her thighs and dipped erotically low at one breast. Because his mouth had gone dry, he could only shake his head.

She smiled then, and held out a hand. "Come to the house with me. Stay with me."

It seemed he still had no choice. He closed his hand over hers.

Sarah awoke with Lafitte licking her face. "Go away," she muttered, and turned over.

"You asked me to stay." Jake hooked an arm around her waist. He watched her eyes fly open, saw the shock, the remembering and the pleasure.

"I was talking to the dog." She snuggled closer. Surely there was no more wonderful way to wake up than in the arms of the man you loved. "He figured out how to climb up, but he hasn't figured out how to get down."

Jake leaned over to pat Lafitte's head. "Jump," he said, then rolled Sarah on top of him.

"Is it morning?"

"Nope." He slid a hand up to cup her breast as he kissed her.

"But the sun's up— Oh…" It dimmed as his hands moved over her.

Day. Night. Summer. Winter. What did time matter? He was here, with her, taking her back to all those wonderful places he had shown her. She went willingly at dawn, as she had on the blanket of hay and then again and again on the narrow cot as the moon had set.

He taught her everything a woman could know about the pleasures of love, about needs stirred and needs met.

He showed her what it was like to love like lightning and thunder. And he showed her what it was to love like soft rain. She learned that desire could be a pain, burning hot through the blood. She learned it could be a joy, rushing sweet under the skin.

But, though she was still unaware of it, she taught him much more, taught him that there could be beauty, and comfort, and hope.

They came together with the sun rising higher and the heat of the day chasing behind it.

Later, when she was alone in the cabin, Sarah cooled and bathed her skin. This was how it could be, she thought dreamily. Early every morning she would heat the coffee while he fed the stock and fetched fresh water from the stream. She would cook for him and tend the house. Together they would make something out of the land, out of their lives. Something good and fine.

They would start a family. She pressed a hand lightly against her stomach and wondered if one had already begun. What a beautiful way to make a child, she thought, running her fingers over her damp skin. What a perfect way.

She caught herself blushing and patted her skin dry. It wasn't right to think that way, not when they weren't married. Not when he hadn't even asked her. Would he? Sarah slipped on her shirtwaist and buttoned it quickly. Hadn't she herself said he wasn't the kind of man who thought of marriage?

And yet… Could he love her the way he had loved her and not want to spend his life with her?

What had Mrs. O'Rourke said? Sarah thought back as she finished dressing. It had been something about a smart woman bringing a man around to marriage and making him think it had been his idea all along. With a light laugh, she turned toward the stove. She considered herself a very smart woman.

"Something funny?"

She glanced around as Jake walked in. "No, not really. I guess I'm just happy."

He set a basket of eggs on the table. "I haven't gathered eggs since my mother—for a long time."

As casually as she could, she took the eggs and started preparations for breakfast. "Did your mother have chickens when you were a boy?"

"Yeah. Is that coffee hot?"

"Sit down. I'll pour you some."

He didn't want to talk about his past, she decided. Perhaps the time wasn't right. Yet.

"I was able to get a slab of bacon from Mr. Cobb." She sliced it competently while the pan heated. "I've thought about getting a few pigs. Lucius is going to grumble when I ask him to build a sty, but I don't think he'd complain about eating ham. I don't suppose you know anything about raising pigs?"

Would you listen to her? Jake thought as he tilted back in her chair. The duchess from Philadelphia talking about raising pigs. "You deserve better," he heard himself say.

The bacon sizzled as she poured the coffee. "Better than what?"

"Than this place. Why don't you go back east, Sarah, and live like you were meant to?"

She brought the cup to him. "Is that what you want, Jake? You want me to go?"

"It's not a matter of what I want."

She stood beside him, looking down. "I'd like to hear what you want."

Their eyes held. He'd had some time to think, and think

clearly. But nothing seemed clear enough when he looked at her. "Coffee," he said, taking the cup.

"Your wants are admirably simple. Take your hat off at my table." She snatched it off his head and set it aside.

He just grinned, running a hand through his hair. "Yes, ma'am. Good coffee, Duchess."

"It's nice to know I do something that pleases you." She let out a yelp when he grabbed her from behind and spun her around.

"You do a lot that pleases me." He kissed her, hard and long. "A whole lot."

"Really?" She tried to keep her tone aloof, but her arms had already wound around his neck. "A pity I can't say the same."

"I guess that was some other woman who had her hands all over me last night." Her laugh was muffled against his lips. "I brought your things over from the shed. Dress is a little worse for wear. Four petticoats." He nipped her earlobe. "I hope you don't pile that many on every day around here."

"I don't intend to discuss—"

"And that contraption you lace yourself into. Lucky you don't pass out. Can't figure you need it. Your waist's no bigger around than my two hands. I ought to know." He proved it by spanning her. "Why do you want to strap yourself into that thing?"

"I have no intention of discussing my undergarments with you."

"I took them off you. Seems I should be able to talk about them."

Blushing to the roots of her hair, she struggled away. "The bacon's burning."

He took his seat again and picked up his coffee. "How many of those petticoats do you have on now?"

After rescuing the bacon, she sent him a quick, flirtatious look over her shoulder. "You'll just have to find out for yourself." Pleased at the way his brows shot up, she went back to her cooking.

He was no longer certain how to handle her. With breakfast on the table, the scents wafting cozily in the air, and Sarah sitting across from him, Jake searched his mind for something to say.

"I saw your pictures on the wall. You draw real nice."

"Thank you. I've always enjoyed it. If I'd known that my father was living here—that is, if I'd known how a few sketches would brighten the house up—I would have sent him some. I did send a small watercolor." She frowned a little. "It was a self-portrait from last Christmas. I thought he might like to know what I looked like since I'd grown up. It's strange. He had all the letters I'd written to him in that little tin box in the loft, but the sketch is nowhere to be found. I've been meaning to ask the sheriff if he might have forgotten to give it to me."

"If Barker had it, he'd have seen you got it back." He didn't care for the direction his thoughts were taking. "You sure it got this far? Mail gets lost."

"Oh, yes. He wrote me after he received it. Liza also mentioned that my father had been rather taken with it and had brought it into the store to show around."

"Might turn up."

"I suppose." She shrugged. "I've given this place a thorough cleaning, but I might not have come across it. I'll look again when Lucius puts in the floor."

"What floor?"

"The wooden floor. I've ordered boards." She broke off a bite of biscuit. "Actually, I ordered extra. I have my heart set on a real bedroom. Out the west wall, I think. My sewing money's coming in very handy."

"Sarah, last night you said something about Carlotta telling you I'd given her some idea about having you sew for her." He watched her stiffen up immediately. "When did you talk to her?"

"I didn't. I have no intention of talking to that woman."

He rolled his tongue into his cheek. He doubted Sarah would be pleased to know that her tone amused him. "Where did you hear that from?"

"Alice Johnson. She works in…that place. Apparently Carlotta had her drive out here to negotiate for my services."

"Alice?" He cast his mind back, juggling faces with names. "She's the little one—dark hair, big eyes?"

Sarah drew in a quiet, indignant breath. "That's an accurate description. You seem to know the staff of the Silver Star very well."

"I don't know as I'd call them staff, but yeah, I know one from the other."

Rising, she snatched up his empty plate. "And I'm sure they know you quite well." When he just grinned, she had to fight back the urge to knock the look off his face with the cast-iron skillet. "I'll thank you to stop smirking at me."

"Yes, ma'am." But he went right on. "You sure are pretty when you get fired up."

"If that's a compliment," she said, wishing it didn't make her want to smile, "you're wasting your breath."

"I ain't much on compliments. But you're pretty, and that's a fact. I guess you're about the prettiest thing I've ever seen. Especially when you're riled."

"Is that why you continue to go out of your way to annoy me?"

"I expect. Come here."

She smoothed down her skirt. "I will not."

He rose slowly. "You're ornery, too. Can't figure why it appeals to me." He dragged her to him. After a moment's feigned struggle, she laughed up at him.

"I'll have to remember to stay ornery and annoyed, then."

He said nothing. The way she'd looked up at him had knocked the breath out of his body. He pulled her closer, holding on, wishing. Content, Sarah nuzzled his shoulder. Before he could draw her back, she framed his face with her hands and brushed her lips over his.

"You're still tying me up in knots," he muttered.

"That's good. I don't intend to stop."

He stepped back, then gripped her hands with his. "Which one did he kiss?"

"I don't know what you mean."

"Carlson." She gave a surprised gasp when his fingers tightened on hers. "Which hand did he kiss?"

Sarah kept her eyes on his. "Both."

She watched the fury come then, and was amazed at how quickly, how completely, he masked it. But it was still there. She could feel it rippling through him. "Jake—"

He shook his head. Then, in a gesture that left her limp, he brought her hands to his lips. Then he dropped them, obviously uncomfortable, and dug his own hands into his pockets.

"I don't want you to let him do it again."

"I won't."

Her response should have relaxed him, but his tension doubled. "Just like that?"

"Yes, just like that."

He turned away and began to pace. Her brow lifted. She realized she'd never before seen him make an unnecessary movement. If he took a step, it was to go toward or away.

"I've got no right." There was fury in his voice. The same kind she heard outside the tent the night before. In contrast, hers was soft and soothing.

"You have every right. The only right. I'm in love with you."

Now he didn't move at all. He froze as a man might when he heard a trigger cocked at the back of his head. She simply waited, her hands folded at her waist, her eyes calm and clear.

"You don't know what you're saying," he managed at last.

"Of course I do, and so do you." With her eyes on his, she walked to him. "Do you think I could have been with you as I was last night, this morning, if I didn't love you?"

He stepped back before she could touch him. It had been so long since he'd been loved that he'd forgotten what it could feel like. It filled him like a river, and its currents were strong.

"I've got nothing for you, Sarah. Nothing."

"Yourself." She reached a hand to his cheek. "I'm not asking for anything."

"You're mixing up what happened last night with—"

"With what?" she challenged. "Do you think because you were the first man that I don't know the difference between love and...lust? Can you tell me it's been like that for you before, with anyone? Can you?"

No, he couldn't. And he couldn't tell her it would never be that way with anyone but her. "Lucius will be back soon," he said instead. "I'll go down and get the water you wanted before I leave."

And that was all? she thought. Damn him for turning his back on her again. He didn't believe her, she thought. He thought she was just being foolish and romantic... But no, no, that wasn't right, she realized. That wasn't it at all.

It came to her abruptly and with crystalline clarity. He did believe her, and that was why he had turned away. He was as frightened and confused by her love as she had been by the land. It was just as foreign to him. Just as difficult to understand and accept.

She could change that. Taking a long, cleansing breath, she turned to her dishes. She could change that in the same way she had changed herself. She embraced the land now, called it her own. One day he would do the same with her.

She heard the door open again, and she turned, smiling. "Jake—"

But it was Burt Donley who filled the doorway.

Chapter 11

"Where's Redman?"

Panic came first, and it showed in her wide, wild eyes. She was still holding the skillet, and she had one mad thought of heaving it at his head. But his hand was curled over the butt of his gun. She saw in his eyes what she had never seen in Jake's, what she realized she'd never seen in any man's, not even in those of the Apache who had kidnapped her. A desire, even an eagerness, to kill.

He stepped inside, and through the thickness of his beard she saw that he was smiling. "I asked you, where's Redman?"

"He's not here." It surprised her how calm a voice could sound even when a heart was pounding. She had a man to protect. The man she loved. "I don't believe I asked you in."

His smile widened into a grin. "You ain't going to tell me he brought you all the way out here last night and then left a pretty thing like you all alone?"

She was terrified Jake would come back. And terrified he wouldn't. She had no choice but to hold her ground. "I'm not telling you anything. But as you can see, I'm alone."

"I can see that, real plain. Funny, 'cause his horse is in town and he ain't." He picked up a biscuit from the bowl on the table with his wide, blunt-edged fingers, studied it, then bit in. "Word is he spends time out here."

"Mr. Redman occasionally visits. I'll be sure to tell him you were looking for him, if and when I see him."

"You do that. You be sure and do that." He took another bite, chewing slowly, watching her.

"Good day, then."

But he didn't leave. He only walked closer. "You're prettier than I recollect."

She moistened her lips, knowing they were trembling. "I don't believe we've met."

"No, but I've seen you." She strained backward when he put a hand to her hair. "You don't favor your pa none."

"You'll have to excuse me." She tried to step to the side, but he blocked her.

"He sure did set some store by you. A man can see why." He pushed the rest of the biscuit into his mouth, chewing as he reached down to toy with the small bow at her collar. "Too bad he got himself killed over that mine and left you orphaned. Smart man would've kept himself alive. Smart man would've seen the sense in that."

She shifted again, and was again blocked. "He could hardly be blamed for an accident."

"Maybe we'll talk about that later." Enjoying her trembling, he tugged the little bow loose. "You look smarter than your pa was."

Lafitte burst in, snarling. Donley had his hand on the butt of his gun when Sarah grabbed his arm. "No, please.

He's hardly more than a puppy." Moving quickly, she gathered the growling dog up. "There's no need for you to hurt him. He's harmless."

"Donley likes killing harmless things." Jake spoke from the doorway. The men stood ten feet apart, Jake backed by sun, Donley by shadow. "There was a man in Laramie—more of a boy, really. Daniel Little Deer was harmless, wasn't he, Donley?"

"He was a breed." Donley's teeth gleamed through his beard. "I don't think no more of killing a breed than a sick horse."

"And it's easier when it's back-shooting."

"I ain't shooting at your back, Redman."

"Move aside, Sarah."

"Jake, please—"

"Move aside." He was over the sick fear he'd felt when he'd seen Donley's horse outside the house. He was cold, killing-cold. His guns hung low on his hips, and his hands were limber and ready.

Donley shifted, settling his weight evenly. "I've waited a long time for this."

"Some of us get lucky," Jake murmured, "and wait a long time to die."

"When I've killed you, I'm going to have the woman, and the gold." His hand slapped the butt of his gun. The .44 was aimed heart-high. He was fast.

The sound of a gunshot exploded, ripping through the still morning air. Sarah watched in horror as Donley stumbled, forward, then back. A red stain spread across his shirt and his leather vest before he fell by the stone hearth and lay still.

Jake stood in the doorway, his face expressionless, his mind calm and cold. He'd never once felt the rush some men spoke of that came from killing. To him it was neither power nor curse. It was survival.

"Oh, God." Pressed back against the wall, Sarah stared. Lafitte leaped out of her limp arms to crouch, growling, by Donley's gun hand. Her vision grayed, wavered, then snapped back when Jake gripped her arms.

"Did he hurt you?"

"No, I—"

"Get outside."

Hysteria bubbled up in her throat. A man was dead, lying dead on her floor, and the one holding her looked like a stranger. "Jake—"

"Get outside," he repeated, doing his best to shield her from the man he'd killed. "Go on into the shed or down to the stream." When she only continued to stare, he pulled her to the door and shoved her out. "Do what I tell you."

"What—what are you going to do?"

"I'm going to take him into town."

Giving in to weakness, she leaned on the rail, dragging in gulps of the hot, dusty air as though it were water. "What will they do to you? You killed him."

"Barker'll take me at my word. Or he'll hang me."

"No, but—" Nausea was churning now, coating her skin with a thin, clammy sweat. "He wanted to kill you. He came looking for you."

"That's right." He took both her arms again because he wanted her to look at him, really look. "And tomorrow, next week, next month, there'll be someone else who comes looking for me. I got fast hands, Sarah, and somebody's always going to want to prove they got faster. One day they'll be right."

"You can change. It can change. It has to." She struggled

out of his hold, only to throw her arms around him. "You can't want to live this way."

"What I want and what is have always been two different things." He pushed her away. "I care about you." It was easy to mean it, hard to say it. "That's why I'm telling you to walk away."

He'd just killed a man in front of her eyes. And killed him coldly. Even through her horror she'd seen that. But it hadn't left him untouched. What she saw now was the frustration and anger of a man caught in a trap. He needed someone to offer him a way out, or at least the hope of one. If she could do nothing else, she could give him hope.

"No." She stepped forward to frame his face with her hands. "I can't. I won't."

Her hands were trembling. Cold and trembling, he thought as he reached for them. "You're a damn fool."

"Yes. I'm quite sure you're right. But I love you."

He couldn't have begun to tell her what it did to him inside when she said that. When he looked into her eyes and saw that she meant it. He pulled her against him for a rough, hungry kiss. "Go away from the house. I don't want you here when I bring him out."

She nodded, took a long breath and stepped back. The sickness had passed, though the raw feeling inside remained. "Once I was sure there was only right and wrong, and that to kill another person was the greatest wrong. But there isn't only right and wrong, Jake. What you did, what you had to do, kept you alive. There's nothing more important to me than that." She paused and touched his hand. "Come back."

He watched her, as he had watched her once before, start up the rise to her father's grave. When she was gone, he went back inside.

* * *

Two days passed, and Sarah tried to follow her daily routine and not to wonder why Jake hadn't ridden back to her. It seemed everyone else had paid her a visit, but not Jake. Barker had come out and, in his usual take-your-time way, questioned her about Burt Donley. It seemed no more than a token investigation to Sarah. Barker, either because he was lazy or because he was a shrewd judge of character, had taken Jake at his word.

The story had spread quickly. Soon after Barker, Liza and Johnny had driven up to hear the details and eat oatmeal cookies. Before she had left, Liza had chased Johnny outside to pester Lucius so that she could spend an hour talking about Will and her upcoming wedding. She was to have a new dress, and she had already ordered the pink silk and the pattern from Santa Fe.

The following morning, the sound of a rider approaching had Sarah rushing out of the chicken coop, eggs banging dangerously against each other in the basket she carried. She struggled to mask her disappointment when she saw Samuel Carlson.

"Sarah." He dismounted quickly, and would have taken her hand, but she used both to grip the handle of the basket. "I've been worried about you."

"There's no need." She smiled as he tied his horse at the rail.

"I was shocked to learn that Donley and Redman had drawn guns right here in your house. It's a miracle you weren't injured."

"I'm sure I would have been if Jake hadn't come back when he did. Donley was...very threatening."

"I feel responsible."

"You?" She stopped in front of the house. "Why?"

"Donley worked for me. I knew what kind of man he was." There was a grimness around his eyes and mouth as he spoke. "I can't say I had any trouble with him until Redman came back to town."

"It was Donley who sought Jake out, Samuel." Her voice sharpened with the need to defend him. "It was he who deliberately provoked a fight. I was there."

"Of course." He laid a soothing hand on her arm. Manners prevented him from stepping inside the house without an invitation. He was shrewd enough to see that something had changed, and that he wouldn't get one. "I detest the fact that you were forced to witness a killing, and in your own home. It must distress you to stay here now."

"No." She glanced over her shoulder. It had been difficult, the first time she had gone inside afterward. There were still traces of dried blood in the dirt, the sight of which had given Johnny ghoulish pleasure. But it was her home. "I'm not as frail as that."

"You're a strong woman, Sarah, but a sensitive one. I'm concerned about you."

"It's kind of you to be. Your friendship is a great comfort to me."

"Sarah." He touched a gentle hand to her cheek. "You must realize that I want to be much more than your friend."

"I know." Regret was in her eyes, in her voice. "It's not possible, Samuel. I'm sorry."

She saw the anger mar his face, and was surprised by the depth of it before he brought it under control again. "It's Redman, isn't it?"

She felt it would be dishonorable, and insulting, to lie to him. "Yes."

"I thought you were more sensible, Sarah. You're an intelligent, gently bred woman. You must understand that Redman is a dangerous man, a man without scruples. He lives by violence. It's part of him."

She smiled a little. "He describes himself the same way. I believe you're both wrong."

"He'll only hurt you."

"Perhaps, but I can't change my feelings. Nor do I wish to." Regret had her reaching out to touch his arm. "I'm sorry, Samuel."

"I have faith that in time you'll get over this infatuation. I can be patient."

"Samuel, I don't—"

"Don't distress yourself." He patted her hand. "Along with patience, I have confidence. You were meant to belong to me, Sarah." He stepped back to untie his horse. Inside, he was boiling with rage. He wanted this woman, and what belonged to her—and he intended to have them, one way or the other.

When he turned to stand beside his mount with his reins in his hands, his face was touched only with affection and concern. "This doesn't change the fact that I worry about you, living out here all alone."

"I'm not alone. I have Lucius."

Carlson cast a slow, meaningful look around the yard.

"He's up in the mine," Sarah explained. "If there was trouble, he'd come down quickly enough."

"The mine." Carlson cast his eyes up at the rock. "At least promise me that you won't go inside. It's a dangerous place."

"Gold doesn't lure me." She smiled again, relieved that they would remain friends.

He swung gracefully into the saddle. "Gold lures everyone."

She watched him ride off. Perhaps he was right, she mused. Gold had a lure. Even though in her heart she didn't believe she'd ever see the mine pay, it was exciting knowing there was always a chance. It kept Lucius in the dark and the dust for hours on end. Her father had died for it.

Even Jake, she thought, wasn't immune. It was he who had asked Lucius to pick up where her father had left off. She had yet to discover why. With death on his mind, Donley's last words had been… A glimmer of suspicion broke into her mind.

I'm going to have the woman, and the gold.

Why should a man like Donley speak of gold before he drew his gun? Why would a worthless mine be on his mind at such a time? Or was it worthless?

Her promise to Samuel forgotten, she started toward the rise.

A movement caught her eye and, turning around again, she scanned the road. Someone was coming, on foot. Even as she watched, the figure stumbled and fell. Sarah had her skirts in her hand and was running before the figure struggled to stand again.

"Alice!" Sarah quickened her pace. The girl was obviously hurt, but until Sarah reached her, catching her before she fell again, she couldn't see how badly.

"Oh, dear Lord." Gripping the sobbing girl around the waist, she helped her toward the house. "What happened? Who did this to you?"

"Miss Conway…" Alice could hardly speak through her bruised and bloodied lips. Her left eye was blackened and swollen nearly shut. There were ugly scratches, like the rake of fingernails, down her cheek, and every breath she took came out with a hitch of pain.

"All right, don't worry, just lean on me. We're nearly there."

"Didn't know where else to go," Alice managed. "Shouldn't be here."

"Don't try to talk yet. Let me get you inside. Oh, Lucius." Half stumbling herself, Sarah looked up with relief as he came hurrying down the rocks. "Help me get her inside, up to bed. She's badly hurt."

"What in the holy hell—?" Wheezing a bit from the exertion, he picked Alice up in his scrawny arms. "You know who this girl is, Miss Sarah?"

"Yes. Take her up to my bed, Lucius. I'll get some water."

Alice swooned as he struggled to carry her up the ladder to the loft. "She's done passed out."

"That may be a blessing for the moment." Moving quickly, Sarah gathered fresh water and clean cloths. "She must be in dreadful pain. I can't see how she managed to get all the way out here on foot."

"She's taken a mighty beating."

He stepped out of the way as best he could when Sarah climbed the stairs to sit on the edge of the bed. Gently she began to bathe Alice's face. When she loosened the girl's bodice, he cleared his throat and turned his back.

"Oh, my God." With trembling hands, Sarah unfastened the rest of the buttons. "Help me get this dress off of her, Lucius. It looks as though she's been whipped."

His sense of propriety was overcome by the sight of the welts on Alice's back and shoulders. "Yeah, she's been whipped." The cotton of her dress stuck to the raw, open sores. "Whipped worse'n a dog. I'd like to get my hands on the bastard who done this."

Sarah found her own hands were clenched with fury. "There's some salve on the shelf over the stove, Lucius. Fetch it for me." She did her best to bathe and cool the wounds. As Alice's eyes fluttered open and she moaned,

Sarah soothed her in a low, calming voice. "Try not to move, Alice. We're going to take care of you. You're safe now. I promise you you're safe."

"Hurts."

"I know. Oh, I know." There were tears stinging her eyes as she took the salve from Lucius and began to stroke it over the puffy welts.

It was a slow, painful process. Though Sarah's fingers were light and gentle, Alice whimpered each time she touched her. Her back was striped to the waist with angry red lines, some of which had broken open and were bleeding. With sweat trickling down her face, Sarah tended and bandaged, talking, always talking.

"Would you like another sip of water?"

"Please." With Sarah's hand cradling her head, Alice drank from the cup. "I'm sorry, Miss Conway." She lay back weakly as Sarah held a cool cloth to her swollen eye. "I know I shouldn't have come here. It ain't right, but I wasn't thinking straight."

"You did quite right by coming."

"You was—were—so nice to me before. And I was afraid if I didn't get away…"

"You aren't to worry." Sarah applied salve to her facial scratches. "In a few days you'll be feeling much better. Then we can think about what's to be done. For now, you'll stay right here."

"I can't—"

"You can and you will." Setting the salve aside, Sarah took her hand. "Do you feel strong enough to tell us what happened? Did a man—one of your customers—do this to you?"

"No, ma'am." Alice moistened her swollen lips. "It was Carlotta."

"Carlotta?" Sarah's eyes narrowed to slits. "Are you saying that Carlotta beat you like this?"

"I ain't never seen her so mad. Sometimes she gets mean if something don't go her way, or if she's been drinking too much you get a slap or two. She went crazy. I think she might've killed me if the other girls hadn't broke in the door and started screaming."

"Why? Why would she hurt you like this?"

"I can't say for sure. I done something wrong." Her voice slurred, and her eyes dropped shut. "She was mad, powerful mad, after Jake came by. They had words. Nancy, she's one of the other girls, listened outside of Carlotta's office. He said something to set her off, I expect. Nancy said she was yelling. Said something about you, Miss Conway, I don't rightly know what. When he left she went crazy. Started smashing things. I went on up to my room. She came after me, beat me worse'n Pa ever did. Eli, he brought me out."

"Eli's the big black Carlotta has working for her," Lucius explained.

"He drove me out as far as he could. She finds out, she'll make him sorry. Took a belt to me," she murmured as sleep took her under. "Kept hitting me and hitting me, saying it was my fault Jake don't come around no more."

"Bitch," Lucius said viciously. Then he wiped his mouth. "'Scuse me, Miss Sarah."

"No excuse necessary. I couldn't agree more." There was a rage running through her, hotter and huger than anything she'd ever experienced. She stared at the girl asleep in her bed, her small, pretty face bruised and swollen. She remembered each welt she'd tended. "Hitch up the wagon, Lucius."

"Yes'm. You want me to go somewheres?"

"No, I'm going. I want you to stay with Alice."

"I'll hitch it up, Miss Sarah, but if you're thinking about

talking to the sheriff, it won't do much good. Alice here ain't going to talk to him like she done with you. She'd be too scared."

"I'm not going to the sheriff, Lucius. Just hitch up the wagon."

She pushed the horses hard, pleased that the fury didn't subside as she approached town. She wanted the fury. Since she'd come west she'd learned to accept many things—the grief, the violence, the labor. Perhaps the land was lawless, but there were times and reasons, even here, for justice.

Johnny raced out of the dry goods as Sarah rode by, then raced back in again to complain to Liza that Sarah hadn't waved at him. She hadn't even seen him. There was only one face in her mind now. She drew up in front of the Silver Star.

Three women lounged in what might have been called a parlor. The late-morning heat had them half dozing in their petticoats and their feathered wraps. The room itself was dim and almost airless. Vivid red drapes hung limp at the windows. Gold leaf glowed dull and dusty on the frames of the mirrors.

As Sarah entered, a heavy-eyed redhead popped up from her sprawled position on a settee. She plopped back again with a howling laugh. "Well, look here, girls, we got ourselves some company. Get out the teacups."

The others looked over. One of them hitched her wrap up around her shoulders. Her hands folded, Sarah stood in the doorway and took it all in.

So this was a bordello. She couldn't say she saw anything remotely exciting. It looked more like a badly furnished parlor in need of a good dusting. There was a heavy floral scent of mixed perfumes that merged, none too appealingly, with plain sweat. Carefully, finger by finger, Sarah drew off her driving gloves.

"I'd like to speak with Carlotta, please. Will someone tell her I'm here?"

No one moved. The women merely exchanged looks. The redhead went back to examining her nails. After a long breath, Sarah tried another tactic.

"I'm here to speak with her about Alice." That caught their attention. Every one of the women looked over at her. "She'll be staying with me until she's well."

Now the redhead rose. Her flowered wrap slid down her shoulders with the movement. "You took Alice in?"

"Yes. She needs care, Miss—"

"I'm Nancy." She took a quick look behind her. "How come somebody like you's going to see to Alice?"

"Because she needs it. I'd be grateful to you if you would tell Carlotta I'd like to speak with her."

"I reckon I could do that." The redhead pulled her wrap up. "You tell Alice we was asking about her."

"I'll be glad to."

While Nancy disappeared up the stairs, Sarah tried to ignore the other women's stares. She had changed to one of her best day dresses. Sarah thought the dove gray very distinguished, particularly with its black trim. Her matching hat had been purchased just before her trip west and was the latest Paris fashion. Apparently it wasn't proper attire for a bordello, she thought as she watched Carlotta descend the stairs.

The owner of the Silver Star was resplendent in her trademark red. The silk slithered down her tall, curvaceous body, clinging, shifting, swaying. Her high white breasts rose like offerings from the scalloped bodice, which was threaded with silver threads. In her hand she carried a matching fan.

As she flicked it in front of her face, the heavy scent of roses filled the room.

Despite her feelings, Sarah couldn't deny that the woman was stunning. In another place, another time, she could have been a queen.

"My, my, this is a rare honor, Miss Conway."

She'd been drinking. Sarah caught the scent of whiskey under the perfume. "This is hardly a social call."

"Now you disappoint me." Her painted mouth curved. "I can always use a new girl around here. Isn't that right... ladies?"

The other women shifted uncomfortably and remained tactfully silent.

"I thought maybe you'd come in looking for work." Still waving the fan, she strolled around Sarah, sizing her up. "Little scrawny," she said. "But some men like that. Could use some fixing up, right, girls? Little more here." She patted Sarah's unrouged cheek. "Little less there." She flicked a hand at the neckline of Sarah dress. "You might make a tolerable living."

"I don't believe I'd care to...work for you, Carlotta."

"That so?" Her eyes, already hardened by the whiskey, iced over. "Too much of a lady to take pay for it, but not too much of a lady to give it away."

Sarah curled her fingers into a fist, then forced them to relax again. She would not resort to violence, or be driven to it. "No. I wouldn't care to work for anyone who beats their employees. Alice is with me now, Carlotta, and she'll stay with me. If you ever put your hands on her again, I'll see to it that you're thrown in jail."

"Oh, will you?" An angry flush darkened cheeks already bright with rouge. "I'll put my hands on who I please." She stabbed the fan into Sarah's chest. "No prim-faced bitch from back east is going to come into my place and tell me different."

With surprising ease, Sarah reached out and snapped the fan in two. "I just have." She had only an instant to brace herself for the slap. It knocked her backward. To balance herself she grabbed a table and sent a statuette crashing to the floor.

"Your kind makes me sick." Carlotta's voice was high and brittle as she leaned toward Sarah. Whiskey and anger had taken hold of her and twisted her striking face. "Looking as though they wouldn't let a man touch them. But you'll spread your legs as easy as any. You think because you went to school and lived in a big house that makes you special? You're nothing out here, nothing." She scooped up a fat plaster cherub and sent it crashing into the wall.

"The fact that I went to school and lived in a house isn't all that separates us." Sarah's voice was a sharp contrast to Carlotta's in its calmness. "You don't make me sick, Carlotta. You only make me sorry."

"I don't need pity from you. I made this place. I got something, and nobody handed it to me. Nobody ever gave me money for fine dresses and fancy hats. I earned it." Breasts heaving, she stepped closer. "You think you got Jake dangling on a string, honey, you're wrong. Soon as he's had his fill of you, he'll be back. What he's doing to you on these hot, sweaty nights, he'll be doing to me."

"No." Amazingly, Sarah's voice was still calm. "Even if he comes back and puts your price in your hands, you'll never have what I have with him. You know it," Sarah said quietly. "And that's why you hate me." With her eyes on Carlotta, she began to pull on her gloves again. Her hands would tremble any moment. She knew it, and she wanted to be on her way first. "But the issue here is Alice, not Jake. She is no longer in your employ."

"I'll tell that slut when she's through here."

It happened so quickly, Sarah was hardly aware of it. She had managed to hold her temper during Carlotta's insulting tirade against her own person. But to hear Alice called by that vile name while the girl was lying helpless and hurt was too much. Her ungloved hand shot out and connected hard with the side of Carlotta's face.

The three women, and the one who had come creeping down the stairs to look in on the commotion, let out gasps of surprise in unison. Sarah barely had time to feel the satisfaction of her action when Carlotta had her by the hair. They tumbled to the floor in a flurry of skirts.

Sarah shrieked as Carlotta tried to pull her hair out by the roots. She had handfuls of it, tugging and ripping while she cursed wildly. Fighting the pain, Sarah swung out and connected with soft flesh. She heard Carlotta grunt, and they rolled across the rug. Crockery smashed as they collided with a table, each trying to land a blow or defend against one. Sarah took a fist in the stomach with a gasp, but managed to evade a lethal swipe of Carlotta's red-tipped nails.

There was hate in Carlotta's eyes, a wild, almost mad hate. Sarah grabbed her wrist and twisted, knowing that if the other woman got her hands on her throat she'd squeeze until all her breath was gone.

She had no intention of being strangled, or pummeled. Her own rage had her rolling on top of her opponent and grabbing a handful of dyed hair. When she felt teeth sink into her arm, she cried out and yanked with all her strength, jerking Carlotta's head back and bringing out a howl of rage and pain. Other screams rose up, but Sarah was lost in the battle. She yanked and clawed and tore as viciously as Carlotta. They were equals now, with no barriers of class or background. A lamp shattered in a shower of glass as the two writhing bodies careened into another table.

"What in the hell is going on here?" Barker burst into the parlor. He took one look at the scene on the floor and shut his eyes. He'd rather have faced five armed, drunken cowboys than a pair of scratching women. "Break it up," he ordered as the two of them tumbled across the floor. "Somebody's going to get hurt here." He shook his head and sighed. "Most likely me."

He stepped into the melee just as Jake strode through the parlor doors.

"Let's pull them apart," Barker said heavily. "Take your pick." But Jake was already hauling Sarah up off the floor. She kicked out, her breath hissing as she tried to struggle away.

"Pull in your claws, Duchess." He clamped an arm around her waist as Barker restrained Carlotta.

"Get her out of here." Carlotta shoved away from Barker and stood, her dress ripped at both shoulders, her hair in wild tufts. "I want that bitch out of here and in jail. She came in here and started breaking up my place."

"Now, that don't seem quite logical," Barker mused. "Miss Sarah, you want to tell me what you're doing in a place like this?"

"Business." She tossed her hair out of her eyes. "Personal business."

"Well, looks to me like you've finished with your business here. Why don't you go on along home now?"

Sarah drew on her dignity like a cape over her torn dress. "Thank you, Sheriff." She cast one last look at Carlotta. "I am quite finished here." She glided toward the door to the secret admiration of Carlotta's girls.

"Just one damn minute." Jake took her arm the second she stepped outside. She had time now for embarrassment when she noted the size of the crowd she'd drawn.

"If you'll excuse me," she said stiffly, "I must get home." She reached up to tidy her tousled hair. "My hat."

"I think I saw what was left of it back in there." Jake ran his tongue over his teeth as he looked at her. She had a bruise beginning under her eye. It would make up to be a pretty good shiner by the end of the day. Her fashionable gray dress was ripped down one arm, and her hair looked as though she'd been through a windstorm. Thoughtfully, he tucked his hands in his pockets. Carlotta had looked a hell of a lot worse.

"Duchess, a man wouldn't know it to look at you, but you're a real firebrand."

Grimly she brushed at her rumpled skirts. "I can see that amuses you."

"I have to say it does." He smiled, and her teeth snapped together. "I guess I'm flattered, but you didn't have to get yourself in a catfight over me."

Her mouth dropped open. The man looked positively delighted. She was scratched and bruised and aching and humiliated, and he looked as though his grin might just split his face. Over him? she thought, and made herself return the smile.

"So you think I fought with Carlotta over you, because I was jealous?"

"Can't think of another reason."

"Oh, I'll give you a reason." She brought her fist up and caught him neatly on the jaw. He was holding a hand to his face and staring after her when Barker strolled out.

"She's got what you might call a mean right hook." In the street, people howled and snickered as Sarah climbed into the wagon and drove off. "Son," Barker said with a hand on Jake's shoulder, "you're the fastest hand I ever saw with those Colts of yours. You play a fine game of poker, and you hold your whiskey like a man. But you got a hell of a lot to learn about women."

"Apparently," Jake murmured. He walked across to O'Riley's and untied his horse.

Sarah seethed as she raced the wagon toward home. She'd made a spectacle of herself. She'd engaged in a crude, despicable sparring match with a woman with no morals. She'd brought half the town out into the street to stare and snicker at her. And then, to top it all off, she'd had to endure Jake Redman's grinning face.

She'd shown him. Sarah tossed her head up and spurred the horses on. Her hand might possibly be broken, but she'd shown him. The colossal conceit of the man, to believe that she would stoop to such a level out of petty jealousy.

She wished she'd torn Carlotta's brass-colored hair out by its black roots.

Not over him, she reminded herself. At least not very much over him.

She heard the rider coming up fast and looked over her shoulder. With a quick gasp of alarm, she cracked the reins. She would not speak to him now. Jake Redman could go to the devil, as far as she was concerned. And he could take his grin with him.

But her sturdy workhorses were no match for his mustang. Nor was her driving skill a match for his riding. Even as she cursed him, he came up beside her. She had a flash, clear as a bell, of how he'd looked when he'd raced beside the stagecoach, firing over his shoulder. He looked just as untamed and dangerous now.

"Stop that damn thing."

Chin up, she cracked the reins again.

One of these days somebody was going to teach her to listen, Jake thought. It might just be today. He judged the timing and rhythm, then leaped from his horse into the wagon.
Surefooted, he stepped over onto the seat, and though she
fought him furiously he pulled the horses in.

"What the hell's got into you, woman?" He scrambled
for a hold as she shoved him aside and tried to jump out.

"Take your hands off me. I won't be handled this way."

"Handling you is a sight more work than I care for." He
snatched his hand out of range before she could bite him.
"Haven't you had enough scratching for one day? Sit down
before you hurt yourself."

"You want the blasted wagon, take it. I won't ride with
you."

"You'll ride with me, all right." Out of patience, he
twisted her into his lap and silenced her. She squirmed and
pushed and held herself as rigid as iron. Then she melted.
He felt the give, slow, easy, inevitable. In her. In himself. As
her lips parted for his, he forgot about keeping her quiet and
just took what he kept trying to tell himself he couldn't have.

"You pack a punch, Duchess." He drew her away to rub
a hand over his chin. "In a lot of ways. You want to tell me
what that was for?"

She pulled away, furious that she'd gone soft with just
one kiss. "For assuming that I was jealous and would fight
over any worthless man."

"So now I'm worthless. Well, that may be, but you seem
to like having me around."

She did her best to straighten what was left of her dress.
"Perhaps I do."

He needed to know it more than he'd imagined. Jake

took her chin in his hand and turned her to face him. "You change your mind?"

Again she softened, this time because she saw the doubt in his eyes. "No, I haven't changed my mind." She drew a long breath. "Even though you didn't come back and you've been to the Silver Star to see Carlotta."

"You sure do hear things. Can't imagine what you'd know if you lived closer to town. Stay in the wagon." He recognized the look in her eye by now. "Stay in the wagon, Sarah, until I get my horse tied on. I'll just catch you again if you run."

"I won't run." She brought her chin up again and stared straight ahead. When he'd joined her again, she continued her silence. Jake clucked to the horses and started off.

"I like to know why a woman's mad at me. Why don't you tell me how you know I've been to Carlotta's?"

"Alice told me."

"Alice Johnson?"

"That's right. Your friend Carlotta nearly beat her to death."

He brought the horses up short. "What?"

Her fury bounded back and poured over him. "You heard what I said. She beat that poor girl as cruelly as anyone can be beaten. Eli helped Alice get out of town. Then she walked the rest of the way to my place."

"Is she going to be all right?"

"With time and care."

"And you're going to give it to her?"

"Yes." Her eyes dared him. "Do you have any objections?"

"No." He touched her face, gently, in a way that was new to him. Abruptly he snatched his hand back and snapped the reins again. "You went into the Silver Star to have it out with Carlotta over Alice."

"I've never been so furious." Sarah lifted a hand to where Jake had touched her. "Alice is hardly more than a child. No matter what she did, she didn't deserve that kind of treatment."

"Did she tell you why Carlotta did it?"

"She didn't seem to know, only that she must have made some kind of mistake. Alice did say that Carlotta was in a temper after you had been there."

He said nothing for a moment as he put the pieces together. "And she took it out on Alice."

"Why did you go? Why did you go to Carlotta? If there's something you..." She hadn't any idea how to phrase it properly. "If I don't know enough about your needs... I realize I don't have any experience in these matters, but I—"

She found her mouth crushed again in a kiss that was half hungry, half angry. "There's never been anyone else who's known so much about what I need." He watched her face clear into a smile. "I went to see Carlotta to tell her I don't care much for having my name used as a reference."

"So she took it out on Alice, because Alice was the one who'd come to talk to me." Sarah shook her head and tried not to let her temper take over again. "Alice only told me what Carlotta wanted her to tell me. It didn't work the way she'd planned, and Alice paid for it."

"That's about the size of it."

Sarah linked her fingers again and set them in her lap. "Is that the only reason you went to Carlotta?"

"No." He waited for the look. The look of passionate fury. "I went for that, and to tell her to stay away from you. Of course, I didn't know at the time that you were going to go and bloody her lip."

"Did I?" She tried and failed to bank down the pleasure she felt at the news. "Did I really?"

"And her nose. Guess you were a little too involved to notice."

"I've never struck anyone before in my life." She tried to keep her voice prim, then gave up. "I liked it."

With a laugh, Jake pulled her to his side. "You're a real wildcat, Duchess."

Chapter 12

Jake learned something new when he watched Sarah with Alice. He had always assumed that a woman who had been raised in the sheltered, privileged world would ignore, even condemn, one who lived as Alice lived. There were many decent women, as they called themselves, who would have turned Alice away as if she were a rabid dog.

Not Sarah.

And it was more than what he supposed she would have called Christian charity. He'd run into his share of people who liked to consider themselves good Christians. They had charity, all right, unless they came across somebody who looked different, thought different. There had been plenty of Christian women who had swept their skirts aside from his own mother because she'd married a man of mixed blood.

They went into church on Sundays and quoted the Scriptures and professed to love their neighbor. But when their neighbor didn't fit their image of what was right, love turned to hate quickly enough.

With Sarah it wasn't just words. It was compassion, caring, and an understanding he hadn't expected from her. He could hear, as he sat at the table, the simple kindness in her voice as she talked to the girl and tended her wounds.

As for Alice, it was obvious the girl adored Sarah. He'd yet to see her, as Sarah claimed her patient wasn't up to visitors. But he could hear the shyness and the respect in her voice when she answered Sarah's questions.

She'd fought for Alice. He couldn't quite get over that. Most people wouldn't fight for anything unless it was their own, or something they wanted to own. It had taken pride, and maybe what people called valor, for her to walk into a place like the Silver Star and face Carlotta down. And she'd done it. He glanced up toward the loft. She'd more than done it. She'd held her own.

Rising, he walked outside to where Lucius was doing his best to teach an uncooperative Lafitte to shake hands.

"Damn it, boy, did I say jump all over me? No, you flea-brained mongrel, I said shake." Lucius pushed the dog's rump down and grabbed a paw. "Shake. Get it?" Lafitte leaped up again and licked Lucius's face.

"Doesn't appear so," Jake commented.

"Fool dog." But Lucius rubbed the pup's belly when he rolled over. "Grows on you, though." He squinted up at Jake. "Something around here seems to be growing on you, too."

"Somebody had to bring her back."

"Reckon so." He waited until Jake crouched to scratch the puppy's head. "You want to tell me how Miss Sarah came to look like she'd been in a fistfight?"

"She looked like she was in a fistfight because she was in a fistfight."

Lucius snorted and spit. "Like hell."

"With Carlotta."

Lucius's cloudy eyes widened, and then he let out a bark of laughter that had Lafitte racing in circles. "Ain't that a hoot? Are you telling me that our Miss Sarah went in and gave Carlotta what for?"

"She gave her a bloody nose." Jake looked over with a grin. "And pulled out more than a little of her hair."

"Sweet Jesus, I'd've given two pints of whiskey to've seen that. Did you?"

Chuckling, Jake pulled on Lafitte's ears. "The tail end of it. When I walked in, the two of them were rolling over the floor, spitting like cats. I figure Carlotta outweighs Sarah by ten pounds or more, but Sarah was sitting on her, skirts hiked up and blood in her eye. It was one hell of a sight."

"She's got spunk." Lucius pulled out his whiskey and toasted Sarah with a healthy gulp. "I knew she had something in her head when she tore out of here." Feeling generous, he handed the bottle to Jake. "Never would have thought she'd set her mind on poking a fist into Carlotta. But nobody ever deserved it more. You seen Alice?"

"No." Jake let the whiskey spread fire through him. "Sarah's got the idea that it's not fitting for me to talk to the girl until she's covered up or something."

"I carried her in myself, and I don't mind saying I ain't seen no woman's face ever smashed up so bad. Took a belt to her, too, from the looks of it. Her back and shoulders all come up in welts. Jake, you wouldn't whup a dog the way that girl was whupped. That Carlotta must be crazy."

"Mean and crazy's two different things." He handed Lucius the bottle. "Carlotta's just mean."

"Reckon you'd know her pretty well."

Jake watched Lucius take another long sip. "I paid for her a few times, sometime back. Doesn't mean I know her."

"Soon plop my ass next to a rattler's." Lucius handed the bottle back to Jake again, then fell into a fit of coughing. "Miss Sarah, I didn't hear you come out."

"So I surmised," she said with a coolness that had Lucius coughing again. "Perhaps you gentlemen have finished drinking whiskey and exchanging crude comments and would like to wash for supper. If not, you're welcome to eat out here in the dirt." With that she turned on her heel, making certain she banged the door shut behind her.

"Ooo-whee." Lucius snatched back the bottle and took another drink. "She's got a mighty sharp tongue for such a sweet face. I tell you, boy, you'll have to mind your step if'n you hitch up with her."

Jake was still staring at the door, thinking how beautiful she'd looked, black eye and all, standing there like a queen addressing her subjects. "I ain't planning on hitching up with anyone."

"Maybe you are and maybe you ain't." Lucius rose and brushed off his pants. A little dirt and she'd have them off him again and in the stream. "But she's got plans, all right. And a woman like that's hard to say no to."

Sarah spoke politely at supper, as if she were entertaining at a formal party. Her hair was swept up and tidied, and she'd changed her dress. She was wearing the green one that set off her hair and eyes. The stew was served in ironstone bowls, but the way she did it, it could have been a restaurant meal on fancy china.

It made him think, as he hadn't in years, of his mother and how she had liked to fuss over Sunday supper.

She said nothing about the encounter in town, and it was clear that she didn't care to have the subject brought up. It was hard to believe she was the same woman he'd dragged off the floor in the Silver Star. But he noticed that she winced now and then. He bit into a hunk of fresh bread and held back a grin. She was hurting, all right, and more than her pride, from the look of it. As he ate he entertained thoughts of how he would ease those hurts when the sun went down.

"Would you like some more stew, Lucius?"

"No, ma'am." He patted his belly. "Full as a tick. If it's all the same to you, I'll just go take a walk before I feed the stock and such. Going to be a pretty night." He sent them both what he thought was a bland look. "I'll sleep like a log after a meal like this. Yessir. I don't believe I'll stir till morning." He scraped back his chair and reached for his hat. "Mighty fine meal, Miss Sarah."

"Thank you, Lucius."

Jake tipped back his chair. "I wouldn't mind a walk myself."

Sarah had to smile at the way Lucius began to whistle after he'd closed the door. "You go ahead."

He took her hand as she rose. "I'd like it better if you went with me."

She smiled. He'd never asked her to do something as ordinary, and as romantic, as going for a walk. Thank goodness she hadn't forgotten how to flirt. "Why, that's nice of you, but I have to see to the dishes. And Alice may be waking soon. I think she could eat a bit now."

"I imagine I could occupy myself for an hour or two. We'll take a walk when you're done."

She sent him a look from under lowered lashes. "Maybe." Then she laughed as he sent her spinning into his lap. "Why, Mr. Redman. You are quite a brute."

He ran a finger lightly over the bruise under her eye. "Then you'd best be careful. Kiss me, Sarah."

She smiled when her lips were an inch from his. "And if I don't?"

"But you will." He traced her bottom lip with his tongue. "You will."

She did, sinking into it, into him. Her arms wound around him, slender and eager. Her mouth opened like a flower in sunlight. They softened against him even as they heated. They yielded even as they demanded.

"Don't be long," he murmured. He kissed her again, passion simmering, then set her on her feet. She let out a long, shaky breath when he closed the door behind him.

With Alice settled for the night and the day's work behind her, Sarah stepped out into the quieting light of early evening. It was still too warm to bother with a shawl, but she pushed her sleeves down past her elbows and buttoned the cuffs. There were bruises on her arms that she didn't care to dwell on.

From where she stood she could hear Lucius in the shed, talking to Lafitte. He'd become more his dog than hers, Sarah thought with a laugh. Or perhaps they'd both become something of hers.

As the land had.

She closed her eyes and let the light breeze flutter over her face. She could, if she concentrated hard enough, catch the faintest whiff of sage. And she could, if she used enough imagination, picture what it would be like to sit on the porch she envisioned having, watching the sun go down every evening while Jake rolled a cigarette and listened with her to the music of the night.

Bringing herself back, she looked around. Where was he? She stepped farther out into the yard when she heard the sound of hammer against wood. She saw him, a few yards from the chicken coop, beating an old post into the ground. He'd taken his shirt off, and she could see the light sheen of sweat over his lean torso and the rippling and bunching of his muscles as he swung the heavy hammer down.

Her thoughts flew back to the way his arms had swung her into heat, into passion. The hands that gripped the thick, worn handle of the hammer now had roamed over her, touching, taking whatever they chose.

And she had touched, wantonly, even greedily, that long, limber body, taking it, accepting it as her own.

Her breath shuddered out as she watched him bend and lift and pound. Was it wrong to have such thoughts, such wonderful, exciting visions? How could it be, when she loved so completely? She wanted his heart, but oh, she wanted his body, as well, and she could find no shame in it.

His head came up quickly, as she imagined an animal's might when it caught a scent. And he had. Though she was several yards away, he had sensed her, the trace of lilac, the subtlety of woman. He straightened, and just as she had looked her fill of him, he looked his of her.

She might have stepped from a cool terrace to walk in a garden. The wind played with her skirts and her hair, but gently. The backdrop of the setting sun was like glory behind her. Her eyes, as she walked toward him, were wide and dark and aware.

"You've got a way of moving, Duchess, that makes my mouth water."

"I don't think that's what the good sisters intended when they taught me posture. But I'm glad." She moved naturally to his arms, to his lips. "Very glad."

For the first time in his life he felt awkward with a woman, and he drew her away. "I'm sweaty."

"I know." She pulled a handkerchief from her pocket and dabbed at his face. "What are you doing?"

She made him feel like a boy fumbling over his first dance. "You said you wanted pigs. You need a pen." He picked up his shirt and shrugged it on. "What are you doing?"

"Watching you." She put a hand to his chest, where the shirt lay open. "Remembering. Wondering if you want me as much as you did."

He took her hand before she could tear what was inside of him loose. "No, I don't. I want you more." He picked up his gunbelt, but instead of strapping it on he draped it over his shoulder. "Why don't we go for that walk?"

Content, she slipped her hand into his. "When I first came here I wondered what it was that had kept my father, rooted him here. At first I thought it was only for me, because he wanted so badly to provide what he thought I'd need. That grieved me. I can't tell you how much." She glanced up as they passed the rise that led to his grave. "Later I began to see that even though that was part of it, perhaps the most important part to him, he was also happy here. It eases the loss to know he was happy."

They started down the path to the stream she had come to know so well.

"I didn't figure you'd stick." Her hand felt right, easy and right, tucked in his. "When I brought you out here the first time, you looked as if someone had dropped you on your head."

"It felt as though someone had. Losing him… Well, the truth is, I'd lost him years and years ago. To me, he's exactly the same as he was the day he left. Maybe there's something good about that. I never told you he had spun me a tale." At the stream she settled down on her favorite rock and listened to the water's melody. "He told me of the fine house he'd built after he'd struck the rich vein of gold in Sarah's Pride. He painted me a picture of it with his words. Four bedrooms, a parlor with the windows facing west, a wide porch with big round columns." She smiled a little and watched the sun glow over the buttes. "Maybe he thought I needed that, and maybe I did, to see myself as mistress of a fine, big house with curving stairs and high, cool walls."

He could see it, and her. "It was what you were made for."

"It's you I was made for." Rising, she held out her hands.

"I want you, Sarah. I can't offer you much more than a blanket to spread on the ground."

She glanced over at the small pile of supplies he'd already brought down to the stream. She moved to it and lifted the blanket.

It was twilight when they lowered to it. The air had softened. The wind was only a rustle in the thin brush. Overhead the sky arched, a deep, ever-darkening blue. Under the wool of the blanket the ground was hard and unforgiving. She lifted her arms to him and they left the rest behind.

It was as it had been the first time, and yet different. The hunger was there, and the impatient pull of desire. With it was a knowledge of the wonder, the magic, they could make between them. A little slower now, a little surer, they moved together.

There was urgency in his kiss. She could feel it. But beneath it was a tenderness she had dreamed of, hoped for. Seduced by that alone, she murmured his name. Beneath her palm, his cheek was rough. Under her fingers, his skin was smooth. His body, like his mind, like his heart, was a contrast that drew her, compelled her to learn more.

A deep, drugging languor filled her as he began to undress her. There was no frantic rush, as there had been before. His fingers were slow and sure as they moved down the small covered buttons. She felt the air whisper against her skin as he parted the material. Then it was his mouth, warmer, sweeter, moving over her. Her sigh was like music.

He wanted to give her something he'd never given another woman. The kind of care she deserved. Tenderness was new to him, but it came easily now as he peeled off layer after layer to find her. He sucked in his breath as her fingers fumbled with the buttons at his waist. Her touch wasn't hesitant, but it was still innocent. It would always be. And her innocence aroused him as skill never could have.

She removed the layers he'd covered himself with. Not layers of cotton or leather, but layers of cynicism and aloofness, the armor he'd used to survive, just as he'd used his pistols. With her he was helpless, more vulnerable than he had been since childhood. With her he felt more of a man than he had ever hoped to be.

She felt the change, an explosion of feelings and needs and desires, as he dragged her up into his arms to crush his mouth against hers. What moved through him poured into her, leaving her breathless, shaken and impossibly strong. Without understanding, without needing to, she answered him with everything in her heart.

Then came the storm, wild, windy, wailing. Rocked by it, she cried out as he drove her up, up, into an airless, rushing cloud of passion. Sensations raced through her—the sound of her own desperate moans, the scrape of his face against her skin as he journeyed down her trembling body, the taste of him that lingered on her lips, on her tongue, as he did mad, unspeakably wonderful things to her. Lost, driven beyond reason, she pressed his head closer to her.

She was like something wild that had just been unchained. He could feel the shocked delight ripple through her when he touched her moist heat with his tongue. He thought her response was like a miracle, though he'd long ago stopped believing in them. There was little he could give her besides the pleasures of her own body. But at least that, he would do.

Sliding upward, he covered her mouth with his. And filled her.

Long after her hands had slipped limply from his back, long after their breathing had calmed and leveled, he lay over her, his face buried in her hair. She'd brought him peace, and though he knew it wouldn't last, for now she'd brought him peace of mind, of body, of heart.

He hadn't wanted to love, hadn't dared to risk it. Even now, when it was no longer possible to hide it from himself, he couldn't tell her.

"Lucius was right," she murmured against his ear.

"Mmm?"

"It's a pretty night." She ran her hands up his back. "A very pretty night."

"Am I hurting you?"

"No." She gripped her own wrists so that she could hold him closer. "Don't move yet."

"I'm heavy, and you've got some colorful bruises."

If she'd had the energy, she might have laughed. "I'd forgotten about them."

"I put some on you myself last night." He lifted his head to look down at her. "I don't know much about going easy."

"I'm not complaining."

"You should." Fascinated, he stroked a finger down her cheek. "You're so beautiful. Like something I made up."

She turned her lips into his palm as her eyes filled. "You've never told me you thought I was beautiful."

"Sure I did." He shifted then, frustrated by his own lack of words. "I should have."

She curled comfortably against his side. "I feel beautiful right now."

They lay in contented silence, looking up at the sky.

"What's an enigma?" he asked her.

"Hmm? Oh, it's a puzzle. Something difficult to understand. Why?"

"I guess I heard it somewhere." He thought of her diary, and her description of him, but couldn't see how it applied. He'd always seen himself as being exactly what he appeared to be. "You're getting cold."

"A little."

Sitting up, he pushed through her discarded undergarments for her chemise. She smiled, lifting her arms over her head. Her lips curved when she saw his gaze slide over her skin. When he pulled the cotton over her, she linked her hands behind his neck.

"I was hoping to stay warm a different way."

With a laugh, he slid a hand down over her hip. "I remember telling you once before you were a quick study." Experimentally he pushed the strap of her chemise off her shoulder. "You want to do something for me?"

"Yes." She nuzzled his lips. "Very much."

"Go on over and stand in that stream."

Confused, she drew back. "I beg your pardon?"

"Nobody says that better than you, Duchess. I'll swear to that." He kissed her again, in a light, friendly manner that pleased and puzzled her.

"You want to go wading?"

"Not exactly." He toyed with the strap. Women wore the damnedest things. Then they covered them all up anyhow.

"I thought you'd go stand in the stream wearing just this little thing. Like you did that first night."

"What first night?" Her puzzled smile faded as he traced his fingertip along the edge of her bodice. "That first— You! You were watching me while I—"

"I was just making sure you didn't get yourself into any trouble."

"That's disgraceful." She tried to pull away, but he held her still.

"I started thinking then and there how much I'd like to get my hands on you. Had some trouble sleeping that night." He lowered his lips to the curve of her throat and began to nibble. "Fact is, I haven't had a good night's sleep since I set eyes on you."

"Stop it." She turned her head, but it only made it easier for him to find her mouth.

"Are you going to go stand in the stream?"

"I am not." She smothered a laugh when he rolled her onto the blanket again. "I'm going to get dressed and go back to the house to check on Alice."

"No need. Lucius is keeping an eye on her."

"Oh, I see. You've already decided that for me."

"I guess you could put it like that. You're not going anywhere but this blanket. And maybe the stream, once I talk you into it."

"You won't talk me into it. I have no intention of sleeping outside."

"I don't figure on sleeping much at all." He stretched out on his back again and gathered her close. "Haven't you ever slept outside before, looked at the sky? Counted stars?"

"No." But, of course, tonight she would. She wanted nothing more. She turned her head to study his profile. "Have you ever counted stars, Jake?"

"When I was a kid." He stroked a hand lazily up and down her arm. "My mother used to say there were pictures. She'd point them out to me sometimes, but I could never find them again."

"I'll show you one." Sarah took his hand and began to draw in the air. "It's a horse. A winged horse. Pegasus," she added. Then she caught her breath. "Look, a shooting star." She watched, his hand held in hers, as it arced across the sky. She closed her eyes quickly, then made a wish. "Will you tell me about your mother?"

For a long moment he said nothing, but continued to stare up at the sky. The arc of light was gone, without a trace. "She was a teacher." Sarah's gaze flicked up quickly to his face. "She'd come out here from St. Louis."

"And met your father?"

"I don't know much about that. He wanted to learn to read and write, and she taught him. She set a lot of store by reading."

"And while she was teaching him, they fell in love."

He smiled a little. It sounded nice the way she said it. "I guess they did. She married him. It wouldn't have been easy, with him being half Apache. They wanted to build something. I remember the way my father used to talk about taking the land and making it work for him. Leaving something behind."

She understood that, because it was what she wanted for herself. "Were they happy?"

"They laughed a lot. My mother used to sing. He always talked about buying her a piano one day, so she could play again like she did in St. Louis. She'd just laugh and say she wanted lace curtains first. I'd forgotten that," he murmured. "She wanted lace curtains."

She turned her face into his shoulder because she felt his

pain as her own. "Lucius told me what happened to them. To you. I'm so sorry."

He hadn't known he needed to talk about it, needed to tell her. "They came in from town…eight, ten of them, I've never been sure." His voice was quiet now, his eyes on the sky. He could still see them, as he hadn't allowed himself to see them for years. "They lit the barn first. Maybe if my father had stayed in the house, let them shoot and shout and trample, they'd have left the rest. But they'd have come back. He knew it. He took his rifle and went out to protect what was his. They shot him right outside the door."

Sarah held him tighter, seeing it with him.

"We ran out. They tasted blood now, like wolves, wild-eyed, teeth bared. She was crying, holding on to my father and crying. Inside the barn, the horses were screaming. The sky was lit up so I could see their faces while they torched the rest."

And he could smell the smoke as he lay there, could hear the crackle of greedy flames and his mother's pitiful weeping.

"I picked up the rifle. That's the first time I ever wanted to kill. It's like a fever in the blood. Like a hand has ahold of you, squeezing. She started to scream. I saw one of the riders take aim at me. I had the rifle in my hands, but I was slow. Better with a bow or a knife back then. She threw herself up and in front of me so when he pulled the trigger the bullet went in her."

Sarah tightened her arms around him as tears ran fast and silent down her cheeks.

"One of them hit me with a rifle butt as he rode by. It was morning before I came to. They'd burned everything. The house was still smoking—even when it cooled there was nothing in it worth keeping. The ground was hard there, and

I got dizzy a few times, so it took me all day to bury them. I slept there that night, between the two graves. I told myself that if I lived until morning I'd find the men who'd done it and kill them. I was still alive in the morning."

She said nothing, could say nothing. It wasn't necessary to ask what he'd done. He'd learned to use a gun, and use it well. And he had found the men, or some of them.

"When Lucius came, I told him what happened. That was the last time I told anyone."

"Don't." She turned to lay her body across his. "Don't think about it anymore."

He could feel her tears on his chest, the warmth of them. As far as he knew, no one had ever cried for him before. Taking her hand, he kissed it. "Show me that picture in the sky, Sarah."

Turning, keeping her hand in his, she began to trace the stars. The time for tears, for regrets—and, she hoped, for revenge—was done. "The stars aren't as big in the East, or as bright." They lay quietly for a while, wrapped close, listening to the night sounds. "I used to jump every time I heard a coyote. Now I like listening for them. Every night, when I read my father's journal—"

"Matt kept a journal?" He sat up as he asked, dragging her with him.

"Why, yes." There was an intensity in his eyes that made her heart skip erratically. "What is it?"

"Have you read it?"

"Not all of it. I've been reading a few pages each night."

He suddenly realized that he was digging his fingers into her arms. He relaxed them. "Will you let me read it?"

Her heart was steady again, but something cold was inching its way over her skin. "Yes. If you tell me why you want to."

He turned away to reach casually in his saddlebag for his tobacco pouch and papers. "I just want to read it."

She waited while he rolled a cigarette. "All right. I trust you. When are you going to trust me, Jake?"

He struck a match on a rock. The flame illuminated his face. "What do you mean?"

"Why did you ask Lucius to work in the mine?"

He flicked the match out, then tossed it aside. The scent of tobacco stung the air. "Maybe I thought Matt would have liked it."

Determined, she put a hand to his face and turned it toward hers. "Why?"

"A feeling I had, that's all." Shifting away, he blew out a stream of smoke. "People usually have a reason for setting fires, Sarah. There was only one I could figure when it came to you. Somebody didn't want you there."

"That's ridiculous. I hardly knew anyone at that point. The sheriff said it was drifters." She curled her hands in her lap as she studied his face. "You don't think it was."

"No. Maybe Barker does, and maybe he doesn't. There's only one thing on this land that anyone could want. That's gold."

Impatient, Sarah sat back on her heels. "But there isn't any gold."

"Yes, there is." Jake drew deep on his cigarette and watched the range of expressions cross her face.

"What are you talking about?"

"Lucius found the mother lode, just the way Matt did." He glanced at the glowing tip of his cigarette. "You're going to be a rich woman, Duchess."

"Wait." She pressed a hand to her temple. It was beginning to throb. "Are you telling me that the mine is really worth something?"

"More than something, according to Lucius."

"I can't believe it." With a quick, confused laugh, she shook her head. "I never thought it was anything but a dream. Just this morning, I'd begun to wonder, but— How long have you known?"

"A while."

"A while?" she repeated, looking back at him. "And you didn't think it important enough to mention to me?"

"I figured it was important enough not to." He took a last drag before crushing the cigarette out. "I've never known a woman who could keep her mouth shut."

"Is that so?"

"Yes, ma'am."

"I'm perfectly capable of keeping my mouth shut, as you so eloquently put it. But why should I?"

There was no way to tell her but straight out. "Matt found the gold, and then he was dead."

"There was an accident…" she began. Suddenly cold, she hugged her elbows. He didn't have to speak for her to see what was in his mind. "You're trying to tell me that my father was murdered. That can't be." She started to scramble up, but he took her arms and held her still.

"Ten years he worked the mine and scratched a few handfuls of gold from it. Then he hits, hits big. The minute he does, there's a cave-in, and he's dead."

"I don't want to think about it."

"You're going to think about it." He gave her a quick shake. "The mine's yours now, and the gold in it. I'm not going to let what happened to Matt happen to you." His hands gentled and slid up to frame her face. "Not to you."

She closed her eyes. She couldn't take it in, not all at once. Fear, hysteria and fresh grief tangled within her. She lifted her hands to his wrists and held on until she felt herself calming. He was right. She had to think about it. Then she would act. When she opened her eyes, they were clear and steady.

"Tell me what you want me to do."

"Trust me." He touched his lips to hers, then laid her back gently on the blanket. She'd given him peace early in the night. Now, as the night deepened, he would try to do the same for her.

Chapter 13

"I'm feeling lots better, Miss Conway." Alice took the tin cup and sipped gingerly.

She didn't want to complain about her back, or about the pain that still galloped along it despite the cooling salve. The morning light showed her facial bruises in heart-wrenching detail and caused the girl to look even younger and smaller and more vulnerable. Though the scratches on her cheeks were no longer red and angry, Sarah judged it would be several days before they faded.

"You look better." It wasn't strictly true, and Sarah vowed to keep her patient away from a mirror a bit longer. Though the swelling had eased considerably, she was still worried about Alice's eye and had already decided to drive into town later and talk with the doctor.

"Try a little of this soft-boiled egg. You need your strength."

"Yes, ma'am." Privately Alice thought the glossy wet

yolk looked more like a slimy eye than food. But if Sarah had told her to eat a fried scorpion she'd have opened her mouth and swallowed. "Miss Conway?"

"Yes, Alice?" Sarah spooned up more egg.

"I'm beholden to you for taking me in like you did, and I can't— Miss Conway, you gave me your own bed last night. It ain't fitting."

Smiling a little, Sarah set the plate aside. "Alice, I assure you, I was quite comfortable last night."

"But, Miss Conway—"

"Alice, if you keep this up I'm going to think you're ungrateful."

"Oh!" Something close to horror flashed in Alice's eyes. "No, ma'am."

"Well, then." Because the response was exactly what she'd expected, Sarah rose. She remembered that the nuns had nursed with compassion tempered with brisk practicality. "You can show your gratitude by being a good patient and getting some more rest. If you're feeling up to it later, I'll have Lucius bring you down and we can sit and talk awhile."

"I'd like that. Miss Conway, if it hadn't been for you and Eli, I think I'd've died. I was hoping… Well, I got some money saved. It ain't much, but I'd like you to have it for all your trouble."

"I don't want your money, Alice."

The girl flushed and looked away. "I know you're probably thinking about where it comes from, but—"

"No." She took Alice's hand firmly in hers. "That has nothing to do with it." Pride, Sarah thought. She had plenty of her own. Alice was entitled to hers. "Alice, did Eli want money for driving you out of town?"

"No, but…he's a friend."

"I'd like to be your friend, if you'd let me. You rest now,

and we'll talk about all this later." She gave Alice's hand a reassuring squeeze before she picked up the empty dishes and started down the ladder. She barely muffled a squeal when hands closed around her waist.

"Told you you didn't need that corset."

Sarah sent Jake what she hoped was an indignant look over her shoulder. "Is that why I couldn't find it when I dressed this morning?"

"Just doing you a favor." Before she could decide whether to laugh or lecture, he was whirling her around and kissing her.

"Jake, Alice is—"

"Not likely to faint if she figures out what I'm doing." But he set her aside, because he liked the way the sunlight streamed through the curtains and onto her hair. "You're mighty nice to look at, Duchess."

It was foolish to blush, but her color rose. "Why don't you sit down, and you can look at me some more while I fix you breakfast?"

"I'd like to, but I've got some things to see to." He touched her again, just a fingertip to the single wispy curl that had escaped from the neat bun on top of her head. "Sarah, will you let me have Matt's journal?"

Both the grief and the dread showed clearly in her eyes before she lowered them. During the night, after love and before sleep, she had thought of little else but what Jake had told her. Part of her wondered if she would be better off not knowing, not being sure. But another part, the same part that had kept her from turning back and going east again, had already accepted what needed to be done.

"Yes." She walked to the hearth to work the rock loose. "I found this the first night. His journal, what must have been his savings, and the deed to Sarah's Pride."

When she held the book out to him, Jake resisted the urge to open it there and then. If he found what he thought he would find, he would have business to take care of before he said anything else to her. "I'll take it along with me, if it's all the same to you."

She opened her mouth to object, wanting the matter settled once and for all. But he'd asked for her trust. Perhaps this was the way to show him he had it. "All right."

"And the deed? Will you let me hold on to it until we have some answers?"

In answer, she offered it to him, without hesitation, without question. For a moment they held the deed, and the dream, between them. "Just like that?" he murmured.

"Yes." She smiled and released her hold. "Just like that."

That her trust was so easily given, so total in her eyes, left him groping for words. "Sarah, I want…" What? he wondered as he stared down at her. To guard and protect, to love and possess? She was like something cool and sweet that had poured into him and washed away years of bitter thirst. But he didn't have the words, he thought. And he didn't have the right.

"I'll take care of this."

She lifted a brow. There had been something else, something in his eyes. She wanted it back, so that she could see it, understand it. "I thought *we* were going to take care of it."

"No." He cupped her chin in his hand. "You're going to leave this to me. I don't want anything to happen to you."

Her brow was still lifted as her lips curved. "Why?"

"Because I don't. I want you to—" Whatever he might have said was postponed. He moved to the window quickly. "You've got company coming." As he spotted the buggy, his shoulders relaxed. "Looks like Mrs. Cody and her girl."

"Oh." Sarah's hands shot up automatically to straighten

her hair. "I must look— Oh, how would I know? I haven't had a chance to so much as glance in the mirror."

"Wouldn't matter much." Without glancing back, he pulled open the door. "Too bad you're so homely."

Muttering, she pulled off her apron and followed him outside. Then memory came flooding back and had her biting her lip. "I imagine they would have heard all about the, ah, incident yesterday."

"I expect." Jake secured the deed and the journal in the saddlebags that he'd tossed over the rail.

"You needn't look so amused." She fiddled nervously with the cameo at her throat, then put on her brightest smile. "Good morning, Mrs. Cody. Liza."

"Good morning, Sarah." Anne Cody brought the horses to a stop. "I hope you don't mind an early call."

"Not at all." But her fingers were busy pleating her skirt. She was afraid there was a lecture coming. The good sisters had given Sarah more than what she considered her share over the past twelve years. "I'm always delighted to see you," she added. "Both of you."

Anne glanced over at the dog, who'd run out to bark at the horses. "My, he's grown some, hasn't he?" She held out a hand. "Mr. Redman?"

Jake stepped over to help her, then Liza, down, remaining silent until he'd slung his saddlebags over his shoulder. "I'd best be on my way." He touched a hand to his hat. "Ladies."

"Mr. Redman." Anne held up a hand in the gesture she used to stop her children from rushing out before their chores were finished. "Might I have a word with you?"

He shifted his bags until their weight fell evenly. "Yes, ma'am."

"My son John has been dogging your heels these last weeks. I'm surprised you put up with it."

Jake didn't imagine it pleased her, either, to have the boy spending time with him. "He hasn't made a pest of himself."

Curious, Anne studied his face. "That's a kind thing to say, Mr. Redman, when I'm sure he's done just that."

"Johnny was born a pest," Liza put in, earning a slow, measured look from her mother.

"It appears my children have that in common." With Liza effectively silenced, Anne turned back to Jake. "He's been going through what most boys his age go through, I expect. Fascinated with guns, gunfights. Gunfighters. I don't mind saying it's given me some worry."

"I'll keep my distance," Jake said, and turned to leave.

"Mr. Redman." Anne hadn't raised two willful children without knowing how to add the right tone of authority to her voice. "I'll have my say."

"Ma." Both Liza's cheeks and voice paled when she saw the look in Jake's eyes. Cold, she thought, and moistened her lips. She'd never seen eyes so cold. "Maybe we should let Mr. Redman be on his way."

"Your mother's got something to say," Jake said quietly. "I reckon she ought to say it."

"Thank you." Pleased, Anne drew off her riding gloves. "Johnny was real excited about what happened here between you and Burt Donley."

"Mrs. Cody," Sarah began, only to be silenced by a look from both her and Jake.

"As I was saying," Anne continued, "Johnny hardly talked about anything else for days. He figured having a shoot-out made a man a man and gave him something to strut about. Even started pestering his pa for a Peacemaker." She glanced down at the guns on Jake's hips. "Wooden grip, he said. Nothing fancy, like some of the glory boys wear. Just a good solid Colt. Mr. Cody and I had just about run clean out of patience with the boy. Then, just yesterday, he came home and told me something." She paused, measuring her words. "He said that killing somebody in a gunfight or any other way doesn't make a man grown-up or important. He said that a smart man doesn't look for trouble. He walks away from it when he can, and faces it when he can't."

For the first time, Anne smiled. "I guess I'd been telling him pretty near the same, but it didn't get through coming from me or his pa. Made me wonder who got him thinking that way." She offered her hand again. "I wanted to tell you I'm obliged."

Jake stared at the hand before taking it. It was the kind of gesture, one of gratitude, even friendship, that had rarely been made to him. "He's a smart boy, Mrs. Cody. He'd have come around to it."

"Sooner or later." Anne stepped toward the door of the house and then she turned back. "Maggie O'Rourke thinks a lot of you. I guess I found out why. I won't keep you any longer, Mr. Redman."

Not quite sure how to respond, he touched his hat before he started toward the paddock to saddle his horse.

"That's quite a man, Sarah," Anne commented. "If I were you, I'd want to go say a proper goodbye."

"Yes, I…" She looked at Anne, then back toward Jake, torn between manners and longings.

"You won't mind if I fix tea, will you?" Anne asked as she disappeared inside.

"No, please, make yourself at home." Sarah looked toward Jake again. "I'll only be a minute." Gathering her skirts, she ran. "Jake!" He turned, the saddle held in both hands, and enjoyed the flash of legs and petticoats. "Wait. I—" She stopped, a hand on her heart, when she realized she was not only out of breath but hadn't any idea what she wanted to say to him. "Are you... When will you be back?"

The mustang shifted and nickered softly as Jake settled the saddle in place. "Haven't left yet."

She hated feeling foolish, and hated even more the idea that he could swing onto his horse and ride out of her life for days at a time. Perhaps patience would do the job.

"I was hoping you'd come back for supper."

He tossed up a stirrup to tighten the cinch. "You asking me to supper?"

"Unless you've something else you'd rather be doing."

His hand snaked out, fast and smooth, to snag her arm before she could flounce away. "It's not often I get invitations to supper from pretty ladies." His grip firm, he glanced back toward the house. Things were changing, he decided, and changing fast, when he looked at the adobe cabin and thought of home. He still didn't know what the hell to do about it.

"If I'd known you'd need so long to think about it," Sarah said between her teeth, "I wouldn't have bothered. You can just—" But before she could tell him he swept her off her feet.

"You sure do get fired up easy." He brought his mouth down hard on hers to taste the heat and the honey. "That's one of the things I like about you."

"Put me down." But her arms encircled his neck. "Mrs. Cody might see." Then she laughed and kissed him again as he swung her down. "Well, will you come to supper or not?"

He vaulted into the saddle in one fluid, economical motion. His eyes were shadowed by the brim of his hat when he looked down at her. "Yeah, I'll come to supper."

"It'll be ready at seven," she called after him as he spurred his horse into a gallop. She watched until dust and distance obscured him. Gathering her skirts again, she ran back to the house. The laughter that was bubbling in her throat dried up when she heard Alice's weeping.

Liza stood by the stove, the kettle steaming in her hand. "Sarah, Ma's..." But Sarah was already rushing up the ladder, ready to defend the girl.

Anne Cody held the weeping Alice in her arms, rocking her gently. One wide, capable hand was stroking the girl's dark hair.

"There now, honey, you cry it all out," she murmured. "Then it'll be behind you." Wanting quiet, she sent Sarah a warning glance. Her own eyes were damp. Slowly Sarah descended the ladder.

"Alice called for you," Liza explained, still holding the kettle. "Ma went up to see what she needed." Liza set the sputtering kettle aside. Tea was the last thing on her mind. "Sarah, what's going on?"

"I'm not sure I know."

Liza cast another look toward the loft and said in a low voice. "Was she...that girl...really beaten?"

"Yes." The memory of it had Sarah touching a fingertip to the bruise under her own eye. "Horribly. Liza, I've never known one person was capable of hurting another so viciously." She needed to be busy, Sarah decided. There was too much to think about. Her father, the mine, Jake, Alice. After running a distracted hand over her hair, she began to slice honey cake.

"Did she really work for Carlotta?"

"Yes. Liza, she's just a girl, younger than you and I."

"Really?" Torn between sympathy and fascination, Liza edged closer to Sarah. "But she... Well, I mean, at the Silver Star she must have..."

"She didn't know anything else." Sarah looked down at

her hands. Honey cake and tea. There had been a time when she had thought life was as ordered and simple as that. "Her father sold her. Sold her to a man for twenty dollars."

"But that's—" The curiosity in Liza's eyes heated to fury. "Why, he's the one who should be beat. Her own pa. Somebody ought to—"

"Hush, Liza." Anne slipped quietly down the ladder. "No one deserves to be beat."

"Ma. Sarah says that girl's pa sold her. Sold her off for money, like a horse."

Anne paused in the act of brushing down her skirts. "Is that true, Sarah?"

"Yes. She ran away and ended up at the Silver Star."

Anne's lips tightened as she fought back words that even her husband had never heard her utter. "I'd dearly love that tea now."

"Oh, yes." Sarah hurried back to the stove. "I'm sorry. Please sit down." She set out the napkins she'd made out of blue checked gingham. "I hope you'll enjoy this honey cake. It's a recipe from the cook of a very dear friend of mine in Philadelphia." As she offered the plate, Philadelphia and everyone in it seemed years away.

"Thank you, dear." Anne waited for Sarah to sit down, then said, "Alice is sleeping now. I wasn't sure you'd done the right thing by taking her in here. Truth is, I drove out this morning because I was concerned."

"I had to take her in."

"No, you didn't." When Sarah bristled, Anne laid a hand on hers. "But you did what was right, and I'm proud of you. That girl needs help." With a sigh, she sat back and looked at her own daughter. Pretty Liza, she thought, always so bright and curious. And safe, she reflected, adding a quick prayer of thanksgiving. Her children had always had a full plate and a solid roof over their heads—and a father who loved them. She made up her mind to thank her husband very soon.

"Alice Johnson has had nothing but hard times." Anne took a sip of tea. Her mind was made up. She had only to convince her husband. At that thought her lips curved a little. It was never hard to convince a man whose heart was soft and open. The other ladies in town would be a bit more difficult, but she'd bring them around. The challenge of it made her smile widen and the light of battle glint in her eyes.

"What that girl needs is some proper work and a real home. When she's on her feet again, I think she should come work at the store."

"Oh, Mrs. Cody."

Anne brushed Sarah's stunned gratitude aside. "Once Liza's married to Will I'm going to need new help. She can take Liza's room in the house, as well…as part of her wage."

Sarah fumbled for words, then gave up and simply leaned over to wrap her arms around Anne. "It's kind of you," she managed. "So kind. I've spoken with Alice about just that, but she pointed out that the women in town wouldn't accept her after she'd worked at the Silver Star."

"You don't know Ma." Pride shimmered in Liza's voice. "She'll bring the ladies around, every one. Won't you, Ma?"

Anne patted her hair. "You can put money on it." Satisfied, she broke off a corner of the honey cake. "Sarah, now that we've got that settled, I feel I have to talk to you about the…visit you paid to the Silver Star yesterday."

"Visit?" Though she knew it was hopeless, Sarah covered the bruise under her eyes with her fingers.

"You know, when you tangled with Carlotta," Liza put in. "Everyone in town's talking about how you wrestled with her and even punched Jake Redman. I wish I'd seen it." She caught her mother's eye and grimaced. "Well, I do."

"Oh, Lord." This time Sarah covered her entire face. "Everyone?"

"Mrs. Miller was standing just outside when the sheriff went in." Liza took a healthy bite of cake. "You know how she loves to carry tales."

When Sarah just groaned, Anne shook her head at Liza. "Honey, you eat some more of that cake and keep your mouth busy. Now, Sarah." Anne pried Sarah's hands away from her face. "I have to say I was a mite surprised to hear that you'd gone in that place and had a hair-pulling match with that woman. Truth is, a nice young girl like you shouldn't even know about places and people like that."

"Can't live in Lone Bluff two days and not know about Carlotta," Liza said past a mouthful of cake. "Even Johnny—"

"Liza." Anne held up a single finger. "Chew. Seeing as you're without kin of your own, Sarah, I figured I'd come on out and speak to you about it." She took another sip of tea while Sarah waited to be lectured. "Well, blast it, now that I've seen that girl up there, I wished I'd taken a good yank at Carlotta, myself."

"Ma!" Delighted, Liza slapped both hands to her mouth. "You wouldn't."

"No." Anne flushed a little and shifted in her chair. "But I'd like to. Now, I'm not saying I want to hear about you going back there, Sarah."

"No." Sarah managed a rueful smile. "I think I've finished any business I might have at the Silver Star."

"Popped you a good one, did she?" Anne commented studying Sarah's eye.

"Yes." Sarah grinned irrepressibly. "But I gave her a bloody nose. It's quite possible that I broke it."

"Really. Oh, I do wish I'd seen that." Ready to be impressed, Liza leaned forward, only to straighten again at a look from Anne. "Well, it's not as if I'd go inside myself."

"Not if you want to keep the hide on your bottom," Anne said calmly. She smoothed her hair, took another sip of tea, then gave up. "Well, darn it, are you going to tell us what it looks like in there or not?"

With a laugh, Sarah propped her elbows on the table and told them.

Scheming came naturally to Carlotta. As she lay in the wide feather bed, she ran through all the wrongs that had been done to her and her plans for making them right. The light was dim, with only two thin cracks appearing past the sides of the drawn shades. It was a large room by the Silver Star's standards. She'd had the walls between two smaller rooms removed to fashion her own private quarters, sacrificing the money one extra girl would have made her for comfort.

For Carlotta, money and comfort were one and the same. She wanted plenty of both.

Though it was barely nine, she poured a glass of whiskey from the bottle that was always at her bedside. The hot, powerful taste filled the craving she awoke with every morning. Sipping and thinking, she cast her eyes around the room.

The walls were papered in a somewhat virulent red-and-silver stripe she found rich and elegant. Thick red drapes, too heavy for the blistering Arizona summers, hung at the windows. They made her think, smugly, of queens and palaces. The carpet echoed the color and was badly in need of cleaning. She rarely noticed the dirt.

On the mirrored vanity, which was decorated with painted cherubs, was a silver brush set with an elaborate *C* worked into the design. It was the only monogram she used. Carlotta had no last name, at least none she cared to remember.

Her mother had always had a man in her bed. Carlotta had gone to sleep most nights on a straw pallet in the corner, her lullaby the grunts and groans of sex. It had made her sick, the way men had pounded themselves into her mother. But that had been nothing compared to the disgust she had felt for her mother's weeping when the men were gone.

Crying and sniveling and begging God's forgiveness, Carlotta thought. Her mother had been the whore of that frigid little town in the Carolina mountains, but she hadn't had the guts to make it work for her.

Always claimed she was doing it to feed her little girl, Carlotta remembered with a sneer. She poured more whiskey into the glass. If that had been so, why had her little girl gone hungry so many nights? In the dim light, Carlotta studied the deep amber liquid. Because Ma was just as fond of whiskey as I am, she decided. She drank, and savored the taste.

The difference between you and me, Ma, she thought to herself, is that I ain't ashamed—not of the whiskey, not of the men. And I made something of myself.

Did you cry when I left? Carlotta laughed as she thought back to the night she'd left the smelly, windowless shack for the last time. She'd been fifteen and she'd saved nearly thirty dollars she'd made selling herself to trappers. Men paid more for youth. Carlotta had learned quickly. Her mother had never known her daughter was her stiffest competition.

She despised them all. Every man who'd pushed himself into her. She took their money, arched her hips and loathed them. Hate made a potent catalyst for passion. Her customers went away satisfied, and she saved every coin.

One night she'd packed her meager belongings, stolen another twenty dollars from the can her mother kept hidden in the rafters and headed west.

She'd worked saloons in the early years, enjoying the fancy clothes and bottles of paint. Her affair with whiskey had blossomed and helped her smile and seduce hungry-eyed cowboys and rough-handed drifters. She'd saved, keeping her mouth firmly shut about the bonuses she wheedled from men.

When she'd turned eighteen she had had enough to open her own place. A far cry from the Silver Star, Carlotta remembered. Her first brothel had been hardly more than a shack in a stinking cattle town in east Texas. But she'd made certain her girls were as young and pretty as she could get.

She'd had a brief affair with a gambler who'd sported brocade vests and string ties. He'd filled her head with talk of crystal chandeliers and red carpets. When she'd moved on, she'd taken his pearl stickpin, two hundred in cash and her own profits.

Then she'd opened the Silver Star.

One day she'd move on again, on to California. But she intended to do it in style. She'd have those crystal chandeliers, she vowed. And a white porcelain tub with gold handles. Gold.

Carlotta felt a pleasure flow through her, a pleasure as fluid as the whiskey. It was gold she needed to bring her dream to full life. And gold she intended to have.

The man beside her was the tool she would use to gain it.

Jim Carlson. Carlotta looked down at his face. It was rough with several days' growth of beard and slack from sleep, sex and whiskey. She knew him for a fool, hot-tempered, small-minded and easily manipulated. Still, he was better-looking than many she had taken into her bed. His body was tough and lean, but she preferred young, limber bodies. Like Jake's.

Scowling, Carlotta took another drink. She'd broken her most important rule with Jake Redman. She'd let herself want him, really want him, in a way she'd never desired another man. Her body had responded to his so that for the first time in her life she hadn't feigned the ecstasy men wanted from a whore. She'd felt it. Now she craved it, as she craved whiskey, and gold, and power.

With Jake, desire was a hot, tight fist in her gut. Not just because he had a style in bed most men who came to her didn't feel obliged to employ. Because Jake Redman held something of himself back, something she sensed was powerful and exciting. Something she wanted for herself. And had been on her way to getting, she thought, before that pasty-faced bitch had come to town.

She had a lot to pay Miss Sarah Conway back for. Thoughtful, Carlotta touched a hand to her bruised cheek. A whole lot. Pay her back she would, and in doing so she would take Jake and the gold.

Jim Carlson, though he was unaware of it, was going to help her on all counts.

Setting the empty glass aside, Carlotta picked up a hand mirror. The bruises annoyed her, but they would fade. The faint lines fanning out from her eyes and bracketing her mouth would not. They would only deepen. She cursed and pushed the mirror aside. With a pleased smile, she ran both hands down her body. It was long, smooth-skinned and curvaceous.

It was her body men wanted and her body she had used,

and would continue to use, to get what life had cheated her of.

She shifted, took Jim in her hand and brought him breathlessly awake.

"God Almighty, Carlotta." Groaning, he tried to roll over and into her.

"In a hurry, Jim?" She evaded him expertly, all the while using her skill to keep him aroused.

"Thought you'd burned the life out of me last night." He shuddered. "Glad to find out it ain't so."

"I want to talk to you, Jim."

"Talk." He filled his hands with her breasts. "Honey, I got better ways to spend my money than talk."

She let him suck and nuzzle, calculating how far she could let him go and keep him in line. Rooting about like a puppy, she thought in disgust while she stroked his hair.

"Your money ran out at dawn, sweetheart."

"I got more." He bit her, hard. Because she knew he expected it, she gave a soft moan of pleasure.

"House rules, Jim. Money first."

He swore at her and considered taking his pleasure as he chose. But if he forced her and managed to avoid getting tossed out by Eli, the doors of the Silver Star would be barred to him. He had money, he thought. And a need that was rock-hard.

When he started to shift, Carlotta trailed a finger down his arm. "Talk, Jim, and I'll..." With a long sigh, she arched back so that he could look his fill. "I'll give you the rest for free."

Sweat beaded on his upper lip as he studied her. "You don't do nothing for free."

Deliberately she ran a hand over her breast and down her rib cage and stroked the soft swell of her belly. "Talk.

We're going to talk first." Her lips curved as she watched him swallow. "About gold." When he stiffened, her smile only widened. "Don't worry, Jim. I haven't told anyone, have I? I've never said a word about how you and Donley killed old Matt Conway."

"I was drunk when I told you about that." He wiped a hand over the back of his mouth as fear and desire twined inside him. "A man says all kinds of things when he's drunk."

That made her laugh. She pillowed her head on her folded arms. "Nobody knows that better than a whore or a wife, Jim, honey. Relax. Who was the one who told you old Matt had finally hit? Who was the one who told you his daughter was coming and you had to move fast? Don't try dealing from the bottom with me, sweetheart. It's business, remember. Yours and mine."

After pushing himself up in bed, he reached bad-temperedly for the whiskey bottle. "I told you once Sam got things worked out you'd get your share."

"And what does Sam have to work out?" She let him take a swallow, two. It never hurt to loosen a man's tongue, but there were some who went from relaxed to mean with whiskey. With Jim the line was all too easily crossed. She took the bottle back.

"We've already been through this," he muttered. He no longer felt like having sex, and he sure as hell didn't want to talk.

"If Sam had some idea about getting that Conway bitch to the altar to get his hands on the deed, he's had time enough. Everybody in town knows she doesn't have her eye on your brother, but on Jake Redman."

"How about you?" He tapped a finger, none too gently, against her bruised cheekbone. "Who do you have those blue eyes on?"

"The main chance, sweetheart. Always the main chance." She ran her tongue over her lips, grimly pleased with the way Jim's eyes followed the movement. The surest way to lead a man, she knew, was from a point just below his gunbelt. She rose, knowing the shuttered light would be flattering to her skin. Slowly she ran her hands up her body, letting them linger on her breasts.

"You know, Jim," she began, slipping into a thin red negligee that was as transparent as glass, "I've always been drawn to men who take risks, who know what they want and take it." She left the negligee open as she walked back toward the bed. "That night you came in and told me how you and Donley had dragged Matt up to the mine and how you'd killed him because he wouldn't hand over the deed. You told me just how you'd killed him, how you'd hurt him first. Remember that night, Jim? You and me sure had ourselves a good time after we came upstairs."

He wet his lips. Her nipples were dark and just out of reach. "I remember."

"It was exciting. Knowing you'd just come from killing a man. Killing him to get what you wanted. I knew I was with a real man." The negligee fell carelessly off one shoulder. "Trouble is, nothing's happened since. I keep waiting."

"I told you. Sam's going—"

"The hell with Sam." She battled back her temper to smile at him. "He's too slow, too careful. A real man takes action. If he wants the Conway girl, why doesn't he just take her? Or you could take her for him." She moved closer, letting the idea take root. "She's all that's in the way, Jim. You deal with her—and I ain't talking about firing one of her sheds." The quick wariness in his eyes pleased her. "Hurt her, Jim. She'll hand over the deed quick enough. Then kill her." She murmured the words like a love song. "When she's dead, you come to me. We can do anything you want." She stood beside the bed, glorious and gleaming. "Anything. And it won't cost you a cent."

She didn't cry out when his hand clamped over her wrist. Their faces were close, each of them aroused in different ways, for different reasons.

"You'll take care of her?"

"Yes, damn you. Come here."

Carlotta smiled bitterly at the ceiling while Jim collapsed on top of her.

From her window an hour later, Carlotta watched as Jake rode into town. Her hands clenched into fists—from anger, yes, but also from a stab of desire. Soon, she thought, very soon, he'd come back to her.

She turned as Jim pulled up his pants. She was smiling.

"I think it's a real good time for you to pay Sarah Conway a visit."

Chapter 14

When Jake walked into Maggie's, she set her fisted hands on her hips and looked him up and down with a sniff.

"Fine time to be strolling in, boyo." What she wanted was gossip, and she hoped to annoy it out of him. "Can't figure why a man would be paying good money for a bed and never sleep in it."

"I pay for your chicken and dumplings, too, but I ain't stupid enough to eat them." He started resignedly up the stairs, knowing she would follow.

"You don't seem to be suffering any from lack of food." With the audacity she'd been born with, she poked a finger in his ribs. "Must be getting meals someplace."

"Must be."

"Sarah a good cook, is she?"

Saying nothing, he pushed open the door to his room.

"Don't go pokering up on me, Jake, my boy." Maggie swiped a dustcloth here and there. "It's too late. Every blessed soul in town saw the way you looked at her at the dance. Then there was the way you rode out of town after her when she socked you in the jaw." The dark, furious glint in his eyes had Maggie cackling. "That's more like it. Always said you could drop a man dead with a look as quick as with those guns of yours. No need to draw on me, though. I figure Sarah Conway's just what you need."

"Do you?" Jake tossed his saddlebags on the bed. He considered starting to strip to get rid of her. But he'd tried that before, and it hadn't budged her an inch. "I reckon you want to tell me why before you leave me the hell alone."

"Like to see the back of me, would you?" She just laughed again and patted his cheek. "More than one man's considered it my best side."

He barely managed to control a grin. He was damned if he knew why the nosy old woman appealed to him. "Why don't you get yourself another husband, Maggie? Then you could nag him."

"You'd miss me."

"I reckon some dogs miss the fleas once they manage to scratch them off." Then he sat by the window, propping his back against one side and his boot against the other.

"Somebody's got to bite at you. Might as well be me. I got something to say about you and Sarah Conway."

Staring out the window, he frowned. "It won't be anything I haven't said to myself. Go away, Maggie."

"Now listen to me, boy," she said in an abruptly serious tone. "There's some who're born to the pretty. They slide out of their mothers and straight into silk and satin. Then there's others who have to fight and claw and scratch for every good thing. We know something about that, you and me."

Still frowning, he looked back at her. With a nod, she continued. "Some go hungry, and some have their bellies full. The sweet Lord himself knows why he set things up that way, and no one else. But he didn't make the one man better than the other. It's men themselves who decide if they're going to be strong or weak—and that's the same as good or bad. Sometimes there's a woman who shoves them one way or the other. You take ahold of Sarah Conway, Jake. She'll shove you right enough."

"Could work the other way around," he murmured. "A woman's easier to shove than a man."

Maggie's brows rose in two amused peaks. "Jake, my boy, you've got a lot to learn about women."

It was the second time in so many days he'd been told that, Jake mused when Maggie clicked the door shut behind her. But it wasn't a woman he had to think about now.

It was gold. And it was murder.

He took Matt Conway's journal and started to read.

Unlike Sarah, Jake didn't bother with the early pages. He scanned a few at the middle, where Matt had written of working the mine and of his hopes for a big strike. There were mentions of Sarah here and there, of Matt's regrets at leaving her behind, of his pride in the letters she wrote him. And always he wrote of his longing to send for her.

He had wanted to build her a home first, a real home, like the one he'd described to her. The mine would do it, or so he had thought. Throughout the pages, his confidence never wavered.

Each time I enter, I feel it. Not just hope, but certainty. Today. Each time I'm sure it will be today. There is gold here, enough to give my Sarah the life of a princess—the life I had wanted so badly to give her mother. How alike they are. The miniature Sarah sent me for Christmas might be my own lost, lovely Ellen. Looking at it each night before I sleep makes me grieve for the little girl I left behind and ache for the young woman my daughter has become.

So there had been a painting, Jake mused. Questions might be answered once it was found. He skipped on, toward the end.

In my years of prospecting, I've learned that success is as elusive as any dream. A man may have a map and tools, he may have skill and persistence. But there is one factor that cannot be bought, cannot be learned. Luck. Without it a man can dig and hammer for years with the vein he seeks always inches out of reach. As I have been. Sweet God, as I have been.

Was it the hand of chance that caused my own to slip, that had me sprawled in the dirt nursing my bruised and bloody fingers and cursing God as I learned to curse him so eloquently? And when I stumbled, half-blind with tears of frustration and pain, was it his hand that led me deeper into the tunnel, swinging my pick like a madman?

There it was, under my still-bleeding fingers. Glinting dull against the dark rock. It ran like a river, back, back into the dark mouth of the mine, narrow, then widening. I know it cannot be, yet to me it seemed to shimmer and pulse like a living thing. Gold. At long last.

I am not ashamed that I sat on the dusty floor of the mine, my lamp between my knees, and wept.

He'd found it, Jake thought as he frowned over the words. It was no longer just a hunch, a feeling, but fact. Matt Conway had found his gold, and he'd died. Perhaps there would be an answer to why and how in the remaining pages.

Do men grow more foolish with age? Perhaps. Perhaps. But then, whiskey makes fools of young and old. There need be no excuses. A man finds his heart's desire after years of sweat. To what does he turn? A woman, and a bottle. I found both at the Silver Star.

It had been my intention to keep my discovery to myself for a little longer. Sarah's letter changed that. She's coming. My own little girl is already on her way to join me. There is no way to prepare her for what she will find. Thank God I will soon be able to give her all that I promised.

It wasn't my intent to tell Carlotta of the gold, or of Sarah's arrival. Whiskey and weakness. Undoubtedly I paid for my lack of discretion with a vicious head the next morning. And the visit from Samuel Carlson.

Could it be coincidence that now, after all these years, he wants the mine? His offer was generous. Too generous for me to believe the purchase was to be made from sentiment on his part. Perhaps my suspicions are unfounded. He took my refusal in good temper, leaving the offer open. Yet there was something, something in the way he held his brother and his man Donley to silence—like holding wild dogs on a leash. Tomorrow I will ride into town and tell Barker about my discovery. It may be wise to hire a few men to help me work the mine. The sooner it is begun, the sooner I can build my Sarah the house she believes is already waiting for her.

It was the last entry. Closing the book, Jake rose. He had his answers.

"Miss Sarah, seeing as you're going into town and all…"

Sarah sighed as she adjusted her straw bonnet. "Again, Lucius?"

He scratched his grizzled beard. "A man gets powerful thirsty doing all this work."

"Very well." She'd managed to cure him of his abhorrence of water. Easing him away from his passion for whiskey would take a bit more time.

"I'm obliged, Miss Sarah." He grinned at her. In the weeks he'd been working for her he'd discovered she had a soft heart—and a tough mind. "You check on that wood you ordered. I'll be right pleased to put that floor in for you when it gets here."

Easily said, she mused, when the wood was still hundreds of miles away. "You might finish building the pen Jake started. I intend to inquire about buying some piglets while I'm in town."

"Yes'm." He spit. He'd build the cursed pen, but he'd be damned if he'd tend pigs. "Miss Sarah, I'm getting a mite low on tobacco."

Whiskey and tobacco, Sarah thought, rolling her eyes heavenward. What would Mother Superior have said? "I'll see to it. You look in on Alice regularly, Lucius. See that she has a bit of that broth and rests."

She heard him grumble about being a nursemaid and snagged her lip to keep it from curving. "I'll be back by three. I'm going to fix a very special meal tonight." She gave him a final glance. "You'll want to change your shirt." She cracked the reins and headed out before she allowed herself to laugh.

Life was glorious. Life was, she thought as she let the horses prance, magnificent. Perhaps she was rich, as Jake had said, but the gold no longer mattered. So many things that had seemed so important only a short time before really meant nothing at all.

She was in love, beautifully, wildly, in love, and all the gold in the world couldn't buy what she was feeling.

She would make him happy. It would take some time, some care and more than a little patience, but she would make Jake Redman see that together they could have everything two people could want. A home, children, roots, a lifetime.

What they had brought to each other had changed them both. She was not the same woman who had boarded the train in Philadelphia. How far she'd come, Sarah reflected as she scanned the distant buttes. Not just in miles. It was much more than miles. Only weeks before she'd been certain her happiness depended on having a new bonnet. She laughed as the hot wind tugged at the brim of the one she wore now. She had come to Lone Bluff with dreams of fine parties and china dishes. She hadn't found them. But she had found more, much more.

And she had changed him. She could see it in the way he looked at her, in the way he reached for her as he slept, just to hold her, to keep her close. Perhaps the words were difficult for him to say. She could wait.

Now that she had found him, nothing and no one would keep her from being with him.

She saw the rider coming, and for an instant her smile bloomed. But it wasn't Jake. Sarah watched Jim Carlson slow his horse to a trot as he crossed the road in front of her. She intended to ride by with a brief nod of greeting, but he blocked her way.

"Morning, ma'am." He shifted in his saddle to lean toward her. The stink of whiskey colored his words. "All alone?"

"Good morning, Mr. Carlson. I'm on my way to town, and I'm afraid I'm a bit pressed for time."

"That so?" It was going to be easier than he'd thought. He wouldn't have to go through Lucius to get to her. "Now that's a shame, since I was just riding out to see you."

"Oh?" She didn't care for the look in his eyes, and the smell of whiskey on his breath didn't seem harmless, as it did with Lucius. "Is there something I can do for you, Mr. Carlson?"

"There sure is." Slowly, his eyes on hers, he drew his gun. "Step on out of the wagon."

"You must be mad." She'd frozen at the first sight of the barrel, but now, instinctively, her fingers inched toward her rifle.

"I wouldn't touch that rifle, ma'am. It'd be a shame for me to put a hole in that pretty white hand of yours. Now, I said get out of the wagon."

"Jake will kill you if you touch me."

He'd already thought that one through. That was the reason he was altering Carlotta's plan to suit himself. He wasn't going to kill Sarah here and now, unless she did something stupid. "Oh, I got plans for Redman, honey, don't you worry. You just step out of that wagon before I have to put a bullet in your horses."

She didn't doubt he would, or that he would shoot her in the back should she try to run. Trapped, she stepped down and stood stiffly beside the wagon.

"God Almighty, you got looks, Sarah. That's why Sam took to you." With his gun still in his hand, Jim slid out of the saddle. "You got those fine lady looks like our mama did. You saw her picture at the house. Sam, he's mighty fond of pictures." He grinned again. When he reached out to touch Sarah's face, she hissed and jerked it aside. "But you, you got some fire. Mama was just crazy. Plumb crazy." He stepped forward so that his body pushed hers against the side of the wagon. "Sam told you she was delicate, didn't he? That's the word he uses. Crazy was what she was, so that the old man would lock her up sometimes for days. One day when he opened up the door he found her hanging dead with a pretty pink silk scarf around her neck."

Horror leaped into her eyes and warred with fear. "Let me go. If Samuel finds out what you've done, he'll—"

"You think I run scared of Sam?" Laughing, Jim forced Sarah's face back to his. "Maybe you figure he's smoother than me, got more brains. But we're blood." His fingers bit into her skin. "Don't forget it. You ever let him get this close, let him do what he wanted? Or did you save yourself for that breed?"

She slapped him with all the force of her fear and rage. Then she was clawing at him, blindly, with some mad hope of getting to his horse. She felt the barrel of the gun press into the soft underside of her jaw and heard the click of the hammer.

"Try that again and I'll leave what's left of you here for the buzzards, gold or no gold. Your pa tried to get away, too." The stunned look in her eyes pleased him, gave him the edge he wanted. "You think on what happened to him and take care." He was breathing quickly, his finger trembling on the trigger. He'd lied when he'd said he wasn't scared of his brother. If it hadn't been for the rage Sam would heap on him, Jim would have sent a bullet into her. "Now you're going to do just like I say, and you'll stay alive a while longer."

"Interesting reading." Barker squinted down at Matt's journal while he fanned the hot, still air around his face with his hat. "Matt had a fine way of putting words on paper."

"Fine or not, it's plain enough." Jake fidgeted at the window, annoyed with himself for coming to the law with something he could, and should, have handled himself. Sarah's doing, he thought. He hadn't even felt the shove.

"It's plain that Matt thought he'd found gold."

"He'd found it. Lucius dug through to where Matt was working. It's there, just the way Matt wrote."

Thoughtful, Barker closed the book and leaned back in his chair. "Poor old Matt. Finally makes the big strike, then gets caught in a cave-in."

"He was dead before those beams gave way."

Taking his time, Barker pushed a cozy plug of tobacco in his cheek. "Well, now, maybe you think so, and maybe I'm doing some pondering on it, but this here journal isn't proof. It's not going to be easy to ride out to the Carlson ranch and talk to Sam about murder with no more than a book in my hand. Now hold on," he added when Jake snatched the book from the desk. "I didn't say I wasn't going out, I just said it wasn't going to be easy." Still fanning himself with his hat, he sat back in his chair. He wanted to think it through, and think it through carefully. The Carlson family had a long reach. He was more concerned about that than about the quick temper and gun of young Jim.

"Got a question for you, Jake. Why'd you bring me that journal instead of riding on out and putting a hole in the Carlson brothers?"

Jake skimmed his eyes over Barker's comfortable paunch. "My deep and abiding respect for the law."

After a bark of laughter, the sheriff spit a stream of tobacco juice into the spittoon. "I once knew a woman—before Mrs. Barker—who lied as smooth as that. Couldn't help but admire her." With a sigh, he perched his hat on his head. "Whatever your reason, you brought it, so I'm duty-bound to do something about it. Got to tell you, nothing's more tiring than duty." He reached unenthusiastically for his gunbelt as the door burst open.

"Sheriff." Nancy stood, darting glances over her shoulder and tugging restlessly at the shoulder of her hastily donned dress. "I got to talk to you."

"You'll just have to hold on to it till I get back. One of them cowboys got a little too enthusiastic over at the Silver Star, I ain't getting worked up about it."

"You'd better listen." Nancy stood firm in front of the door. "I'm only doing this 'cause of Alice." She glanced at Jake then. "Carlotta'd strip my skin if she found out I come, but I figured Miss Conway done right by Alice, I ought to do right by her."

"Quit babbling. If you're hell-bent on talking, say it."

"It's Carlotta." Nancy kept her voice low, as if it might carry back to the Silver Star. "She's been feeling real mean since yesterday."

"Carlotta was born feeling mean," Barker muttered. Then he waved to Nancy to continue. "All right, finish it out."

"Last night she took Jim Carlson up. She don't usually let men stay overnight in her room, but he was still there this morning. My room's next to hers, and I heard them talking."

Jake took her arm to draw her farther into the room. "Why don't you tell me what you heard?"

"She was talking about how Jim and Donley killed Matt

Conway, and how he was supposed to take care of Matt's girl." She yelped when Jake's fingers bit into her arm. "I didn't have no part in it. I'm telling you what I heard 'cause she took Alice in after Carlotta near killed her."

"Looks like I'd better have a talk with Carlotta," Barker mused, straightening his hat.

"No, you can't." Fear for her own skin had her yanking free of Jake. "She'll kill me. That's the God's truth. Anyways, it's too late for that."

"Why?" Jake caught her again before she could dash out the door.

She'd gone this far, Nancy thought, dragging the back of her hand over her mouth. She might as well finish. "Carlotta said Jim was to scare Miss Conway good, hurt her. Then, when he had the deed to the mine, he was to kill her. He rode out an hour ago, and I couldn't get away till now."

Jake was already through the door and halfway to his horse when Barker caught up with him. "Will and me'll be right behind you."

There had been times when killing had come easily to Jake, so easily that after it was done he'd felt nothing. This time would be different. He knew it, felt it, as he sped down the road toward Sarah's house. If Jim Carlson was ahead of him and he got within range, he would kill him without question. It would be easy. And it would be a pleasure.

He heard the horses behind him, but he didn't look back.

His own mount seemed to sense the urgency and lengthened his strides until his powerful legs were a blur and the dust was a yellow wall behind them.

When Jake saw the wagon, the cold rage dropped into his gut and turned into a hot, bubbling fear. He vaulted from the saddle beside the two horses, which stood slack-hipped and drowsy.

Surprisingly agile, Barker slipped down beside him. "Take it easy." He began to place a hand on Jake's shoulder, but then he thought better of it. "If he took her off somewhere, we'll track him." He held up a hand before any of the men with him could speak. Along with Will were three men from town, including John Cody, who still wore his store apron. "We take care of our own here, Jake. We'll get her back."

In silence, Jake bent down to pick up the cameo lying facedown in the road. Its slender pin was snapped. There were a few pale blue threads clinging to the broken point. The signs told him she'd struggled, and the picture of her frightened and fighting clawed at him. The signs also told him where she was being taken. With the broach in his pocket, he jumped into the saddle and rode hard for the Carlson ranch.

Her hands were bound together and tied to the saddle horn. If it had been possible, she would have jumped to the ground. Though there was nowhere to run, at least she would have had the satisfaction of making him sweat.

Everything Jake had said was true—about the gold, about her father's death. Sarah had no doubt that the man responsible for it all was sitting behind her.

At first she thought he was taking her into the hills, or to the desert, where he could kill her and leave her body hidden. But she saw, with some confusion, the graceful lines of the Carlson ranch house in the shallow valley below.

It was a peaceful scene, lovely despite the waves of radiant heat rising up from the ground. She heard a dog bark. As they approached, Samuel burst out of the house, hatless and pale, to stare at his brother.

"What in God's name have you done?"

Jim loosened the rope around the saddle horn, then lifted Sarah to the ground. "Brought you a present."

"Sarah, my dear." His mouth grim, Carlson tugged at her bonds. "I'm speechless. There's no way I could ever…" He let his words trail off and began to massage the raw skin of her wrists. "He must be drunk. Stable that horse, damn you," he shouted at Jim. "Then come inside. You've a great deal to answer for."

It stunned her, left her limp, when Jim merely shrugged and led his horse away. It must be a joke, a bizarre joke, she thought, bringing her trembling hands to her lips. But it wasn't. She knew it was much too deadly to be a joke.

"Samuel—"

"My dear, I don't know what to say." He slipped a supporting arm around her waist. "I can't begin to apologize for my brother's outrageous behavior. Are you hurt? Dear Lord, your dress is torn." He had her by the shoulders then, and the look in his eyes froze her blood. "Did he touch you, molest you?"

She managed to shake her head, once, then twice. Then the words came. "Samuel, he killed my father. It was for the gold. There's gold in the mine. He must have found out and he—he murdered my father."

She was breathless now, her hands clinging to his trim black vest. He only stared at her, stared until she wanted to scream. "Samuel, you must believe me."

"You're overwrought," he said stiffly. "And no wonder. Come in out of the heat."

"But he—"

"You needn't worry about Jim." He led her inside the thick adobe walls. "He won't bother you again. You have my word. I want you to wait in my office." His voice was quiet, soothing, as he led her past his mother's portrait and into a room. "Try to relax. I'll take care of everything."

"Samuel, please be careful. He might—he could hurt you."

"No." He patted her hand as he eased her into a chair. "He'll do exactly what I tell him."

When the door shut, she covered her face with her hands. For a moment she let the hysteria she'd fought off take control. He'd intended to kill her. She was certain of it, from the way he'd looked at her, the way he'd smiled at her. Why in God's name had he brought her here, where she would be protected by Samuel?

Protected. After letting out a shaky breath, she waited until her heartbeat leveled and the need to scream passed. She was safe now. But it wasn't over. She closed her eyes briefly. It was far from over.

It was madness. Jim Carlson was as mad as his poor mother had been, but instead of killing himself he had killed her father. She wanted to weep, to let the new, aching grief come. But she couldn't. She couldn't weep, and she couldn't sit.

Rising, she began to pace. The room was small but beautifully furnished. There were delicate porcelain figurines and a painting in fragile pastels. It reflected Samuel's elegant taste and eye for beauty. How unalike the brothers were, she thought.

Cain and Abel.

With a hand on her heart, she rushed to the door. She could never have borne the guilt if one brother killed another over her.

But the door was locked. For a moment she thought it was only her nerves making her fumble. After a deep breath she tried the knob again. It resisted.

Whirling around, she stared at the room. Locked in? But why? For her own protection? Samuel must have thought she would be safer behind a locked door until he came back for her.

And if it was Jim who came back with the key? Her heart thudding in her throat, she began a frantic search for a weapon.

She pulled out desk drawers, pushing ruthlessly through papers. If not a pistol, she thought, then a knife, even a letter opener. She would not be defenseless. Not again. She tugged open the middle drawer, and the brass pulls knocked against the glossy mahogany. Her hand froze when she saw the miniature. Her miniature.

Like a sleepwalker, she reached for it, staring blindly.

It was the self-portrait that she had painted the year before, the one she had shipped to her father for Christmas. The one, Sarah realized as her fingers closed over it, that he had shown with pride to his friends in town. The one that had been missing from his possessions. Missing because it had been taken by his murderer.

When the key turned in the lock, she didn't bother to close the drawer or to hide what she held in her hand. Instead, she rose and faced him.

"It was you," she murmured as Samuel Carlson closed and locked the door behind him. "You killed my father."

Chapter 15

Carlson crossed the room until only the desk was between them. "Sarah." His voice was almost a sigh, a sigh touched with patience. In his hand he carried a delicate cup filled with fragrant tea. But she noted that he had strapped on his gun. "I realize how upset you must be after Jim's inexcusable behavior. Now, why don't you sit down, compose yourself?"

"You killed my father," she repeated. It was rage she felt now, waves of it.

"That's ridiculous." The words were said gently. "I haven't killed anyone. Here, my dear. I've brought you some tea. It should help calm you."

The quiet sincerity in his eyes caused her to falter. He must have sensed it, because he smiled and stepped forward. Instantly she backed away. "Why was this in your desk?"

Carlson looked at the miniature in her hand. "A woman should never intrude on a man's personal belongings." His voice became indulgent as he set the cup on the desk. "But since you have, I'll confess. I can be faulted for being overly romantic, I suppose. The moment I saw it, I fell in love with you. The moment I saw your face, I wanted you." He held out a hand, palm up, as if he were asking for a dance. "Come, Sarah, you can't condemn me for that."

Confused, she shook her head. "Tell me how this came to be in your drawer when it belonged to my father."

Impatience clouded his face, and he dropped his hand to his side. "Isn't baring my soul enough for you? You knew, right from the beginning, you knew the way I felt about you. You deceived me." There was more than impatience in his face now. Something else was building in him. Something that had the bright, hot taste of fear clogging her throat.

"I don't know what you're talking about, Samuel." She spaced her words carefully and kept her eyes on his. "But you're right. I'm upset, and I'm not myself. I'd prefer to go home now and discuss all of this later." With the miniature still clutched in her hand, she stepped around the desk and toward the door. The violence with which he grabbed her and shoved her back against the wall had her head reeling.

"It's too late. Jim's interference has changed everything. His interference, and your prying. I was patient with you, Sarah. Now it's too late."

His face was close to hers—close enough for her to see clearly what was in his eyes. She wondered, as the blood drained slowly from her face, how it was that she'd never seen it before. The madness was bright and deadly. She tried to speak and found she had to swallow first.

"Samuel, you're hurting me."

"I would have made you a queen." He took one hand and brought it up to stroke her face. She cringed, but his eyes warned her not to move. "I would have given you every-thing a woman could want. Silk." He traced a finger over her cheekbone. "Diamonds." Then he ran it lightly down her throat. "Gold." His hand tightened abruptly around her windpipe. Before she could begin to struggle, it was loosened again. "Gold, Sarah. It belonged to me, truly to me. My grandfather had no right to lose that part of my heritage. And your father…he had no right to deny me what was already mine."

"He did it for me." Perhaps she could calm him, if only she could remain calm herself, before it was too late. "He only wanted to see that I was taken care of."

"Of course." He nodded, as if he were pleased that she understood. "Of course he did. As I do. It would have been yours as much as mine. I would never have let you suffer because I had taken it back. As my wife, you would have had every luxury. We would have gone back east together. That was always my plan. I was going to follow you back east and court you. But you stayed. You should never have stayed, Sarah. This isn't the place for you. I knew it the moment I saw your picture. It was there, in that miserable little cabin, beside the cot. I found it while I was looking for the deed to the mine."

His face changed again. He looked petulant now, like a boy who had been denied an extra piece of pie. "I was very annoyed that my brother and Donley killed Matt. Clumsy. They were only to…convince him to turn over the deed. Then, of course, it was up to me to think of causing the cave-in to cover up what they'd done. I never found the deed. But I found your picture."

She didn't think he was aware of how viciously his fingers were digging into her arms. She was almost certain he was no longer aware of how much he was telling her. She remained silent and still, knowing her only hope now was time.

"Delicate," he murmured. "Such a delicate face. The innocence shining in the eyes, the soft curve of the mouth. It was a lie, wasn't it, Sarah?" The violence sprang back into his face, and she could only shake her head and wait. "There was no delicacy, no innocence. You toyed with me, offering me smiles, only smiles, while you gave yourself to Redman like a whore. He should be dead for touching what belonged to me. You should both be dead."

She prepared to scream. She prepared to fight for what she knew was her life.

"Sam!" The banging on the door brought with it a mixture of fear and relief.

Swearing, Carlson dragged Sarah to the door to unlock it. "Goddamn it, I told you to go back and get rid of the wagon and team."

"Riders coming in." The sweat on Jim's face attested to the fact that he had already ridden, and ridden hard. "It's Redman and the sheriff, with some men from town." He glanced at Sarah. "They'll be looking for her."

When Sarah tried to break away, Samuel locked an arm around her throat. "You've ruined everything, bringing her here."

"I only did it 'cause you wanted her. I could've taken care of her back on the road. Hell, I could've taken care of her the night we torched her shed, but you said you didn't want her hurt none."

Carlson tightened his grip as Sarah clawed at his arm. Her vision grayed from lack of air. As if from a distance, she heard the voices, one mixing into the other.

"How long?"

"Ten minutes, no more… Kill her now."

"Not here, you idiot… Hold them off… In the hills."

Sarah's last thought before she lost consciousness was that Jake was coming, but too late.

"You listen to me." Barker stopped the men on the rise above the Carlson ranch. But it was Jake he was looking at. "I know you'd like to ride in there hell-bent, but you take a minute to think. If they've got her, we've got to go slow."

"They've got her." In his mind, the Carlson brothers were already dead.

"Then let's make sure we get her back in one piece. Will, I want you to break off, ease on over to the barn. John, I'd be obliged if you'd circle around the back. I don't want any shooting until it's necessary." With a nod, he spurred his horse.

Jim watched them coming and wiped the sweat off his brow. His men were all out on the range. Not that they'd have been any good, he thought. The only one who'd have backed them against the sheriff was Donley. And he was dead. Wetting his lips, he levered the rifle in the window.

He had to wait until they got close. That was what Sam had told him. Wait until they got close. Then he was to kill as many as he could. Starting with Redman.

Sweat dripped down into his eyes. His fingers twitched.

Sam had sent Donley to kill Redman, Jim remembered. But it was Donley who'd been buried. Now he was going to do it. He wet his lips when he caught Jake in the sight. He was going to do it right. But nerves had his finger jerking on the trigger.

Jake felt the bullet whiz past his cheek. Like lightning, he kicked one foot free of the stirrup to slide halfway down the side of his horse. Gun drawn, he rode toward the house while Barker shouted orders. He could hear the men scrambling for cover and returning fire, but his mind was on one thing and one thing alone.

Getting inside to Sarah.

Outside the doors, he leaped off. When he kicked them open, his second gun was drawn. The hall and the foyer were empty. He could hear the shouts of men and peppering gunfire. With a quick glance for any sign of her, he started up the stairs.

Jim Carlson's back was to him when he broke open the door.

"Where is she?" Jake didn't flinch when a bullet from outside plowed into the wall beside him.

From his crouched position, Jim turned slowly. "Sam's got her." With a grin, he swung his rifle up. For months he'd wanted another chance to kill Jake Redman. Now he took it.

He was still grinning as he fell forward. Jake slid his smoking guns back in their holsters. Moving quickly, he began to search the house.

Barker met him on the steps. "She ain't here. I found this on the floor." In his hand he held Sarah's miniature.

Jake's eyes flicked up to Barker's. They held there only seconds, but Barker knew he would never forget the look in them. Later he would tell his wife it was the look of a man whose soul had gotten loose.

Turning on his heel, Jake headed outside, with Barker close behind.

"Oh, God." For the first time since Jake had known him, Barker moved with speed. Pushing past Jake, he raced to where two of his men were carrying Will Metcalf.

"He isn't dead." John Cody laid Will down and held his head. "But we have to get him back to town, to the doc."

Barker crouched down as Will's eyes fluttered open. "You're going to be all right, son."

"Took me by surprise," Will managed, struggling not to gasp at the pain as Cody pressed a pad to the hole in his shoulder. "Was Sam Carlson, Sheriff. He had her—I saw he had her on the horse. Think they headed west."

"Good job, Will." Barker used his own bandanna to wipe the sweat off his deputy's brow. "One of you men hitch up a wagon, get some blankets. You get this boy to the doctor, John. Redman and I'll go after Carlson."

But when he stood, all he saw of Jake was the dust his mustang kicked up as he galloped west.

Sarah came to slowly, nausea rising in her throat. Moaning, she choked it back and tried to lift a hand to her spinning head. Both wrists were bound tight to the saddle horn.

For a moment she thought she was still with Jim. Then she remembered.

The horse was climbing, picking its way up through dusty, dung-colored rock. She watched loose dirt and stones dislodged by the horse's hooves fall down a dizzying ravine. The man behind her was breathing hard. Fighting for calm, she tried to mark the trail they were taking and remember it. When she escaped—and she would—she didn't intend to wander helplessly through the rocks.

He stopped the horse near the edge of a canyon. She could see the thin silver line of a river far below. An eagle called as he swooped into the wide opening, then returned to a nest built in the high rock wall.

"Samuel, please—" She cried out when he pulled the rope from around her wrists and dragged her roughly to the ground. One look warned her that the calm, sane words she had meant to use would never reach him.

There was a bright, glazed light in his eyes. His face was pale and drenched with sweat. His hair was dark with it.

She watched his eyes dart here and there, as if he expected something to leap out from behind a huddle of rock.

The man who had swept off his hat and kissed her fingers wasn't here with her now. If he had ever been part of Samuel Carlson, he had vanished. The man who stood over her was mad, and as savage as any beast that lived in the hills.

"What are you going to do?"

"He's coming." Still breathing rapidly, Carlson swiped a hand over his mouth. "I saw him behind us. When he comes for you, I'll be ready." He reached down to drag her to her feet. "I'm going to kill him, Sarah. Kill him like a dog." He pulled out his gun and rubbed the barrel against her cheek, gently, like a caress. "You're going to watch. I want you to watch me kill him. Then you'll understand. It's important that you understand. A man like that deserves to die by a gun. He's nothing, less than nothing. A crude gunslinger with Indian blood. He put his hands on you." A whimper escaped her as he dragged a hand through her hair. "I'm going to kill him for you, Sarah. Then we're going away, you and I."

"No." She wrenched free. The canyon was at her back when she faced him. If she had stumbled another step she would have fallen back into nothing. There was fear. The taste of it was bitter in her throat. But it wasn't for herself. Jake would come, she knew, and someone would die. "I won't go anywhere with you. It's over, Samuel. You must see that. They know what you've done, and they'll hunt you down."

"A potbellied sheriff?" He laughed and, before she could evade him, closed his hand over her arm. "Not likely. This is a big country, Sarah. They won't find us."

"I won't go with you." The pain when he squeezed her arm nearly buckled her knees. "I'll get away."

"If I must, I'll keep you locked up, the way my mother was locked up. For your own good."

She heard the horse even as he did and screamed out a warning. "No, Jake, he'll kill you!" Then she screamed again, this time in pain, as Carlson bent her arm behind her back. Calmly he put the gun to her temple.

"It's her I'll kill, Redman. Come out slow and keep your hands where I can see them, or the first bullet goes in her brain." He twisted her arm ruthlessly because he wanted Jake to hear her cry out again. He wanted Jake to hear the pain. "Now, Redman, or I'll kill her and toss her body over the edge."

"No. Oh, no." Tears blurred her vision as she watched Jake step out into the open. "Please don't. It won't gain you anything to kill him. I'll go with you." She tried to turn her head to look into Carlson's eyes. "I'll go anywhere you want."

"Not gain anything?" Carlson laughed again, and it echoed off the rocks and air. "Satisfaction, my dear. I'll gain satisfaction."

"Are you hurt?" Jake asked quietly.

"No." She shook her head, praying she could will him back behind the rock, back to safety. "No, he hasn't hurt me. He won't if you go back."

"But you're wrong, my dear, quite wrong." Carlson bent his head close to hers, amused by the quick fury in Jake's eyes when he brushed his lips over Sarah's hair. "I'll have to, you see, because you won't understand. Unless I kill him for you, you won't understand. Your gunbelt, Redman." Carlson drew back the hammer for emphasis and kept the gun tight against Sarah's temple. "Take it off, slowly, very slowly, and kick it aside."

"No!" She began to struggle, only to have him drag her

arm farther up her back. "I'll kill you myself." She wept in rage and fear. "I swear it."

"When I'm done here, my dear, you'll do exactly what I say, when I say. In time you'll understand this was for the best. Drop the belt, Redman." Carlson smiled at him and jerked his head to indicate that he wanted the guns kicked away. "That's fine." He took the gun away from Sarah's temple to point it at Jake's heart. "You know, I've never killed a man before. It always seemed more civilized to hire some-one—someone like yourself." His smile widened. "But I believe I'm going to enjoy it a great deal."

"You might." Jake watched his eyes. He could only hope Sarah had the sense to run when it was over. Barker couldn't be far behind. "Maybe you'll enjoy it more when I tell you I killed your brother."

The muscles in Carlson's cheek twitched. "You bastard."

Sarah screamed and threw her weight against his gun hand. She felt the explosion, as if the bullet had driven into her. Then she was on her knees. Life poured out of her when she saw Jake sprawled on the ground, blood seeping from his side.

"No. Oh, God, no."

Carlson threw back his head and laughed at the sky. "I was right. I enjoyed it. But he's not dead yet. Not quite yet." His lips stretched back from his teeth as he lifted the gun again.

She didn't think. There was no room for thought in a mind swamped with grief. She reached out and felt the smooth grip of Jake's gun in her hand. Kneeling in the dirt, she balanced it and aimed. "Samuel," she murmured, and waited for him to turn his head.

The gun jumped in her hand when she fired. The sound of the shot echoed on and on and on. He just stared at her.

Afraid she'd missed, Sarah drew back the hammer and calmly prepared to fire again.

Then he stumbled. He stared at her as his hand reached up to press against the blood that blossomed on his shirt-front. Without a sound, he fell back. He groped once in the air, then tumbled off the edge and into the canyon.

Her hand went limp on the gun. Then the shudders began, racking shudders, as she crawled to Jake. He'd pushed himself up on one elbow, and he held his knife in his hand. She was weeping as she tore at her petticoats to pad the wound in his side.

"I thought he'd killed you. You looked—" There was so much blood, she thought frantically as she tore more cloth. "You need a doctor. I'll get you on the horse as soon as—" She broke off again as her voice began to hitch. "It was crazy, absolutely crazy, for you to come out in the open like that. I thought you had more sense."

"So did I." The pain was searing, centering in his side and flowing out in waves of heat. He wanted to touch her, just once more, before he died. "Sarah…"

"Don't talk." Tears clogged her throat. His blood seeped through the pad and onto her hands. "Just lie still. I'm going to take care of you. Damn you, I won't let you die."

He couldn't see her face. Tired of the effort, he closed his eyes. He thought, but couldn't be sure, that he heard horses coming. "You're a hell of a woman," he murmured, and passed out.

When he awoke, it was dark. There was a bitter taste in his mouth and a hollow throbbing at the base of his skull. The pain in his side was still there, but dull now, and constant. He lay still and wondered how long he'd been in hell.

He closed his eyes again, thinking it didn't matter how

long he'd been there, since he wouldn't be leaving. Then he smelled her, smelled the soft scent that was Sarah. Though it cost him dearly, he opened his eyes again and tried to sit up.

"No, don't." She was there, murmuring to him, pressing him gently back on a pillow, then laying a cool cloth against his hot face.

"How long—" He could only manage two whispered words before the strength leaked out of him.

"Don't worry." Cradling his head with her arm, she brought a cup to his lips. "Drink a little. Then you'll sleep again. I'm right here with you," she continued when he coughed and tried to turn his head away.

"Can't—" He tried to focus on her face, but saw only a silhouette. It was Sarah, though. "Can't be in hell," he murmured, then sank back into the darkness.

When he awoke again, it was daylight. And she was there, leaning over him, smiling, murmuring something he couldn't quite understand. But there were tears drying on her cheeks, cheeks that were too pale. She sat beside him, took his hand and held it against her lips. Even as he struggled to speak, he lost consciousness again.

She thought it would drive her mad, the way he drifted in and out of consciousness that first week, with the fever burning through him and the doctor giving her no hope. Hour after hour, day after day, she sat beside him, bathing his hot skin, soothing when the chills racked him, praying when he fell back into that deep, silent sleep.

What had he said that day when he'd awakened? Pacing to the window, the one Maggie had told her Jake had sometimes sat in, she drew the curtain aside to look down at the empty street. He'd said it couldn't be hell. But he'd been wrong, Sarah thought. It was hell, and she was mired in it, terrified each day that he would leave her.

So much blood. He'd lost so much blood. By the time Barker had ridden up she'd nearly managed to stop it, but the ride back to town had cost him more. She had stanched still more while the doctor had cut and probed into his side to remove the bullet. She hadn't known that watching the bullet come out of him would be as bad as watching it go in.

Then the fever had raced through him, vicious and merciless. In a week he'd been awake only a handful of minutes, often delirious, sometimes speaking in what Lucius had told her was Apache. If it didn't break soon, she knew, no matter how hard she prayed, no matter how hard she fought, it would take him.

Sarah moved back to the bed to sit beside him and watch over him in the pale light of dawn.

Time drifted, for her even as it did for him. She lost track of minutes, then hours, then days. When morning came she held his hand in hers and thought over the time they'd had together. His hands had been strong, she thought. Biting back a sob, she laid her forehead on his shoulder. And gentle, too, she remembered. When he'd touched her. When he'd taught her.

With him she'd found something lovely, something powerful. A sunrise. A fast river. A storm. She knew now that love, desire, passion and affection could be one emotion for one man. From that first frantic discovery in the hay to the soft, sweet loving by the stream, he'd given her more than most women had in a lifetime.

"But I'm greedy," she murmured to him. "I want more. Jake, don't leave me. Don't cheat me out of what we could have." She blinked back tears when she heard the door open behind her.

"How is he?"

"The same." Sarah rose and waited while Maggie set a

tray on the bureau. She'd long ago stopped arguing about eating. It had taken her only a few days to realize that if she wanted the strength to stay with Jake she needed food.

"Don't worry none about this breakfast, because Anne Cody made it up for you."

Sarah dashed away the hated, weakening tears. "That was kind of her."

"She asked about our boy here, and wanted you to know that Alice is doing just fine."

"I'm glad." Without interest, she folded back the cloth so that steam rose fragrantly from the biscuits.

"Looks like Carlotta skipped town."

"It doesn't matter." With no more interest than she had in the biscuits, she looked at her own face in the mirror. Behind her reflection, she could see Jake lying motionless in the bed. "The damage is done."

"Child, you need sleep, and not what you get sitting up in that chair all night. You go on and use my room. I'll stay with him."

"I can't." Sarah ignored the biscuits and took the coffee. "Sometimes he calls for me, and I'm afraid if I'm not here he might…slip away. That's foolish, I suppose, but I just can't leave him, Maggie."

"I know." Because she did, Maggie set a comforting hand on Sarah's shoulder. The noise at the door had her turning back. "What are you doing sneaking around here, young John Cody?"

Johnny slipped into the doorway and stood with his hat crushed in his hands. "Just wanted to see him, is all."

"A sickroom ain't no place for nasty little boys."

"It's all right." Sarah waved him in and summoned up a smile. "I'm sure Jake would be pleased that you'd taken the time to visit him."

"He ain't going to die, is he, Sarah?"

"No." She found the confidence she'd lost during the night. "No, he isn't going to die, Johnny."

"Ma says you're taking real good care of him." He reached out a hand, then balled it at his side again.

"It's all right, boy," Maggie said, softening. "You can pet him as long as he don't know it. I do it myself."

Gingerly Johnny stroked a hand along Jake's forehead. "He's pretty hot."

"Yes, but the fever's going to break soon." Sarah laid a hand on Johnny's shoulder. "Very soon."

"Will's better," he said, giving Sarah a hopeful smile. "He's got his arm in a sling and all, but he's getting around just fine and dandy. Won't even let Liza fuss no more."

"Before long Jake won't let me fuss, either."

Hours later she dozed, lulled by the afternoon sun. She slept lightly, her head nestled against the wing of the chair and her hands in her lap on top of her journal. She'd written everything she felt, hoped, despaired of on those pages. Someone called her name, and she lifted a hand as if to brush the voice away. She only wanted to sleep.

"Sarah."

Now her eyes flew open, and she bolted out of the chair. Jake was half sitting up in bed, his brows drawn together in annoyance or confusion. And his eyes, she noted, were focused, alert and direct on hers.

"What the hell's going on?" he asked her. Then he watched, astonished, as she collapsed on the side of the bed and wept.

It was three weeks before he had the strength to do more than stand on his own feet. He had time to think—perhaps too much time—but when he tried to do anything he found himself weak as a baby.

It infuriated him, disgusted him. When he swore at Maggie twice in one morning, she told Sarah their patient was well on the road to recovery.

"He's a tough one, Jake is," Maggie went on as they climbed the steps to his room together. "Said he was damn sick and tired of having females poking him, pouring things into him and trying to give him baths."

"So much for gratitude," Sarah said with a laugh. Then she swayed and clutched the banister for support.

Maggie grabbed her arm. "Honey, are you all right?"

"Yes. Silly." Shrugging it off, Sarah waited for the dizziness to pass. "I'm just tired yet, I think." One look at Maggie's shrewd face had her giving up and sitting carefully on the riser.

"How far along are you?"

It surprised Sarah that the direct question didn't make her blush. Instead, she smiled. "About a month." She knew the exact moment when she had conceived Jake's child, on the riverbank under the moon. "I had the obvious sign, of course. Then, for the last few days, I haven't been able to keep anything down in the morning."

"I know." Pleased as a partridge, Maggie cackled. "Honey, I knew you were breeding three days ago, when you turned green at the sight of Anne Cody's flapjacks. Ain't Jake just going to fall on his face?"

"I haven't told him," Sarah said quickly. "I don't want him to know until he's...until we've..." She propped her chin in her hands. "Not yet, Maggie."

"That's for you to decide."

"Yes, and you won't say anything...to anyone?"

"Not a peep."

Satisfied, Sarah rose and started up the stairs again. "The doctor said he'd be up and around in a couple of days. We haven't been able to talk about anything important since he's been healing." She knocked on the door to his room before pushing it open.

The bed was empty.

"What— Maggie!"

"He was there an hour ago. I don't know where—" But she was talking to air, as Sarah was flying down the stairs again.

"Sarah! Sarah!" His hand wrapped around a licorice whip, Johnny raced toward her. "I just saw Jake riding out of town. He sure looked a lot better."

"Which way?" She grabbed the surprised boy by the shoulders. "Which way did he go?"

"That way." He pointed. "I called after him, but I guess he didn't hear me."

"Damned hardheaded man," Maggie muttered from the doorway.

"So he thinks he can just ride off," Sarah said between her teeth. "Well, Jake Redman is in for a surprise. I need a horse, Maggie. And a rifle."

He'd thought it through. He'd had nothing but time to think over the last weeks. She'd be mad, he figured. He almost smiled. Mad enough to spit, he imagined, but she'd get over it. In time she'd find someone who was right for her. Who was good for her.

Talking to her wouldn't have helped. He'd never known a more stubborn woman. So he'd saddled up and ridden out of Lone Bluff the way he'd ridden out of countless towns before. Only this time it hurt. Not just the pain from his still-healing wound, but an ache deeper, sharper, than anything that could be caused by a bullet.

He'd get over it, too, he told himself. He'd just been fooling himself, letting himself pretend that she could belong to him.

He'd never forget how she'd looked, kneeling in the dirt with his gun in her hand. His gun. And there had been horror in her eyes. He'd taught her to kill, and he wasn't sure he could live with that.

The way he figured it, she'd saved his life. The best he could do for her was return the favor and get out of hers.

She was rich now. Jake remembered how excited Lucius had been when he'd come to visit, talking on and on about the mine and how the gold was all but ready to fall into a man's hands. She could go back east, or she could stay and build that big house with the parlor she'd told him about.

And he would…he would go on drifting.

When he heard the rider coming, instinct had him wheeling his horse around and reaching for his gun. He swore, rubbing his hand on his thigh, as Sarah closed the distance between them.

"You bastard."

He acknowledged her with a nod. There was only one way to handle her now, one way to make certain she turned around and left. Before just looking at her made him want to crawl.

"Didn't know you could ride, Duchess. You come out all this way to tell me goodbye?"

"I have more than that to say." Her hands balled on the reins while she fought with her temper. "Not a word, Jake, to me, to anyone? Just saddle up and ride out?"

"That's right. When it's time to move on, you move."

"So you're telling me you have no reason to stay?"

"That's right." He knew the truth sometimes hurt, but he hadn't known a lie could. "You're a mighty pretty woman, Duchess. You'll be hard to top."

He saw the hurt glow in her eyes before her chin came up. "That's a compliment? Well, you're quite right, Jake. I'll be very hard to top. You'll never love another woman the way you love me. Or want one," she said, more quietly. "Or need one."

"Go on back, Sarah." He started to turn his horse but stopped short when she drew the rifle out of its holster and aimed it heart-high. "You want to point that someplace else?"

For an answer, she lowered it a few strategic inches, smiling when his brow lifted. "Ever hear the one about hell's fury, Jake?"

"I get the idea." He shifted slightly. "Duchess, if it's all the same to you, I'd rather you pointed it back at my chest."

"Get off your horse."

"Damn it, Sarah."

"I said off." She cocked the lever in two sharp movements. "Now."

He leaned forward in the saddle. "How do I know that's even loaded?"

"How do you know it's loaded?" She smiled, brought it up to her eye and fired. His hat flew off his head.

"Are you crazy?" Stunned, he dragged a hand through his hair. He could almost feel the heat. "You damn near killed me."

"I hit what I aim at. Isn't that what you said I should learn to do?" She cocked the rifle again. "Now get off that horse before I shoot something more vital off you."

Swearing, he slid down. "What the hell are you trying to prove with all this?"

"Just hold it right there." She dropped to the ground. Giddiness washed over her, and she had to lean one hand against her mount.

"Sarah—"

"I said hold it right there." She shook her head to clear it.

"Are you sick?"

"No." Steady again, she smiled. "I've never felt better in my life."

"Just crazy, then." He relaxed a little, but her pallor worried him. "Well, if you've a mind to kill me after spending the better part of a month keeping me alive, go ahead."

"You're damn right I kept you alive, and I didn't do it so you could leave me the minute you could stand up. I did it because I love you, because you're everything I want and everything I intend to have. Now you tell me, you stand there and tell me why you left."

"I already told you. It was time."

"You're a liar. Worse, you're a coward."

Her words had the effect she'd hoped for. The cool, almost bored look in his eyes sizzled into heat. "Don't push me, Sarah."

"I haven't begun to push you. I'll start by telling you why you got on that horse and rode away. You left because you were afraid. Of me. No, not even of me, of yourself and what you feel for me." Her chin was up, a challenge in her eyes as she dared him to say it was untrue. "You loved me enough to stand unarmed in front of a madman, but not enough to face your own heart."

"You don't know what I feel."

"Don't I? If you believe that, you're a fool, as well as a liar." The fresh flash of fury in his eyes delighted her. "Don't you think I knew every time you touched me, every time you kissed me?" He was silent, and she drew a long breath.

"Well, you can get on that horse and you can ride, you can run into the hills, to the next town. You can keep running until you're hundreds of miles away. Maybe you'll be fast enough, just fast enough to get away from me. But before you do you're going to tell me."

"Tell you what?"

"I want you to tell me you love me."

He studied her. Her eyes glowed with determination, and her cheeks were flushed with anger. Her hair, caught by the wind, was blowing back. He should have known then and there that he'd never had anywhere to run.

"A man'll say most anything when a woman's pointing a rifle at his belly."

"Then say it."

He bent to pick up his hat, slapping it against his thighs twice to loosen the dust. Idly he poked his finger through the hole in the crown.

"I love you, Sarah." He settled the hat on his head. "Now do you want to put that thing away?"

The temper went out of her eyes, and with it the glint of hope. Without a word, she turned to secure the rifle in the holder. "Well, I had to threaten it out of you, but at least I heard you say it once. Go ahead and ride off. I won't stop you. No one's holding a gun on you now."

She wouldn't cry. No, she swore to herself she wouldn't hold him with tears. Fighting them back, she tried to struggle back into the saddle. He touched her arm, lightly, not holding, when he wanted more than anything he'd ever wanted in his life to hold her.

"I love you, Sarah," he said again. "More than I should. A hell of a lot more than I can stand."

She closed her eyes, praying that what she did now would be right for both of them. Slowly she turned toward him, but she kept her hands at her sides. "If you ride away now, I'll come after you. No matter where you go, I'll be there. I'll make your life hell, I swear it."

He couldn't stop the smile any more than he could stop his hand from reaching up to touch her face. "And if I don't ride away?"

"I'll only make your life hell some of the time."

"I guess that's a better bargain." He lowered his head to kiss her gently. Then, with a groan, he crushed her hard against him. "I don't think I'd've gotten very far, even if you hadn't shot at me."

"No use taking chances. Lucky for you I was trying to shoot over your head."

He only sighed and drew her away. "You owe me a hat, Duchess." Still amazed, he drew it off to poke at the hole. "I guess I'd have to marry any woman who could handle a gun like that."

"Is that a proposal?"

He shrugged and stuck his hat back on his head. "Sounded like it."

She lifted a brow. "And it's the best you can do?"

"I haven't got any five-dollar words." Disgusted, he started back to his horse. Then he stopped and turned back. She was waiting, her arms folded, a half smile on her face. So he swore at her. "There's a preacher comes into town once every few weeks. He can marry us proper enough, with whatever kind of fuss you figure would satisfy you. I'll build you a house, between the mine and the town, with a parlor if that's what you want, and a wood floor, and a real bedroom."

To her it was the most eloquent of proposals. She held out her hands. "We'll need two."

"Two what?"

"Two bedrooms," she said when his hands closed over hers again.

"Listen, Duchess, I've heard they've got some odd ways of doing things back east, but I'm damned if my wife is going to sleep in another room."

"Oh, no." Her smile lit up her face. "I'm going to sleep in the same room, the same bed as you, every night for the rest of my life. But we'll need two bedrooms. At least we will by spring."

"I don't see why—" Then he did, so abruptly, so stunningly, that he could only stare at her. If she had taken the rifle back out and driven it butt first into his gut he would have been less shaken. His fingers went slack on hers, then dropped away. "Are you sure?"

"Yes." She held her breath. "There's going to be a child. Our child."

He wasn't sure he could move, and was less sure he could speak. Slowly, carefully, he framed her face with his hands and kissed her. Then, when emotions swamped him, he simply rested his forehead against hers. "Two bedrooms," he murmured. "To start."

Content, she wrapped her arms around his waist. "Yes. To start."

* * * * *